THE
FALLING
OF
STARS

ALSO BY TRACI FINLAY

The Rules of Burken

THE
FALLING
OF
STARS

TRACI FINLAY

To everyone suffering from depression and feelings of worthlessness...
I understand you. I see you. I love you.
And I am so, so proud of you.

Stay strong, tiger. You got this.

IF YOU OR A LOVED ONE ARE STRUGGLING WITH
SUICIDAL THOUGHTS OR DEPRESSION, PLEASE CONTACT
THE NATIONAL SUICIDE PREVENTION HOTLINE.

CALL 1-800-273-8255

OR TEXT HOME TO 741741

YOUR WORTH IS NOT DETERMINED
BY THE LIES IN YOUR MIND.

I

EVE

Malik holds my hand as we walk toward the gravesite. He hasn't held my hand since he was about ten. Is it awful that I'm finding a silver lining at this teenage funeral because my sixteen-year-old son is holding my hand? I duck my head as my eyes well for the nine-hundredth time in two days. Something else for me to feel guilty about.

Malik is spooked; I see it in his eyes. Jordan's passing is tragic. A child taking his own life is never easy, but this hits home for Malik, I can tell. Childhood friends—nostalgia. Distanced with age—guilt. The thought of sweet, fourteen-year-old Jordan, fresh out of puberty, with a gun to his head—unfathomable.

My grip on his hand tightens as we head toward the tent and chairs and gathering people. Not too hard—it may remind him that he's holding his mommy's hand, and he might let go. But hard enough to let him know he's not alone. Every single person drooping over that hole feels some sort of guilt. We all feel we could've prevented it somehow. We all take blame for Jordan's suicide, regardless of our degree of separation.

I'm surprised when Malik returns my squeeze hard enough that it borderline hurts. I turn my eyes up to him. Up. I'll never be cool with my kid being taller than I. "I can't look at his mom," he whispers, swiping his hand roughly over his mouth and down his chin. His eyes dart in all directions—the hearse, a patch of trees, headstones, people—anything that is not the mother of Jordan Sawyer.

"I know," I whisper back, and forcefully turn my eyes in the direction he can't—Jill Sawyer molded into a folding chair, her feet planted on the turf leading up to the hollowed earth that waits to envelop her son. "I can't even imagine, Malik." I swallow hard because Malik is already breaking down, and one of us needs to hold it together.

I see the tight group of teenagers the same time Malik does, because I feel his hand releasing mine to go join them, but I'm not ready. While their presence gives him strength, it's tearing mine down, and if he lets go of my hand I'll cry. "Malik?" I say desperately. His head swivels toward me at the sound of my voice cracking, and he's looking at me like he's concerned, and it's disconcerting that we're switching roles right now, but we're still connected by the fingertips and frozen at arm's length, and he needs to know. "If you ever—" I involuntarily swallow.

Malik lets go of my hand but steps toward me, shoving his hands in the pockets of his dress pants. "What, Mom?"

I glance back and forth from the ground to his chest—his black dress shirt, his silver tie. I can't meet his eyes. "If you ever do ... what Jordan did. If you ever feel like, like that's what life's become. That you need to—to do that. I mean, please don't. I hope you never do. But if you do, just ... put the gun to my head first. Okay?" And now I look into his eyes. Silver-blue, just like mine. The only part of us that looks alike. Only now, mine are pleading and his are registering. "I'd rather you blow my brains out than to turn me into..." I can't say Jill's name.

THE FALLING OF STARS

Malik's face sobers, assuming the parental role as quickly as I relinquished it. He gazes over my head toward Jill and pulls me into a hug. "I promise, you drama queen. Now stop being so extra."

I hate how soft I've become; I'm the parent. *I* should be comforting *him*. Now I feel even more guilty because my actions made him look at Jill when he just said he can't look at her.

I release him and dab at my face, forcing a smile. "Go see your friends." There. I'm a parent again.

He chuckles, though, and shakes his head, putting his hand on my back and guiding me toward the turf. "We need to talk to Jill, Mom. She needs all the support she can get. Those guys can wait."

I sigh. I hate when he adults better than I do.

We wait awkwardly as a mute Jill receives hugs from people I don't recognize. Any other day, I'd ask her who they were, but not today. At least a hundred people are standing around, and yet I can hear each of their heartbeats, the blood swooshing through everyone's veins. The whispers are monotone, the condolences so hushed and repetitive they've become background noise. A breeze sneaks through the herd of us, causing palm trees to rattle above our heads and putting a damper on the heat that is a Miami autumn. October is just as scorching as July, but today is unseasonably cool. And by cool, I mean eighty degrees.

The couple moves on, and Malik leans down first to hug Jill. She immediately reacts to his embrace, crying and wrapping her arms around his neck as she stands. "Oh, Malik. You were his best friend growing up. You were like his big brother. He loved you so much. Thank you for loving him and for being such a good friend." She's looking him up and down and tracing her hands along his arms, his shoulders, as if Jordan would manifest from Malik's teenage body. As if visions of their sleepovers and bike rides and bonfires are radiating from him. She touches his face—his jaw is quivering—like it's the only teenage boy's face she'll ever touch again.

"I'm sorry," is all Malik can manage, and my heart breaks. Malik hadn't hung out with Jordan since middle school three years ago. And even so, each phone call and every visit was initiated by Jordan, who at that time was an eleven-year-old desperate to salvage a childhood friendship with a hormone-raging, thirteen-year-old Malik waging wars in his head over girls and sports, and there wasn't much room for the immaturity that was Jordan Sawyer.

Jill turns to me. "Eve!" she sobs into my shoulder. "Eve, why did he do this?" She pulls away and stares into my eyes. Waiting. She actually wants me to answer this question.

Time halts, and I can't breathe. I finally manage to shake my head. "I don't know, Jill. I'm so sorry." I glance at Malik—who also seems to be experiencing this horrific time-annihilating phenomenon—and flick my gaze toward his friends. He graciously bows out just as Jill's wife, Petra, approaches and puts her arm around Jill's shoulder.

Petra and I lock eyes and smile sadly before she gazes back toward the ground, her hand rubbing Jill's back. I've never been able to break through Petra's shell, even though I'm Jill's oldest friend. I'd known Jill before she even knew she was gay. I tell myself Petra is simply an introvert and not to take it to heart. She seems to really love Jill, and that's all that matters.

Jill buries her head in my shoulder again, and I wrap my arms around her. There's nothing to say to a mother whose child took his own life, so I just say, "I love you, Jill. I'm so sorry," over and over until Petra gestures toward the others waiting to give condolences. Like a robot, Jill turns to the people behind me.

I move toward Petra. "How are you holding up?"

Petra sighs and tugs a curly strand of hair. "I'm okay. Thanks for asking, Eve. You're the first person to ask me how I'm doing."

I give her a sympathetic look. "Don't take it personally. It's just that Jill is, you know, the biological mom. Stepparents always get pushed to the side, I'm sorry."

She clicks her tongue. "Nah, I get it. Jill and I've only been together a few years. I guess people would think Jordan and I weren't close. But I loved that kid, Eve. I did." Her eyes mist and she shifts her feet, her hand returning to Jill's back to absently rub.

"I know you did." I glance over at Malik, who's gelled right into his group of friends. Population: two boys from Malik's JV football team, and four girls. I know them all from the sophomore English classes I teach at their high school.

I'm just about to turn my attention back to Petra when I see Malik's hand graze across the back of one of the girls—a cheerleader, probably. Her back is to me, so I can't tell who she is. But she turns her head to whisper to Malik, and I recognize her profile. It's Creed Holloway. Definitely not a cheerleader.

I'm trying to figure out what this anomaly of sophomores is doing at a freshman funeral when I feel a hand being shoved into mine and is shaking it. I look at my hand, my eyes following past the connected one, up the arm, and into the eyes of a woman who looks identical to Petra, only with longer hair. "...this is Eve Hunter. Eve, this is my twin sister, Mallory."

"Mallory," I repeat. "Nice to meet you." I'm confused as to why I'm being introduced to Petra's sister, but apparently I missed an entire conversation spying on my son, so who knows what I agreed to?

Petra turns to Jill, who's hugging Jeremiah Lorrey, the high school superintendent and my boss, and I realize Petra's just pawned me off on her sister so she can get back to Jill and the condolences.

"So, Petra says your son was friends with Jordan?" Mallory's sustained blinks indicate her high level of curiosity toward my answer.

I nod. "Yes, Malik grew up with Jordan. He's right there." I gesture toward his group.

She turns back to me with a puzzled look. "The blonde one?"

Now I feel guilty. She doesn't know our story. "No, the darker-haired one."

She looks at me again, and I can tell it's just not registering. "The who now?"

"The boy with the dreadlocks."

She masks the inevitable shocked look, her eyes darting from my pale skin and reddish-blonde hair to my honey-colored son with light brown, shoulder-length dreads pulled back in a low ponytail. I clear my throat. "His dad was ... *not* Irish, like I am," I say and pray she doesn't ask questions about Malik's father.

"Ah! How old is he?"

"Sixteen."

I wait for the second look of shock that always comes after realizing we're different ethnicities—the one that says I barely look older than sixteen myself, thanks to my petite stature and the freckles across my nose. "You must've been a child when you had him. How old were you?"

"Sixteen."

She blinks rapidly as she does the math that makes me thirty-two. She hasn't upset me; I'm used to this. The events that led to Malik don't matter, because he's my son and I love him beyond comprehension. But I really, really, *really* don't want her to ask about it. I pretend to scratch my face with my left hand, giving her a glimpse of my wedding ring so she can conclude that I'm happily married. I really wish my husband were here right now.

"He's breathtaking, Eve." She turns back to Malik, who's swaying next to Creed and inching closer to her with each sway.

THE FALLING OF STARS

I thank her just as the minister begins reading from Psalms, and the crowd hushes. I feel a small hand slip into mine—Jill's. Holy crap, how did I end up next to the grieving mother during the most horrible time of her life? Should I move and let someone closer to her stand here? I look at my colleagues—Mr. Lorrey and a few other teachers who taught Jordan's freshman classes—but in order to join them, I'd have to abandon the grieving mother who grabbed my hand in the first place.

Besides, I *am* the closest thing to family. Jill hasn't been close with hers since she came out twelve years ago, so I straighten my shoulders and accept my fate at her right hand with Petra at her left as we hear about valleys of shadows of death.

The minister finishes, and the casket is mechanically lowered into the ground. I hear sniffling and soft sobs throughout the gathering; Jill is a stone. I close my eyes and try to remember the last time I saw Jordan, but I can't. It must've been July when I gave him his acceptance letter to Liberty School of Excellence. I pulled some strings for Jill, bypassing a waiting list to get Jordan enrolled in the most prestigious private school in Miami-Dade County for his freshman year—the perks of being staff. I remember how she peeled around the room, clapping and cheering, and Jordan looked back and forth from me to the letter, his crooked grin waxing wider with each second. "Malik goes to school there?" he'd asked in his squeaky, pubescent voice.

No, that couldn't've been the last time, because I ran into him the first week of school and asked him how he was doing. I try to remember his response, if he'd given any indication of being suicidal. I just don't remember. I'm angry with myself. I should've been more involved. I should've sought him out. I should've—

My thoughts are interrupted by Mallory saying it was nice to meet me, although not under the circumstances, and she hopes to see me again sometime, although not under the circumstances. I return her sentiments and turn to Jill. She's hugging the last of the mourners, and I can tell she's exhausted. I look at Petra. "She needs to rest."

Petra nods just as Jill pivots toward me, her eyes having gone from glazed to fiery in about two seconds. "I need to tell you something, Eve."

I start. "What is it?"

"The cops don't want to hear it because they deal with teen suicide every day, and they don't care. But something happened to Jordan to make him do this. I know it."

Petra rolls her eyes behind Jill and shakes her head at me. I hesitate before responding. "What do you mean, Jill? What happened?"

Jill shakes her head frantically, and for a second I think she's having a seizure. "I don't know. Something, someone was putting a bug in his ear. I'm going to find out. Will you help me?"

Petra looks attentive now, her droll dismissal of Jill's conspiracy morphing quickly to unease at her call to action. She puts her hands on Jill's shoulders. "Jill, you have to stop this," she whispers like she's speaking to a five-year-old. "Let the cops do their investigating. You can't ask Eve to involve herself in something that you don't know is true."

Jill shrugs Petra's hands off. "I *do* know." She's staring at me. They're both staring at me, waiting for my response.

But I don't know what to say. Jill *is* acting pretty erratic right now, and it *does* sound like a desperate plea for a mother to have some sort of closure after her son's suicide. But what sort of monster would I be to say that to her right now? Her son just lowered into the earth moments ago? I bite my lip as Malik saunters toward me, his friends long gone.

"Why don't you go home and rest, Jill? We'll talk about this tomorrow, okay?"

2

EVE

I cower in my backyard, leaning against the house and taking a long hit off a cigarette. It's ironic that as a kid, I had to hide smoking from my parents, and now as a parent, I have to hide it from my kids.

It's dinnertime, I know. But I need a break. That funeral was emotionally draining, and it's taking my entirety not to cry. Besides, on my counter sits a Crock-Pot, and in that Crock-Pot are all the ingredients for chili. It's been simmering for hours, and I'm grateful for Crock-Pots on days when funerals just suck the life out of you. I've got a cornbread in the oven—so domesticated and Octoberish! Misleading, I know, since Miami doesn't have fall, and I'm feeling far from domesticated right now.

I peek in the kitchen window as I flick ashes off my cigarette and watch my husband, Alex, grating a block of cheese into a bowl and dicing up onions. Thank God for wonderful husbands.

I scamper toward the side of the house, stepping through wet grass and avoiding scattering lizards, and glance into Malik's bedroom window. He's at his computer, a YouTube video streaming as he tips back in his chair.

Xander, my eight-year-old son with Alex, bursts into the room, causing Malik's chair to nearly topple over. I twist away from the window before I'm caught spying and smoking.

"Get out, Xander!" Malik's voice muffles through the window. I hear Xander's high-pitched arguing ("I'll show you the dark side!") and peek in just in time to see Malik jump from his chair, causing Xander to rush out the door. I chuckle and exhale a stream of smoke.

But my shoulders deflate and the smoke swirls off into oblivion as I hear Xander's squealing— "Mooooooom!"— and Malik's baritone harmony. I drop my cigarette and stamp it out, heading toward the patio door. Duty calls.

"What's the problem?" Alex is hollering as I step inside. He glances up from his dicing, apologizing with his eyes for the chaos that's managed to cut short my cigarette break. I shrug and smile at him while Xander continues acting like everyone's being murdered in front of him.

"Malik's watching porn!" Xander squeals, his eyes dancing below a mop of fiery red hair, despite that blatant lie.

Malik shuffles in, rolls his eyes, and pulls a Gatorade from the fridge. "I am not. You don't even know what porn means."

"You'd better not be watching porn," Alex says, and I stiffen amongst Xander's chirps of, "What's porn? What's porn?"

"Leave him alone, Alex. Xander's being a little stinker." I pop a piece of gum in my mouth and try scrubbing the cigarette smell off my hands at the sink. Alex's knife stops chopping—I know it's because he's bothered by my rebuffing, so I glance over my shoulder and wink at him. "We've had a rough day, Malik and I," I remind him softly.

THE FALLING OF STARS

"I'm not a stinker!" Xander's chanting, and he's wearing a Kylo Ren costume without the mask. He looks so cute, I chuckle. "Go take that costume off and get ready for dinner, Cutie Ren."

"What're we eating? I'm starving," Malik says as Xander darts to his room. I can tell by his voice that he's just as exhausted as I am. I gesture toward the Crock-Pot and dry my hands, reaching up to accept the kiss Alex is aiming at me as he dumps his chopped onions into a bowl.

"Chili, and we're eating now," Alex replies. "Help me carry these dishes to the table, please. Malik."

Malik sighs but doesn't argue, and I pull the cornbread from the oven. It's burnt.

"How was the funeral?" I hear Alex asking Malik as I curse and pick off the blackened edges. Malik mumbles a reply, but I can't understand it. I hope he's not getting an attitude with Alex; I can only defend him so much, and neither Alex nor I have a very high tolerance for backtalk.

It's not like I have to spend my life defending Malik against Alex—Alex is a fantastic stepdad. Alex is a fantastic everything: teacher, husband, father … I truly believe he loves Malik just as much as Xander. But he's also a fantastic temper-loser, and toss in a smartass remark from Malik, that's a recipe for disaster. I prefer to call my constant guard *mitigating*.

I cut the cornbread into ridiculous-looking squares to detract from the missing burnt chunks and toss them in a bowl, scurrying into the dining room because it's too quiet in there. I stop short when I see Malik leaning on the table, his palms propped on the surface and his face hovering over the pot of chili. He looks like he's about to cry.

Alex sets the salad down and reaches an arm across Malik's broad shoulders to give him a quick massage/hug/masculine-yet-sympathetic pat on the back in an awkward way that only a stepdad whose stepson just got home from a funeral can pull off. Even though Malik is six feet tall, Alex still towers four inches over him. All this height is making this picture even more awkward.

Malik ignores his sentiments in an attempt to regain composure. "Let's not talk about it now," I mumble as I place the cornbread chunks next to the salad. I squeeze Malik's arm and shoot him a smile. He's already poker-faced, and it's almost scary how quickly he morphed back into normalcy.

Alex calls for Xander (who's been abnormally quiet back there) as Malik and I sit at the table. "Xander!" he calls again.

"What?"

Malik and I giggle as Alex flattens his lips to hide a smile. "Let's go! It's dinnertime!" He shakes his head as he lowers in his chair. "I swear that kid's gonna be grounded off everything until Christmas if he doesn't start listening."

Malik scoffs and I roll my eyes. We take his threats just as seriously as Xander does, obviously. Xander runs in the room, devoid of any Kylo Ren paraphernalia and complete with a sweater and combed hair.

"Wow! Don't you look nice?" I gush as he plops in the chair next to me. He smiles unabashedly and smooths his hair with his palm.

Alex begins scolding him for his dinner tardiness, but Malik interrupts. "You look like you have a hot date, Xander. You got a hot date?"

"Pshh. No, I don't have no hot dates," he replies in the voice he uses when he tries to sound grown up. "You have all the hot dates, Malik. I don't even have cold dates."

Alex chuckles as he ladles chili into everyone's bowls. "That's a pretty tight schedule squeeze for Malik during football season, isn't it? You still managing to date between schoolwork and football?"

Malik laughs. "Yeah, I'm pretty much married to Coach Jay for the next couple months."

"Well, hopefully he'll put a ring on it at the end of the season. A championship ring." Alex winks and Malik snickers and suddenly my heart is full. I feel like crying. "When's your next game?" I ask Malik, scooping copious amounts of cheese into Xander's bowl, because cheese is his favorite part of chili.

"Friday."

"Friday night lights! Let's go, Liberty Lords!" Alex says excitedly through a mouthful of salad. "Coach Jay told me he's got you and Javier learning some new plays."

Malik nods as he wipes his face with his napkin. "Yeah. Javi cuts a post. As long as the O-line does its job, I should be able to put the ball right in his hands."

"You're still the quarterback, Malik?" Xander asks.

"I'm always the quarterback," Malik answers with slight irritation, and I'm not sure if it's because Xander asks that every week, or because Malik doesn't really want to be QB anymore. I don't ask. Malik has the best arm in high school football in all Miami-Dade County, including Varsity. He can throw a perfect spiral over fifty yards—in motion. So no matter how much he wants to run the ball, his unswerving throw and precise aim condemns him to quarterback. Especially when you have a receiver like Javier Acosta.

Alex picks up on Malik's tone, too. "You should have gone to Varsity when they asked you to. You wouldn't have to be quarterback."

Malik smirks. "Right, I'd have a starting position right on the bench the entire season."

Alex nods. "Yeah, I understand. Have you studied for your history test tomorrow?"

My phone sings in my pocket, and I smash any button through my pants to get it to stop. Malik turns his face down to his food and begins shoveling it in his mouth, clearly avoiding Alex's stare. "Not yet."

Alex's silence is loud and clear—Malik is to study for his history test tonight. It's the fine line he teeters, being Malik's father as well as his history teacher, and he refuses to give Malik any special treatment because of this conflict of interest.

I don't think Malik would want special treatment, anyway.

"Can I be done?" Xander asks, and my phone chirps a text from my pocket. I ignore it as I assess Xander's bowl—still full of chili and void of cheese, and that's dinner.

"Fine, but no dessert."

Xander grumbles and stomps into the living room as Malik excuses himself to his room to do homework. Alex and I are left alone at the table, and we look at each other.

We smile.

He drags the back of his fingers down my jaw and runs his thumb along my bottom lip. "Rough day, huh?"

I nod and feel my eyes drooping. "You have no idea."

"I'm sorry I wasn't able to go with you to the funeral. You know, with the thing…"

I nod again; I know the thing—a nasty bout of pink eye Xander had up until this morning. I can't blame him for not wanting to take any risks, but this was a funeral and there are no repeats.

I push my face into his caresses, closing my eyes and absorbing the comfort of his warm hand. "It was so awful, Alex. I don't ever want to experience a day like this again as long as I live." All the emotion I've held back rushes to the surface, and Alex pulls me into his lap as tears build in my eyes.

"I'm sorry, Eve. I'm sure Jill was a wreck." Alex rubs my back as my phone manifests in my pocket—again. I squeeze my pocket—again.

"She actually asked me why Jordan did this. She looked me in the eye—a grieving mother whose son took his own life—and waited for an answer. I never want to see eyes like that again. I don't know how such oceans of pain can fit into such a small face."

"Damn. What did you tell her?"

THE FALLING OF STARS

I shrug. "I don't even remember. I think I just told her how sorry I was."

"Why don't you get a glass of wine? Go take a bubble bath? I'll clean this up."

I kiss him. Hard.

He kisses me back, and after nine years you'd think the fire would've died down a little. But we're just as hot and heavy as we were back in the teachers' lounge, before we got caught by Jeremiah Lorrey and he wrote us up. We were engaged the following month. Then as a wedding present, Jeremiah removed the infraction from our files.

He's still the charming, adorable creature that had all the high school girls giggling when he was hired nine years ago. Even the teachers—full-fledged conversations turning to hushed murmurs when Alex Hunter, the new strawberry-blonde history teacher, would enter a room. The whole thing was romanticized; Alex is cute, but he's no Hemsworth brother. I mean, he's a history teacher, for crying out loud.

He fell hard for the "hot literature teacher" (as I was known amongst the students, and which wasn't true) and the "single mom to the cute little exotic-looking boy" (as I was known amongst the staff, and which *was* true). And, not immune to his charm, I fell equally as hard. I'll never forget the day he paraded into my classroom—smack in the middle of sixth period when my desks were full of senior butts—and handed me a rose, asking me to dinner.

He'd made a scene on purpose, knowing the effect we both had on the students. The cheering and hooting lasted until the day we came back from our honeymoon, and if we weren't already, we were instant favorite teachers. Scholastic celebrities. Oh, it was totally blown out of proportion; they called us Barbie and Ken. And let's be realistic. I'm way too plain to be Barbie, and Alex is entirely too dorky to be Ken.

His hands move down between my thighs, and I flip my leg over to straddle him. But my phone goes nuts again. "Who's the cock block?" he asks amusedly, and I finally pull my relentless phone from my pocket.

"Two missed calls and three texts. All from Jill." I look at him wide-eyed.

Alex raises his eyebrows. "Oh, boy. What do her texts say?"

I open them.

I'm so sorry to bother you. Can you call me when you get a chance?

I'm sorry, Eve. I just need to talk to you.

???

I jump off Alex's lap and pace. "Oh, crap. What've I done?"

Alex smiles sympathetically as he clears dishes from the table. "Go call her back and take your bath."

"Love you," I mumble as I head toward the bathroom. What does Jill need so desperately? I'm nervous.

She answers on the first ring. "Eve, hi. I'm sorry to bother you. I know you're with your family."

Tears flood my eyes, and I swallow. "Hi, Jill. Don't be sorry. Are you okay? What can I do?"

She hesitates. "I know you're busy with the boys, but if you have a few minutes, can you come over? I want to talk to you about something."

I abandon thoughts of a bubble bath and grab my keys off the dresser. "Of course. I'll be right there."

3

EVE

If Miami had the proverbial railroad tracks that divided the good and bad parts of town, I'd be crossing them now. Instead, it's a canal.

A canal that's been known to host an alligator or two, and flanked by two highways. I'm driving over a bridge that ascends above them all—a bridge that Xander calls "The Bump." A city should never have so many highways and alligator canals that people need to build bridges and bumps just to go to a friend's house two miles away, safely.

As I coast down the other side, I pass a cemetery on the right and plain, small homes with well-manicured lawns on the left. See, the proverbial railroad tracks insinuate that one side is "good" and the other is "bad." Sometimes that's not the case. Sometimes there are gray areas in between. And those areas are my favorites.

Just north of the Section 8 housing, Jill's neighborhood is inexpensive (for Miami real estate), simple, and often avoided—probably due to the proximity of the Section 8 housing. But Jill is the proud owner of this modest, 1980-something ranch she purchased all on her own after the falling out with her family, and my heart swells with pride for her every time I pull up to her house.

Both Jill's and Petra's cars sit in the driveway; their elderly neighbor is raking fallen leaves from the mango tree in his front yard. I flash him a smile, and he gives a friendly wave. I cruise up to Jill's front door, giving it five hard raps and wondering if the neighbor knows about Jordan.

Petra opens after a moment, and her face draws into a long, horizontal line, like she can't imagine what must've transpired to result in Eve Hunter appearing on her doorstep the evening of her stepson's funeral. She opens the door wider, edging aside to allow me to enter.

My feet stumble over the threshold as I mutter, "Sorry, it's just—Jill wanted—I didn't—"

"Jill's in the kitchen," she states. "I don't know why she's bothering you with all this. She needs to just mourn in peace."

Petra's slamming of the door and forward trudging propel me even more quickly toward the kitchen. "I'm happy to help in whatever way I can, Petra," I call over my shoulder with a hint of disappointment I try very hard to hide. Why is Petra trying to dictate how Jill mourns?

My heart flips when I see Jill seated at the table, a lot more slack in her body than the rigid pose she held at the cemetery. She's put sweatpants on, and what I think is one of Jordan's Miami Hurricanes T-shirts. A cup of tea sits in front of her that I feel she's barely tolerating; I'm assuming Petra told her to *drink this, it'll make you feel better.*

"Jill?"

"Hi, Eve," she says without looking up.

I slip into a chair across from her and clear my throat. "How ya holdin' up?"

"This sucks."

"I know."

THE FALLING OF STARS

Petra sighs from the entryway. Silence follows, and I watch Jill as she fingers the swerving handle of her teacup. She's so wispy. A tiny brunette thing whose only indication of her thirty-five years is the lines in her forehead and mouth. But she's pretty much the strongest person I know.

"Why did you name your boys their names?" she finally whispers.

I'm thrown by the randomness of the question, and I think Petra is, too, because she joins us at the table, as if preparing to intercede if Jill flies off the handle.

"Malik—" I jar the phlegm from my throat. "Malik was supposed to be Malachi, but I couldn't fit it on this … this snowman mug I wanted to personalize."

Petra looks at me sideways, and I shrug. "I was sixteen. A child. Things like that are important to a child."

Jill snorts a soft giggle. She stays quiet, as if waiting for me to continue with the origins of Xander's name, although I think it should be fairly obvious. "And Xander is short for Alexander. He was named after his father."

Jill sighs from somewhere far away. "Jordan was the name of my first love."

I swallow and shift in the chair. "His dad?"

Jill looks at me and smiles wistfully. "No, the girl I met after his dad. I was pregnant with Jordan. She helped me through that really hard time in my life. I never told you about her." She rests her chin in her hand, her elbow propped on the table. I don't dare look in Petra's direction while Jill talks about an ex, but I imagine the awkward tension shooting from her ears like a smokestack.

"Do you think I ruined him? By naming him after a girl? Do you think that's why he did it, Eve?"

Oh, my god. How tortured Jill's mind must be that she's going through every decision she's made as his mother, even before he was born, trying to determine why he killed himself. I can't fathom the depths of pain her mind is enduring.

"No! Jill, you're not the reason Jordan did this."

"It couldn't've been easy being a boy with two gay moms."

"Don't—"

"Do you think he was gay?" Her hand drops from her chin, and she analyzes me.

I pinch the bridge of my nose and squeeze my eyes shut. Petra's chair scrapes on the floor. "Jordan wasn't gay, Jill. You know that," she says. "He had that girlfriend last year."

I look up to see Jill shrugging. "I had boyfriends up until my twenties."

Petra shakes her head. "It was different for Jordan. He knew if anyone understood, it was us. He knew we would've helped him through that."

"But it's not the same for boys," Jill bounces back. "They would've made fun of him at school. Bullied him. You know what it's like. It's not easy, especially for a kid."

Petra studies Jill then shoots me a glance. "What do you need from Eve, love? She's here to help you, but unfortunately, she can't answer these questions."

I breathe a sigh of relief. Maybe Petra doesn't hate me, after all. Jill nods through a loud exhale, leaning back and looking toward the ceiling. "I wouldn't wish this upon my worst enemy." And she bursts into tears.

Petra moves to her and rubs her hands up and down her arms. Jill drops her head on Petra's shoulder, and I don't know what to do. My heart is breaking as my tears drip onto the table.

"Someone did this to him." The words rip through Jill's gritted teeth.

Petra's hands halt for a moment before resuming their up-and-down motion along Jill's arms. "There's no proof of that," she whispers.

"That's just it. There's no evidence. Nothing. In fact, there's so much *nothing*, it's suspicious."

Petra and I exchange a confused look. "What do you mean?" I ask.

Jill leaps from the chair and swipes an iPhone off the counter, tossing it to me. "Be my guest. Snoop. Dig. Go through Jordan's phone."

I look down at the little rectangle like I'm holding a voodoo doll. "Um, okay..." An ominous feeling shoots through me as I open his home screen, devoid of any passcodes. It looks as any other teenage boy's phone should, with Sebastian the Ibis—the Hurricane mascot—as the background. All the typical social media icons—Twitter, Snapchat, Instagram—line perfectly amongst Spotify and ESPN and YouTube.

I gulp and touch his texting icon. Four names cascade from the top:

Mom

Isaac

Janice

And a 305 number that apparently wasn't in his contacts.

I open that one first. There are only a few exchanges, dated from three days ago. It's a brief conversation about some French homework. I go back and click on Janice's (whom I don't know). Same thing—five texts total between the two of them; Janice asks about going to a movie and he says he has to study. Isaac's (whom I also don't know) conversations are just as anticlimactic, and the few texts between him and Jill are about the proper size of an air filter to buy from Publix.

"Where are all his text messages?" I ask, exiting and going to Instagram.

"Exactly," Jill sighs.

I don't follow Jordan on Instagram, but I know Malik does because I see that he liked his posts every now and then. But there's only one post on Jordan's profile—a random stock photo of a galaxy he posted three days ago with the hashtag, *#shootingstar* as the caption. "He deleted all his Instagram posts," I announce, exiting out. I don't even go to Snapchat. There's no way anything's there, because within the last twenty-four hours, he hasn't even been...

I lock the phone and set it on the table, scooting it toward Jill and farther away from me. I don't need to see anything else to get the gist of what she's saying.

Petra stands and circles Jill. "That doesn't mean anything. Who knows why he felt the need to delete everything three days ago ... the day he ... killed himself?"

"Jordan is a hoarder, Petra," Jill states, then whispers, "Was."

"Well, what do you think this means?" I prompt.

"Jordan had photos on here from when he first got his phone at age eleven!" Jill snatches his phone, swiping until she's in his photos. She steers the phone toward me, and I see an empty album. No pictures. "He was a nostalgic, little old soul. He never got rid of anything. For Christmas, he asked me to pay for more gigabytes of storage because he was running out."

"What about iCloud or Google Drive or the likes? Maybe he stored everything there to clear up space on his phone," I suggest.

Jill drags her fingertips across the phone before shoving it back in my face. I have to back up a tad to see the iCloud screen and the only option available: *Set up iCloud on this device.* She jerks it back and manically swipes and clicks some more, shoving it back toward me. *Download Google Drive Now!*

My eyebrows shoot up, and she opens her fingers and lets the phone plummet to the table like a mic drop. "This is why I need your help."

I take a moment to let those words sink in, and she lets me.

Petra halts behind Jill and rests her hands on her shoulders. "This still doesn't mean—"

"I don't know anything about modern technology!" Jill interrupts. "Are there other places besides these and

Dropbox he could've saved everything to? And if there are, and he did, why did he do it?"

I'm stuck at Dropbox. I forgot about that; I'm an English teacher, not an IT technician or even a detective, and I have no idea why Jill's sought me out to play these parts. I clear my throat and try to sound smart, digging deep into my experience with the Internet, outside of Amazon and Pinterest. "What about Snapfish? Or Shutterfly?"

Petra laughs. "He's not a domesticated, scrapbooking, middle-aged mom."

"Hey! I—" She's absolutely right.

We sit in silence. Again.

Petra plops down in her chair. "It's probably typical for a suicidal teenager to do this. A phone is a teenager's lifeline. It's social suicide to delete everything on a phone, so actually, if you think about it … it does make sense."

Jill glares at Petra. "You. Are. Wrong."

I tense.

"You are Jordan's mom, too. You know him better than this. Jordan was happy, sweet, caring, and he never threw anything away!" Jill's voice is escalating as well as her body as she rises from her chair and hovers over Petra. "Go look in his room! Go! Now!" She turns to me with crazy eyes. "Go look in his room, Eve!" She snatches my arm, dragging me from the kitchen.

I turn to Petra, who is just as wide-eyed as I am.

I stumble down the hall behind a fast-paced Jill and run into her when she stops in front of a doorway and flips on the light. "Tell me he deleted everything on his phone!"

My eyes drape across his bedroom, and I burst into tears. His dirty clothes lie on the floor, and sports posters cover every inch of his wall—Jose Fernandez, the Marlins pitcher who died in a boating accident. Jamal Carter, a Hurricanes football player who graduated years ago. Trophies and trinkets clutter his desk, his dresser, his nightstand—fifth grade spelling bee, sixth grade science fair, seventh grade soccer. A laptop next to an older laptop next to an extinct laptop … Jill's right. Jordan didn't throw things away.

But I can't speak because I'm crying outside Jordan Sawyer's bedroom that he'll never enter again. Jill will have to do that laundry on the floor, and she'll fold it, knowing he'll never wear it. She'll have to take down these posters—eventually—and assess the darker paint behind them, the large squares and rectangles that haven't seen the sun since Jordan was a small, hopeful child, awed and inspired by the athletes he splayed amongst the walls wherein he dwelled.

A glass of water adorns his nightstand. He was thirsty before he decided to shoot himself with a Glock .43.

I can't take it anymore. I need to see Malik and Xander. My arms ache for them. I have to go hug my sons.

I back away from the bedroom and head toward the kitchen, wiping my eyes and suppressing hiccups. "Have you told the cops this theory?" I manage.

"Yes, they said the same thing Petra did. Symbolism. Committing technological suicide before actual suicide."

"And everything was the day he … did this. Right?" I grab my purse from the table and retrieve my keys.

"Yes. I asked him to check the size of the A/C filter while I was at Publix, and that was literally four hours before." Jill eyes my keys lobbing up and down in my hand. I'm not trying to be rude, but no joke—I gotta get outta here. For my own sanity.

I stop momentarily, everything I saw on Jordan's phone running through my head in summary. "And what did they say about the stars? The one post he had on Instagram, the last thing he posted before he…?"

Jill shrugs one shoulder. "Cryptic suicide letter."

I scratch my chin with my car key. "Is there any way to contact your phone service provider and get those deleted texts?"

Jill looks at me like I just spouted some riddle, and Petra steps out from behind her. "Eve, please. We appreciate you stopping by, and we appreciate your support. But this..." Petra glances at Jill, who's still pondering my "riddle," and I realize she never discussed the deleted texts with the cops. I've set off a fire alarm in her head.

"Now look what you've done." Petra tosses a hand toward the frozen Jill. "You can't feed into these ideas. What's done is done, and now she's searching for peace by conjuring up some conspiracy about Jordan. All that'll lead to is more disappointment. She needs therapy and time, that's all."

Petra's been guiding me toward the door throughout her entire scolding, and from the looks of it, I won't even get to hug the mourning mother goodbye. Seeing I've been pushed out the door, I look up at Petra, gearing up for my rebuttal.

But she speaks again. "If you want to give support, send her some stupid flowers," she says through a clenched jaw. "Or make a damn casserole. But don't encourage this behavior."

I can't see Jill at all; Petra's body is blocking the entire doorway. "Petra, I—"

And the door closes in my face.

"What did I do?" I say to the door. Tears begin welling, and I entertain thoughts of knocking again to give Jill a proper goodbye. But it's dark out now, and the friendly neighbor has harvested all his mango leaves and is gone.

What if he's crouched in my backseat?

I jerk my head—that's ridiculous. I need to hug my boys. I trot to my car and hit the unlock button; the lights flash, lighting up the dark streets of the *in between*. The *other side* of the *canal*.

The backseat is clear, just as I suspected. *Silly, Eve.* I jump in and lock the door, starting my car and swinging it in reverse. I call Malik's cell as I race out of the neighborhood.

"Hey, Mom," he says.

I sigh. "Hi, baby."

Malik is alive, and weird things happened in Jill's house.

4

MALIK

"Oye, *pendejo! Dale!* Hurry your ass up!"

I look up from Creed's texts on my phone to see Javier Acosta trotting toward me, twirling a towel. I jump from the locker room bench just in time for the thwack of his towel to crack against the air and not my thigh.

"Oh, shit! I'm still faster than you, jit," I tease, tossing my phone in my locker and shutting it before Javi can see the pictures Creed just sent. And the sight of the twirling towel eliminated any indication my own body might've given away as to the content of the pictures Creed just sent.

She's so fucking hot.

"Bro. What the hell are you doing? Practice starts in five minutes. You know if you're on time, Coach says you're late." Javier's Cuban accent is thickened by the panic in his voice. "And you missed practice yesterday, you and those fat linemen. So you're already on his shit list."

I toss my shoulder pads on, shaking off the last memory I have of hanging out with Jordan. It keeps popping up in my mind like those annoying ads online. I wish I could pay the ninety-nine cents to get rid of it, but my brain's not about subscribing to upgrades and shit. "That was for a funeral. It's not like I was fucking around."

"It don't matter, bro. Your ass better be on that field in, like, eleven seconds." And Javier Acosta—the five-foot-six fastest sixteen-year-old running back in Miami-Dade County—dashes out the door toward the field. Tiny little shit.

"Fuck!" I yell through the empty locker room, but I don't know why. Maybe 'cause my childhood friend is dead, and I'm late to football practice. Maybe 'cause the girl I've been talking to for a couple months just sent me the hottest pictures of her ass in a thong, and I'm late to football practice.

Maybe 'cause I give zero fucks that I'm late to football practice.

I canter out onto the field, the scorching Miami sun sizzling through my dreads, and I hurry to put my helmet on.

"Malik Hunter!" Coach Jay yells from the fifty-yard line, pacing along the entire team lined up doing stretches. King and Lopez, the offensive and defensive coaches, stand a few feet away from him, their arms crossed over their chests like they're Jay's bodyguards, even though that monster of a man doesn't need protection. I do, though.

Javi stands in his captain's position at the head of the lines, my space next to him glaringly empty. I upgrade from cantering to sprinting.

"You're late, Hunter," Coach Jay says, smacking my helmet.

"Sorry, Coach." I take my spot next to Javi, facing the rest of the JV team that stands in four lines of five.

"To the left! Begin! Ten!" Javi yells, but Coach holds up a hand.

"Whoa, hold up. Our quarterback has better things to do than show up to practice and be a leader."

Ah, shit. The rest of the team rectifies themselves from *the left*, and all helmets turn toward me. Even King and Lopez twist their sunglasses- and whistle-clad faces in my direction.

Coach Jay circles me like a shark. "Malik, do us a favor and tell us what you were doing that was more important than being a leader for your team."

I bite hard on my mouthpiece before spitting it out. "I'm sorry, Coach. I'm still just a little out of it today." I scan my eyes across my teammates and raise a hand in a peace treaty. The majority of them nod their forgiveness and begin toward *the left*, but Coach has to keep going and can't shut the fuck up.

"Is this what we should expect from our team captain?"

No, Coach!

"Should this be tolerated from our QB?"

No, Coach!

"Hunter! Hit the buckets! Acosta, finish the drills."

Javier gives me a sympathetic look as he shouts, "To the left! Begin! Ten!" And I groan because the buckets suck ass. I sprint past King and Lopez—whose faces are so stuffed with sunglasses and whistles that there's no room for sympathetic looks—to the sideline, where Coach Jay always has two buckets full of sand sitting next to the water bottles. I listen to the team chanting *nine, eight, seven…* as I grab a twenty-pound bucket in each hand, extending my arms out to the side like a crucifix, and let the torture begin.

I wonder how long he's gonna make me stand like this as I watch Javi run the warmup drills solo. What was I thinking? Did I really think I'd get away with being on time—AKA late—to football practice? It's been thirty seconds, and pain is creeping pretty damn quickly into my delts. I can't tell if it's icy pain or fiery pain yet. I feel my arms descending toward the ground as the team finishes warmups and circles around Javier, hands in, and grunts *LORDS!* before sprinting to the water bottles for the first water break.

The water bottles that are right next to my punished ass.

And by the way, it's fiery pain. For *real*, for real.

I dart my arms upward, trying to keep them parallel to the ground with these thousand-pound buckets as the team approaches and shoots me apologetic glances while squirting water into their gaping pie holes like a bunch of baby fucking birds.

Two minutes and my arms feel like Jell-O shots. My hands are shaking and it's transferring to the buckets; I can hear the rattling. If it's not humiliating enough to be the team captain standing here like a frickin' scarecrow, now I have shaking sand buckets shouting my pain and misery to everyone. I drop my head back and close my eyes against the blinding sun, licking my lips that suddenly feel dry.

My delts are in hades.

The pain is spreading to my forearms as the team trots back onto the field, Coach Jay shouting at them to *Run! Don't walk on my field!* I had to do the buckets once before in middle school, for fighting with a teammate, and I vowed never to do it again. I've watched zillions of athletes do stupid shit that landed them with the buckets, and looked at them with the same pity I'm receiving now, thankful it wasn't me and that it'd never be me.

My delts are in hell.

King walks over, assessing the hot mess that is me, and I hope he offers me water. But he offers something better— "Towel?"

I jerk my head up and down, sweat dripping into my eyes. He grabs an ice-cold cloth from the cooler and shoves it in my mouth. I bite down as he walks away and let the tension release through my clenched jaw as the icy towel cools my thick, dry tongue and water rolls down my throat.

The release is temporary. One minute, tops.

I try distracting myself by reciting The Lord's Prayer and panning my gaze across the football field. I stop on two figures—Mrs. Hendrick, the school counselor, and Alex, my stepdad and history teacher. They're both looking at me, Alex shaking his head in disgust. Fuck. He's gonna kill me.

I spit the towel out, now hot and suffocating. I hope my mom's home when he lights into me later. She always negotiates his punishments, and shaves *years* off my grounding sentences. I can't believe I did this. Xander'll have more freedom than I will.

And just as I think my life can't go any more to shit, this damn memory pops back into my head, the Jordan one. Tears burn my eyes, and I try forcing them back.

It was my thirteenth birthday, and Jordan was running up our walkway carrying a gift in his eleven-year-old arms. I saw him through the window, but when the doorbell rang, I looked at my mom and jostled the PS4 controller in my hand. These autos weren't going to grand theft themselves.

She greeted Jordan like it was his birthday instead of mine, and he jogged up to me with the gift outstretched. "Happy Birthday, Malik!"

I glanced at him and smiled, even though the cops were chasing me for punching a hooker. "Thanks, man. That's awesome."

"Malik?" That was my mom.

I looked up at her. "Huh?"

"Jordan got you a present." She pronounced her t's especially hard.

I begrudgingly set my controller down and reached for his gift, and was pleasantly surprised to open a new headset to use with my PS4. "Oh, yes! Thank you!"

Jordan beamed. "Now we can talk to each other and play GTA online. It'll be so fun!"

I grinned back. "I can't wait!"

But I never did. I never played with him.

"Hunter! Up!"

I jerk to attention and realize my arms have dropped to forty-five-degree angles. I try lifting them, but I physically can't. They feel like metal weights and the earth's a huge magnet planet.

"Hunter! UP!"

I grit my teeth and pray that my arms rise, crying out in agony when they don't. "I'm trying, Coach!" I shout to cover up my bitch-like crying. My entire body is shaking, and I think I'm gonna piss myself. I'm fully conscious of every single grain of sand in these goddamn buckets. They all have names and they're mocking me, all eleventy-gazillion of 'em, all fucking and multiplying and giving birth to more grains of sand and these buckets are getting heavier.

I open my eyes to see Coach Jay marching up, his face mangled in anger. He grabs my facemask and jerks me toward him. "Are you being a little bitch, Malik?"

"No, Coach!"

"Get your arms up, now!"

"Yes, Coach!"

But they don't move.

"NOW!"

And I strain so hard, I fall to my knees like a pathetic pussy.

Coach Jay knocks the buckets from my hands and lifts me to my feet by my facemask. I'm staring into his eyes that are basically shooting flames at me. What the hell's wrong with his face? He looks like he wants me dead. I purposely don't watch John Malkovich movies to avoid shit like this.

But the anger drains from his face and is replaced with the same sympathetic look the rest of my teammates have been giving me throughout this torture. "I know you're going through shit with the kid killing himself," he says quietly and respectfully, despite his rough words and his fingers locked around my facemask. "But you are the leader on this team. Do you understand?"

"Yes, Coach!"

He shakes my facemask, making my head jostle around inside my helmet. "No, you are *the* leader. It's not Acosta. It's you. And leaders are always held to a higher standard. You are the quarterback; the team looks to you for everything. They rely on you to execute every frickin' play properly, and they blame *you* if it fails. They praise *you* if it doesn't. This team is yours, Hunter. And don't you frickin' forget it."

"Yes, Coach!" Although I find it funny that he just fucked me up so hard he could probably be arrested for child abuse, yet he refuses to say *fuck*.

"Now get your butt on the field and practice the bootleg."

"Yes, Coach!"

I don't even get excited when he makes us practice the bootleg anymore—the one play where I get to run the ball—because as much as we practice it, he hasn't called it in a game in the two years he's been our coach.

"How're your arms, bruh?" Javi asks in the locker room after practice, CJ and Gabriel—the two linemen who came to Jordan's funeral yesterday—standing close by.

I purposely spent an extra ten minutes in the shower, waiting for everyone to leave to avoid this line of questioning. But I'm not surprised these three waited for me.

"Fucking wrecked."

"Bro, you got the buckets, bro!" Javi shakes his hand like he's packing an imaginary pack of cigarettes, causing his thumb to slap loudly against his fingers. "What the hell were you thinking? You know you can't be late to practice, man. You know Coach don't tolerate that shit."

I huff as I step into my boxers and sweatpants, slipping my feet into my slides and throwing a *Liberty Lords* hoodie on that feels like a straitjacket because my shoulders are so fried. "I'm sorry I let you down."

They shake their heads. "Nah, man. Don't be sorry," CJ says. "Me and Gabriel got to practice extra early, since we missed yesterday for Jordan's funeral. We figured you'd be early, too."

"Why were you late?" Gabriel asks.

And in some Freudian slip, I grab my phone from my locker and check the home screen.

All three guys burst into barbaric baboon laughter.

"That's what's up!" Javier cackles. "You got pics! We knew there was no way you could do a static hold with those buckets for fifteen minutes—that's a record! — without some driving force! Who is *la puta*?"

CJ pauses his high-pitched laughter to say, "It's Creed!"

"Creed? That's a dude's name. Malik, you poking dudes, you *maricón*?"

Gabriel punches him in the arm. "Creed Holloway, you dumbass. The crunchy little hipster with the glasses in our English class." He pulls up her Instagram on his phone.

Javier's face contorts into a look of disgust when he sees her picture. "What the—you're kidding, right, Malik? What're you messing around with that loser for?"

I clench my jaw and snatch my bag from my locker. This is what I hate about Javi and the team. Yeah, we're close—going through such emotional highs and lows of the games, wins and losses, has caused us to form a camaraderie the rest of the student body doesn't understand. But it also fits us into a mold. A stereotype where athletes only date cheerleaders. I purposely don't watch 90s teen movies to avoid shit like this.

I hate the cheerleaders. For one, I can't tell them apart. They all look like the same soulless, mass-produced creature. You kiss one, it's like kissing them all. I know— I've kissed pretty much all of them. And two, I'm just so attracted to Creed, even though she's not athletic in the slightest. She's artsy and smart and unassuming. I met her in my mom's English class at the beginning of this year, which is strange, since we've been in the same class for two years now. But she's so quiet, it's easy to miss her. So when we were stuck sitting next to each other while my mom rambled about Greek Mythology and literature, and this gorgeous little girl with glasses and brown hair started cracking jokes about how Oedipus and Midas were "motherfucking gold," how could I not be intrigued?

"Bro, I can see Camila Rodriguez's panties soak every time you walk by her. You give her and the rest of those cheerleaders wet pussy syndrome. And you're fucking this thing?" Javi shoves Gabriel's phone in my face, and I'm looking at the worst picture of Creed.

I have no time or desire to play these games. I hike my bag on my shoulder and shoot all three of them a couple birds. "Shorty. Fatasses. Fuck you all." I grin and wink as I back toward the door.

"Hey!" Javi calls right before I hit the exit.

I turn around with my hand on the door, waiting for him to insult me back.

"Icy Hot. For those shoulders tonight."

Shocked at his lack of insults, I nod and turn back to the door, pushing it open.

But just before the door slams behind me, he continues. "And maybe that tight-ass smoke show you got for a mama can massage them for you later." Followed by more baboon laughter.

There it is.

"The sheep says beep! Beep-beep-beep!"

I shut my eyes and try to refocus after Xander just interrupted my studying with whatever the hell that was. I glance up from the dining room table to see him sprawled on the couch, glued to his iPad. Such is the life of a second-grader.

"Malik," my mom calls from the kitchen. "White or dark meat with your dinner?"

"Both."

"'Kay."

I turn back to my homework and plant my palms over my ears, trying to factor the algebraic expression of $6x^2-21xy+8xz-28yz$.

"The cow says meow! Meow-meow-meow!"

"Dammit, Xander!" I slam my fists on the table. "Sheep and cows don't even make those noises! Can you just—"

My mom's head shoots around the corner, and she glares at me. "Stop it." Then she disappears back into the kitchen.

I roll my eyes just as Alex walks through the front door. Now *he's* glaring at me. I forgot he saw me with the buckets. I turn back to algebra. Algebra questions never glare at you or tell you to stop it. It's pretty sad that I'm finding solace in algebraic expressions.

Sometimes, when Alex is mad at me, he likes to loom silently in anger because he thinks I'll suffer more by having to wait for his wrath. He's even doing it to Xander now, when Xander gets in trouble, and it pisses me off because Xander's too young for his mind games, but I think Xander's oblivious to it, anyway.

And today, I don't give two fucks if Alex is pissed. I think he knows, too, because he drops his briefcase on the table and starts right in.

"What was that?" he asks.

"What was what?" I know exactly what he's talking about.

"The sheep says beep! Beep-beep-beep!"

My mom comes in and sets my food on the table before turning to Alex. "Hi," she says blatantly. "What, we don't greet our family members anymore when we come home?" She leans up to kiss him, but halts when she sees the look on his face and follows his gaze to his target— me. She bites her lip and inflates her chest. She's gearing up to defend me, even though she has no idea why. I didn't tell her.

"You know what," Alex growls, his fingertips strumming on the back of a chair. "Football practice. What did you do that landed you with the buckets?"

My mom shoots me a questioning/accusatory stare. "Buckets? What buckets? What happened, Malik?"

I put my pen down and turn toward them, because they find it disrespectful to have a conversation with someone and not make eye contact. They find the dumbest things disrespectful, but it really doesn't bother me. I'm generally pretty easygoing, and asking Alex, "What was what?" is the mouthiest I get. And it's already so passive-aggressive they rarely notice.

"The cow says meow! Meow-meow-meow!"

Alex already knows the reason I had the buckets; I know he spoke with Coach. He's trying to catch me in a lie, so I look him in the eye and answer, "Coach Jay wants us at practice at least ten minutes early. I showed up right on time. He said I was late."

My mom's face scrunches up like it does when she thinks something's unfair, but Alex doesn't give her a chance to speak. He folds his arms and says, "Why were you late?"

I shrug and look to the floor before remembering the eye contact, and look back up. "Just lost track of time, I guess."

"What are the buckets?"

"The sheep says beep!"

"You've never lost track of time, Malik. Since you were eight, you've never been late to practice. What happened?"

I shift in my seat. "I'm sorry, I really don't know. It's just been a rough couple of days, and—"

"What the hell are the buckets!"

"The cow says meow!"

"Xander!" Alex bellows, and I shoot my mom a look that says, *I told you so.*

She suppresses a smile because she's supposed to be mad at me.

Alex turns to her and puts his hands in prayer position, pointing them at her like he's really trying to control his temper. "*The buckets* are two steel buckets filled with twenty pounds of sand. When they screw up, they have to hold them out to the sides, like this, for however long Coach deems necessary." He mimes the position I held for twenty hours today, and my arms ache just looking at him. I don't think I could reenact it if I tried.

My mom looks at me as I absently rub my shoulder. She puts her hands on her hips. "What the actual fuck?"

Aaanndd, that's the first time I've ever heard my mom say *fuck.*

She looks back and forth between Alex and me. "They actually do that to kids? That's abuse! They did that to you, Malik?"

Alex and I glance at each other as my mom storms behind me and starts massaging my biceps, which don't even hurt. I immediately remember Javi's crude comment from the locker room and shrug her off. "It doesn't hurt there, Mom."

She starts squeezing my neck and traps, and I'm about to shrug her off again, but sweet Jesus—they're in nearly as much pain as my delts. My face freezes in agony as my mom stabs her knife-blade finger bones into muscles I didn't even know were assaulted during my punishment— muscles I didn't even know I had.

Alex monitors my facial expression—still frozen agony—and holds a hand up. "Take it easy, Eve. That's too much." She drops her hands as he comes to stand next to her, and he pokes my left delt like I'm some sort of science experiment.

I wince and duck my shoulder away.

I hear my mom's hand land harshly against Alex's chest. "You let them do this to your son? Alex, we don't even punish our kids like this, why would you allow someone else to?"

Alex shrugs. "It's football, honey. You wouldn't understand."

"Ugh! Do they do this all the time?"

"Nah, only for disrespect or direct disobedience. So once every few weeks, someone ends up with the buckets," I reply. I have to agree with Alex—Mom's a diva and doesn't understand football. As much as I hated that today, it's football—and I disobeyed.

"Have you ever had to do it before?" she demands.

"Once, in eighth grade."

"Alex, did you know about that?"

Alex nods. "He and that Colombian kid got in a fight, and the coach made them both do it." Then his voice falters as he asks, "Didn't we … tell you about that?"

She smacks his chest again. "No one told me that my son and his teammates are physically abused at practice!"

Oh. I see what she's doing. She's turning this into an injustice so Alex won't punish me further. I mean, I'm sure she really is anti-buckets, but she's not gonna march in DC or create a hashtag movement. She'll get back at Coach Jay in her own little way, and save me from my stepdad at the same time.

I watch the angry sparks die out in Alex's eyes as she continues ranting about how this is what's wrong with society and this sets children back a hundred years, and don't get her started on the fact that I'm a minor and Jay needs to acquaint himself with Florida Child Labor Laws.

Then Alex starts in with, "Actually, the Federal Fair Labor Standards Act deals strictly with the workplace and not football, and maybe you should acquaint yourself with child labor laws," and I punish myself by retreating to my room with my algebra and dinner plate.

Creed calls as soon as I land on my bed.

"Hey," I answer.

"Hey. What's up? How was practice?"

I swallow food before replying. "Sucked."

"I'm sorry. You better now that you're home? What's going on there in Pleasantville, population: The Hunters?"

I consider that question as I shovel the rest of my food in my face. "Well, my parents are currently arguing about child labor regulations, and my brother is beeping and meowing like … sheep and cows, apparently."

She pauses before she bursts out laughing. "World's most interesting family."

"Speaking of interesting, what's up with those pictures you sent me today? What are you trying to do to me, girl?" Now that I'm thinking of those pictures, I disregard all thoughts of going back out and getting more food. Not with this tent.

Creed's quiet. I know it's because she's embarrassed. She's not that kind of girl. That's what I love about her. She doesn't fit into stereotypes; if she wants to try something new, she does. Today, she wanted to be the type to send nude pics to the JV quarterback. That doesn't make her a slut—trust me.

"Did you like them?" she asks softly.

THE FALLING OF STARS

"Did I *like* them? Are you crazy? You drove me insane. The only reason I'm not looking at them now and jerking off is because I'm using my phone to talk to you." I laugh and hear her sigh of relief.

"That was the reason I was late to practice today and got my ass handed to me. You wouldn't believe what Coach—"

"What? You were late to practice?"

"Creed, are you serious? You sent me those just as I was headed out of the locker room. You gotta be more careful—"

"Malik, I sent you those photos at two fifty-five. You're supposed to be in practice at two fifty, because it technically starts at three, right? I purposely sent those *after* you should've been on the field, I'd never try to get you in trouble. Why weren't you already at practice?"

Whoa. She's right. It wasn't her fault I was late today; I was already late before she sent them. But why?

"Malik? You there?"

I clear my throat. "Yeah, yeah. I just—you're right. I don't know what I've been thinking. Maybe I really did just lose track of time or something."

Creed laughs. "I doubt it. Not Mr. Captain-of-the-football-team. Not the high and mighty quarterback. Your coach would kill you. Your dad would kill you. He's always bragging in class about how responsible you are, how you're taking football and your grades so seriously. What's wrong? Why were you late?"

I think about what she said about Alex. It's true, football and grades have always been my first priority, ever since he came into my life when I was eight and instilled those principles in me. Except today at two-fifty. What was possibly going through my mind, knowing I should've been on that field? Knowing I'd be penalized because I wasn't?

Nothing. I wasn't thinking about a damn thing. I can't blame it on Jordan's death, I can't blame it on Creed's photos, because I prioritized *nothing* before football today. Then it hits me—it's not that I'm frustrated with being quarterback. Not that I'm overwhelmed with being the leader of the team.

I just don't want to play football anymore.

5

EVE

I gaze across the gymnasium full of solemn high-schoolers seated in the bleachers. Some do signs of the cross, some stare at the floor. But most are gazing attentively at Mr. Lorrey at the podium, giving his Jordan Sawyer Memorial/Suicide Awareness speech.

He's harping on how Liberty was "founded upon the idea of perfectionism," and that "this moral theory should be strived by all humans to reach the optimum pinnacle of humanity…" Normally I'd throw the nobody's-perfect card, but I can't even find one kid among these hundreds of students who's being disrespectful. Jeremiah Lorrey is like Dumbledore.

I sit in the row of faculty situated behind Jeremiah and facing the student body. I'm anxious, and I realize this when Alex gently places his hand on my unconsciously bouncing knee. I return his light smile, but this is a conflict of interest for me. Jordan—regardless of the drift—was like family to me. And while I understand schools have protocol when a student commits suicide, I also want to scream out, *"WHY DIDN'T YOU HAVE THIS SPEECH LAST WEEK, WHEN JORDAN WAS STILL ALIVE????"*

I glance down at Mrs. Hendrick, the school counselor, who's sitting rigidly with her legs crossed, and I imagine that's the same way she sits during her counseling sessions. I wonder if she feels guilty because she's a counselor and should've known Jordan was suicidal. Her poise says otherwise—she looks quite confident, and I'm sure she'd muster up some psychological excuse as to why she didn't burst in like Wonder Woman moments before Jordan…

Stop it, Eve. This is no one's fault.

I'm still staring at her when she nods, and I realize Jeremiah just addressed her. I snap back to attention.

"…her door is always open. And all of these teachers—" Jeremiah turns to the rest of us— "care about each and every one of you, and are always willing to talk."

I see in my peripheral vision the staff pantomiming their agreement, including Alex, and I'm scanning the crowd again for Malik. I find him in a sea of *Liberty Lords* hoodies. The football teams—both JV and Varsity—are huddled together, as usual. He sits between Javier Acosta and Gabriel Menendez, not a girl around for miles.

I wonder if Malik will ever get a girlfriend.

"…dismissed to your seventh periods."

I'm snapped back to attention again when the gymnasium fills with the sounds of rising humans and sneakers pounding down bleachers amongst hushed communication. Alex grazes an inconspicuous hand across the back of my neck and gives me chills. "I'm off to teach eleventh grade social studies."

My lips form a sly grin. "I'm off to the teachers' lounge. This is my free period."

He stares at my smirk with a vulturine glint in his eyes. "You have a smart mouth, you know that?"

"I do, Mr. Hunter."

THE FALLING OF STARS

He growls as we approach the double doors, students and staff brushing past us, and I lose him in the crowd.

Great. Now I'm horny.

I head toward the teachers' lounge, praying it's empty so I can drink coffee and fantasize about my husband, with whom I haven't had sex since the night before Jordan's passing. This must be some sort of record for us.

But when I enter, there's the brand-new science teacher—fresh out of college, long curly hair, and the sparkling eyes and goofy grin of a toddler at Disney World.

"Hey, Mrs. Hunter!" she says in a syrupy-sweet southern accent as she pours coffee in a paper cup.

"Hi, Miss Dupree." I move to the corner, pull out my hidden stash of K-cups, and turn to the Keurig.

"You can call me Kendall."

"That's a pretty name. It's also what they call part of southwest Miami." I smile as I snap the K-cup into the Keurig and press the button, and the little machine revs up. "Did you want ... you can call me Eve, by the way, but would you like this coffee instead? It's much better than that industrial stuff." I don't even share my K-cups with Alex, so I don't know what's come over me.

"No, this is fine. Thank ya, though! And yeah, can you tell I didn't grow up here? I'm from South Carolina. Probably not many Miamians would name their child after a census-designated zone. Not to mention my accent. Ha, ha!"

I chuckle and place my hand on my chest. "Well, Eve Hunter. Also not a Miami name. I grew up in the Keys. And Alex is from Lakeland. A gringo if I ever met one."

"Oh." She sits at the table and sips her coffee while I cream and sugar mine. "What was your last name before you married Mr. Hunter?"

I sit at the table with her. "Ryan," I say behind my cup.

"That doesn't sound very Miamian, either."

I smile. "Nope. So how do you like Liberty so far?"

She nods so hard, she bounces in her seat. "I love it here! Everyone's so nice, and the kids are great. All of 'em are well-behaved and respectful. Ya'll are doin' a great job here."

I beam.

"So. What brought you to Miami from the Keys?"

My beam quickly fades. I thought I'd successfully changed the subject. "My parents moved here when I was a teenager."

"Oh. Your dad get transferred or somethin'?"

Oh, sweet mother of…

"No."

Kendall waits for me to continue. I've told myself a thousand times I have nothing to be ashamed of, I have nothing to hide. Besides, she's sweet. I could use some of her southern hospitality. I'll just be honest. "I'd just gotten pregnant with Malik, and—"

"Oh, that's right!" she squeals. "Malik's your son! I have him in fifth period, and he's such a doll. You and Mr. Hunter are doin' such a good job raisin' him."

"Th-thank you."

"Now, Malik's tan with brown hair, and ya'll are reddish blonde and super pale. Is Malik adopted?"

I'm pressing my fingertips into my eyes, trying to ward off this inevitable mental warfare.

She's being rude.

No, she's not. She's being overly friendly.

But that's rude.

So? You've nothing to hide, anyway.

Touché.

"No. He's mine. His biological dad isn't around anymore."

She dips her head sympathetically. "I'm sorry to hear that. But Mr. Hunter's just fantastic."

I'm pretty sure her pupils morphed into hearts for a second, and I thought it was Malik I was going to have to keep her away from, but apparently it's my husband, too.

"You can call him Alex."

She scoffs. "Oh, no. I couldn't. He's like my dad's age."

Oh, son of a—

The door opens and Ruben DeSoto—our IT guy—strolls in and heads for the refrigerator. He raises a hand at us. "Hola, Señoritas," he says with an American accent, even though he's Puerto Rican and speaks perfect Spanish.

Kendall barks some pleasant greeting, and I remember something. "Hey, Ruben. Can I ask you a computer question?"

"Hit me, buttercup."

I glance at Kendall and decide to alter my question—I don't need her cute, perky ears concocting theories. "Malik got a new phone a couple days ago, and it's missing some important texts from his old phone. Something for football. I don't know, exactly. But I was wondering if there's any way to ... you know, get those back."

Ruben is slightly overweight, so when he takes a drink of water and spills it, it drips right down his tie and onto his dress shirt covering his protruding belly. He curses and looks for a napkin, and Kendall takes advantage. "Did he back it up to the Cloud? You can get 'em from there."

Ruben gestures toward her. "See? Ask a millennial those questions. That's not a computer question, Eve."

I take a long, angry chug of coffee. That stupid scenario didn't work, considering Jordan didn't use iCloud, and now I'm a tad insulted because I, too, am a millennial, and Ruben basically just called me old and stupid. I need to find out how to get deleted texts without making Jill look like a crazy person or making it sound like I don't trust my husband or son.

"Yeah, for some reason, they didn't transfer. Oh, well." I shrug as my face blooms an artificial smile.

Ruben throws his hands up—"What can you do? Bye, ladies—" and he leaves.

Kendall leans forward. "That's really weird about his phone. Maybe I can look at it tomorrow durin' fifth period—"

"Psh, no. Don't worry about it. I think, um, yeah, Malik's grounded off his phone anyway, so he won't have it. Tomorrow. During fifth period." I make a mental note to watch Malik like a hawk tonight, so I can ground him off his phone tomorrow.

She blinks like she's about to ask more questions.

"Well, I gotta go. Nice chatting with you." I jump from the table and flee the room, searching for which way Ruben DeSoto went.

I see him heading toward the east wing. "Ruben!"

He waddles along—quickly, for a waddler—and I pick up my pace. "Ruben!"

He finally turns around and pushes his glasses up his nose. "Yeah?"

"Listen," I whisper as I approach him. "I didn't want to say anything in front of that new teacher, but I'm wondering if there's a way to recover deleted texts. Not lost or transferred ... purposely deleted." I throw my hands up in a melodramatic shrug and chuckle nervously. "It's—it's nothing to do with Alex or Malik. I'm ... I'm asking for a friend." This is humiliating...

A sly grin curls up around his mustache. "Of course, you are. Well, it all depends on your *friend's* reasoning. If it's an emergency, you should talk to your phone provider or the authorities to see the proper way to go about recovering them. But if you're scheming and trying to keep it on the DL—or your *friend*, rather—there may be some apps. You could jailbreak the phone. There are lots of apps that Apple hasn't approved for their store if you jailbreak it."

My mind's going a mile a minute.

"There're recording devices to put on phones, if you're trying to catch him cheating—"

"He's not—" I shut my mouth and my eyes, counting to ten. "He's not cheating on me. This really is for a friend."

It's funny that the one truth I told today is the one nobody believes.

The final bell rings as I'm sitting at my desk, going through the App Store. I hear the students in the halls, packing to go home or to after-school activities.

There are two apps for recovering deleted texts, and both have one star. The reviews are horrible and full of expletives. I sigh.

I open a new text for Jill: *I'm trying to figure out how to recover deleted texts, but not getting much luck. We can find a hacker, or we can always go to the police. Thoughts?*

I lock my phone and set it on my desk, strumming my fingers as anxiety builds as to whether Malik made it to practice on time. I covered for him once, and I'll let Alex go ham on him if he does something stupid like that again.

I'm going to check.

I grab my purse and lock up. My heels clip on the tile as I scurry to the back of the building and shove the double doors open, brisking down the sidewalk toward the football field.

Alex is standing at the twenty-yard line in his typical stance: arms folded, bouncing on the balls of his feet, his mouth a grim line because JV football is *soooo serious*. I scan all the blue jerseys, and thank God—I see Malik's big *10* as he jogs from Coach Jay on the sidelines to the O-line huddled behind the ball.

I relax and watch them execute a couple plays. After each one, Malik trots over to Coach Jay, who puts both hands on Malik's shoulders and gazes intently into his facemask while giving him instructions. A couple times, he pulls him into a hug, and I smile. Then he smacks his helmet and shouts an encouraging, "Let's go, Hunter!" each time Malik heads back to the huddle.

My smile fades as I retreat back into the school. It's obvious he and Alex adore Malik, so why are they so hard on him? Alex never cuts him any slack. I asked him about it before, and he said: "Eve, no one's perfect. People should constantly strive to become better. Yes, Malik's a great athlete and student. But there are a lot of those. He's gotta surpass *great* to stand out and get a football scholarship."

I get it, I do. I'm grateful for the promise he and Coach Jay see in him. But ... and I hate saying this, because I know I'm his mom, but ... Malik's still just a kid.

I feel a headache forming in my pituitary gland as I walk past the athletic offices, and my phone chimes with a text. It's Jill.

No need. I have all his texts here. Come over later.

I have to read it twice and say two different swear words before I can comprehend it. She has all his texts? Has she found anything in them? I start to text back, but realize I'm still standing outside the athletic department. I get an idea.

I glance around the hallway and sneak through the door. The lights are off, so I flip them on and see the sign for *Coach Jay* mounted on the first door to the left.

The best thing to happen today is when I turn the handle and find it unlocked. I scan the room: trophies, volleyball nets, track uniforms ... bingo. They're sitting in the corner. He must've forgotten them today.

Biting back a grin, I drop my purse and seize a bucket of sand, sifting it all over the floor. I grab the other and dump it on his desk and chair, tossing the buckets in the garbage. I grab my purse, kill the lights, and tiptoe out into the parking lot toward my car.

No one punishes my son with sand buckets.

6

EVE

I'm already four miles away from Xander's elementary school, which is two miles farther than Alex is. That's one of the many valid points I make during our current phone conversation.

"Eve, you can't just spring these things on me. I can't always drop everything to cook dinner or go pick up Xander, in this case. Our deal was I'd take him to school in the morning, and you'd pick him up in the afternoon. Just turn around."

I zip through a yellow light, putting me officially four and a half miles from Xander. "What do you have that's so important? You're watching Malik's football practice. I have to go see Jill. She found something of Jordan's she wants to show me."

Alex sighs, because in the battle of inconvenienced husband versus grieving mother, grieving mother wins. "Malik has a game tomorrow night," he says as a last-ditch effort.

"Xander has dismissal now." *Mic drop.*

"Dammit, Eve."

"I'm sorry, but Malik isn't going to die if you're not watching him practice. It's just a walk-through today, anyway. Please?" I pause before purring, "I'll make it up to you later."

"So Xander's ready to be picked up now, then? Because I'm already halfway to the car."

I giggle. "Thank you, love."

"I'm taking you up on that offer," he says softly, and I actually hear him running through the parking lot.

"Alex? One more thing?"

"What is it?"

"I have pork tenderloins marinating in the fridge. Could you cut up some vegetables and preheat the oven around, like, five, five-thirty?"

He hesitates, and I can hear the evil grin crawling up his face. "That's going to cost you."

I roll my eyes as I turn into Jill's neighborhood, pretending the butterflies in my stomach haven't just migrated south to my crotch. "Prepare yourself, Hunter."

"I love when you talk dirty to me."

"Yeah. Well, I'm at Jill's so, gotta run." I hang up and notice that Petra's car isn't in the driveway.

Jill opens the door before I even knock. I don't know what I expected her face to look like, but it certainly wasn't this. She's devoid of any emotion whatsoever. My heart sinks. What did she find in his texts?

"I got here as fast as I could. What happened?" I give her a quick hug and step inside. I look around the living room, searching for who knows what—messages on the walls, evidence of a séance—but all I see are his school pictures hanging where they've always been, and slightly crooked.

Jill exhales a deep, soul-stirring sigh and shuffles toward the kitchen. "Apparently, he had his phone synced up to his iPad."

"Okay…"

THE FALLING OF STARS

She sits at the table—the same chair she sat in the other night—and opens an iPad I'm assuming is Jordan's. I slip into the chair next to her and tuck my hands in my lap, peeking over at the screen as she maneuvers her fingers to bring up iMessages.

My heart is pounding.

"Look." She scrolls through pages and pages of texts, dating back three years when he first got his iPhone. "They're all here. He even labeled the contacts."

"So wait, any time he'd get a text on his phone, it would also come to his iPad?"

"Yes."

"Well, what did you find?"

She finally looks at me, chandeliers of pain glistening in her irises. "There's nothing, Eve. I spent the entire night and all morning reading through every single one of his texts." She tosses the iPad onto the table and whispers, "There's nothing."

My heart sinks to the floor. "You read every single text Jordan ever sent and received in the last three years?"

Jill wipes her nose and nods. "Well, obviously not mine or Petra's. I know there's nothing threatening in those, and my eyes felt like frying pans."

Red flags burst like fireworks in my brain, and I have to actually put my hand over my mouth to avoid blurting out something detrimental. Jill didn't read Petra's texts. And not that I'd ever in a million years think Petra would be involved in Jordan's death, but ... Petra's been acting strange—she was adamant against Jill going to the police about retrieving deleted texts. She'd get angry when Jill would start in with her conspiracy theories. If not for that, I wouldn't even think twice about Jill skipping over them. But Petra changed—she physically changed—when we'd discuss Jordan's texts. Is she hiding something?

But if I'm wrong...

If I'm wrong, I'd be accusing Petra of murdering her stepson. I'd never gotten any indication that Petra's capable of murder, much less that she didn't love Jordan like her own.

Besides, it's not like Petra's stance on Jordan's suicide is wrong—there's really no indication that foul play was involved. There's a good possibility Petra's absolutely right, and Jill's creating these conspiracies in her head because she refuses to deal with her son's death.

I have to steady my voice before I speak, because I refuse to ruin Petra's life and marriage if I'm wrong. And it's not like Jill needs this right now, either.

"Are those the only ones you didn't read? Yours and Petra's? Were there other family members you...?" I have to stop because my voice—it's starting to shake.

"No. I read everything else. My family doesn't speak to me, remember?" Jill sits so forlorn, wave after wave of pain crashing over her and there's nothing she can do about it. There's no way I can suggest she read Petra's messages.

"Does Petra know about these?" My voice barely chokes through my throat.

Jill shakes her head. "No. She's working a twenty-four-hour shift at the hospital. She'll be home soon, and she doesn't like talking about Jordan's texts."

"Hey, do you mind if I take this home and read through them myself? I might be able to find some clues. Malik, even—he might recognize something, you know, some teenage lingo we don't understand—that may give us any indication..."

Jill's frozen in her seat, staring unblinkingly at the iPad on the table. I wonder if she hears my heart pounding. Does she know what I'm thinking about Petra? She finally sighs, leans forward, and tosses the iPad on my lap. "Be my guest."

When I walk into my house an hour later, I'm not even upset at the absolute chaos that's going on. This place is a zoo and a warzone.

While the oven is preheating, about six different vegetables are spread around with a butcher knife glistening next to them. Some of them are untouched, but most are halfway chopped. I grimace at the variety— tomatoes, carrots, broccoli, and seriously with the head of cabbage? Alex emptied the fridge of vegetables. The best part is that Corn Pops are all over the floor. Corn Pops.

I hear feet pounding like a stampede and Malik's laughter floating from the back of the house. Then Xander screams like a girl, and Alex yells in his maniac way he does when he's tickling Xander.

My family is here. They're happy. That's all that matters.

But Corn Pops on the floor? Hell, no.

Before I can announce my arrival, Malik flies around the corner, his socks slipping on the tile. He puts a finger in front of his boyish grin, warning me to stay quiet. His eyes sparkle as he presses his back against the pantry, waiting for someone to round the corner.

I play nonchalant and set my things on the counter as Xander tiptoes in the kitchen. Malik jumps out and tackles him, tickling him while Xander screams and damn near pisses himself.

Alex bursts in the kitchen and starts when he sees me. "Hey, hon!" His eyes dart around the mess they made, and Malik and Xander follow suit. Alex points to the counter. "I cut veggies to have with the chicken!"

I smile coldly. "It's pork."

He swings his pointed finger toward the stove. "Pre-heated. Just like you asked." Then his finger swings to Xander. "Look! It's Xander, straight outta dismissal."

"Yeah, this is great. You guys did an amazing job. I mean, you went over and above with my request for people to dump cereal all over the floor." I take a step, but crunching happens under my foot, and I stop.

"Uh, that's my bad." Malik places a hand on his chest, his eyes still shining. "Sorry, Mom. I'll clean it up. I was hungry after practice, so I got cereal. I didn't put the box away."

Xander clears his throat pretentiously, like he needs everyone's attention. "And I am guilty for knocking the box of cereal on the floor." Unlike Malik's apologetic tone, Xander's sounds like he's pretty proud of himself.

I laugh loudly. "Well, it looks like this was a team effort, then. Way to go, team!" They all look at me funny, like they're not sure if I'm pissed off and sarcastic, or genuinely laughing.

I shuffle across the floor and slide the meat into the oven. Then I turn to hug and kiss each of them.

They're shocked.

"Ohhh," Alex says, enlightened, and turns to Malik. "She was just at Jill's."

Malik's mouth opens in realization. "Okay, it makes sense now." He had initially accepted my hug stiffly and nervously, so he pulls me back into his embrace. He rests his chin on top of my head, and I'll never be okay with the fact that he can do that.

I squeeze his torso with all my might before smacking him in the chest. "Now clean this mess up. All of you." I turn toward the bedroom with my purse and Jordan's iPad.

Xander gasps and points to the iPad. "What's that? Is that for me?"

"Jit, you already got an iPad. I didn't have an iPad at your age, and you want two, now?" Malik scoffs as I stuff the iPad in my purse, as if that would make Xander un-see it.

Alex gives me a questioning look, and I shake my head. "It's um, it's Jordan's iPad."

"Why do you have Jordan's iPad?" I don't even know who asked that.

"I—I'm doing something for Jill. I'm—she needs me to do something for her." And I march right through the Corn Pops back to the bedroom.

Of course, Alex isn't far behind. He sneaks in and shuts the door as I'm taking off my shoes. "Hey, is everything okay?"

"You're going to leave those two out there to clean up by themselves?"

"Hell, yeah. I'm the dad. They do what I say." He winks.

I toss my shoes in the closet and unbutton my blouse. "Alex, you can't breathe a word of this to anyone. I mean, if I'm wrong, then I'm a horrible person. But if I'm right…"

Alex crosses his arms, his eyebrows dipping in concern as he waits for me to continue.

I toss the blouse on the bed and unbutton my pants. "Petra's been acting strange. She's very supportive of Jill, but she shuts Jill down the moment she starts talking about someone assisting in Jordan's suicide. She doesn't want Jill recovering his deleted texts." I drop my pants on the bed and pull my hair out of its bun, letting it flow freely down my back.

"Jill found Jordan's iPad and discovered all his text messages on there. Only she didn't read the ones from Petra, because, well, Petra's his mom also, and she trusts her. So … I asked Jill if I could bring home the iPad to see if Malik could find any *clues*." I use air quotes and shrug. "Do you think I'm a horrible person?"

Alex is chewing his bottom lip thoughtfully as he assesses me, then covers his face with his hands. "I'm not gonna lie, I'm having a hard time listening to what you're saying when you're standing there with no clothes on." He steps forward and fingers my hair, reaching back to unsnap my bra.

Okay, then.

It falls to the floor, and he runs his fingers over my breasts, dragging his hand up to the back of my neck. He kisses me—hard. He's backing me toward the bed, his other hand traveling down my hip and grabbing my butt.

"Alex," I moan as he lowers me on the bed. "Alex, please. I can't do this right now."

He exhales enough to shrivel his lungs, staring at me like he can't believe I'm rejecting him. He inflates his depleted lungs to capacity and mutters, "I picked up Xander for you today. I was promised this." And he nestles his face into my neck.

I pull away. "I know, and you'll get it. But not right this second. I just walked in the door, the kids are in the kitchen, dinner's in the oven, and I'm trying to tell you something important about Jill and you're not even listening."

He jumps back like I told him I have herpes. "You're naked, Eve. You really expect me to hear about Jill when your clothes are falling off your body?"

"I didn't ask you to come back here while I changed! You should be out there helping your kids clean up the mess you assholes made! *You* came back here on your own, and *you* asked me about the iPad. So I'm telling you and you're not listening."

"Whatever." And he storms out of the room.

I rip a pair of sweatpants from my drawer. All men think with their dicks. All of them.

7

EVE

Xander and I are heading to the high school for Malik's football game, and I'm exhausted. I didn't get a chance to look at Jordan's iPad last night, because after dinner everyone had homework, then I had to grade papers, then I had to pay my dues to Alex.

Not that I'm complaining. We needed it. Previous dick behavior forgiven.

"When can I play football, Mom?" Xander asks from the backseat.

I look at him in the rearview mirror. "Whenever you want. Malik started playing around your age, a little younger, actually. He probably would've started earlier, had Alex been around."

That was one of the first things Alex did when he met Malik—that and melt into a puddle of love the moment I introduced him to my seven-year-old boy with the huge blue eyes and thick brown hair. Alex said on our wedding day that he knew he wanted to marry me the day he met Malik; that not only was I the love of his life, but Malik was the son of his life. There wasn't a dry eye in the reception hall.

He registered Malik in a peewee football league at one of the county parks, attending every practice and every game, and even coaching a few seasons until Malik started playing in school. He worked with him in the off-season— running track, doing strength and conditioning programs … it's no wonder Malik is such an amazing athlete.

"So *Alex* isn't Malik's real dad, right?"

Shoot. Did I say that out loud? I could've sworn I thought it, especially because I called him Alex. "Xander, we've talked about this. Your *daddy*—don't call him Alex— is Malik's daddy, too. Okay?"

"So why doesn't my *daddy* put me in football like Malik?"

God, this kid has a smart mouth. "I don't know, Xan. You have to ask him." I pull into a parking space with a little more force than necessary because I want to escape this car of eight-year-old interrogation.

We walk toward the stadium, which is hands-down the nicest high school stadium in all South Florida, possibly the entire state. The field used to be turf, until the players complained it was too hot. It's been replaced with Bermuda grass so green, it glows. The Liberty Lords symbol engulfs the center of the field, and each end zone is painted royal blue with *Liberty* in silver at one end and *Lords* at the other.

Lafayette Hall—the tallest building on campus at four stories—looms nearby, in-ground spotlights illuminating it majestically. It hovers like a guardian, bringing a sense of safety to the home team and a reverent fear to the visiting team. Home games are the best.

The stands are already getting crowded, and we weave through people toward the center of the bleachers, waving to students who call out, "Hey, Mrs. Hunter!" just as the marching band comes onto the field and begins playing the

Liberty Fight Song, which sounds like every other fight song in the history of fight songs.

"Where's Dad?" Xander yells.

I point toward the field, where Alex is standing with a few other dads and staff members near the forty-yard line, opposite of the benches.

"Hi! Can I sit here?"

I look up to see Kendall Dupree grinning down at me.

"Of course. Kendall, this is our other son, Xander. Xander, say hello to Miss Dupree."

"Greetings," Xander says.

I roll my eyes as Kendall chuckles. "He's so cute! He looks like your husband, but he's got your red hair and freckles. What a wonderful family y'all have!"

I do.

All the lights turn out on the field. The crowd starts cheering, and the marching band is silenced by some rapper—Drake, maybe? —blaring over the loud speakers. A spotlight shines at the south end of the field, where the cheerleaders have spread a massive banner across the entryway from the locker room. *LET'S GO LIBERTY LORDS #THISISOURHOUSE*

Xander stands and claps with the rest of the crowd, and suddenly the banner splits and the JV football team sprints onto the field, led by Malik and Javier Acosta. The crowd goes crazy.

For twenty seconds.

Then Drake is silenced, the lights turn back on, and the cheerleaders clear the field of their torn banner, the climax swiftly cantering downhill as the team arrives at the benches, and Malik and Javi meet with the refs and the opponent's captains for the coin toss.

"Wow, that was pretty cool!" Kendall says breathlessly.

"Is this your first game?" I ask her.

"Yes!" And she's got that Disney look in her eye again.

Xander looks at me and rolls his eyes, and I have to bite my cheek to keep from laughing.

"Awww, look at Malik over there with Javi!" she coos like she's watching a kitten and duckling video on YouTube. "Look at his dreads comin' out the back of his helmet. Why'd he get dreads, anyway?"

I shrug. "He wanted them about a year ago. He thought he'd look like an NFL player. And now I'm stuck twisting them every month," I mumble.

"My dad doesn't like them," Xander announces, perfectly poised.

Kendall pokes him in the rib. "Hey, kiddo, you think you could broadcast the game for me? Give me play-by-play coverage?"

Xander and I nod dramatically. "I have to do this for my mom, too."

And he does. He tells us everything that happens in the first quarter, which isn't much. Then shortly into the second, Malik receives a snap and throws it up field, right into Javier's hands. It was the best throw—Javi, with his back to Malik, literally stuck his hands out and the ball landed in them, like clockwork. The crowd goes wild as he runs it into the end zone, but I'm staring in horror back at Malik, who got tackled just after he released the ball.

No one notices. No one even says what a great throw that was. Everyone's cheering for Javi, but my son is on the ground.

"Look! Malik! He's hurt!" I scream like crazy, though no one can hear me over the crowd. I look down to where Alex was standing, but he's not there.

Finally, a ref blows the whistle and the players take a knee as Coach Jay jogs onto the field, but Malik waves him off and gets up. Alex appears next to Jay, signaling something to Malik, but Malik's insisting he can play. The sportsmanlike clapping ensues as Alex and Jay acquiesce and the teams line up, and my jaw drops. Why don't they take him out? At what point does the woman who pushed him out her vagina get a say in whether he plays or takes a break?

Kendall looks at me with raised brows. "I can't imagine how hard it is havin' your kid out there playin'."

I nod. "I physically hurt right now."

She smiles sympathetically, and the ball is snapped for the conversion. I force myself to relax—this isn't Malik's first game, and he's smart enough to sit out if he were really hurt. And yet all everyone talks about is what a great touchdown Javi just scored. I'll never understand football.

At halftime, I take Xander to the bathroom and text Alex to see how Malik is. He doesn't respond, and Xander takes so long that by the time we get back onto the bleachers, the third quarter has started and the opponents have scored.

Xander's face falls as Kendall relays what happened. "Well, did they get the conversion?"

Kendall stares at him.

Xander rolls his eyes. "Never mind, I can see on the scoreboard they did." He points to the giant sign that says we're losing 7-6.

The minutes tick by, and I'm getting more and more nervous. Malik's playing his heart out, and if he loses, he'll be upset for days. Alex will, too. They're finally in the fourth quarter with just a few seconds on the clock, and we're on offense. My foot bounces on the bleachers, and I chew my thumbnail as I see Malik instructing the O-line before they line up.

"What down is this, Xander?"

"Fourth."

Crap.

They're on the forty-yard line. Too far for even Javier to kick a field goal.

Malik shouts "Hut!" and the ball is snapped. Javier is running for his life down the field, and Malik is dancing around, watching between him and the other receiver,

Tyler Something. I grit my teeth as a lineman breaks through the O-line and is bearing down on Malik.

Malik takes one look at him and begins running horizontally, looking for Tyler but he can't find him. He looks to Javier, and Coach Jay is screaming at Malik to *"THROW THE GODDAMN BALL!"*

But Javier is dancing around in the end zone with the corner, and within a split second, Malik shakes off the lineman and is hauling ass down the field at twice the speed of Javier.

I—along with the entire stadium—jump up and scream my ass off as Malik takes the ball in the end zone and the buzzer announces the end of the game.

"We won! We won!" Xander jumps up and down. "My brother scored the winning touchdown!"

Kendall and I high-five, and I realize I have tears streaming down my face.

I am so fucking proud of my son.

I watch his teammates run toward him and slap his helmet, and I look over to see Alex flailing his arms, throwing punches into his fist, screaming and pointing at Malik. He looks pissed.

My clapping slows as I watch him, but I remind myself that men get very emotional when it comes to football, and their victorious sentiments are often mistaken as anger. Just in case, I look over at Coach Jay, who just took off his *Lords* hat and threw it on the ground, looking just as pissed as Alex.

Men are so weird, and I swear to God I'll never understand football.

THE FALLING OF STARS

Xander is watching *Karate Kid* in bed.

I had texted Malik right after the game: *Congratulations! I'm so proud of you! You looked so awesome scoring that touchdown. Go out and celebrate! Ask Dad for some money so you can eat. XOXO*

I wanted to see him after the game, but it takes him forever to have the post-game meeting with the coaches, shower, and then he'll want to watch Varsity.

I have texts to read.

I take a quick shower and pour a glass of Pinot Noir before attacking the iPad. On my way back from the kitchen, I peek in at Xander, and he's already asleep. Excellent. Mr. Miyagi's still kicking ass and taking names, decades later.

I climb into bed and unlock the iPad, sipping my wine while tapping the Messages icon. I can't believe how many texts are here. I know teenagers use their phones a lot, but sweet Jesus.

Malik's name surfaces as I'm scrolling, and I click on it. His last message to Jordan was three months ago: *Welcome to Liberty, buddy!*

My heart twinges, and I don't know if I'm smiling or grimacing. *Compose yourself, Eve. You're a detective now. And detectives don't cry over texts.*

I power through and scroll back up, and I'm taking another sip of wine when my eyebrows dip. Something isn't right. When I looked at his phone yesterday, the last four people he texted were his mom, an Isaac, a Janice, and a 305 number. But I'm not seeing Isaac or Janice on here. Jill is at the top, and then the 305 number.

Where are Isaac's and Janice's texts?

I open the 305 number and see the same exchange I saw yesterday. However, there are about ten additional exchanges, all about homework. The very first text was initiated by the other person, about three weeks ago: *Hi Jordan, it's Daisy. U have the notes for history?*

I'm confused why Isaac and Janice aren't in this lineup. I need more wine. I take a longer sip, then stop because I should probably be sober when I read Petra's.

My hands begin shaking as I find her name and tap on it. I scroll all the way to the bottom before allowing my eyes to read anything—the last thing I need is to read part of a conversation out of context.

Their first exchanges were the same day he got his phone, apparently, three years ago.

Petra: *Happy birthday, Jordie!*

Jordan: *Thx* ☺

Petra: *Store my number. I've already got yours. And use it whenever. I love you.*

Jordan: *Kk luv u 2*

I grab a pillow and sob into it. This is so much harder than I thought. How in God's name did Jill read every single text? My stomach is churning, and I take another gulp of wine.

"Suck it up, Eve," I say as I wipe wine and tears off my mouth with the back of my hand. "You've got to do this. You owe this to Jill. And hopefully it's nothing. Hopefully it's nothing."

That becomes my internal mantra as I continue scrolling up, up, up through Petra's and Jordan's exchanges throughout the years. Most of it's small talk— *Where are you guys?* from him, and, *When are you coming home?* from her. There are *Happy Birthday* texts and *Merry Christmas* texts, and an entire conversation about getting a puppy.

Jordan: *Can you talk to my mom? Please? It's a little Yorkie, and Troy is giving it away.*

Petra: *It's cute, I saw the pic! I'll do what I can, but if your mom says no, it's no.* ☹

Jordan: ☹ ☹ ☹

"I can stop, right?" I mutter. "Petra is a saint. Petra is a saint!"

That's my new internal mantra, and I cozy down into the ice-cold sheets. The texts are becoming more recent—within the last month. They slow down substantially and become very short. Clipped, even.

Then suddenly they're not short. Not at all. They're very long.

I close my eyes and shake my head. No, no. I must have read that wrong. *Go back, Eve. Scroll back down and start over.*

But I'm not wrong. I'm not.

Oh, my god.

8

MALIK

I'm actually scared for my life.

Listen, that last play … it was what it was. It was a judgment call I wouldn't wish upon anyone. And it worked, right? I scored. We won.

My teammates were hella supportive, even Javier—who was supposed to receive that touchdown—hugged me and tried picking me up. I mean, he didn't, considering he's five-foot-six and scrawny, and I'm six feet tall and lean, but it was a valiant effort.

The post-game meeting in the locker room was lit. We yelled our asses off. Coach recognized me for my passes and leadership, Javi for his runs and catches, and a few other guys for sacks and great blocking.

So now that we've put our hands in and I just finished leading the team in our victory chant, I'm pretty fucking shocked to hear Coach Jay say, "Hunter, come here," in his deep, cringy voice while the rest of the team hits the showers.

I haven't even removed my cleats or shoulder pads when he grabs me by the jersey and drags me to the other end of the locker room where the urinals are. Thank God I took off my helmet, or he'd be dragging me by the facemask.

When we're out of sight from everyone else, he transfers his grasp to the V of my jersey and shoves me into the wall.

Whoa.

"What the hell was that, Malik? What the frick was that?"

What the...

He tightens his grip on my jersey, and I think he might spit in my face. "Boy, you better answer me, boy, or I'll knock you into next week!"

I really don't think he will, since coaches aren't allowed to hit kids, and knocking someone into next week isn't chronologically or physically possible, but I think I should answer him, anyway. "Sir, I'm—I'm sorry. I don't know what you mean."

"What was the last play I called? Huh?" At least he lets go of my jersey. But his eyes are wild and fucked off his rocker, and I'm about to piss myself. I purposely don't watch horror movies to avoid shit like this.

"The post, Coach."

"You're goddamn right! So why the hell can't you take directions?"

"Coach, you know why I did what I did, right? I mean, you saw the same thing I saw. Javi was covered. I couldn't risk throwing a pick. Not with seconds left and us being down by one."

"You had two men, Hunter. Javi and Tyler. Why did you take it upon yourself to throw the play out the window?"

"Tyler was double teamed! I had that lineman chasing me, he would've sacked me!"

Coach Jay is snarling. He's literally snarling at me. See? This, right here, is why I didn't watch *The Shining*. I got *Here's Johnny!* all up in my face.

"Sir, I'm not being disrespectful, but don't you think you should trust me? I've been a pretty decent quarterback, right, Coach?"

He puts his teeth away and nods.

"Then why are you all up in my ass? My plan worked, right? We won, didn't we?"

He pooches his bottom lip out and stares at the floor, nodding along.

"You haven't called one of my running plays all season, and I've never complained about it. I've done everything you've told me, even though I'm faster than Javi. I've been condemned to quarterback because I'm also more versatile and can throw the ball, and Javi can't. Right? Have I complained once, Coach?"

He looks at me, one eyebrow arched toward his *Lords* cap. "You have not."

"Then why the hell would I risk running the ball in the last play of the game if I didn't know for a fact that was the only option?"

He stares at me. He's surrendering, I can tell.

"Coach, I scored. I was just trying to get those last five yards to get a first down, then hope for some miracle or Hail Mary if there was any time left. I swear on my life I was not trying to defy you. If Tyler and Javi were open, I could understand your frustration. But they weren't, and you know they weren't. We won, Coach."

The side door slams open and Alex storms in. He stops short when he sees me against the wall with Coach Jay slumping in front of me.

Coach ignores Alex and extends his hand to me. "You're a true leader on this team. I'm sorry, Malik."

I shake it, and he pulls me into a hug. But what the hell just happened?

"What's going on, Jay? Was it him? Did he do it?" Alex asks.

"Did I do what?"

Jay releases me and holds a hand up to my stepdad. "Alex, I got everything under control." He turns back to me and actually smiles. "Congrats, kid. On a great game."

I bust out a shit-eating grin. "Thank you, Coach."

He walks away, and Alex approaches with a suspicious look. "So it wasn't you?"

I shake my head. "Still don't know what you're talking about, Dad."

"The sand? You didn't—?"

"Sand? What sand?"

"Did Coach talk to you about your rebellious behavior?"

I look at him sideways. What the fuck is happening? "You mean my only option of running the ball? The one that saved our asses and made us win the game? Yes, yes. He did. And you saw him congratulating me just now." I can't believe I have to defend myself so hard to the two people I want to please the most. I single-handedly won the game, and Javier Acosta is getting his dick sucked by everyone while I'm getting my ass chewed out.

That moment during the game when I had to make that decision—the one that would determine the outcome of the whole game and the odds were against me—I don't wish that upon my worst enemy. It was a kick in the 'nads. I'm pretty sure I'm gonna suffer from PTSD after that shit, and I actually made the right decision! I should be getting medals! Honors! Blowjobs! And these grown-ass men want to kill me. Is "Congratulations, Malik" so hard to say?

Alex's face contorts from pissed-off-mofo to this creepy, happy clown face. "I'm proud of you, son. Great job today. Way to keep your head in the game."

"Thank you, Dad," I say cautiously.

"Let's go home."

"What? I want to watch the varsity game."

Alex marches toward the other side of the locker room, and I follow until I get to my locker to grab my stuff.

"Are you sure he didn't ask you about the sand?"

I look at him like he's crazy as I get my phone from my locker. "Why do you keep saying that?"

Alex shifts his feet. "Apparently someone pulled a prank on Coach Jay. He thought it might've been you, since you were the last person…"

I'm half-hearing him because I'm reading a text from my mom. I'm disappointed, at first, that she didn't stay to see me after the game. She's always my number one cheerleader. But then I finish reading her text. "Yes! Look here, you have to give me money!" I point my phone toward Alex. "Have fun at home. I'm staying to watch varsity."

Alex chuckles the way he does when he's been humbled by my mom and digs a twenty out of his wallet. "Here. Enjoy. You deserve it."

I'm on cloud nine for the rest of the night. Everyone I know (and don't know) congratulates me on winning the game for us. Not Javi, not Coach Jay … me.

"That's using your head, Hunter!"

"Way to work under pressure, Hunter!"

"You've got to be the best quarterback in the nation after a play like that, Hunter!"

I haven't said thank you this much since my birthday a month ago.

Varsity wins, and there's a party at Javi's house after. He lives in Pinecrest because his parents are rich lawyers.

They have a huge backyard with a pool that's all lit up at night, and an outdoor kitchen full of beer.

I text my mom that I'm going to Javi's (strategically omitting the party aspect) and call up Creed. She agrees to come after a little persuading, and I can almost forget that Coach Jay and Alex nearly skinned me alive tonight.

I'm happily buzzed while waiting for Creed, and there're at least a hundred people in Javi's backyard. I'm pretty much a wallflower, so when Javi and a few varsity guys decide to go skinny-dipping, I politely decline their offer to join, and relax in a lounge chair with my beer, ignoring all their flailing dicks.

Creed finally shows up. "Hey, handsome." She tucks her short, brown bob behind her ear. She looks nothing like the cheerleaders and other girls walking around here—so much so that she stands out. While they all look like they're in slutty Halloween costumes, Creed's wearing jean shorts and an off-the-shoulder top with long sleeves and these big flowers printed on it, and I want to rip it off and fuck her. And don't get me started on that sexy-ass choker or her purple glasses.

She knows she stands out. She's glancing around uncomfortably, trying to make herself as small as possible. I grab her by her belt and pull her down next to me, wrapping my fingers behind her neck and pulling her in for a kiss. "Did you watch my game?" I ask against her lips.

I feel her smiling. "I did. I pretty much had multiple orgasms, watching you run that ball and win the game."

And now I have a full-blown boner.

I took Creed's virginity a few weeks ago, here at Javi's house actually, at his last party. After a month of second base, I finally just said something like, "I want to fuck you so hard."

I realized, as soon as I said it, how disrespectful it was. I thought she was gonna slap me when she looked at me all serious and said, "I need to be honest, Malik," and I freaked out 'cause I thought she was gonna say she had

The Clap or something. But she said, "I'm a virgin," and she bit her lip. It couldn't have been hotter if it were actual porn. I wanted to tell her she'd be my first, but there was that one time last year when Camila Rodriguez backed me into a corner at her birthday party and had her way with me. I certainly didn't hate it, but I wanted this so much more, and it was so worth it.

We make out in the lounge chair for a while until even the drunk people start noticing, and I can no longer hide this raging boner. "Let's go to the guest room."

"Are you drunk?"

I chuckle. "No. But I *am* going to fuck you again."

I literally feel her pussy shiver and her panties getting wet. "Oh, my gosh, Malik. I've been so scared. I thought you hated it the first time because I was bad or something." Her entire body quivers every few seconds. Javi and the guys would find her insecurities a turnoff. I find them adorable. She couldn't be bad if she tried.

I pull into my driveway at four a.m. I'm not drunk, but I fucked Creed Holloway, so it's kinda the same thing. I grab my phone and text her as promised: *I'm home now, sexy.*

She replies right away: *Good. Thank you for tonight. I'll never forget it. Sleep tight.* ☺

I send her a kissy emoji and head inside. I'll never forget tonight, either.

Alex is standing in the kitchen when I walk in and scares the hellfire out of me. "Oh, crap. You—you're up." I hesitate between the kitchen and dining room, because I'm sure he has things to say at this bewitching hour.

"It's four in the morning. Where've you been?"

"I texted Mom and told her I was at Javi's."

"And you decide to come strolling in at four in the morning?"

I can't help it. I'm pissed. He ruined my victory after the game and now he's ruining my Creed-fucking. "You wanna read the texts, Dad? Mom told me to go out and celebrate. She didn't say what time to be home, and I told her where I was going. You haven't even texted or called. I haven't done anything wrong. You know what? I can't even get a 'congratulations' from you. I won the game tonight, and you and Coach Jay lit me up like I'd lost the game. What's your problem? I do everything I can to make you proud and it's never good enough. So what the hell do you want from me?"

He stares at me while I go off on him, his face getting tighter and tighter. He finally pushes off the counter and heads toward his den. "Come with me."

Fuck.

I follow him, and he sits at his desk and points to the chair across from it.

I sit.

He just stares at me, and now I'm enraged because he's doing his stupid game where he tries punishing me by making me wait. "You know what? No. Fuck this." I stand. "You just brought me in here so you can have some power trip. Whenever you decide to say what you need to say, I'll be in my room." I storm out and head to my bedroom, shutting the door and jumping into bed.

Maybe I'm drunker than I thought. I've never spoken to Alex like that in my life.

The door cracks open, and I see his silhouette enter and perch on the edge of my bed. I'm lying on my back and drop my arm over my eyes. I don't want to see him, and I don't care what he's gonna say.

He clears his throat. "Malik, you played a fantastic game tonight. That last play … I'd never want to be in that position."

My hand darts straight up in the air. "Thank you. That's what I've been saying all night. Now was that so hard?"

"You showed true leadership on the field, and it paid off. I'm sorry for my reactions. The reason we reacted that way was because someone dumped sand all over Coach's office, and we thought it might be you. Since you were the last one punished with the buckets."

I sit up on my elbows. "You thought I did what?"

"We should've talked to you first before jumping to conclusions and assuming you changed the play on purpose, and I'm sorry. It's just that you were late to practice Wednesday, and then Thursday was when the prank happened, and then this…"

I fall back onto my bed. This is such bullshit. They ruined this game for me because they thought I dumped sand in Coach's office? Don't they know me better than that? Do they really think that lowly of me?

"And I'm sorry," I say. "I'm sorry that you got stuck with me as a son and not Javier Acosta. I'm sure you'd be much happier with him."

He turns to me. "Now Malik, that's not true."

"Whatever, Alex." I roll over in bed, away from him. I haven't called him Alex to his face since he married my mom.

He stands, and I feel him hovering over my bed. "I know you're upset, but I'm still your parent, whether you like it or not. And you will not speak to me that way."

He waits for me to apologize or say "Yes, sir" or something, but screw that. He finally leaves.

I'm too pissed to sleep. I jump out of bed and sit at my computer, logging onto libertynet.org—our school's own intranet.

It's actually pretty cool—Mr. DeSoto, the IT guy, created the entire thing and launched it at the beginning of the year. It's like a social media platform for students and faculty, and you can post forums about homework or do study groups, or just chat online with your friends. You can ask teachers questions and even upload homework and do practice quizzes. My favorite is the video streaming, where they upload videos of the games and people can comment on them.

I navigate to JV Football and click on the link for tonight's game—it's already up. There are two hundred comments.

Hunter is so badass.

Wow! Our QB won the game for us tonight!

I'd hit #10 all day, every day.

I actually blush at that one. I'd click on the profile to see if I'd hit it back, but I'd rather watch my play. I click the video, drag the cursor to the last few seconds of the game, and watch myself execute the game-winning touchdown.

I watch it again. And again.

A chat pops up from a name I don't recognize. In fact, it's just a bunch of numbers. Like twenty different numbers.

Great game tonight. You're a star.

My eyebrows scrunch up. *Thank you. Who is this?*

A fan.

Ah, geez. I almost log off, but it's four in the morning. What's this person doing on here at this hour? I type: *A fan of what? Insomnia?*

I could ask you the same thing.

I scoff. They didn't even LOL at my joke. *Well at least you know who I am. I have no idea who you are. What grade are you in? How did you get your profile name to be all those numbers?*

I'm sorry about the way Coach Jay treated you tonight. That wasn't fair. I bet that made you feel really unappreciated, especially after all you do for the team.

What the ever-living fuck. Who is this? A teammate? *Javi? Is that you?* I type, but I know it isn't, because I have Javi's screenname saved to my favorites, and I just left his house and he was shit-faced. Certainly not coherent enough to spell out *unappreciated* properly.

No, I'm definitely not that pompous asshole.

I almost come to his defense, but nah—that jit needs to sit down. *Tyler? CJ? Gabriel? Who is this?* I ask, but I get nothing.

It bothers me that Coach picks you out of the entire team to make an example of. You're the best student, the most talented athlete, and the most respectful kid out there. You really are a star. Why would you have the buckets Wednesday, and not Acosta?

This fucker knows about the buckets. I'm clearly not going to find out who this is, so I'm ghosting this fool.

I go to read more comments on the video, but another message pops up: *You wanna hear a secret?*

I don't, but apparently I'm gonna hear it anyway, 'cause here comes another message.

I heard Coach and Mr. Hunter talking about you tonight. They said you probably ran the ball at the end because your arms were still store from the buckets and you didn't think you could throw it.

This is crazy. This complete stranger is telling me all the shit my own dad and coach talked about me. It's probably all lies, and I don't know why I'm entertaining this clown, but now my ego is all like, the hell with ghosting! I type: *That's ridiculous. I threw a perfect forty-yard pass to Javi in the second quarter. Right before that linebacker cheap-shotted me.*

Enough. I'm really ghosting him now, for real. I exit out of the chat window, but that little fucker just pops right back up again.

Do you ever feel like an outsider?

I exit out again.

Up it pops again: *I can tell you do.*

I log off without responding. I'm done.

9

EVE

It's the one day I get to sleep in, and I swear to God Alex is reenacting *Jumanji* in our bedroom at eight in the morning.

I slice my eyelids apart and glare at him. "Why are you being so loud? What could you possibly be doing this early on a Saturday?" Then I remember what I found in Jordan's texts and immediately sit up to tell him.

"We need to talk," Alex announces, springing from the bathroom with a towel around his waist. His face looks urgent, so I peel my gaze from the steam emitting from his body and the water dripping down his chest, and ignore the piney smell of his body wash and deodorant.

And that's how you think with your brain and not your dick.

"Okay. What's up?" I yawn and put Jordan's texts on the back burner, along with sex.

"It's Malik. He was out until four in the morning."

I blink. This is his urgent matter? "He told me he was going to Javier's house. I told him it was fine."

"Until four a.m.?"

I shrug and pull the covers up to my chest. "I mean, it's not like Malik has a set curfew. We agreed, once he turned sixteen, that as long as he's keeping his grades up and excelling in football, we trust him to behave and act responsibly when he goes out. He rarely goes out, Alex. His entire life right now is school and football. And he played such a good game last night!" I smile at the memory of my son—*my son!* —tearing a hundred miles an hour down the field and causing an entire stadium to erupt.

"And you think coming home at four a.m. is responsible? And being late to practice Wednesday, was that responsible?"

"Oh, for the love of God, will you get over that already? It's not that big of a deal, Alex. So he was late to practice one time, who cares? And the coach took care of it with his stupid buckets." I bite my lip before spilling the fact that I, too, took care of it with his buckets.

"He mouthed off to me pretty bad last night," Alex states with a stone expression, as if presenting the final piece of condemning evidence to the jury.

My jaw opens, then I close it. I clear my throat and squirm in bed. "What did he say?"

Alex turns and drops his towel, giving me a nice view of his bare ass before grabbing a pair of boxers.

And I'm still thinking coherently.

"I told him to talk with me in the den and he said, 'fuck this' and went to his room."

My eyes must look like a couple of bloodshot saucers.

He nods at my response. "Yeah, then when I went to his room to talk to him, he told me he's sorry that I have him as a son and not Javier Acosta, then he called me Alex."

Alex's face falls at that last part. I'll never forget the first time Malik called him Dad at the age of nine—the day Alex officially adopted him—and the joy I saw in Alex's eyes was the same joy I would see in them the day Xander was born.

But I still think he's overreacting.

"Hon, try to cut Malik some slack. He's had a really rough week. Jordan just passed away, and he hasn't even had time to mourn properly. And speaking of Jordan, I have something—"

"That's something else he said!" Alex claps and drops the jeans he was about to slide on. "He wanted to know why Coach and I were so upset with him after the game last night, and he went off on this tangent—"

And back on the burner go Jordan's texts. "I'm sorry, what? You were *upset* with him after that amazing game he had?"

Alex retrieves his jeans and shoves each leg in them. "Well, it wasn't so much the game as much as what we *thought* his motives were. See, that last play was supposed to be a pass to either Tyler or Javi. And Malik just did his own thing. Which—whatever, we won the game. But when I went in the locker room, Coach had him up against the wall and had been yelling at him. We … we thought Malik had…"

"What? You thought Malik had what? What did you possibly think he could've done that was worthy of you both ruining that game for him by screaming at him?"

Alex sighs and places his hands on his hips, his jeans hanging a few inches below. "Well, someone dumped the sand buckets all over in Jay's office, and we thought it was Malik."

I went from sitting cross-legged to standing on the bed in two seconds. "Fuck, Alex! Malik did *not* do that!"

He eyes me. "You're acting like you know this already. How do you know this?"

"Because I dumped the sand in his office, asshole!"

Alex face-palms. "Eve, tell me you're joking."

I stomp through pillows to the edge of the mattress and stand over him. "You accused him of dumping sand in the coach's office after he played one of his best games of his life?"

Alex blinks at me. "N—no. I mean, we screamed at him because we thought he purposely disobeyed Jay. And we thought he disobeyed Jay because he dumped the sand..." He trails off once he realizes how stupid he sounds, causing his hand motions of dumping sand to look like he's sprinkling fairy dust around like freaking Tinkerbell.

We both stare at each other. "You sicken me," I say quietly, folding my arms.

Alex stutters like he has all the letters of the alphabet stuck in his throat. "We apologized!" he finally squeaks.

"Right. *After* you ruined his game for him."

"You know, I admit I was wrong in that situation, but you're always taking Malik's side, even when he's wrong."

"Because you always want to punish him over the stupidest things! By all rights, he should be a lot worse, considering his background. Malik's a pretty damn good kid!"

"It's *because* of his background that the kid needs structure. You don't have to tell me Malik's a great kid, I know that. But he's got the genes of—of *him*."

Alex might as well have slapped me in the face. I can't even speak.

He must see the horror on my face because he immediately reaches for me. "Baby, I'm sorry. You know I didn't—"

"How dare you?" I whisper. It's been years since I've cried over Malik's father, yet tears are rushing to my eyes as quickly as they did back then.

Alex lifts me from my standing position on the bed and sets me on the floor, cupping my face in his hands. "You know I love Malik like my own child, right?"

I just stare at him through my tears.

"Eve, please. I didn't mean to—I'm so sorry."

I drag my face out of his hands and trudge back to bed.

"What are you doing?" he asks desperately.

I don't answer. I crawl back into the warm little nest and throw the blankets over my head.

I wake up two hours later, and pain bombards me—Alex's words. Jordan's texts. I'm overwhelmed and I have no one to talk to. I have to do something, but I don't know if going straight to Jill is the answer. She's already dealing with so much. I need to just confront Petra. Tell her I know.

I get her number off Jordan's iPad and create a new text message on my phone.

Petra, this is Eve Hunter. I need to talk to you. It would be better if Jill weren't with us.

I stare at my phone until it's obvious she's not responding right away. I stumble out into the kitchen to make coffee; the house is empty. I've no idea where everyone is, but I can come to a few conclusions: Alex never punished Malik, because Malik is gone. Also, Alex and Malik are fighting, so I'm sure they're not together. And lastly, I wonder who has Xander. I'll text Malik to find out.

I open Malik's text threads on my phone when Petra responds. *What is this about?*

I bite my lip and think of how to reply. *It's about Jordan.*

This time she responds right away. *Is it about what I think it's about?*

My heart starts pounding. *I'm not sure what that means, but I'd like to talk to you soon, so can we just arrange for that to happen, please?*

The text bubble flickers a few times before: *I get off shift in an hour. Meet me at that sushi place down the road from Dadeland Mall.*

Me: *Not public enough.*

Petra: *The food court in Dadeland Mall?*

Me: *Perfect. I'll see you in an hour.*

The food court is packed. Why would I agree to come here? It's Saturday, and it took me damn near twenty minutes just to find parking. But I remind myself—I may want half of Miami here at the food court as witnesses. I don't know how Petra will react when she knows I know. Also, there's a sale at Bath and Body Works.

I manage to find an empty table (with crumbs that I brush over to Petra's side) near the Cuban Coffee kiosk at the entrance of the food court, so I'll be able to see Petra when she comes.

And she's certainly not hard to see—a woman in green scrubs is beelining down the hallway right toward me. She pulls the chair out and plops down, her eyes immediately drawn to the crumbs, and she brushes them to the floor. "What do you know?" she says, crossing her arms on the table. She looks terrified.

I hold up Jordan's iPad. "Did you know all Jordan's text messages go to his iPad?"

And Petra just took a shit in her pants, right here in the food court of Dadeland Mall, right next to Chick-fil-A, Subway, and Pedro's Cuban Café.

"What did you read?" she whispers.

I turn on the iPad and navigate to their messages. "Well, it seems about three weeks ago, you texted him the following: 'Jordan, it's not what it looks like. Brandy is a coworker.' To which Jordan replied, 'I don't know what kind of asshole you think I am, Petra. I know what I saw. You kissing that bitch. Does my mom know?' And you answered, 'No, please don't tell her. What you saw in the car was nothing. If you tell your mom, it'll just upset her.'"

I look up to see tears streaming down her face. But I don't care. I keep reading. "'You're cheating on my mom. Why should I help you?' And you, Petra, replied with, 'Because if you tell her, it'll kill her. And you'll be responsible for killing your mother.'" My voice catches and I have to stop because I, too, have tears streaming down my torture-twisted face.

I turn my burning eyes back to Petra, and she's covering her face with her hands. Her entire body is shaking through her sobs. I force myself to focus on my anger because I need to finish reading these aloud to her. "Jordan said, 'She will die because you cheated on her. Not because I confessed it.' And you said, 'So you're basically pulling the trigger.'"

"Stop, stop. Eve. Please stop."

"You did it, didn't you? You killed Jordan. So he wouldn't tell Jill."

As hard as Petra's lost it, she suddenly gains enough control to glare at me. "I did *NOT* kill Jordan. I did *NOT* make him kill himself."

"Is this why you were so adamant against Jill reading the old texts? Why you didn't want her snooping around his phone or getting the cops involved?"

Petra stares at me like I'm about to shove a sword through her heart.

"Did you delete all his texts on his phone?"

She shakes her head. "I didn't. He really did delete everything the day he shot himself. But I swear to you, I never wanted that to happen. I had no idea he was suicidal!"

"Are you still cheating on Jill with her?"

"No. Once Jordan found out, I stopped it. I do love Jill, Eve. I know you don't believe me, but people make mistakes, people cheat all the time. I'm not trying to make excuses, but I don't want my marriage to end."

I roll my eyes because I don't need to hear her justifications. "Where are the rest of the texts? Between you and Jordan? That was the last one. You mean to tell me you guys just stopped talking about it, and didn't text again for another three weeks?"

Petra wipes her nose with the sleeve of her scrubs and looks at the iPad with one scrunched eyebrow. "What do you mean? Of course, we texted more."

"Well, they're not here," I snap. "And he has no texts on his phone."

Petra pulls her phone from her bag and begins scrolling. "Here. Look. Same day, three weeks ago. There are a bunch more. I mean, you understand I deleted those ones about Brandy off my phone, right? The ones you just read on his iPad? I—I didn't want Jill seeing them."

"Oh, of course. God forbid."

"Scroll up and read them." She hands the phone across the table.

I snatch it from her and sure enough, there are more messages here that weren't on the iPad. These texts were sent the following day.

Petra: *I'm at work. I need to know if you said anything.*

Jordan: *I already told you I didn't say anything.*

And the cryptic questioning continues and tapers off until a few days before he died. "Why aren't these on his iPad?" I scroll to the old ones, past where the cheating texts should have been, and see conversations that I did read on his iPad. All the way to the puppy he wanted a year ago. "Why are these ones blue, and the ones up top green?"

"What do you mean?" Petra leans across the table to look at the phone.

"Look, the messages down here about ... the puppy, these old ones ... are all blue. But these most recent ones, the ones you still have, they're all green."

She looks at me like I'm stupid. "Blue means it's an iMessage, and green's just an SMS message. I'm a nurse at Baptist Hospital, which has very poor reception. So a lot of times, I have to send my messages as SMS, and vice versa." She finally blinks at me. "You do know iPads only receive texts from other iPhones, right? Through iMessages?"

Apparently, I'm the only idiot in the world who doesn't know this. "So Isaac and Janice. Those people don't have iPhones? Like they have a Samsung or something?"

"Right. Any time he'd get a message in green, it wasn't delivered to the iPad."

So there could still be hundreds of texts Jordan had on his phone that were never delivered to his iPad. And if I've already found incriminating evidence that was probably a huge asset to his suicide, who knows what else was on his phone? Maybe Jill was right—this could at least point toward why Jordan did what he did, even if there was no conspiracy or bullying involved.

I place the iPad on the table and slide Petra's phone toward her. "I'll make a deal with you," I say with such authority, Petra freezes. "You get me Jordan's texts. All of them. I don't care how you do it. If you go to the authorities, if you call your service provider, or if you go back in time and handwrite them from his phone. You have three days to get me every single text Jordan ever laid his little eyes on, and every message his little fingers typed out and sent, and I won't say anything to Jill."

Petra starts. She looks like she's about to say something, but I'm not finished.

"But here's the catch. When we're finished, if there's nothing to show her—I mean, if you're right, and there's no evidence that Jordan was coerced into committing suicide—you have to confess that you cheated on her."

And she's sobbing again. Sweet Jesus.

"Do we have a deal?"

"And if we do find something in his texts?" she asks.

I lay my palms flat on the table, set my jaw, and stare into her soul. "Then we find the fucker and we kill him."

10

MALIK

My life is divided into two stages: pre-Alex and post-Alex.

Pre-Alex is harder to remember, obviously, 'cause I was just a little kid. I do have vivid memories, though, of those days when it was just my mom and me, and our last name was Ryan. When I was really young, we lived with my grandparents down in the Redlands on this big-ass farm. My mom's parents owned an orange grove, and I remember running up and down the rows of trees, climbing them until my shins were bloody, and throwing oranges at iguanas.

I'd run down to the pond and find toads—these huge, massive, diabolic-looking things—and try to skip them across the pond, like they were rocks. I'd jump on my grandpa's ATV and tear around their eighty acres, until I broke my arm crashing it into this barn that was destroyed back in the nineties by Hurricane Andrew. I wasn't allowed to ride it anymore.

I was a mischievous little shit, and that's probably why my grandparents didn't like me. I remember lying in bed at night, listening to my mom fight with them. Especially once when I accidentally hit a feral cat with an orange and cried for like ten hours.

"Look what you've done," they sobbed. "He nearly killed one of those cats today, Eve. You think that's normal for a little boy?" And she responded, "It was an accident, he didn't mean to. There are like a zillion feral cats running around, and you always say how much you hate them. Leave him alone; he's your grandson and my child, whether you like it or not."

I always thought they were nice to my face, until other children—distant cousins, random family members—would get together for some birthday party or holiday, and I'd watch the way my grandparents would treat them versus the way they'd treat me. I got blamed for every fight, and I was always the last person to get a hug or a piece of birthday cake. My gifts were always crappier than the other cousins—one Christmas I got Battleship, and they all got new rollerblades.

I was five when that happened, and I asked my mom later why everyone else's gifts were so nice. I'll never forget the look on her face—like every person she'd ever known slapped her. Her voice quivered when she answered, "Malik, it's only because Grandma and Grandpa don't see that side of the family often. If you think about it, you get presents all year from them. But with these kids, they have to cram a full year's worth of presents into one visit." She fake smiled and blinked a lot.

But my grandparents didn't give me gifts all year. Sure, I lived in their house, and I had a lifetime supply of oranges, and there were frogs and iguanas and feral cats for days, but I didn't have any rollerblades. I was five—I was no idiot.

"Is it because I look different?"

THE FALLING OF STARS

My mom's face did weird things—first, she smiled. But her eyes didn't; they were frantic, wild, angry. "Absolutely not, Malik. No one should ever treat you differently because of your appearance."

"Why do I look different than you? And Grandma and Grandpa?"

"Your daddy was from South America. His parents were ... lots of different things."

"Where is he? Why don't he live with us, like daddies do?"

It was the first time I ever saw my mom chew on her lip. She's done it a million times since then, but I specifically remember noticing that time. "He—he died. When you were a baby."

"Oh." My heart hurt. I'd never have a dad like my friends and cousins. I looked different, people treated me different. Why couldn't I be like everyone else?

"But you have a grandma and grandpa that you live with! That's even better than a daddy, because that's two people who love you!" she said.

I thought about that. If dads loved their kids like my grandparents loved me, then I probably didn't want a dad. "And what if one day, Grandma and Grandpa don't love me anymore?"

"Then we'll move out."

And we moved out the following year, when I was six. My mom had just finished college, and she got the teaching position here at Liberty. We rented an apartment in a crappy area in Kendall, and that's where we lived until she met Alex and married him two years later, and they bought a house near The Falls in a modest little neighborhood where everyone has pools and white sheds in their backyards—the house we live in to this day.

Post-Alex life was a dream come true. I finally had a dad. I finally understood how all the other kids in my class felt when they'd talk about their dads playing with them—

dads are fun! —and yelling at them—*dads are strict!* —and I loved Alex so much.

He made us happy. He made our last name Hunter, and then they had a baby—I finally had a little brother who was cute, chubby, and laughed at everything I did.

Alex registered me for a Pop Warner football team at one of the parks down the street, and I met a hundred other kids just like me—multi-ethnic families, some with just a dad, some with just a mom, black kids, white kids, Hispanic kids, and none of them batted an eyelash at the fact that Alex was my stepdad or that we all looked different, because that's how the majority of Miami was, anyway. It was great! I finally fit in somewhere. Life was perfect.

When I lived at the orange grove, I thought my life was perfect, then. But once we left and Alex entered, I realized how toxic living with my grandparents was. Why did I think I had it so good? My life became perfect *after* Alex.

But as I lie here in bed, staring at the ceiling at eight in the morning and wondering why I've only slept three hours, my life feels far from perfect.

I head to the bathroom and hear my parents arguing in their bedroom. I pause to listen; it's about me and how I came home late last night. It's always about me. Just like with my grandparents. I don't want to hear it. I take a piss and go back to bed, and a thought hits me that makes me sick. Is my life toxic now and I don't realize it, just like when we lived at the orange grove? Will I look back on this life with Alex and Xander and Mom, and shudder, wondering how I survived this?

But why? Two lives, polar opposite, and I'm *still* miserable? What sort of life would make me feel … I don't know … loved, happy? Is it my fault? Am I being selfish? A discontented little bitch?

I collapse onto my pillow as I hear Xander thumping down the hall—he's awake. A few seconds later, I hear my parents' bedroom door shut and Alex's signature sauntering toward the kitchen, and soon I smell pancakes and hear Xander laughing his little ass off. Probably because Alex is flipping pancakes up to the ceiling again. *Dads are fun!*

My stomach is growling, but I don't want to go out there and face Alex. He's gonna ground me, and for sure he'll point his spatula at me while he does it. *Dads are strict!*

I grab my AirPods and listen to music, zoning out for a good hour until I'm being shaken and open my eyes. It's Xander. I pop out my AirPods. "What's up, Little Dude?"

"Malik!" he whisper-yells with gigantic eyes. "Dad's looking for your car keys! He's tryin' to take them because he said you were 'disrespectful and rebellious last night,'" he says in a mock-authoritative voice, pointing his finger like he's lecturing me.

I laugh because he's eight going on thirty, and I dart my eyes around the room for my keys. I got this car on my sixteenth birthday last month, and Alex has already grounded me from it once. I swear, the only reason he agreed to get me a car was so he could have leverage. "Damn," I mutter. "Where did I put them?"

"I don't know, but he's coming in here soon, so you'd better hide them and just fake sleep. He's taking me to Dolphin Mall to buy shoes, but save yourself!" And this clown I have for a baby brother scampers out the door.

Xander just saved my life.

I find my keys in my jeans and slide them under my pillow, jump into bed, and pretend to be in a deep REM cycle when I hear Alex come in. I peek through one eye to see him scanning his laser-beam eyes across my desk, my dresser, and then picking up my jeans and checking the pockets. He huffs and looks around the room again before leaving and closing the door.

Xander's my fucking hero.

If I'm gonna be grounded, I better make these last few hours of freedom worth it.

I won't argue with Creed. If she doesn't want to go to South Beach, then who cares. "So what do you want to do?" I say into the phone between bites of cereal (those fatasses ate all the pancakes). I'm trying to keep my voice down—I noticed my mom's asleep in bed. She didn't look well. It sucks that she's sick, but I really need her well to be my defense attorney later when Alex tries confiscating my keys.

Creed yawns. "Who's going to the beach?"

"A lot of the same people from the party last night." I thought that'd be comforting, since she has no problem putting out within a hundred-foot radius of them, but it sounds like she's having a panic attack over the phone.

"Malik, your friends don't like me. Especially Javier Acosta."

She's right, but I'm not going to admit that. "What do you mean? You were just at his house last night. You had sex in his house last night." I chuckle, but she's not finding this amusing. "Why don't you think they like you?"

"Well, for one, Javi told me he didn't. During PE last year." Her voice has a bitter undertone, and she pauses, waiting for me to say something, but I really don't know what to say. "He didn't even acknowledge me last night. None of them did. It's like they looked right through me. I don't fit in with your group of friends, Malik."

"They were drunk." I roll my eyes because I have douchebags for friends.

"It's a wonder *you* even talk to me."

I let out a long, Corn Pop-scented breath. I've been waiting for her to address the fact we're in two different worlds when it comes to high school. "I'm not like them. You should know that by now."

She sighs. "I'm sorry. I do know that. Sometimes I just feel like you're too good to be true. Like I'm going to wake up and Malik Hunter was just a dream. Or that this is all one big joke and you guys are going to dump pig's blood on my head at prom."

Milk shoots through my nose and I'm hacking on cereal. "Fuck, Creed!" I finally manage. "Are you a psycho? Listen, I like you *because* you're not like those girls from the party. I play sports, and the athletes hang out with the athletes. I don't like it, but it's just the way it is. I hate cheerleaders."

"You dated Lidia Valdes for four months last year."

"Yeah, and we broke up." I toss my bowl in the sink, cringing at those four months I dated that idiot. We never had sex, but she did suck my dick almost every day after school. Which was basically the only reason I stayed with her that long.

I'm obviously not telling Creed that, either.

"I want to go to Wynwood. There's an art walk today by the Wynwood Walls," she announces.

I blink. A lot. "Oh—okay." I've been to Wynwood once with my parents to some restaurant that blew. I've never hung out there. My friends and I usually go to South Beach or Lincoln Road or Sunset Place.

"This better not suck," I say on the way to my bedroom to get dressed in whatever's appropriate for lots and lots of art. Damn. I purposely didn't watch *Waste Land* to avoid shit like this.

"It won't!" she says, super bubbly. "There's a farmer's market, too. And an antique show."

Great. So maybe I can see some old tractors and a shit ton of oranges before being verbally berated and chastised by parental authority. Because *that's* never happened before…

I've never seen so many beanies and Dr. Martens in my life. Am I the only dude who's not rocking plaid or cut-off denim shorts? What the ever-living fuck? I'm dressed like all the old men here—jeans and a polo. And I thought I was relatively stylish, considering my purple Stephen Curries match perfectly with my shirt.

The ambiance, though. It's so chill here. No tension, no pressure, no one looking at me and expecting me to pull some miracle outta my ass to win a game or score a touchdown ... this is actually pretty fuckin' lit.

Creed fits in pretty damn well; she's wearing this little sundress with Birkenstock sandals (I'm pretty sure Alex has the same pair he wears with socks when he goes to the pool). She's rocking these half-framed cat-eye glasses that single-handedly turn me on, and I want to stick each one of her black-nail-polished fingers and toes in my mouth and suck on them until she melts.

She had this clunky mustard-yellow cardigan on until I told her to take that shit off. It's a hundred degrees outside, and more importantly, I can't enjoy the way her sweet little body moves around in that dress. I watch her as she approaches each art exhibit on the sidewalk, admiring her just as intently as she admires the art.

"Look, Malik," she'll say, pointing to a graffiti mural or some seven-armed sculpture made out of chicken wire, and the life in her eyes is what makes the art inspirational. I'd stare at chicken wire all day if it meant Creed's face shining like a portal straight outta heaven.

We stroll down the sidewalk past a guy with a blonde, scruffy beard sitting on a stool outside the Wynwood Walls, and he's going ham on this green ukulele and singing the shit out of a Twenty-One Pilots song.

I actually stop before Creed does. He's gathered a nice little crowd, everyone bobbing along and tossing money in a cardboard box beside him. I'm captivated by the atmosphere he's created. I mean, it's such a happy little bubble we're in—no competitions, everyone just wants everyone else to succeed in whatever the hell they're pursuing in life.

Creed glances up at me every now and then, her little foot tapping to whatever song this guy's squealing out now—Imagine Dragons, I think. When he finishes his set, everyone claps and scatters as he gets off his stool, massages his ass, and shocks me when he heads straight over to Creed.

"What's up, chickadee?" And he wraps her in a hug. He's a little thing—five-foot-eight, a buck fifty soaking wet, but Creed still ascends on her tiptoes as she hugs him back.

"It's so good to see you!" she gushes. "You did amazing, as always."

"Thanks!" he chirps and turns to me with the same shit-eating grin he's had for the last twenty minutes.

"This is Malik," Creed says. "Malik, this is Tray."

We shake hands, and I say something dumb like "Sup, man" or something.

"Malik Hunter. The great QB over at Liberty. Great game last night, man. Great game."

Now I'm shook, because not only is he a talented musician, but he knows high school football!

"Thank you. And great set just now. That was pretty legit."

He acts truly flattered. I like this guy. He doesn't make a big deal out of shit. He doesn't cum on himself because I'm the Liberty QB like a lot of these asshats do, and he probably has more talent in his little finger than most guys do in their entire bodies, combined. Yet he's so humble. He doesn't make sexual comments about Creed and me being here together, like Javi and the guys would. To him, it's completely natural that this six-foot jock is chilling in Wynwood with this precious little hipster. No questions asked. *You do you, Boo.* I finally understand that ridiculous statement.

But then he puts his arm around her shoulders. *Boo* better check himself before it gets all primal up in here.

"So when are you gonna play with me again?" he asks her.

She blushes and ducks her head. "Oh, well now that you went and got all famous on me, you don't want this little ol' nobody up there singing with you."

Tray acts like someone just punched him in the stomach. "Nah, that's bull. You're amazing." He turns to me and points to Creed. "Have you heard chickadee sing, Malik?"

I shift my feet and rub my chin harshly. "Can't say that I have." I didn't even know she sang.

He drops his arm from her shoulder and points his ukulele at her. "Next week I'm playing at Bougainvillea's by Sunset Place. You're singing with me." Then he swings the ukulele at me like a sword. "You gotta come, too. You need to hear her. She's doing the world a disservice by not singing."

I look at Creed with the world's biggest grin. She's blushing something fierce. "I'd love to," I say more to her and less to Tray.

This tiny hint of a smile reflects on her lips. "We'll see," she whispers.

His arm returns to her shoulder and he laughs loudly, pulling her in to kiss her forehead. It doesn't even bother me anymore, because this guy is like a modern-day Santa Claus, just spreading all sorts of cheer and shit around town. He releases her and extends his hand toward me again. "Malik, it's been a pleasure."

"Hey, great meeting you, my man. Take care."

He strolls off toward his cardboard cash box, and Creed scurries in the opposite direction.

"Hey, slow down," I call, and I actually have to jog to catch up with her. "Why didn't you tell me you sang?"

She pushes her glasses up her nose, her face dipped toward the sidewalk. "I—I don't—it's never really come up in conversation." She finally looks up at me and slows to a normal pace, her face so blank it's raw.

"Will I ever get to hear you?" I shove my hands in my pockets as we turn a corner, and she almost collides with a Husky, its owner oblivious and speaking loud, angry Spanish on his phone.

"No," she says.

"Oh, c'mon. You watch me play football all the time. At least tell me what songs you like to sing. Halsey? Taylor Swift? Snoop Dogg?" I grin at my joke, but she doesn't find it funny.

"I write my own music." She's been scratching her arm relentlessly, and there are long, red lines running along her forearm. Before I can make her elaborate, she ducks inside an unassuming brown building that I probably wouldn't've noticed if she didn't just disappear in it. I look up at a sign that says *Panther Coffee*.

I step in behind her, and this place is eighty shades of amber. The walls are thick, brown, horizontal planks that stretch up to an equally brown wooden ceiling. These huge yellow orbs hang from the rafters, accounting for at least thirty of the eighty amber shades lighting up the place. Behind the bar are square shelves of all sizes fitting together against the wall like puzzle pieces, holding organized clutter: tea boxes, coffee tins, and all sorts of overpriced shit they want you to buy. This place would be cool if there weren't a thousand people inside. This is why there can't be nice things in Miami. Too many people.

Creed is staring up at the menu and chewing on her thumb. "Do you want coffee?"

"Uh, no. I'll just get this." I grab a Monster Energy drink from a cooler.

She rolls her eyes and orders some latte with organic almond milk and raw beet sugar, and I pull out my wallet to pay seven dollars for her glorified fertilizer. We have to stand in a clusterfuck of people while we wait for them to call her name, and I'm halfway done with my Monster when they finally do.

She looks around the area and turns her eyes up to me. "Wanna sit outside?"

Yup.

It's hot out, but there's a massive Banyan tree hovering over a couple tables, so we sit at one and I stare awkwardly at her as she sips her hot, vegan garbage. I try being considerate, but I honestly find it a little messed up that she never told me she writes music and sings.

"So when were you gonna tell me about your hidden talent?" I ask, tossing my empty can in a recycle bin.

Her face squishes up and she looks down at her coffee. "I didn't know you wanted to know about it."

I lean toward her and speak in that soft voice she says turns her on. "Why wouldn't I want to know that, Creed? I want to know everything about you."

She stares at my lips and says, "Tell me a secret." Then sips her sewer coffee. She's smiling, even though she's hiding behind her cup. I can tell because her eyes are twinkling.

I lean back in my chair. "What kind of secret?"

She shrugs and sets her cup down. "Everyone knows everything about you, Malik. Your life's an open book. We know your parents, everything you do on campus, which cheerleader you date, what you eat for lunch … tell me something no one knows."

I tug on my bottom lip as I stare at her. "I'll tell you one if you promise to sing for me."

She raises an eyebrow in surrender. "Deal."

"But you can't tell anyone, Creed. It's serious."

Her face drops all teasing insinuations and she sits up. "I promise."

"I don't want to play football anymore," I say before realizing what a stupid idea this is.

Her jaw drops and she glances around, like she's scared someone might've heard. "Malik, did you say what I think you just said?"

I nod.

"You—but you're like, the best football player ever. You're gonna get a scholarship! What would your dad say? Oh my gosh, he'd die. Your teammates would die! The entire school would go under."

I hold up a hand, laughing nervously. "Okay, okay. See why I didn't want to say anything? You've just described the apocalypse."

"But why? Don't you love football?"

I nod as a leaf flutters from the tree onto the table. "Do you have any idea how much pressure I'm under, twenty-four, seven?" I glance at her as I pick at the leaf. "So many people rely on me for so much, and … I just want to relax sometimes, you know? Just be a kid and fuck around. Take off the pressure, just do my own thing."

"Well, what is your own thing? What would you be doing instead?"

"I don't know, anything. I don't want to be associated with something so severely, you know? I mean, you hear my name and you immediately think 'football.' I'm not allowed to be human. To make mistakes. I gotta be like a soldier, on guard at all times. And I take a lotta heat if other people fuck up, too. I—it's just—"

I stop and look at her, and she's assessing me. I can't believe I just spoke all these words aloud. To another person. What have I done?

"Football season's only a few months, though. You have the rest of the year to relax."

I scoff and crumble the remainder of the leaf, throwing it on the cement. "You'd think that. Then I have to do track for three months, then a strength and conditioning program for three months at this gym that trains college athletes. Then Alex has me doing seven-on-seven with a bunch of guys from Goulds. Then we start conditioning for tackle again. No days off, Creed. No days off."

She pushes her cup away and folds her hands on the table. "Malik, no one is going to force you to do anything you don't want to do. You're not anyone's slave. You're a kid, and your dad thinks you like football. He's just encouraging you. I know this because he talks about it all the time in class."

"You see? He'd be so disappointed if I told him I wanted to quit."

She shrugs. "He may be a little sad, but he's still your dad. He's not going to stop loving you."

I sigh. She clearly doesn't know my luck with father figures. "It's the difference between going to college on a full-ride scholarship, and making my parents pay thousands of dollars in tuition. I think he'd be more than 'a little sad.' He'd be a lot pissed."

Creed's eyebrows drop, and she leans forward. "Tell me about your biological dad. Have you ever met him?"

I should be surprised at this question, but I'm not. "My mom said he died when I was little."

"How?"

"I don't know. I asked about him when I was really young, but once Alex showed up, I never really thought much about my biological dad anymore. It didn't really matter."

I wait for her to ask more questions, but she doesn't.

"I wrote you a song."

I jerk my eyes to her face. "What?"

She nods solemnly. "I did. A few weeks ago."

I sit up attentively and look around, trying to decide if this is an appropriate setting to just burst into song. "Do I get to hear it?"

She shrugs. "I promised you I'd sing if you told me a secret. And you did. Come on." I follow her to a small building down the street. She grabs my hand and pulls me inside, and we pass through a pizza restaurant with a full bar, the bartender being the only person in the entire place. She waves at him and he at her (like this is all routine and everyone is BFF with everyone) and hauls me up some stairs in the back that look like no one's ever ascended them, ever.

The upstairs is small and empty—a studio with a stage on the far wall. It's dark in here; the walls are painted black and decorated with old posters of local indie bands that probably aren't even around anymore. A little light comes in from the slits of windows on one side. She leads me to an old trunk sitting next to a grand piano. "Sit down here."

Okay.

Then she sits at the piano and starts moving her fingers across the keys.

I love the way you love my hair,
And tell me things when we're alone.
I love the way you look at me
Even from across the room.

You always think I'm beautiful
Even on my worst days
But if only, if you only knew
My worst days are without you.

I'll be your secret, it's okay
Since we are who we are.
I'll be your secret, it's okay
Since secrets are never shared.

Her fingers come to a stop, her head bowed over the piano. I don't know what to say. The song was beautiful, her voice is beautiful. But she's not my secret, and I don't really know what she means by that. But this moment is perfect, and I don't want to talk. So I reach my hand to brush her hair out of her face and cup her cheek, and I wait for her to look at me so I can kiss her.

II

EVE

The aloneness is torture. It's not that I'm lonely. I mean, I am, but I can handle that. I can't handle feeling *alone*. I haven't spoken to my family in ten years—not since we moved out after my parents accused Malik of stealing money. He was freaking six. I never told him that; I don't want him knowing his grandparents wish I would've aborted him.

Alex and I aren't speaking. He loves Malik and all, but sometimes he says dumb, insensitive shit that pisses me off. No one gives Malik a chance.

It's Sunday, and it's rainy. I need to tell someone about Petra. I need to talk about Jordan. And Alex. And Malik. I have nobody to talk to. I'd go back to my therapist if I knew she wouldn't chuck a bottle of antidepressants at my head as soon as I stepped through the door.

Then it hits me—Alondra Hendrick. The school therapist. We're pretty good acquaintances; I'd even say we're almost friends, even though she's twenty years my senior. I roll over in bed and grab my phone, shooting her a quick text to see if she has any availability tomorrow. She writes back promptly—*Hello, Eve. Can you come during your break?* I send her a thumbs-up emoji and go back to sleep.

It's Monday, seventh period, and I'm about to head down to Alondra's office when I'm intercepted by three senior girls, bombarding me and shouting, "Mrs. Hunter! You have to come to Mr. Hunter's classroom!" They grab my arms and are tugging me down the hall.

I'd be worried, but their faces are mischievous and playful—the seniors have been plotting. I can't get caught up in the excitement, though, because I'm still mad at Alex and I don't want to go in his room. Especially if he told them about our fight, and this is their attempt to make us reconcile. His big mouth tells his classes everything about everything. Malik and I have no privacy because Alex cannot shut the hell up and leave our home life at home, and now I'm even more mad at him.

Until I step in the room and see that he, too, is being bombarded.

"We got her!" one of the girls announces, presenting me like a scavenger hunt item. "Mrs. Hunter, stand by Mr. Hunter." She directs me next to him, and we look at each other.

He shrugs, and I just look away. Students are gathered around, grinning and taking videos with their phones. What's going on?

Sarah, the student body president, steps forward and holds up her hands. "We have a present for you, because you're both the most amazing teachers ever..." She stops because she's crying, and I really have no idea what's so fucking amazing about us and I'm missing my appointment with Alondra.

THE FALLING OF STARS

Another kid approaches carrying a cardboard box with a towel draped over it and thrusts it at us. Alex and I look at each other again—he's clearly just as lost as I am—and the kid prompts us to open it. I turn to Alex a third time.

He gestures to the box. "Be my guest."

I pinch the towel between my thumb and index finger and timidly lift it off the box, then immediately drop it and cover my mouth. "Oh, my god!"

Alex bursts into the most infectious laughter as this adorable gray kitten with blue eyes pops its head out, and the class erupts in cheers and laughter. The cell phones creep closer, and this is quite possibly the cutest little rascal I've ever seen.

Sarah claps giddily. "We know you guys lost Pumpkin, and you didn't deserve that. You're the nicest, best teachers, and you guys would do anything for us. So we wanted to do this for you."

They all applaud, and the cameras keep rolling. But I'm shocked they knew about Pumpkin. It was Xander's cat, really—super cute with orange fur, and the stupid thing ran away a few months ago. Xander was beside himself over that little turd, and Alex's big fat face must've told the seniors about it.

I'd be even more angry with him except I'm enamored with this fur nugget, and Alex is nearly in tears, or pretending to be, anyway. This is one of the most thoughtful things anyone has ever done for us, especially a bunch of teenagers, and I'm truly touched.

"Xander's going to love him!" I gush. "He's got the Liberty Lord colors—gray and blue!"

"Yeah, that's why we picked him! He can be our new mascot!"

A few chuckles and coos flutter through the room, then someone yells, "What about Malik?" pretty facetiously, and more laughter ensues.

"Malik hates cats!" someone else yells, and Alex has gathered the little gray fluff in his hands and is snuggling it.

109

I'm turning my head back and forth between the students and Alex with his fur. "N—no, Malik doesn't—"

"Yeah, Malik is NOT a cat person. But he'll get used to it," Alex says melodramatically like it's some sort of inside joke, and I have no idea where this theory that Malik hates cats came from. I mean, he was fine with Pumpkin. I wouldn't say he *loved* the thing, but he certainly didn't hate him, like the entire senior class and Alex have unanimously decided.

Alex dismisses seventh period only ten minutes in. He's loving the kitten and the seniors are happy to get out of class early, and they hug me as they file out of the classroom, phones tucked away, the surprise finished and successful.

And we have a cat. Xander will probably name this one Cupcake.

I try sneaking out the door before Alex catches me, but no such luck.

"Hey! Eve!" he barks right before my escape.

I turn to look at him.

"Where are you going?" The kitten is crawling all over his neck and shoulders, like a Boa Constrictor only shorter and cuter, and he blinks at me with his fake grin still plastered on his face.

"I have an appointment I'm late to." And I leave the room, straight for Alondra's office. I tap on her door before cracking it open. "Hi. Sorry I'm late. We had … a surprise."

She peers up from her desk and smiles. "No worries. Come on in." Her Spanish accent is beautifully methodical. It's like she speaks perfect English but insists on staying true to her Latinx roots.

I shut the door and sit across from her, blowing air straight up my face and shooting my bangs upward.

She gives me a sympathetic smile. "What's up, Eve? You've looked stressed the last few days."

"I don't even know where to begin. This whole Jordan Sawyer thing. And I'm close to the family, you know, so there's all this other drama I'm stuck in the middle of."

"Well, it's not your drama. Why feel like you have to carry it on your shoulders? Just be supportive." She smiles like she just solved all the problems in the world.

I glance around her office. It's not like a regular psychologist's office. It's not homey with comfy couches and lamps. It's like a regular office with a few stupid motivational posters on the wall. But I guess she's just a school guidance counselor, so I'm not really sure why I expected it to look like a shrink charade.

"I know, it's just—well, I—I just need someone to talk to, I guess."

Instead of looking flattered, she looks concerned. "Why can't you talk to your husband?"

I roll my eyes. "Alex, he's ... I'm not too happy with him right now. He and I have different ideas on how to ... parent our children. Malik, specifically."

Alondra looks like I just squirted her with a water gun. "What? Malik? But he's such a good kid."

I clap at her. "Thank you! That's exactly what I said. But Alex is always on edge, thinking Malik has these ulterior motives. He's so strict with him, and Malik's been through enough in his life already." I stop before getting carried away.

She props her chin on her fist and pouts her lip. "And Alex doesn't do this with Xander? Do you think it's because Malik isn't his biological child?"

I sigh. "Xander's still young. It's hard to compare the two. Alex has never given me a reason to believe he doesn't love Malik. He's the best thing ever to happen to him. And Malik loves him. It's obvious. But I'm scared Alex's strictness will eventually push Malik over the edge."

She gives me a blank look that's unbecoming of a therapist. "Eve, you don't need me to tell you that you need to talk to Alex. As parents you should be on the same page. These are your children's lives we're talking about, and by being childish and fighting with Alex, you're only hurting your children."

I sit back like she just spit in my face. "So that's your solution? I need to stop being childish? You don't think maybe I *have* tried talking to Alex, and that's why I'm here?"

She blinks at me, stuttering and flicking her fingers around.

Is this how she talks to students? If so, no wonder Jordan…

I narrow my eyes, those negative vibes I felt at the assembly rushing back. "Did Jordan Sawyer ever come in here and talk to you?"

She takes a deep breath. "Yes, he did."

I nod slowly. "Did he ever show signs of suicide?"

She drops her fluttery fingers to the desk, where they lie motionless—dead, apparently. I killed them. "I'm not supposed to talk about sessions with students. But I will say, I knew he was troubled, but I had no … idea…"

And she's fighting back tears.

I was right—she does feel guilty, no matter what her rigid posture said in the assembly. "What was he troubled about, Alondra?"

She grabs a tissue out of her desk—why wouldn't she have tissues out for students? —and dabs her eyes. "I'm sorry. I really can't get into what my sessions with Jordan were about."

I picture Jordan sitting in this same chair, confiding in her about Petra cheating on his mom. And Alondra saying something insensitive: *You should've never gotten involved in your lesbian parents' affairs.* So far, she and Petra make one hell of a tag team.

"Alondra, Jill Sawyer believes that Jordan was bullied into killing himself. I've been helping her some, just to appease these theories while she's mourning. If there are any answers I can give her, anything that Jordan was going through that could help give Jill even a little peace, I want to do that for her."

Alondra is pinching the bridge of her nose. "I wish I could help you, Eve. But I'm sorry. There's nothing I can do for you." She looks at me with such finality, it's clear our "session" is over.

I don't say a word as I walk out the door. I wish I never came here. I don't feel better; I actually feel worse. And now she knows Alex and I are having problems. Great. She's the worst counselor ever.

I run to my room to grab my purse and lock up, and as I'm heading to the parking lot, I see Kendall Dupree and Jeremiah Lorrey walking about twenty feet ahead. They don't see me, but that Kendall is a flirty little fruitcake. Either that or her southern belle disposition has left her hopelessly clueless. I don't even speak that casually with our boss, and I've been working with him for ten years.

They pause in the parking lot, consequentially allowing me to intrude on their conversation en route to my car. I turn my lips in the direction of what I hope is a genuine smile.

"Hi, Eve!" Kendall says in her sweet tea accent.

"Eve, how have you been?" Jeremiah says in a methodical, professional tone that he's hoping Kendall picks up on.

"Splendid, thank you," I respond, surpassing professionalism and touching on royalty. I look at Jeremiah, who is clearly irritated with Kendall's immaturity.

He turns back to Kendall with a forced smile. "Ms. Dupree, enjoy your evening." He bows at her, and she's been dismissed.

That weird Disney look riddles her face again, but she takes the hint and meanders to her car.

I'm stifling a laugh when Jeremiah turns back to me, and he's too professional to address her behavior, so he sighs and joins me as I head toward my car. "How is everything, Eve? I know you're close with Jordan's family. How are they doing?"

I shake my head. "It's too soon to tell. Jill's coping, but it's going to be a long road."

He nods sympathetically and switches his briefcase to the other hand. "Why are you leaving so late? You're usually gone by now."

I glance over at the football field and see all the silver and blue helmets bobbing around, and wonder briefly which one is mine. "I was chatting with Alondra Hendrick about all this."

Jeremiah stops. "About what? Jordan Sawyer?"

I nod. "Yeah, kind of. It was brief."

"May I ask if she divulged information that may be considered inappropriate?"

I blink. "No, she told me nothing at all. Why?"

He resumes walking, shifting his briefcase again. "This must stay between you and me, but Ms. Hendrick is under investigation."

Now it's my turn to stop in my tracks. "What? Why?"

"Well, she's obviously the first person to which fingers point when a student commits suicide. She's the counselor, and Jordan had been having meetings with her. She's trained to detect these sorts of things, and she didn't."

"Ouch. That seems harsh." And I thought my accusations were insensitive.

He looks at me with a smirk—a professional smirk, nonetheless. "The moment one of my students committed this heinous act, I started asking questions. This is a school of excellence, Eve. You know that. I expect one hundred percent from my staff and students alike, and this, well … Jordan Sawyer's mentality does not coincide with what we are about here at Liberty. Someone dropped the ball somewhere. And she was the first person I looked into."

I gulp. "Have you found anything on her?"

He stops, looks at the sky, then at me. He's considering me. Monitoring me. Deciding how much he should say. "Perhaps. It's still not entirely clear."

Thank God I'm at my car, otherwise I'd throw up. I reach for the door handle, but he places his hand on my wrist. "Eve, please don't mention this to anyone. I've told you because I trust you and your husband, but nothing has been exposed yet. I just wanted you to know that she is, in fact, under investigation."

I look up at him. "Does she know?"

He nods. "She does."

So that explains why she was so abrupt when I was trying to con her into telling me things about Jordan. She probably thought I was sent in as bait by Jeremiah to see if she would spill.

This just got really weird.

12

EVE

I lied. I didn't leave the school after talking to Jeremiah like I made it look; I drove over to the football field to watch Malik's practice until I saw Jeremiah's car leave.

Xander will be dismissed in about ten minutes, and I'll be late picking him up if I don't hurry. I drive back to the faculty parking lot that's quickly emptying and scan it for Alex's truck. It's gone. I'm sure he wanted to get that kitten home to surprise Xander. Now I really can't be late.

I sneak back into the school, rushing past a few parents and lingering staff who all smile at me, and to whom I give a brief wave. Stepping into the office, I expect to see Mrs. Steinson, the little old secretary, sitting at her desk. But she's not, and I don't even take time to wonder where she is before ducking into the back office where the employee files are.

Thankfully, *Hendrick* is right before *Hunter*, so if anyone catches me, I can easily say I'm getting into my own file. Until I actually pull hers out and open it, scanning over her resume and the notes Jeremiah had taken during her interview. I don't spend much time on those—they're obviously positive, since he hired her—and sift to a manila envelope labeled CLASSIFIED.

And now I'm beyond the point of no return.

I'm so frantic, I don't even know what I'm looking at. Her fingerprints, a signed affidavit, a background check, and various documents and someone's coming. I grab my phone and snap pictures of every document and cram them back in the envelope just as Mrs. Steinson walks in and catches me red-handed.

She places a wrinkled hand on her chest. "Oh, Mrs. Hunter. You scared me."

She's not acting suspicious, so I chuckle and wave the folder at her. "Just had to check something on my resume." I casually return it to the H section and stand back up, throwing my hands out to the side theatrically. "Can you believe I couldn't remember the name of that preschool I interned at down in Homestead? A friend was asking about it, and I just plumb forgot!" I bump my palm into my forehead like I'm some dumb imbecile, and Mrs. Steinson gets a real kick out of that because she's old-school and loves her some slapstick humor.

Her hand goes from her chest to her mouth as she starts giggling. "Oh, dear. You sound like me. So, what was the name of it?"

Oh, damn. I honestly don't remember, and as I'm glancing around the room, my eyes stop on an artificial tree in the corner. "Oak—Oakwood. Oakwood Preschool."

She looks at me funny.

I do my best Laurel and Hardy impression and scamper out of the room.

I'm home five minutes late with Xander—enough to blame on traffic. Crisis averted.

I don't know if Alex is setting up some elaborate surprise, but I couldn't tell Xander about the kitten if I wanted to, because the kid talked my ear off the entire way home. Bria broke up with Matthew and now she's boyfriend/girlfriend with Grayson, and can I believe the audacity, and Xander wonders when he's gonna get a girlfriend and if she's gonna be pretty or not. And I don't know who any of these people are, but Bria sounds like a ho.

"Let's just stay away from Bria, okay, Xan?"

Xander rolls his eyes as he steps through the front door. "Don't worry, Mom. Bria has a dog face."

"Wait, that's not nice, Xan—"

And there's Alex standing in the kitchen, gallantly presenting the kitten like Simba. Xander drops his backpack and squeals, rushing to grab the kitten. "Is it for me?"

Alex chuckles. "Sure is. She's a gift from the senior class. You should write them a thank-you card."

Xander doesn't speak, and I look to see he's crying. I swallow back tears of my own and kneel next to him. "Do you like it?"

"I love her so much, Mommy."

I hug him, and my heart feels full again. This hasn't happened since the day of Jordan's funeral, when we were eating chili at the dinner table. The kitten meows and Xander wipes his eyes, then turns his shining face to me. "I'm gonna take her to my room and show her her new bed. Thank you, Mommy." He gives me another hug before running to Alex. "Thank you, Daddy."

I stand from my crouched position as he hightails to his room, and suddenly I'm enveloped in Alex's arms.

This feels so amazing; I've missed his hugs and his smell and the all-around comfort, but I have a position to uphold, and right now that position is disgruntled wife.

He releases me and squeezes my arms as he looks down at me. "I know you're angry, and what I said was stupid. But Eve, I'm sorry. They always say, 'actions speak louder than words,' and I think my actions over the last nine years have proven my love for you and Malik way more than a few stupid words Saturday morning."

I drop my gaze. I've never doubted his love for us, but that doesn't change the fact that we're on two different pages. "Alex, when you make those comments ... about Malik and about his father ... it just reminds me that... ugh. Look, I hate it that you tell your class everything that goes on here at home."

He releases my arms and steps back, clearly surprised—maybe even a little hurt—at my blatant turn of conversation. I kind of am, too, actually. But it's one step at a time, and apparently I feel this should be addressed first.

"You're open and outgoing, and that's fine, but I ... I have my secrets, Alex. I'm a closed person, and for good reason. I have things in my past that need to stay where they are. And I feel completely exposed when I hear from other students all the things they know about us." I lower onto a barstool at the island.

He sits next to me, placing one hand on the island and one on my thigh. "You think I don't know that? Eve, do you honestly think I would tell a bunch of students the truth about you? Our kids don't even know the full truth, why would I—"

I clap my hand over his mouth. "Shhh! Xander's in his room!"

He rubs my back and leans in to kiss my cheek. "Eve, I'm so happy with my life. I'm so thankful and so in love with you and our kids, it's all I want to talk about. You and Malik and Xander make me happier and prouder than I ever thought I could be, and I'm sorry, but I love this life I've built with you. I'm sorry if that makes me seem insensitive about your past, but you three are all I think about, every second of every day, and I want everyone to know how lucky I am, because even the smallest things that happen among the four of us changes me, as a person, on a daily basis."

Tears are running down my face and I surrender into his chest, basking in his arms as they wrap around my body, and I smell him—breathing Alex into my lungs and my heart and my soul. I absolutely and irrevocably love this man. "Thank you, Alex. I love you. I'm sorry."

He kisses my forehead. "I love you more," he whispers.

"I have to tell you something," I say into his chest, and as much as I don't want to, I back out of his embrace. "I've been wanting to tell you this since Friday. It's about Jordan."

His eyes grow wide. Cautious. Like he's scared *of* me and not *for* me.

"Petra is having an affair. I found Jordan's text messages, and he knew. Petra bullied him into not telling Jill."

Alex blinks and darts his eyes around the room, like he just woke up and doesn't know where he is. Then he zeroes in on me. "Whoa, hold on. Did you tell Jill this? She needs to know."

I hold up a hand. "No, but I confronted Petra."

And now he's scared *for* me. "You did *what*?"

"I met up with her Saturday. She's willing to help me if she promises to tell Jill after it's all over."

His jaw snaps shut. "Help you with what?"

"I want all of Jordan's texts. There are a lot missing on his iPad and he deleted everything from his phone. If I could find that huge role to his suicide in Petra's texts, I'm sure there are more."

Alex is breathing heavily and staring at the ground. He finally rubs his face harshly and shakes his head. "I don't know if this is a good idea. I don't like the sounds of this. We don't know Petra, and you have this incriminating evidence against her. I mean, that's some serious blackmail."

"This isn't about blackmail. It's about Jordan and giving Jill the closure she deserves. What if it were Malik? Wouldn't you want to know?"

Before he can answer, the front door opens and Malik walks in, dripping sweat and wearing his football pants. He drops his bag and heads to the kitchen, glancing from me to Alex, back and forth. "Yo," he says, tossing his head up, and he grabs a Gatorade from the fridge, emptying the entire bottle down his gullet in a matter of seconds.

"How was practice?" Alex asks.

"Fine. Same. What's for dinner?"

I clap my hand over my mouth. "I forgot to defrost the steaks. I'm sorry! I'll order pizza."

Malik gives no reaction; he just continues moving about the kitchen to throw the bottle in the recycle bin and wash his hands.

"We got another kitten today, Malik," I say, navigating to the pizza app on my phone and clicking on *past orders*.

He grins from the sink. "I heard. How's Xander like it?"

"He cried when he saw it. It's his new best friend." *Click*. Twenty minutes until pizza time. Thank God for modern technology.

Malik snickers and grabs a towel. "Crazy kid. What'd he name it?"

"I don't know. It'll probably be after some superhero," Alex says.

I look at him as Malik heads to the bathroom to shower. "You think? I think it'll be some sort of baked good. Let's make a bet." I glance down the hall and wait for Malik to shut the bathroom door. "Winner receives oral gratification."

"Deal."

Alex waits for the shower to turn on before whispering, "Eve, you need to be careful with this whole

Jordan thing. You don't know what you could uncover. We don't know what drove Jordan to do what he did."

I bite my lip and assess him. He doesn't get it. "Alex? A teenage boy is dead. And no one knows why. We deal with teenagers all the time—we have one of our own. Don't you want to know what triggered it? How it could've been prevented? This is little Jordan Sawyer we're talking about, not Lucifer. And besides, I owe this to Jill."

Alex sighs. "Well, it sounds like you have your mind made up. Please just keep me in the loop, okay? Speaking of which, what was this appointment you had today?"

My head shoots back up. "Oh! That's something else! I spoke with Alondra Hendrick. I set up an appointment with her because I've been depressed all weekend since you were being a dick Saturday."

He rolls his eyes. "Great, thanks."

I wave him off. "Don't worry, I didn't get into much detail, but guess what? Jeremiah told me she's under investigation for Jordan's suicide."

Alex nods. "Yeah, I know."

My jaw drops. "How did you know? Why didn't you tell me?" I continue rebuking him as I open my phone and go to the photos. "I was able to sneak in the office after school and look in her file."

Alex literally jumps off the stool. "Eve, tell me you're lying!"

"No, look." I try zooming in on the shots I took of the documents, but they're too blurry. "Dammit! I went to all that trouble and wound up with nothing to show for it!" I lock my phone and toss it on the island.

Alex grabs my chin and turns my face toward his. "Do you realize what you've done? It's illegal to go into someone else's files and snoop through their personal information, Eve! What is the matter with you?" He releases my chin and begins pacing, then stops next to me, putting his hands on his hips. "What did you see in her file? Jesus Christ, I can't believe you did that." And he's pacing again.

"Nothing, I swear. I tried getting these photos, but they're too blurry."

"What were you looking for?" he nearly yells.

"Will you be quiet? I was trying to find something to help in the investigation."

Alex slaps his hands over his face. "I wish you would've just asked me about this. I was in the board meeting when they decided to open the investigation. They got an anonymous tip that Alondra Hendrick worked under a different name at an unaccredited facility that shut down, and she didn't include it in her resume. But we don't know for sure, because nothing came up in her background check. It *looks* suspicious, that's all."

"Well that's a shit ton of information I could've used earlier. What school was it? Why'd it shut down? Why'd she change her name?"

Alex shuts his eyes and rubs the back of his neck. "Please, Eve," he says tiredly. "She's only been a citizen for five years, and she came here ten years ago. That leaves five years unaccounted for because she didn't have a social security number. She had a perfectly legitimate reason for not using her current name and not putting it on her resume—I wouldn't want people associating me with a shady, unaccredited school, either—and now, because Jordan committed suicide, she's under fire for everything she's ever done, ever."

It all makes sense... Unless she was the reason the school was shady. But Alex is clearly Team Alondra, so I'm not telling him that. "Who would give the school this information?" I ask instead.

He shakes his head. "I don't know. But this investigation should be closed out by the end of the week, so let's just ride it out. Please don't tell people this, and please leave her alone about it."

I jump off the stool and yank paper plates from the cupboard. "You have no problem telling your students all our shit, and you can't even tell me this stuff you know about Alondra. I told you the same day I heard about it."

He's grabbing a beer from the fridge and stops. "You're just now telling me two days later about Petra. Are you serious right now?"

"Because you were being a dick!"

"I'm always a dick, Eve!" He throws his hands up. "You just decided you weren't going to speak to me!"

I slam the drawer after pulling out the napkins. "That doesn't change the fact that you vomit our personal lives to your students and you can't tell me this piece of information."

"Think about it! I tell the kids fun, cute little stories that go on in our home. What happened to Alondra isn't a fun, cute little anything. Just like I don't tell everyone your and Malik's business, I don't tell everyone Alondra's."

"I'm not everyone," I snap.

"It's gossip, Eve. That's all." The doorbell rings, and we retreat to our mutual corners.

Malik trots out from the bedroom to get the door, walking into the kitchen with two pizzas. He calls Xander, who comes running with his gray furball, and I stomp out of the kitchen and into the bedroom.

This is twice in one day I can't stand Alex. A new record.

13

MALIK

If "Malik is such a good kid," why am I always feeling like I'm one decision away from the world caving in on me?

I'm standing in the shower in the locker rooms after practice with the water almost all the way hot. I mean, this shit's scalding, and I'm pretty sure I've single-handedly fogged up the entire locker room, and no one can breathe. But nobody says anything. They let me be, for whatever reason. I'd like to think it's because I'm their motherfucking captain and they have to let me do what I want, but I know it's because no one really cares the temperature or length of my shower, no matter how extreme either one is.

I could be dead in here and no one would know or care.

"Yo, Hunter."

Well, except for Javier.

"What's up?" I call.

"You good, man?"

I stand up straight when I realize I've been leaning against the wall as this aqua-hell assaults me. "I'm good."

It's quiet, and I think he's left until he says, "You sure?"

Am I sure? I don't know. I twist the water off and grab my towel, stepping out to see Javier chilling in shorts and slides, his bag on his shoulder and his hands elbow-deep in the pockets of his hoodie. The rest of the locker room is empty.

"Shoot. How long have I been in here?" I mutter.

Javi nods, laughing nervously. "About a half hour. Everyone dipped."

"Why are you still here?" I slip into basketball shorts and throw a *Liberty Lords* T-shirt over my head.

Javier pulls his hands from his pockets and rubs the back of his head. "Keeping an eye on you. You seem kinda out of it lately."

I snicker as I step into my slides. "You noticed, huh? It's that bad?"

We walk out of the locker room toward the student parking lot. As luck usually has it, Javier and I are two of the few sophomores with cars, considering we turned sixteen before most of our class. His new Mustang is way nicer than my used Nissan, but again, with the luck.

"So, what's been going on with you?" he prompts.

I pause. "Not really sure. Just dealing with a lot of shit. That kid, Jordan, that whole situation's kinda fucked me up. My parents are fighting a lot, and then school and football—it just doesn't stop. You know?"

"Yeah," he says in a tone that indicates he has no idea what I'm talking about. I know Javier couldn't care less about Jordan; he didn't know him. And with Javi's lifestyle and the fact that everything he touches turns to gold, I don't think he's ever had a bad day in his life.

"You just need to get laid, brother."

Yeah, that's it. I give him a courtesy laugh anyway, and think of Creed. I miss her. I haven't really seen her since she sang to me at Wynwood, and I laid her across that piano and gave her the fucking of a lifetime.

Of course, Javi has no idea about Creed because he was drunk both times she came to his house, and he's currently listing off all the girls he's fucked and telling me their strengths and weaknesses in bed. He honestly thinks I want his sloppy seconds.

I laugh out loud. "I'm good, man. Thanks, though. You keep all your hos." I get to my car and throw my bag in the trunk.

Javier's looking at me with a confused grin, like he really doesn't understand why I wouldn't want to stick my dick in all the same holes his has been. "Well, just take care of yourself, brother. I'm serious."

I slam the trunk and nod at him. Maybe Javi isn't such a douche after all. Maybe he really does care. I mean, he's noticed I've been a little out of it lately, right? He waited for me in the locker room, didn't he? Maybe he does think of someone other than himself.

"...because I need you to help me win this game Friday. Those Braddock *come mierdas* have been talking mad shit, and we gotta whoop that ass."

There it is.

The traffic in Miami is shit-tastic. Twenty-four, seven.

I swear to God, every car in the world is on US-1 right now, and I'm stuck behind the one idiot in a red Mazda blasting reggaeton and shaking my entire car. I flip the radio to *103.5 The Beat* and let Kendrick Lamar rap his way through this complete standstill and into whatever sane part is left of my brain. Except I keep it at a reasonable decibel with my windows rolled up.

I don't know which things to stress about, but the first two that come to mind are Creed and Friday's game.

Creed first. I haven't seen her since Saturday. We've talked and texted here and there, but fucking football, man. They want a bunch of celibates out there tossing pigskin, apparently. I hope she doesn't think I'm being an arrogant prick. Some douche who fucks her on weekends and that's it. But what exactly do I want with her? What sort of couple would we make?

I try to picture taking her to prom or homecoming, and I can't. The thought of walking through the halls with her at school, holding hands, kissing between classes ... I realize I'm gritting my teeth as the Metrorail goes pounding by, and I should take public transportation to avoid shit like this.

Maybe I am a douche, because I can't figure out why I like her so much but can't picture us together. Have I really fallen victim to the whole high school stereotypical crap? Or am I just being a normal sixteen-year-old guy who doesn't want to commit?

God, I can't. Football, then—Friday's gonna be insane. Coach Jay's been putting so much pressure on me. It's like when everyone else fucks up, that's just more responsibility for me to handle. *The O-line can't block? Well then, Hunter, just use your agility and throw the ball and don't get sacked and don't throw a pick and don't fumble.* I mean, why can't the offensive coaches just teach the O-line to fucking block instead of forcing me to ward off the entire defense while the rest of my teammates jack off? Why can't I just suck at football so people would leave me the fuck alone and stop with all the expectations?

A clean-cut, overweight guy walks up to my car holding a piece of cardboard that says HOMELESS. NEED MONEY. GOD BLESS. And he's being championed by a Haitian walking around selling bags of lychees. I have no cash for either of them. Same song and dance at every stoplight.

And it's like the heavens open and light pours down because there's a break in traffic and I can actually move around this Mazda ass-clown and drive like a normal person. I can almost hear the Hallelujah Chorus amidst all this Migos on my radio.

But I jump at the sound of three short blasts of a cop siren, and look in my rearview mirror to see that damn strip of blue light flashing in my retinas.

"Shoot." I pull my car off the road, and he follows right behind. I shift into park and reach in my pocket for my wallet, monitoring the driver-side mirror as this tan-uniformed mustache gets out of his car and jaunts toward mine.

I turn down the radio and roll down my window.

"Good afternoon, young man."

"Afternoon, sir."

"License, registration, and proof of insurance, please."

I hand him my license and reach for the glove compartment for my registration, but stop when he makes a sudden move that I see in my peripheral vision.

"Whoa. Easy, buddy," he says, and his hand goes right to his holster.

My eyes widen—mostly because this idiot's *already* going for his gun, and not even *because* he's going for his gun—and I put my hands up. "D—did you want my registration and proof of insurance? Because they're in there." I point to the glove compartment.

He releases his holster and hovers over it, instead. "Yes, of course."

I wait until I'm reaching for the Ziploc bag my mom put all this stuff in before rolling my eyes. I pull out both papers and hand them over.

He inspects all three before asking, "Do you know why I've pulled you over?"

"No, sir."

"Welp, the speed limit here is forty, and you were doing sixty."

I sigh. I was just doing negative five for twenty minutes back there in that traffic jam—why can't this shit just average out? How come no one's pulling over the assholes who were making everyone go negative five to begin with?

He heads back to his car, and I roll my window up because it's hot as balls.

Fuck.

I shut my eyes 'cause this day blows, but I hear commotion and open them back up. A crap load of blue lights is in my rearview mirror now, and I jerk my head around to see three more cop cars have joined. What the hell's going on? I wonder if I should get out and investigate—something clearly happened because the officers are multiplying.

I unbuckle my seatbelt and open the door, and no sooner does my foot hit the earth than I hear, "Get down, young man!" And three of these fuckers are sprinting toward me and they're all aiming guns at me.

"Shit!" My heart is pounding as I twist back into my car, my hands automatically going up, and these dreadlocks are going to be the death of me. I'm going to jail.

"Hey!"

I look in my rearview mirror to see the first cop—the one with my license and stuff—getting out of his car and waving them off. "Nah, guys. Wrong call. The robbery was south. That was an African-American male, just been picked up. This is just a kid. Speeding violation."

My hands are frozen next to my skull as I watch this all go down in my driver-side mirror. The three fuckers hem and haw and put their shit away, avoiding eye contact with me in the mirror, until one of them meanders over sheepishly and leans down.

I haven't even shut my door yet, since my hands are still locked near my head.

"Our apologies, son," he says.

I manage to jerk my head a couple inches to the left, slowly bringing my hands down into my lap. "What just happened?"

The officer chuckles like I'm some sort of comedian at gunpoint, and apologizes again. "Miscommunication, that's all. You're fine."

Translation: they saw my dreads and jumped to conclusions.

"Where you go to school?"

And now I turn my head the full ninety degrees. "Liberty."

His eyes trail down my body, like he doesn't believe I go to a private school. "You play basketball? You look like a basketball player."

"Football."

"Ah, football! What position?"

Sweet Jesus. "Quarterback."

He starts rambling about how the chief's niece goes to Liberty, and her name is Natalia and do I know her.

I don't.

The first officer finally approaches and hands me my stuff. "Mr. Hunter. Here. I'm giving you a ticket for speeding. However, instead of marking the twenty miles over you were doing, I put you as only going ten over. The fine is cheaper, and the points on your license are much lower."

I look up at him as I take the papers. I just had three guns pointed at my head, and he's acting like he's doing me a favor?

I turn to the other cop, the one who was just chatting me up, and he's straight-up powerwalking back to his car, following the other two that already left. Yeah, I get it— duty calls. These minorities aren't going to judge themselves.

"I need you to sign here, please," he responds.

I don't know what the hell I signed, but it sure as hell wasn't my name.

He grabs the pen from me and circles a bunch of shit in the fine print. "If you go to this website and enter your citation number, you'll be able to do an online driving course. If you do this, the ticket will be eradicated from your record and you won't have to pay a fine or receive any points."

I twist my head up to him. "You mean it'll come off completely?"

"Your driving record will remain clean, yes. This is the website, and if you have any questions, or if you want to confirm completion, call this number here when you've finished." And he circles something else.

Then why doesn't he just not give me a ticket?

I don't say that, but he must read the confusion on my face because he stands tall and looks at me sternly. "I need you to slow down. This is how accidents happen, people get killed. You're young, you're an athlete, and it would be quite a tragic story to read in the *Miami Herald* if something happened to you."

"Yes, sir." I wonder if he thinks I look like a basketball player, too.

He taps the citation with his pen. "Take this online course. And no more speeding. Have a great day." And he's gone.

You know how you can get people to stop speeding *without* fake tickets? Put a bunch of guns to their head.

I promise you, Alex's eyes are the dwelling places of Satan when he's pissed. I'm staring at them now while he's bawling me out, and it's one of those things where I don't want to be staring, but I can't peel my eyes away because they're so phenomenal. Eyes should never, ever look that diabolical. I purposely didn't watch *Saw* to avoid shit like this.

I zoned out a while ago, maybe ten seconds after he jerked the speeding ticket from me and asked, "What's been going on with you lately?" because nothing's been going on—I haven't done anything wrong. Not worth this magnitude of lecturing, anyway. I could understand if I came home drunk or high, or with bad grades, or if I killed someone. But for the love of God, am I the first person in the world to get a speeding ticket? What would he do if I really did commit some horrible crime?

He must have just asked me a question because I realize it's quiet, and I have no idea what it was, so I just shrug.

He slams the citation on the counter and throws his hands up, turning to my mom. She's leaning against the counter, her arms folded, chewing on her lip. I wish I knew what she's thinking—if she's mad at me or about to defend me.

"You're grounded, Malik. Two weeks. No phone, no car," Alex says.

Now I'm listening. "What? Two weeks? Why my phone? I wasn't texting and driving. And I told you, the cop said I can get everything taken off! No points, no fees, and the insurance will never know."

"It has nothing to do with points and fees, son. You were speeding, and you've already been on very thin ice with me." He taps his middle finger on the countertop—four times—that's where he wants my keys and my phone. Now.

I turn to my mom and throw my hands out as a last resort. "Mom, come on! Do something!"

She eyes me for a moment before shrugging and shaking her head. "I don't know, Malik. I've been very understanding with you lately. But there's no excuse for speeding. Your car is a privilege, and if you abuse privileges, you lose them."

Alex stands a little taller, gesturing harder at the countertop, if that's possible. "Now, son."

"Neither of you have ever gotten pulled over for speeding before? Isn't this like a rite of passage? I didn't do it on purpose! Javier gets pulled over all the—"

"Would you like to make it three weeks?"

This is fucking bullshit. I throw the keys on the counter and toss my phone next to it, grabbing my bag and storming to my room. Cops treating me like a black kid, my parents treating me like a white kid. And yet I am neither one. Who knows what the fuck I am.

It takes me about ten minutes to contact all the people I need to that I'm phoneless for two weeks through LibertyNet. Some of them are on chat, the rest I send messages to.

Creed's on chat, and she keeps sending me sad faces.

I'm sorry, Creed. I hate this. But my parents are pissed.

She writes back: *Are you still able to play in the game Friday?*

I huff and type: *Let's get one thing straight. No punishment will ever eliminate football from my life. I could be on death row and my dad would come bust me out every Friday night and tell me to suit up.*

She says she has to do homework, and I have to study, anyway. So we say our goodbyes and I navigate to my homework menu for history, because I'm not going to ask Alex. He'd probably ground me more for not having it memorized and tattooed on my ass.

And if that's not irritating enough, that stupid video of the seniors giving my parents that cat has gone viral. I hate it. Why'd they even take video if they were trying to do something nice? It makes my parents look like these vulnerable dipshits who were charity cases for these stupid teenagers. They didn't give us a cat because they love my parents, they did it to post their good deed all over the

Internet and make themselves look good. Bunch of arrogant assholes.

How's football going?

The chat message pops up so randomly, I flinch. It's that weird number again. Who the hell has manipulated their profile name to a bunch of numbers? And why don't they leave me alone? *Who is this?* I type.

I told you before, it's a fan.

Yeah, screw that. I exit out and continue scouring the homework menu. But it pops up again.

I bet if you play well Friday, your dad will give your phone and car back.

I'm tipping back in my chair, but I immediately slam the two front legs into the ground. How the hell does this person know I'm grounded? I literally told, like, seven people. Like, five minutes ago.

He does that sometimes, doesn't he? Removes punishments for a good game?

I'm wracking my brain, trying to figure out who this is. I told Creed, Javier, Tyler, CJ, Gabriel, and two kids I'm partnered with for an English project. I didn't tell my English partners about the car—I'm not that close with them, and they only needed to know about my phone, since we text about assignments.

So that leaves the other five.

Or is it your mom who always fights him for your privileges? They fight over you a lot.

Okay, I've never told anyone that. My fingers are shaking, but I manage to type: *I'm not telling you a damn thing until you tell me who this is.*

You've already told me things. You feel like an outsider. Remember? The last time we spoke.

Hell, nah—he asked me that weird question, but I never answered. Just like I'm not going to now. I should've blocked his stupid ass back then.

You know who else felt like an outsider? Jordan Sawyer. You two were so much alike. He was a star, too.

137

And now my hands are shaking so hard, I couldn't type if I wanted to. He kept calling me a star the last time, and I thought he meant in football. But if Jordan was a star, then I have no idea what this means.

You want to hear another secret?

Nope. I don't. But I'm too frozen to type, to log off. I just stare at the screen.

Jordan confided in me. A lot. I tried helping him, but he was too weak. That's where you two are different. You're so strong, Malik. I can help you, if you'd let me.

Nope. Nope. No.

I can tell you want to quit football.

My pencil hits the floor. Creed? She's the only person who knows this. And Creed's weird and all, but she'd never hide behind some shady profile. Right? I click over on the chat window to see that Creed is logged on, but is away. Is it possible to be logged on at the same time with two different accounts? I message her anyway.

Creed?

Her name goes from gray and italicized to black and normal. *Yeah?* she responds.

I start to type out like a zillion different sentences but erase them all. I don't even know what to ask. "Are you fucking with me from a different profile?" just doesn't do it for me. Besides, I can see this other chat window is blinking with new messages, so there's no way she could be doing both.

I'm doing history. What do you need? she asks as the other chat window continues going nuts.

Sorry. Never mind. And I ex out of her's.

I really don't think it's her messing with me, but did she tell someone? I'm super disturbed right now. I look over to see the book this creep has written me.

I understand your frustrations with football. How you feel like there's no way out. If you quit, you'd be disappointing your team. Your coach. Your dad. People would be angry with you. You'd lose friends, popularity status. Scholarships. Just think—try to think of the only way you could stop playing football, and no one would be mad at you. You could give it all up, Malik. Everything that weighs you down, all the stress and pressure placed on you. You can get rid of it all, and people would understand. And everything would be okay. Because no one would ever expect you to be a leader or throw another football for the rest of the season.

My cursor blinks in the text box like a hypnotic heartbeat. He couldn't be suggesting what I think he's suggesting. My body is suddenly very still, every nerve ending alert, on edge.

Jordan's answer was suicide, but he was wrong. He was a different star than you.

I let out an audible breath.

My inbox pings with a new message.

I just sent you a video. Watch it and tell me what you think.

I steeple my fingers in front of my mouth. It's like Pandora's Inbox. My hand steers to the mouse and I click on the red circle that says *New Message!* Sure enough, it's from all those numbers @libertynet.org. I click the attachment.

My knee is quivering as the video loads, and when it does, it's a football clip. I relax for a sec until I see it's black and white, maybe from the forties or fifties. The clip is forty seconds. I click PLAY.

I feel like I'm watching through a Snapchat filter with a vintage theme, and you can hear the projector reel spinning. I'm waiting for some old Vaudeville music from one of those haunted piano roll thingies, or even an old-fashioned sports commentator who talks with some antiquated American accent where they don't pronounce their *r*'s.

But there's no sound outside of the spinning reel. The footage is choppy, and all the lines and spots blinking in and out are making me sick. I expand it so the video engulfs my entire screen.

I'm twenty seconds in and watching a shotgun snap to the quarterback, when some huge monster-looking dude comes out of nowhere and trucks him, and the camera angle's so perfect that I actually see the quarterback's leg snap at the shin.

I wince and back away from the screen, but the video isn't over. For the next twenty seconds, I'm subjected to watching slow-motion, close-up replays of this guy's leg just shattering—one second it's normal, and the next it's at a ninety-degree angle and bones are splintering out the sides. In addition, the sound has changed from the reel spinning to this creepy, forlorn music. It's not even music—it's like sounds you'd hear on a horror movie trailer (that I purposely don't watch to avoid this shit). The only reason I'm able to watch it on this twenty-second continuous loop is because it's black and white and faded, so it's not as gory and realistic as if I were watching it in, like, modern-day HD or anything.

It's like a train wreck or Alex's sadistic eyes—I want to look away, but I can't. When it's over, I exit out quickly. The chat window blings.

Feel sorry for him, Malik? Do you blame him for not playing the rest of the season?

I don't breathe. Don't blink. Is he really suggesting I break my leg to get out of football?

What do you think, Malik?

I'm finally able to respond. *I think you're one sick son of a bitch.*

Then I block his ass.

14

EVE

This stage of limbo while waiting on Petra is really screwing up my communication with Jill. She hasn't asked about Jordan's iPad or if I've found anything on it, but I know I eventually need to say something. And it's hard to have a normal conversation with her when I know her wife was cheating on her, and her deceased son knew about it.

I feel like a damn liar.

Petra's had three days to get me Jordan's texts, and on day three she texts me: *Eve, I need more time. I'm sorry but I've been working doubles at the hospital.*

It's simple. I respond with: *I'm telling Jill, then.* And she has the messages the same day.

She calls me when she gets off work at six p.m. "There are thousands of texts here, Eve. It's overwhelming. I don't know how we're going to attack this. But I've already started."

"Anything so far?" I ask between sips of Pinot Noir and grading English compositions.

"Not much. There's a girl named Katie he was having sex with, but I don't know who Katie is."

Pinot Noir comes out my nose, and it burns like a mother. "Jordan was having sex? At fourteen?"

"Do you know any Katie from school?" She's saying the name like she's never heard it before, like it sounds foreign to her. I don't know why she has to make things so difficult.

Regardless, I wrack my brain. I can't think of any Katies in the freshman class, and I know there are none in Malik's sophomore class. I scan through the juniors and seniors, but would upper-classmen really sleep with a fourteen-year-old? "What about in your neighborhood, friends, anything?" I ask. "Maybe he knows a Katie outside school? Or even the middle school?"

I hear Petra exhale. "Not that I know of. But I gotta read more of the texts. What could that stand for? Katherine Something? Kathleen Something?"

"I don't know, Petra. It stands for whore." And I take the biggest sip of wine in the world.

Petra huffs. "Well, when can we meet up? This thing is huge, and I can't hide it from Jill for long."

I correct a *who* to a *whom* on a junior composition. "Can you swing by my house on your way home?"

She rings the doorbell right in the middle of dinner with my family. God, she's difficult. I made Beef Wellington, Malik's favorite—because he got in big trouble and I'm beginning to feel sorry for him.

I open the door with beef in my mouth. "Hey, Petra," I say behind my fist.

She hands me a stack of papers. "Here, good luck."

"Oh ... wow." She wasn't joking about the quantity. This thing is like a literary landslide. We say our goodbyes and I shut the door, heading back to the dining room. My appetite's gone to hell.

"What was that all about?" Alex asks.

"It was just Petra. I'm not feeling well. I think I'm going to lie down for a while." I stop on my way out and turn back to Malik. "Malik, if you do the dishes, you can have three days removed from your sentence."

"One day!" Alex counters as I continue through the living room, flipping through these Franken-texts. Fine. One day. And that's how you negotiate punishments.

Malik will be off the hook in a week, at this rate.

This thing is my Everest. It's just spreadsheet after spreadsheet, and none of the contacts are listed, just their phone numbers. So I don't know who's who, or how Petra found any Katie. I'm trying to keep straight which ones he sent and which ones he received, and I'm gonna need more wine.

The good thing is they're all in descending order, so it's not like I have to start from the bottom and work my way up, like on the iPad. I'm finally starting to form some semblance of this, thanks to the recognition of the texts I read on his iPad. I skip past the photos he sent to girls, as well as the photos they sent back, shivering at the fact that he was thirteen sending nudes. I wonder if Malik's ever done anything like this, but that's not something I can think about right now. And Xander never will. He'll stay eight forever.

There's one number that seems to resurface once he started this semester at Liberty, and I'm wondering if this is Katie because she says really dirty things and then asks about biology homework. "So it's someone in his biology class," I whisper, and I'm actually getting a headache because I can't think of a Katie in the freshman class. But where the hell did Petra see Katie written anywhere? I slow down, reading those specific texts more carefully, but there are so many abbreviations and teenage lingo that I'm gonna need Urban Dictionary to decipher this.

She seems to have come on pretty strong with him, always initiating the sexting, and poking fun at him when he responds shyly or declines. Who is this brazen ho? For kicks, I punch the number into my phone to see if a contact comes up. I'm not surprised when it doesn't, but I save the number, anyway, under *Katie*.

I've already been at this for two hours, and I have to stop. My brain hurts, and I have to go be a mother.

I come out and peek across the hall into Malik's room; he's sitting at his computer, doing homework on LibertyNet. He doesn't see me, but I watch him for a few seconds as he glances at the screen and turns back down to his notebook. He's so perfect.

I sneak in and wrap my arms around his neck, kissing his temple. "I love you, my baby."

He jumps initially, but then relaxes and looks up at me. "Love you, too, Mom. What're you doing? You scared me."

I kiss his temple again. "Nothing. Just watching you be awesome. Are you almost finished with homework?"

"Almost. I lost that worksheet you handed out in English. Do you have another one?"

"I do, but not here. I can email it to you, though."

"Thanks." His shoulders visibly relax, and I wonder why he's so stressed over English.

"Wow, done with homework by eight o'clock. You're not going to have anything to do. What will you do with all that free time?" I chuckle as I look around his room: his unmade bed, his football gear everywhere, his trophies lining an entire wall.

He gives me a crooked, roguish grin and winks. "I'm gonna play Call of Duty. Maybe some Madden, if there's time. Don't want to get too crazy, though."

I laugh and tell him to have fun, leaving his room and thinking how Xbox is probably on the list of things he's grounded from, but what the heck. Let the boy be a boy for once.

I enter the kitchen, and Xander's sitting at the island with a concentrated look, his tongue forced out the side of his mouth as he hovers over a spelling paper and Alex hovers over him. "Dragon, Xander. Spell Dragon. No, there's no *e* in dragoooooon."

"Need help?" I ask, and they both look up.

"Want to give me a sentence for *dragoooooon*?" Xander asks.

Alex ruffles Xander's hair. "Hey, Buddy? You think you got this? You think I can go have a talk with Mommy?" Xander nods, and Alex looks at me, gesturing to the living room.

Puzzled, I follow and sit next to him on the couch. He leans in and hooks his finger under my chin. "I have something for you that will make you happy with me."

I bite my lip and grin. I hope it's a new sex toy.

He pulls a slip of paper from his pocket and hands it to me.

I crinkle my eyebrow and open it, staring down at his handwriting. "Evelyn Gomez. What's this?" It certainly doesn't sound like a vibrator.

Alex taps the paper with his fingertip. "This is Alondra Hendrick. I did some stalking. This was her name when she first came here from Venezuela."

"Whoa!" I look back down at the paper. "How do you go from Evelyn Gomez to Alondra Hendrick?"

Alex shrugs. "Who knows? Middle names, maiden names, whatever. Hendrick is probably her married name."

"She married a gringo, it sounds like. Hendrick certainly isn't Hispanic."

Alex reaches next to the sofa and pulls out his laptop. "Look what I found." I snuggle into him as he navigates through all sorts of search engines and Pinellas County (which is two hundred miles away) school websites.

Finally, he pulls up an article. "Bingo! Read this. It's dated from six years ago." He sets the laptop on my lap.

Private School Investigated After Four Student Suicides

Beaumont Christian School is under investigation after four of the sixty students committed suicide in the time span of two years. The first occurred twenty months ago, when a ninth-grade girl was found hanged in her bedroom. The tragedies continued when nine months later, two tenth-grade girls, best friends, were discovered dead in a running car parked in the garage of one of the girls. The final act was when a boy, age 15, shot himself on campus, leaving no note or any indication as to why he took his own life. Parents took matters to authorities when they felt the school was unresponsive and unsympathetic toward these tragedies. There is currently no word on what police have discovered. However, so far, one employee of Beaumont Christian has been arrested. Evelyn Gomez, the enrollment director and interim guidance counselor, was taken into custody Tuesday.

I gulp. "This is insane. But how do you know that Evelyn is Alondra?"

Alex takes the laptop and clicks things, handing it back to me. And behold, I'm staring at a mugshot of Alondra Hendrick, a few years younger with lighter, shorter hair, under the name of Evelyn Gomez. I turn to Alex with my jaw swinging into my clavicle. "No. Freaking. Way."

Alex nods solemnly. "Look, it's dated shortly after this article was published. But I don't see what she was charged for. Whatever it was, it was expunged. No one else knows about this, so I haven't been able to validate it or follow up on it yet."

"Oh, my gosh. Alex, what are you going to do with this information? I mean, this is huge." My heart is pounding. Jill may be right. Poor, grieving, insane Jill. Despite losing her son, despite being cheated on, this chick knows her conspiracies.

Alex shakes his head. "I don't know yet. I need to just think about it." Then he turns to me, pointing his favorite lecturing finger. "And you are not to say a word to anyone. I told you this as a peace treaty. And because you're my wife. Alondra was caught in some sort of suicide scandal, then changed her name. Jeremiah is very thorough with his background checks before hiring anyone, so she went to quite the extent to avoid him discovering this."

I nod. "I promise I won't say a word." Then I kiss him and tell him I'm going to bed, fully intending on texting Alondra to schedule another appointment with her tomorrow.

The following day, I'm extra careful to keep my appointment with her a secret from Alex. She isn't able to see me until halfway through seventh period, so I decide to hang out in the teachers' lounge for those first thirty minutes.

I'm sipping from my favorite mug, scrolling through Instagram and willing my foot to stop bouncing when Kendall waltzes in, waving at me and heading toward the coffee.

"Hi, Eve," she says.

"Hi, there," I return.

"Is Malik ready for the game Friday?"

I drain my mug. "He's always ready."

"I heard this one's gonna be a doozy." Oh, her accent.

I nod. "Yeah, I'll be taking a Xanax beforehand."

She laughs and sits across from me. "I heard Malik's grounded from his phone and car," she says sympathetically. "For speedin'? Was it speedin'?"

I look at her cockeyed. "Yes, unfortunately. Where did you hear that?"

She sips her coffee and looks like she's thinking really hard. "I'm not sure. Your husband, maybe? Maybe some of the other kids. But he's so quiet in my class, I never hear a peep out of him. I don't know how he could ever get in trouble."

I roll my eyes. "You don't know Malik very well. Or my husband, for that matter."

She giggles. "No, I guess not. Hey, do you mind if I sit with you again at the game Friday? It's just that, I don't really know a lot of people yet, and I don't like sittin' with students. It's unprofessional, ya know? And to be honest, I like havin' your other son there, commentatin' everything for me." She laughs.

"Of course, Kendall. You're always welcome to sit with me."

"You're so kind." And it sounds so much more genuine with her drawl. "Can I get your number?" She pulls out her phone and starts clicking things, and I tell her of course she can. I rattle it off as she stores it in her phone, and she says, "I'm gonna text you so you have mine, is that okay?"

Before I can respond, my phone chimes. I look down, but something isn't right.

I just got a text from Katie.

What the fuck.

I swipe it open, and it's a single line: *This is Kendall.* ☺

"There ya go, and you can save my number, too," she's saying, but I'm doing my damnedest not to projectile-vomit all over the table.

I squeeze my phone and stand. "I gotta go." And I run from the room before she can ask questions. Forgetting my appointment with Alondra, I sprint to my car and drive straight home. I'm leaving early, but I don't care. I pull in the driveway and beeline into the house, grabbing Jordan's texts and scouring it for that same number.

I read a couple pages worth of various degrees of sexting and see nothing about Katie.

I call Petra.

"Hello?"

"Petra, tell me about this Katie. I'm not seeing her name anywhere."

"Yeah, Katie. It's all those sexting texts. See how he addresses her. Sometimes it's BB, and sometimes it's Katie."

I run my finger over the texts, and I see BB, but I'm getting pissed because I don't see Katie anywhere. "Petra, I don't know what you saw, but Katie isn't in this list anywhere."

"Yes, it is," she says irritably. "Capital letters. Just like BB. Look for them. I gotta go." And she hangs up.

I continue searching the page, and my fingers stop because this dumb idiot wasn't saying Katie. She's been saying the initials. KD.

As in, Kendall Dupree.

15

EVE

I can't even wrap my head around all this. I've seen how ugly this world can be, firsthand, and I still cannot believe what Jordan Sawyer went through before he died. I've been sprawled on my bed, sobbing for the last hour, when I get a call from Xander's school.

I forgot to pick him up. Oh, my gosh.

Petra was cheating on Jill, Kendall was defiling Jordan, and I'm the worst mom ever.

I rinse my face and grab my sunglasses and go harvest my child from his elementary school.

I don't even know what to do. I want to call Alex, but once Xander's in the car (telling me all about a science project they did today with balloons and xanthan gum and he ruined his art shirt and I need to get him a new one and please don't forget like I forgot to pick him up today), it's impossible to even focus on this pedophile preying throughout the school disguised as a sweet, innocent southern belle.

We get home, and thank God Alex isn't home yet. "Hey, Xan? Why don't you go play with your kitten in your room while I fix dinner, okay?"

"I was going to do that anyway, Mom." He rolls his eyes and runs off, and apparently he doesn't need a parent anymore because he's got his shit together.

I wait until Xander's door slams before calling Alex, who's not answering. I'm going to explode. Then it hits me—I can call Petra. She hung up on me before I could enlighten her earlier.

She doesn't answer either, so I leave a voicemail. "Petra, it's Eve. What's the matter with you? Why didn't you tell me Katie was initials? I thought you were saying the name. Anyway, KD is, get this—his biology teacher, Kendall Dupree. Jordan was sleeping with his teacher. I don't even know what to do. Call me."

I set my phone on the counter and turn around, and Alex is standing there, staring at me. "What did you say?" he says.

I nod and start crying again. "What's going on? Who are these people surrounding our children? We bust our asses trying to protect our kids, and we're feeding them to the wolves."

Alex gathers me in his arms, and I cry into his chest. He's still trying to absorb this, I can tell by the way he doesn't speak and how his movements are jittery and sharp, not soft and reassuring, as he strokes my hair.

"How do you know about Miss Dupree?" he asks.

I take him in the room and show him the messages. "She gave me her phone number today. It's the same one."

"Oh, my god." Alex pushes his fist against his mouth. "We have to do something. I need to tell Mr. Lorrey. We can't let this go on." He kisses me and storms out of the room.

Tacos! I have to make tacos for dinner, because my kids need sustenance. Alex has closed himself in the den, and I hear him talking on the phone as I move about the kitchen, browning the ground beef and dicing up tomatoes on autopilot because I can't function on my own right now.

Malik walks in the front door, waving to whoever dropped him off. I hear good-natured yelling from the driveway, and I can tell it's Javier Acosta. Malik hollers something back, laughs, and flips him off before shutting the door and dropping his bags. "Hey," he says, his smile lingering. But when he looks at my face, he starts. "What's wrong? Have you been crying?"

I abandon the pan and set the spatula down. "Has Miss Dupree ever come on to you?"

Malik's face twists into eighty knots of disgust. "Ew, Mom! What are you asking?"

I cover my mouth. He's just a child. Why did I say it like that? "I'm sorry. But, I mean, she's young and pretty, right? Do the guys flirt with her?"

He shrugs. "I don't know. They talk about how hot she is, but they do that about you, too." He does his ritualistic walk to the fridge for a Gatorade. "I just think she's dumb."

I heave a sigh of relief. "So she's never like, flirted with you? Texted you inappropriately? She's never touched you, has she?"

Malik chokes on his Gatorade. I wince and pat him on the back until he gains composure. "Okay, Mom? I don't know what you're doing, but you need to stop. Get your mind out of the gutter. She's my teacher."

"Oh, thank God." I wrap my arms around his sweaty, smelly torso.

At that moment, Alex comes out of his den, running his fingers through his hair. He nods at Malik. "Hey, son. How was practice? You guys ready for Friday?"

"Mom's saying some messed up shit about Miss Dupree."

Alex turns alarmed—and angry—eyes to me. "What? You told him?"

"No, I haven't *told* him. I only asked him if he's ever been … a victim."

Alex sighs, and Malik is shooting looks between the two of us. "What's going on? What happened with Miss Dupree?"

"She was sleeping with Jordan Sawyer before he killed himself."

"Eve! Will you shut up?" Alex throws his hands out, and Malik has to brace himself on the island.

"He needs to know, Alex! It's going to get out! Oh, god. We're all gonna be on the news!" I put my hands on my head and start circling the kitchen.

"No, it's not! And no, we won't! I just got off the phone with Mr. Lorrey. We have a schoolboard meeting tomorrow morning at seven, and you and I both have to be there. We'll determine the proper discipline for Kendall, which will obviously be termination. But we're not telling the kids, we're not telling the parents, and we sure as hell aren't telling the news. This could ruin our school."

I cock my head. "And then what? She goes and does it at other schools? Who knows if there are other kids here at Liberty she hasn't done this with? We need to call the police, Alex! She's a criminal!"

Alex holds out his hands like he's trying to calm me down, but he's really trying to calm himself down. "We're going to the authorities, Eve. Don't worry. She'll be tried and sentenced. Our first concern is getting her away from our kids. Let the cops handle the rest. We have to confront her tomorrow and see if she even confesses."

Malik has plopped down on a barstool and is staring at the wall. I move to him and take his face in my hands, forcing him to look at me. "Malik? You have nothing to worry about, okay? You're not in trouble. Now for the last time, are you sure you don't know anything about her messing around with students?"

His eyes search mine, and he takes three uneasy breaths before answering. "I'm sure."

THE FALLING OF STARS

My heels click defiantly on the tile at seven a.m. sharp as I enter the schoolboard meeting. I didn't sleep at all. And the few times I did drift off, nightmares. I haven't had nightmares in years. This is all Kendall's fault.

Part of the beauty of working at a school with money is that everything is elaborate—including this courtroom replica for board meetings. The size of an auditorium, the room is dimly lit and hosts rows of pews in the back. The front holds a semi-circular mahogany table that wraps halfway around a podium. It's scary and intimidating, and I can't wait for Kendall to stand behind that podium for judgment.

We're all in formal business attire: suits, blazers, dress shoes ... we don't play, here at Liberty School of Excellence.

Alex follows me as I march through the room toward my seat at the circular desk. Jeremiah is already seated at the center, his hands folded and looking as stern as ever. Alex seats himself to the right of Jeremiah and I to his left as the rest of the faculty files into the room, solemn-faced and professional.

We sit in silence and wait for Kendall, who shows up four minutes late. She's never been to a board meeting, so when she steps into the room for the first time, her face immediately drops as intimidation takes over. Her eyes dart from one end of the circular mahogany desk to the other as her colleagues and superiors stare at her. She smiles uncomfortably. "Where do y'all want me to sit?"

Jeremiah returns a self-assured smile—almost a leer—and leans forward. "Why don't you take your place right there behind that podium, Miss Dupree?"

Her eyes jerk to the center of the room to the podium the rest of us are circling like sharks. I see her swallow as her body tenses, and she stumbles her shaking limbs to the podium, raking fearful eyes across calm, accusing ones.

Jeremiah waits an excruciating ten seconds before addressing her. "Miss Dupree, how well did you know Jordan Sawyer?"

Kendall grips the sides of the podium. Her jaw is quivering, and I think she's going to vomit her heart up any second because that shit's not staying in her chest. "I—I had him in my freshman biology class."

"Mmm. How about on a more personal level? Did the two of you speak outside of class?"

Kendall can barely breathe, let alone speak.

Alex leans toward his microphone and says, "Miss Dupree? You've been addressed."

"I—I—Yes, we did." Kendall starts crying, and something inside me sparks.

"How would you describe this outside relationship? Was it an appropriate relationship between a grown woman and a teenage boy? Between a teacher and her student?"

She reaches a shaky hand to wipe her face. "Probably not."

Jeremiah squeezes his folded hands until they start changing color. "*Probably* not? Please elaborate."

"Um … uh … are y'all gonna have me arrested?"

Jeremiah's fist comes down on the table. "Answer the question!"

"J—Jordan and I, we … we had sex in my classroom. Twice."

Gasps erupt through the room, and I'm going to throw up. Alex slaps his hands over his face, and Jeremiah looks like he's going to explode. Ruben DeSoto, the IT guy, is cursing next to me and I hardly hear him.

When the noises die down, Jeremiah stands, smoothing down his tie. "Kendall Dupree. Do you understand the lawsuit this school could face because of your illegal, immoral, and disgusting actions? Are there any other students with whom you've engaged in sexual intercourse while under our employment?"

She shakes her head frantically. "No, sir."

Jeremiah is losing his professionalism quickly. He's turning into a pissed off motherfucker. "You do know that is illegal, correct? I mean, you know it's wrong to have sex with students!"

Kendall is convulsing, she's crying so hard she's barely able to hold herself up. "I was raped!" she screams. "I was raped in college, and it messed me up! I need help!"

The room has fallen completely silent.

Jeremiah clears his throat. "What do you mean, you were raped?"

"Yeah, I was. And I never told anyone and I never got counselin', but I'm pretty sure I was date raped and now I have all these mental disorders and I guess I'm actin' out by sleepin' with students—"

Jeremiah holds up both hands. "Miss Dupree, I am very sorry to hear that this happened to you. No one should ever have to suffer such a tragedy, and in silence, nonetheless. However, that is not an excuse to justify what you did with Jordan. Since this happened to you in college, you are still within the statute of limitations. I encourage you to disclose this information to the authorities once you're in custody and press charges against the rapist."

Kendall looks more freaked out than ever. "Wait, what? I gotta tell on him?"

"I—I'm sorry?"

"I don't really wanna get any authorities involved…"

Jeremiah is massaging his temples, and I'd pay good money to see what sort of thought mechanism he's using to keep his sanity intact. "Miss Dupree, why in God's name wouldn't you want justice against this perpetrator? You realize by keeping your silence, he will continue doing this to other women?"

Kendall's shaking her head so hard, her curls are flipping around her shoulders. "Oh, 'cause I was just kiddin'. I wasn't really raped. I don't think, anyway."

My vision zeros out until I see nothing but her. And red. Noise spreads throughout the room as teachers groan and shake their heads at this plot twist and victim mentality, and I'm gripping the sides of my chair, every muscle in my body about to explode.

Jeremiah quiets the room and turns back to Kendall. "I think that—"

"How dare you?" I stand up, knocking my chair over. "How dare you claim you fell victim to one of the worst things a woman could endure, just to make excuses for your poor decisions?" My voice is shaking, raspy, I'm marching around the table, my gaze targeted on her because she just caused me to snap and I'm no longer in control of my actions. "You were not raped! I was raped! I was raped when I was sixteen years old, I was wide awake, attacked, abducted, and I felt every sort of fear and pain there is and I never once touched a child inappropriately, *you sick, sick fuck! You raped Jordan Sawyer!*"

People are pulling me away, pulling my hands from around her neck. She's screaming. I'm screaming. She's a fraud. She was never raped. *I* was raped.

I was.

16

MALIK

I don't know what's going on. My parents were so frantic last night, but everything's so calm and normal at school today that I wonder if I just imagined that whole conversation about Miss Dupree.

But she's not here today. Neither are my parents. Substitutes for all three classes. I don't get it. My parents left early this morning for a board meeting, and never mentioned anything about missing school. In fact, my mom apologized for forgetting to email that worksheet and said she'd give me a new one in class.

I don't even have my phone to text them because I'm grounded. But I don't care about that—the problem is, they have my phone. They can read my texts, and they'll see that I lied to them about Miss Dupree.

She did come on to me. It was like the second or third week of school. I told myself it was all my imagination, but then when Javi was a witness, we started texting about it, and those texts are still on my phone.

The first time, it was so subtle I almost missed it. See, I'm an athlete, right? I'm a dude who's always in locker rooms, and we're Neanderthals who constantly slap each other on the ass for encouragement. My coaches, my teammates, everyone slaps my ass like a hundred times a day. Two hundred on game days. I don't even notice it anymore. So when I ran into Miss Dupree one day after school on my way to practice, she stopped to chat me up for a sec.

"Hey, look at you all decked out in your football gear! Lookin' good!"

I honestly didn't think anything of it. I mean, she'd only ever seen me in my school uniform, so I get it—when you finally see someone wearing something besides the same shit day in and day out, you comment on it. Like, if she walked up wearing yoga pants and a tight little tank top, I probably would have said something, too. Or at least thought something...

Anyway, I remember switching my helmet to my other hand so I could high-five her. She asked me like, two super general questions about football. Maybe what position I played and when the next game was, I don't even remember. Then she said, "Well, good luck today," and slapped me another high-five.

But this time, it was like a high-five in passing because we were already walking our separate ways. So when her hand came down, it landed on my ass. It took me a second before I realized that wasn't appropriate. I mean, do you know how many times I've high-fived someone and gotten smacked on the ass immediately after? And by that time, we were already, like, ten feet apart. And besides, what would I possibly say?

Then I started justifying it in my mind. She didn't mean to. It's just that my ass was probably right where her hand would have landed, and she's probably super embarrassed about it and just didn't want to say anything.

But then a couple weeks later, it happened again. This time during her chemistry class. We were in the science lab, and Javi and I had partnered up to look at some shit in the microscope. I'm pretty tall, right? So I had to bend over to get my eye down to the lens. Next thing I knew, my ass was getting smacked. I thought it was Javier, but when I stood up, freaking Miss Dupree's standing right there next to us. "How's it goin' over here, fellas?"

I felt my face reddening and I couldn't even say anything, because my teacher just deliberately hit my ass, so Javier answered her. I didn't hear him, but he asked her a question about the worksheet we had to fill out.

"Let me see," she replied, and she stood between us to look at the paper. She rested her hand on my waist, right below my belt. I was fully conscious of her hand lingering just above my butt, and I looked over to see if she was doing it to Javier, too. But he was too far away, and her hand was burning a hole through my skin.

And she fucking left it there. For like, ten hours.

When she finally moved to the next table, she grazed her hand across my lower back and I had to think really bland thoughts while Javier nudged me with his elbow. "Bro, did she slap your ass?"

I turned to him and whispered, "Yes! You saw her? Dude, I thought it was my imagination. But she totally slapped my ass and then rested her hand right here." I placed my hand on Javi's hip, right under his belt (or where his belt should have been, because his punk-ass wasn't wearing one, and anyone else would have gotten demerits for that).

He did that stupid thing where he packs an imaginary box of cigarettes, his mouth making a huge O. "No shit! She wants your dick! She wants to sit on your face!"

I immediately stuck my face back down into the microscope. "Shut up, man. She does not." Then the bell rang and class was over. But he wasn't finished. He texted me later that night, asking if I was fantasizing about my chemistry teacher molesting me and jerking off in the shower. I sent him the middle finger emoji, and he sent back, *LMAO you didn't answer the question.*

And I wasn't going to.

Instead, I wrote: *Bro, you need to STFU because the last thing I need is my dad hearing some rumor about me and a teacher for him to really kill me.*

Javi: *Relax, LOL it wasn't your fault. You didn't do anything. She came on to you.*

Me: *Doesn't matter. He'll still kill me.*

And back and forth our texts went about how my dad likes everything to be perfect and the ruined reputation would piss him off more than the fact that my chemistry teacher smacked my ass and touched me inappropriately, and it would somehow be my fault.

And I lied to my parents about it.

And now they have my phone with all those texts on it. Why didn't I delete them?

At lunch, I'm not hungry. I'm at the same table where I always sit, with both JV and varsity football players ... and of course, cheerleaders. Javier slams his tray across from me, and I jump.

"You asleep, Hunter?" he asks, dropping into the seat so hard he shakes the entire table.

"Naw, man. Just tired." I rub my face and glance across the cafeteria to where Creed is sitting with her friends. I can't see her that well, but it looks like she's reading. I feel like an asshole. I haven't seen her since Wynwood, and I obviously haven't spoken with her because I don't have my phone.

And we just don't interact in school. It's too hard; we don't run in the same circles. We sit next to each other in English and algebra. But those are the only classes we have together, and it's not like we can talk during class. She probably hates me. She probably thinks I'm another Javier Acosta—a walking STD.

THE FALLING OF STARS

Speaking of which, he's scooping mashed potatoes in his face and talking about Friday's game. "Bro, Malik! You remember the new play, or nah?"

I nod.

"Hey, what's wrong with you? Are you getting sick?" He's eating a corndog like it's a dick, and that's single-handedly making me sick.

"Yeah, I'm not feeling too hot."

He slams his hands on the table. "Yo, someone get this pussy an orange juice! Malik needs Vitamin C. We gotta whoop Braddock tomorrow, and I'm gonna kick your ass if you miss it and we lose."

Tyler throws his half-empty bottle of orange juice in my direction, and I bat it away. "I don't want your backwash, Tyler," I say, and Camila, who's sitting next to me, touches my forehead.

"You feel warm, Malik." She drags her fingers down and caresses my neck. "Yeah, you feel feverish. Do you want some Advil? I have some in my bag."

"Is that why your parents are out today? Are they sick, too?" CJ asks as Camila doesn't wait for me to answer and is shaking pills into her hand.

I shake my head as I cup my hand for Camila to drop a couple tablets in it. "I don't know where my parents are." I regret it as soon as I say it. I pop the pills in my mouth and chase them with my water, feeling at least four sets of eyes on me.

Javier's the first to speak. "Dude, what's going on? Both your parents are out, and so is Miss Dupree..." His face lights up mischievously. "Yo! Do you think they found out about...?"

I drop my head in my hands as everyone perks up and starts chirping, "What? What? Found out about what?"

"Nothing!" I shout, but it's muffled by my hands and ignored by Javier, who continues.

"Miss Dupree is wet for Malik!" He's cackling like one of those stupid Halloween decorations that doesn't shut the fuck up. "She slapped his ass and groped him in chemistry. I saw it."

Jaws are dropping and eyes are popping and I'm so fucked.

"No, she didn't," I insist. "Javier *thought* he saw that, because he would *love* to get his ass smacked by a hot teacher." I'm glaring at him, threatening him by telepathy to shut his goddamn mouth.

He's eyeing me. He knows exactly what I'm telling him. But he's an asshole who doesn't know how to stop. "If there's any teacher I want slapping my ass, it's your mom. She's making her way through ethnicities, but has she ever had Cuban dick?" And he grabs his Cuban crotch.

A chorus of "ohhhh!" breaks out across the table, and I stand up and chuck my water bottle at him. "You need to shut the fuck up before I shut you the fuck up."

His eyes are raging—he's pissed, but fear flashes through them because I'm twice his size and I'll fuck him up in a second. "A'ight, relax. Chill. I won't talk about your mom anymore." He laughs it off and turns back to his potatoes, but I'm on fire.

Half the cafeteria is staring at us now, because I'm kinda making a scene. But I can't help it. There's no way I can sit back down and pretend like nothing happened, because I want to beat Javi's face in. If I sit down, I'll end up flipping the table. I know he's gonna make another smartass comment and I'll wind up beating the shit out of him and getting suspended. Then grounded for life.

I storm out of the cafeteria. I'm pretty sure everyone's watching me at this point, but that's nothing new. *Why's Malik being so extra?*

And where the *fuck* are my parents?

I bust through the locker room door and kick a trash can. A guttural roar rips from my core through my mouth and impales the walls, and I punch a locker. I punch it until my knuckles are as raw as my throat, then I spin toward a bin of dirty towels and shove it, and the towels fly. I grab a cleat and chuck it at the mirror over the sinks, and it shatters in a zillion pieces while adrenaline pummels my pumping blood like guerilla warfare. I hate this locker room. I hate how much time I've spent in here. All the times I've cried in here, stressed in here, pissed in here, and showered in here. I've bitched people out and been bitched out in here. This is a torture chamber for me. And I'm some sort of masochist, because this is the first place I thought to come to. Not to seek solace, but to feel even worse.

The bell rings for lunch to end, but I don't care. I'm not going to class. I'll sit in here however long I want. I don't even know why I'm so upset. I don't give a shit about Javier. I don't even care that Miss Dupree did what she did, or that I lied to my parents about it and Alex would fuck me up if he read my texts. This isn't about any of that.

I sit on a bench and start sobbing. "Jordan, I'm sorry. I'm so sorry," I wail between sobs. "Jordan, please. Forgive me." Over. And over. And over.

I steer clear of Javier during practice that afternoon. I see him eyeing me, and I walk away whenever he tries to approach. I know he's gonna apologize, but I don't want to hear it. Or his jokes about my mom. Wherever she is.

Practice sucked for everyone. Coach Jay kept screaming that we have a game tomorrow and we need to wake the frick up, but when the D-line kept breaking through and sacking me, I was praying for him to yell at me so I could throw the ball in his face and quit. Only he screamed at the O-line and told them I can't carry this team by myself. He even yelled at Javier to stop showing off and run up the sideline instead of trying to impress the safety by juking him. That made me feel a little better.

Now practice is over and I've locked myself in the shower again, wondering how I'm gonna get home because I'm grounded from my car and I fucking hate Javier. God knows how many minutes have gone by when I finally turn the shower off and step out, and sure enough, Javi's sitting there. Goddammit.

He stands as I wrap my towel around my waist. "Look, man. I'm really sorry. I didn't realize how bad you're going through shit right now. I messed up, and I'm sorry."

"Can I borrow your phone?"

He pulls it from his pocket and hands it to me. I dial my mom's number. She doesn't answer. Then my dad's. He doesn't answer, either. I shove the phone back toward him, biting my cheek to keep from crying.

"You ready to ride home?" he asks.

"Naw. I'm good."

"You sure?" he asks, alarmed. He knows he's been my ride for the last few days and is supposed to be for the next week.

"I'm good," I say a little more firmly.

Javi throws his arms out and lets them fall to his sides. "Malik, please. Your parents didn't answer just now. How are you gonna get home, man?"

"I got this." I slip into my shorts and shirt, tossing my towel in my bag.

Javier grabs the back of his head. "All right, if you say so. Let me know if you need anything, brother. Let's kick some Bulldog ass tomorrow, a'ight?" Then he sticks his fist out for me to fist-bump it.

I do.

I don't know how the hell I'm getting home. There are still a few people on campus for whatever reason—cheerleading practice, varsity football, afterschool clubs—I'm sure I can find someone to drop me off. I head back into Lafayette Hall, upstairs to my locker in the mezzanine. Maybe there's someone there I can bum a ride off of. But the mezzanine's empty. I decide to go down to the office and use the phone to blow my parents' phones up.

I'm heading toward the stairs when I hear crying. I slow down to listen, because the voice sounds familiar. "I don't know what to do. He hates me."

Oh, god. It's Creed. I know it. I follow the sound of her voice and find her sitting on the floor, leaning against a classroom door with two of her friends next to her, rubbing her back and giving her tissues. All three of them freeze when I approach.

"Creed? Oh, my god. What's wrong?" I say, crouching next to her. "Why are you crying?"

Her friends stand and walk away, and I'm watching them, thinking what crappy friends they are, when Creed turns her tortured face to me. I've never seen her upset before, let alone crying like this. I don't know what to do, so I help her up and cup her face in my hands. "Is it me? I'm so sorry, Creed. I never meant to hurt you. I really do like you, but I don't think I'm ready for a commitment."

She jerks her face from my hands. "Shut up, Malik! Not everything is about you! You selfish piece of shit!" Then she punches me in the arm.

It doesn't hurt, but it does kinda. I just don't know why she hit me or why she's so mad at me. "Okay, okay you're right. It's not about me. What's it about, Creed? Tell me."

"I'm pregnant."

My mouth goes dry. Shivers burst through my body in spurts. I—I can't—can't comprehend what she just said. There's no way. We're kids. Sophomores. We don't even eat lunch together—we can't have a baby together.

I reach out to touch her, then drop my hands. My jaw, it's moving, but nothing's coming out. I'm just blinking like a wack job.

She throws her hands out. "What now, Malik? Tell me more about your commitment issues. Is this inconvenient for you? Too much football for you to take care of your child? Too busy being Mr. Popular to settle down and be a family man? Don't worry about me. Old Creed'll just carry your kid in her womb for the next nine months. No one will even have to know it's yours. I won't tell a soul. I'd never do that to you, because I love you too damn much."

I'm shaking my head at her, but all I'm able to mutter is "No, no." But it's not for the reason she thinks it is.

She's sobbing. Gut-wrenching wails. "I fucking love you, Malik Hunter. And I hate it that I love you so much." Then she slaps me across the face and I'm seeing stars. By the time I'm feeling any senses outside of this overwhelming pain in my cheek, she's gone.

"Creed! Creed!" I'm turning circles, looking everywhere for her. But I can't see out my left eye, and my right one just isn't picking up signs of her at all. I plop down right in the middle of the mezzanine, absorbing this bomb she just dropped.

Creed's pregnant. She has a child living inside her. My child. What the hell are we gonna do? I never wanted this. Oh, god. Her parents. What are they gonna say. Oh, god. My parents! They're gonna kill me. My mom's gonna cry and say things like, *Why, God, why?* And my dad. He's never hit me before, but if there were ever a time for him to start beating the shit out of me, it'd be now. Why am I such a fuck-up?

I can't get off the floor. I have no reason to. I don't want to go home. Besides, I have no way to get home. I'm stuck here forever.

I have a game tomorrow.

Oh, god. I still play football. I planted my seed in a woman, and I have to go play football tomorrow in one of the biggest games of the season. I gotta get out of here. I stumble to my feet and stagger toward the railing for support.

She must have gotten pregnant the first night we did it. Why didn't I use a condom then? What's wrong with me? We only had sex three times. How the fuck?

I drag myself along the railing. I remember when I thought lying to my parents about Miss Dupree was the worst thing in the world. That seems like a million years ago. I want my mom and dad. I don't care what they'll say, I need them right now. I actually want Alex to punch me right in the face. The sting of Creed's slap is wearing off, and I need to feel something. I'm going numb. I grab at my dreads and pull as hard as I can.

Nothing.

Then I open my eyes, and stare down the concrete staircase.

You could give it all up, Malik. Everything that weighs you down, all the stress and the pressure placed on you. You can get rid of it all, and people would understand. And everything would be okay.

I think of the video of the guy's leg breaking. I deserve to have my shin splintering out of my skin. I screwed everything up. I don't deserve to play football. I don't deserve Creed. I don't deserve to be anyone's dad. I don't deserve to be anyone's son. I shut my eyes, embracing the numbness that runs through my veins, freezing them in this state of horror, trying to remember what it felt like to feel things.

I close my eyes and open them. And stare down the concrete staircase.

17

EVE

S*leep,* they said. *You'll feel better,* they said. But the moment I doze off, the nightmares begin.

"Eve, run to the store and buy everything for enchiladas," my dad said with a grin.

"Dad, it's ten forty-five at night."

He threw a twenty-dollar bill and his keys at me. "Just run, hurry. Your ma's sleeping. I'll make them for us and we can have a fiesta." Bigger grin. Wink.

I drove the four miles to the closest grocery store in Marathon Key, about halfway from the mainland to Key West. It was so dark on the one-lane highway, I turned the radio up just to feel like I wasn't the only person in the world.

I was in and out of Publix in ten minutes. I threw my grocery bag in the trunk and jumped in, revving the engine and already counting the minutes until I'd be home.

I didn't even make it out of the parking lot.

A figure emerged from the backseat and slapped his hand over my screaming mouth. I felt something cold and hard pressed against my temple. "Turn the other way."

I did—I turned left instead of right. Away from my home.

He made me drive for miles along the lone highway of A1A before directing me to pull off onto the shoulder. He dragged me into the passenger's seat, moved to the driver's seat, and began driving. Farther and farther from home. From the continental U.S.

My body shook. I was going to die. And it was going to hurt. I was crying. "How will this end?"

He didn't answer. He was so big. Massive.

I looked out the window at the swamps and forests whizzing by, going farther out into the ocean. Away from civilization. Out of Marathon. Past Little Duck Key. Big Pine Key. Sugarloaf Key. I would not let him kill me this way. If tonight was the night I'd die, then I'd do it myself. Fight or flight. He was going at least sixty miles an hour. I opened the passenger door and threw myself out.

I rolled. And rolled. And rolled. Forever. I would die rolling.

When I finally stopped, I stood and ran through the thick marshland. Sideways. Stumbling. Dizzy. And he was chasing. He caught me. Knocked me down. Hit me. I hit back. I hit and kicked and punched until I couldn't anymore.

It hurt. Pain I'd never felt. Relentless. I gazed into his face. He had light eyes. I stared at them—memorized them.

He carried me back to the car. Said he had friends for me.

No. I was torn and bloody, but no. I jumped out of the car again. I ran. It was like running underwater. But I saw a house. I'd make it. He was following me. I banged on the door. "Help me! Please! Help me!" It was the middle of the night. He was coming. Reaching for me.

The door opened and I was pulled inside.

"Eve. Eve! Wake up!"

I open my eyes, and they're wet. My heart is pounding. I'm drenched in sweat. Alex stands over me, one hand gripping my arm, the other caressing my face. "You're dreaming again. Everything's okay. You're here."

I sit up and stare at the wall, huffing and puffing and regaining clarity. "I told them. Why did I tell them? I never wanted them to know. Alex? What have I done?" I turn my frantic eyes to him.

He sits on the bed, grasping my shoulders. "Eve, it's okay. Nothing's changed. It's just now people know what happened to you."

"But Malik—"

"Malik doesn't know, and no one will tell him. Now I need you to listen to me. Are you listening?"

I nod.

"There's been an accident."

My hand goes directly over my heart. "Oh, my god."

"Shhh, everything's okay. Malik fell down a flight of stairs at school."

"Oh, my god!"

"He's fine. An ambulance came and took him to the hospital, because he hit his head and may have broken his wrist. He's got bumps and bruises, but that's all. We need to go see him."

"Xander. What about Xander? Where is he?"

Alex softens his voice like he's talking to the damn cat. "He's in his room. Everything's fine. Okay? You need to trust me. You're okay, Malik is okay, and Xander is okay."

But he's wrong. Malik's in the hospital. I snapped today and confessed something I never wanted anyone to know. Not to protect me, but to protect Malik. Who's in the hospital. I jerk the covers off and jump out of bed. My son needs me.

I feel like I'm pushing through crowds of Liberty students and staff in the hallways of the hospital, and why are they here and I'm his mother and I've just heard about it?

They're judging me. I know it. Then I realize it's only three people—Coach Jay, Javier Acosta, and Mr. Lorrey.

"Where is he?" I ask the collective three. And they collectively nod toward room 1407, the same room I was headed toward anyway because the nurse told me he was in there, so I have no idea why I asked them that. I halt just before entering and turn to Alex. "Maybe Xander should wait until we see what sort of shape Malik's in."

Alex agrees. "Xan, stay here with Coach Jay and Mr. Lorrey until Mommy and I say it's okay to come in."

We ignore Xander's crowing inquiries and step in to see Malik stretched out on the hospital bed—similar to the one I lay in at his age—an immobilization device around his neck and a splint on his arm. He has scrapes and bruises on his face and arms, and I have to dig deep to find the strength not to cry.

Alex propels me toward the bed. Malik's eyes are closed, but they open when we approach and tears well in them.

My heart breaks. I'd rather it be me back in that bed than having to see my child lying there so miserable and in so much pain. I gingerly kiss his forehead and run my hand down his face.

"Where've you been?" he asks, wiping his eyes. It always fascinates me how quickly he can gain composure.

I sniff. "I took the day off. I'm so sorry I didn't tell you."

"Why didn't either of you answer your phones?" He's looking between me and Alex, and I can see his broken soul through the windows that are his eyes. His heart is just as bruised as his body. And I did this to him.

Alex and I glance at each other. "I—I've been sleeping, Malik. I'm so sorry. I haven't been feeling well today."

He assesses me, and I can't tell if he believes me. He turns to Alex. "What about you? Are you sick, too?" And he definitely has an accusatory tone in his voice.

"No, buddy. It's just that ... well, you know we had that board meeting this morning for—" he glances toward the door and lowers his voice— "Miss Dupree. It didn't go well. But don't worry about that. What happened to you?" Alex squeezes Malik's hand.

Malik looks down at his hospital gown. "I don't know."

I blink. "Did you really fall down the stairs?"

He tries to nod, but the immobilization device. "Yes," he says instead.

"How did you do that, son?" Alex asks, and there's so much intonation in his voice that it's obvious he's trying to sound sincere and not angry like he usually is when he says a sentence like that.

Malik swallows. "I don't know."

I lower onto the edge of his bed. "Do you remember it? Was it after practice? During practice? Did it mess up your memory?"

"No."

I glance at Alex with concern. "No, what? Malik?"

"It didn't mess up my memory."

"So you *do* remember it?" Alex prompts.

"Yes."

"Baby, can you tell us what happened?" I run my fingernails up his arm.

He watches my fingers drift along his forearm. "I don't know."

Alex shifts uncomfortably. "Who saw it happen? Who called 911?"

"Mr. Lorrey."

We hear a tap at the door. "Hello? Can I come in?" It's Xander, and how many times can I forget about that child?

"Yeah, come on in, Xan." I reach for him as he trots in the room, eyeing Malik with a downcast face.

"What happened to you, Malik? Are you okay?"

Malik smiles for the first time. "I'm okay, Little Dude."

Xander is raking his eyes up and down Malik's body, stopping on each bruise before landing on his face. "Does this mean you can't play football anymore?" he asks sadly.

Malik starts to respond, but Alex beats him to it. "He's not playing tomorrow. Probably not for a few weeks."

Malik stares at Alex. "I'm sorry, Dad."

Alex leans down. "For what, buddy? You have nothing to be sorry about."

"For disappointing you. I know you were looking forward to tomorrow."

Alex chuckles awkwardly. "I'd rather have you healthy. Let's focus on making sure you heal properly. We'll deal with football later."

Malik sighs.

Xander curls up on the bed next to him and snuggles into his chest. "Are you gonna die?"

We chuckle, but Malik's is almost a full-blown laugh. "Not today, junior. Not today."

I want to punch the coach and that little Acosta shit in the face. They're pretending to be supportive, but I can see the frustration in their faces because they're worried about that stupid game tomorrow. Malik could have gotten really hurt—hell, he could have died—and they're worried about the Braddock Bulldogs.

When they're leaving, Alex steps out of the room to thank them for coming and for helping Malik, and he's still out there chatting them up ten minutes later. I'm sitting in a vinyl recliner watching Malik sleep with Xander curled into his side, and I lean toward the door to eavesdrop. They're talking about freaking football. Strategizing. Filling in the gaps now that their all-star quarterback has inconvenienced them by being hospitalized with an immobilization device and a bruised kidney and pending CT scans and X-rays to rule out internal bleeding and broken bones. Monsters.

I'm concerned. Why did he fall down a flight of stairs? Did he have a seizure? He's never had a seizure. He gets an EKG every year, and there's never an issue. Did he trip? He's an elite athlete; he doesn't trip and fall down stairs—he's never done that in his life, even as a toddler. Why does he keep saying he doesn't know how it happened?

I hear blankets scraping and look toward the bed. Malik is fidgeting, and he opens his eyes. Xander doesn't move an inch—his eyes are locked on the TV suspended from the wall and the Cartoon Network it's broadcasting. "You okay, Malik?" I ask.

"Can't sleep."

Xander finally pulls out of inertia and turns his head up to Malik. "Am I bothering you?"

Malik pulls him into his chest. "Not at all."

I smile. They've both always been snugglers. But they haven't lain like this since Malik was a tween and Xander was in Pull-Ups. "Do you want me to see if the nurse can give you anything to help you sleep?"

Malik shifts again. "Sure. Thanks."

I stand and head toward the door, and have a flashback of my mom fighting with nurses, telling them I needed sleeping pills and they said I was already on too many painkillers and she said it wasn't enough because I was awake and screaming. I have to stop and grab onto the doorway because I'm having vivid and horrific déjà vu.

"Mom? You all right?"

I haven't had one like this in years.

Rustling noises are coming from the bed. "Mom? Mom!"

TRACI FINLAY

I have to stop. I force myself to turn and observe Malik sitting up in bed, Xander stuck to his side like a fetus, both of them gaping at me. I force my face muscles to split in opposite directions until I'm sufficiently smiling at them.

Relax, Eve. The only reason you're having these panic attacks is because you were triggered today by Kendall's stupid statement. That's all. The therapists all said this is a long journey. You're doing fine.

"Sorry. I just—whew. I'm good. Okay, then!" I swing into the hallway and nearly collide with Alex and the collective assholes. Jeremiah's standing a few feet away, talking on his phone.

Alex's smile drips off his face the moment he sees me. "You okay? You're really pale."

Coach Jay and Acosta are looking at me, too, and they don't get to look at me when I'm like this. I take a deep breath and split my face muscles again. "Yep. I'm going to find a nurse." I scurry through their huddle toward the nurses' station.

Jeremiah ends his call and approaches me as I zip past the others, a look of concern laced across his face. "Eve, hello. How are you holding up? Rough day, huh?"

I scoff. "You can say that again. Thank you so much. For helping Malik when we weren't there for him. This could've been so much worse if you weren't there." I feel like crying again.

His eyebrows shoot down to the bridge of his nose. "I was just doing my job as a human citizen by getting help when another human tumbled down the stairs. What would I be had I just left him, Eve? A Braddock Bulldog?" He rolls his eyes toward Coach Jay and Javier and chuckles. I do, too.

"Malik will be fine. I'm just glad I was there. He never blacked out or mumbled incoherently or anything, so I'm confident the CT scans will come back normal. A small concussion, at the worst. He'll be back on the field in no time." He smiles reassuringly.

I swallow back tears as I smile and nod. "Well, thank you, anyway." There's an awkward silence and only one last thing to address.

He clears his throat. "As far as Kendall Dupree, she's been terminated. We've turned this over to the authorities, and the testimony we will give students is simply that Miss Dupree is no longer under our employment. If questions arise, which they will, just send them to me. I'll take care of it." He winks and gives an even more reassuring smile, but it lasts only a second before it folds into a grimace. "And, Eve? As far as your … outburst? Confession? Both? Likewise, that stays amongst staff. No questions asked. Is that okay?"

"Mr. Lorrey, I'm sorry about that. I didn't mean to snap. She just made me so angry, I—"

"No explanations needed. I understand." He clasps his hands. "Tomorrow is a new day. Because Malik is hospitalized, I understand that either you or Alex will want the flexibility of being with him. However, I expect at least one of you at school tomorrow. You both received the day off today. And, assuming Malik goes home this weekend, both of you there Monday. I already have a position to fill, and I can't continue bringing in substitutes."

I start at his sudden change of mood—Mr. Fairy-Godfather morphed right back into Mr. Strictly-Business. "Yes, sir. I'll speak with Alex tonight to see which one of us will attend tomorrow. And Monday, we'll be there."

He nods. "Good. Just let me know this evening so I can make arrangements for coverage." He smiles like he's doing me a favor, but I can't bristle—he saved Malik today. Besides, he's right—we did both take today off, last minute, because I snapped. And he'll be busy trying to hire a new science teacher. Not to mention having to deal with all the gossip and drama involved in what could very well become the biggest scandal Liberty has ever seen.

"Thanks again, Mr. Lorrey."

He nods again, gives a little wave—to me then over to Alex and the collective assholes—and turns to stride down the hall.

I snap my fingers. Sleeping pills. To the nurses' station.

I'm utilizing the wait while the nurses are preoccupied with others to calm myself down, when I glance up to see a familiar shape in a familiar pair of scrubs brisking down an adjacent hallway. "Petra!" And I jog after her.

18

EVE

"Petra!"

She turns, sees me, and stops, making a complete about-face. "Eve, what are you doing here? Is everything okay?"

I shake my head as I approach. "Malik had an accident at school today. He fell down some stairs."

Petra winces. "Is he okay? He's here?"

"Yes, he's in the ER right now, waiting to get a CT scan and X-rays on his wrist. Do you have a minute? I need to tell you something." I cock my head apologetically.

She looks more hospitable than ever, probably because she's in work mode. "Sure, I'm going on break right now. Come with me to the cafeteria. Want coffee or something?"

I take a deep, cleansing sigh. "Yes."

We head downstairs and I grab a cup of what they claim is Starbucks coffee, but I think they're a bunch of damn liars. I grab a table while Petra piles a sandwich, soup, and a diet Coke on a tray. She finally seats herself across from me. "You sure you don't want anything to eat?" And she takes a monstrous bite of an egg salad sandwich.

I smile. "I'm good. Listen, that science teacher admitted to sleeping with Jordan. According to her, it happened twice. In her classroom."

The hospitable contour of her eyes quickly melts as she drops her sandwich on her tray. Tears form in her eyes as her mouth shapes into a horrific rectangle.

I just ruined her lunchbreak. What was I thinking, blurting out information like that? That was super insensitive of me, whether she's a cheater or not.

"This is so hard, Eve. It's not getting better. Jill's not doing well. I don't know if she's gonna make it through this. I miss him so much. The house ... his absence physically hurts. It's like a thousand knives in my eyes when I look around and he's not there. A thousand knives in my feet when I walk through the hall and he's not walking back. A thousand knives in my heart because I smell him, hear him, feel him, but he's not there. And he never will be ... and I probably played a big part in his decision to do this." Her eyes are orbs of guilt and pain swirling in her skull, staring into my soul. Tortured, writhing. We're sitting in a hospital cafeteria surrounded by staff, doctors, nurses, family members, and Petra is right in the middle of her own personal hell that no one can see but me.

A tear drips down my cheek. "I'm sorry," I whisper.

She looks down at her soup. "What am I supposed to do with this information? About his teacher? What do I do? Do I tell Jill?"

"What do you think she'll do?"

Petra's shaking her head, her mouth open and eyes aimed toward the ceiling. "I don't know. She may finally lose it. She may sit there and pretend I didn't say anything."

I swirl my coffee absently. "Do you think she'll take action? Call a lawyer? Sue the school?"

Petra turns glaring eyes to me.

I hold up my hands. "I don't care, either way. I mean, she has every right to file a lawsuit against them, and I'll support her. I mean, I don't *want* her to, but—"

"No lawsuit is going to bring Jordan back, Eve," Petra scolds. "Look at us. We're a very unassuming couple. We don't want money, we never have. We just want our son back." She pushes her tray away and looks at me with tears along her eyelids. "Why don't *you* tell her?"

My hand flies to my chest. "Me? I don't—I can't—"

"Sure, you can. Just like you told me. You can tell Jill."

I consider blackmailing her with her cheating, but I don't have the energy. "Petra, I have so much going on in my life right now. Malik in the hospital, this whore of a teacher we have to handle, a guidance counselor with a questionable past ... and I've been dealing with some personal things that I have to get straightened out."

She eyes me, then nods. "I understand." But her eyes accuse; they say, *nothing you're going through is anywhere near the magnitude of what we're going through.* She gathers her tray and heads for the trash, and I follow her.

"I don't mean to interrupt all the shit you got going on in your life," she calls sarcastically over her shoulder. "But I found another text message of Jordan's that seems interesting. I don't know what it means. It could be nothing, but it stuck out to me."

Oh, lord. We still have to do this. Petra's scouring those messages to find something, anything, that will support Jill's theory so she doesn't have to confess her infidelity. Part of me doesn't blame her, but part of me says karma's a bitch, isn't it?

"What is it?" I ask.

She looks at her watch. "I have fifteen minutes. C'mon. I have the texts in my car." I follow her from the cafeteria, through the lobby, and out the main entrance of

Baptist Hospital. We walk through valet and past the massive fountain toward the parking lot full of wandering geese from a nearby lake. I'm already sweating—it's easily ninety degrees out.

Petra wipes her forehead as she presses her key fob, sending one of the many dormant cars into flash/chirp mode. I lean on a neighboring car as she pulls the Franken-texts from her backseat, flipping through and licking her finger every few pages. "Here it is. Page nine. Look."

I step closer and follow her finger.

"It's this one number, just one time. One week before he died. It looks like a weird email address."

204679311148060025@libertynet.org: Log on now. Don't reply. Delete immediately.

I officially have a migraine.

"Like I said, it might not be anything. I just thought it was weird that it was from that number-email address thing, and not a phone number. And the fact that it says to delete immediately is kinda fishy."

I squint at it like it's a hieroglyphic. "That *is* strange. Maybe because it was sent to a phone, it came up as numbers. People's names are their profiles on LibertyNet. Like, it should've said Malik Hunter at LibertyNet dot org, or something. I didn't know you could message phones from LibertyNet."

"Right? It's kinda weird."

"Ugh. Petra, do you have any cigarettes?"

She gives me a disgusted, judgmental look. "No, Eve. That's an awful habit."

"You know what's not an awful habit? Monogamy. You should try it."

She rolls her eyes. "Touché. Let's go."

We walk back to the hospital in silence. She goes back to her wing, and I head to Malik's room. Coach Jay and Javier are gone, thankfully, and I step into room 1407 with the rest of my family.

THE FALLING OF STARS

Alex, Malik, and Xander all look up.
"Did you get sleeping pills?" Malik asks.
Ah, crap.

Malik does have a concussion. It's not serious, but he needs to stay out of football for a few weeks (duh—he doesn't need a doctor to tell him that when he has me for a mother). Also, his wrist is sprained—not broken, thank God. There's no internal bleeding, just that bruised kidney and all the superficial scrapes, bumps, and bruises. They want to keep him overnight to make sure he doesn't start hemorrhaging.

The doctor tells him he was very lucky those were the only injuries he suffered. Broken bones are usually inevitable when taking such a serious fall. Then he and Alex make hilarious jokes about how Malik's probably been hit harder by linemen than those stairs, and he should've just juked a little more, and congratulations on making it all the way into the end zone, but it's not a touchdown if you don't have the ball. Freaking comedians.

I tell Alex Jeremiah's expectations of us, and he says he'll go to school tomorrow so I can stay with Malik. Xander kisses my cheek and Alex hugs me and says, "I'll see you tomorrow. I love you."

I hug him with all my might. "Love you more."

They leave, and I curl up in this god-awful recliner where I plan on spending the next twelve to sixteen hours. I watch Malik sleep while thinking about that text. The good thing is we know it's from someone at school, thanks to the @libertynet.org. I wonder if all those numbers somehow translate into someone's name? Or a student ID maybe? Perhaps it was Kendall? If they were having sex

185

and carrying on through texts, there's a good possibility it carried over onto LibertyNet, as well.

But why would she text him to get on LibertyNet and then tell him to delete it, when he had way more incriminating texts and never deleted those? Was there more involved in their relationship than just sex? Is she smart enough to be the culprit of Jill's conspiracies?

I think back to the day in the teacher's lounge when I asked Ruben DeSoto about recovering deleted texts, and she knew right away. So she's either pretty tech savvy, or she's experienced in the art of devious manipulation. Or both.

I decide to call Alex.

"Hey, honey?" I say when he answers. "Do me a favor. When you get home, go in the bedroom and get Jordan's texts. On the ninth page, there's a text about halfway down from an email address. It's a bunch of numbers at LibertyNet dot org. Can you take a picture of that and text it to me, please?"

"What the heck? He got a text from a LibertyNet profile?"

"Yeah, it's weird. Petra found it."

"Okay. I'm home now, give me a couple minutes."

Within five minutes, my phone chimes with his text. I open it, and he sends immediately after: *Now that's weird as fuhh.*

I roll my eyes. I hate when he talks like a teenager. I reply, *We need to find out whose profile that is and what happened online after Jordan logged on. Assuming he did log on.*

Alex: *Well, let me know what you find, super sleuth. Putting Xander to bed.*

I stare at the number: *204679311148060025*

I can't even begin to form any rhyme or reason how that would translate into someone's name. I mean, it's eighteen digits. There's nothing in the history of the world that has eighteen of anything. Unless you're the Duggars, and they didn't even stop there.

Malik inhales a sharp breath and rolls over, waking from what I hope was a great drug-induced nap. He groans and stretches the one arm that's not locked in a sling.

"Hey," I say cheerfully. "How was your nap?"

"Sucked. Where's Dad? And Xander?"

"They went home. Dad has to go back to school tomorrow. You hungry?"

"No."

"Have you eaten anything since you've been here?"

He pauses. "I don't think so. I don't feel well. I wish I could just sleep forever."

"That's the painkillers talking." *I know from experience.* I stand and approach him, grinning and tracing my finger along the curvatures of his face.

His eyes flutter shut. I used to trace his face like this when he was a baby and wouldn't fall asleep. As soon as my fingertip would touch his face, his eyes would flutter just like that. I remember giggling as I'd watch his pacifier bounce up and down, then slow down and stop completely after thirty seconds of caressing his face. A few seconds later it'd start bouncing again, then stop, and so forth until he was in a deep sleep. His pacifier's been replaced with a masculine jawline, but he still looks like that baby from so many years ago.

He opens his eyes. "Any chance you can get me more pills?"

I frown. "I doubt it. You have a concussion."

He shuts his eyes and sighs. "I just don't want to be awake."

I sit on the edge of his bed. "Why not?"

"The pain."

"I'm sorry. Where does it hurt?"

"It's everywhere, Mom," he snaps.

Okay, then. Yikes. He's so weird when he has a concussion. I stand and walk back to my recliner. "Hey, Chicken Little. I have something for you." I pull out his phone from my purse, tossing it on his bed.

He looks at me with wide eyes. "I get my phone back?"

I giggle and nod. "You've been through enough, I think. Your friends are worried. You should let them know you're okay."

"Thanks," he says pseudo-enthusiastically, and barrels into his phone in a way that reminds me of Xander's hamsters when he finally remembers to feed them after three days.

I watch him a few minutes before interrupting his reunion. "Hey, Malik? Can I ask you something? What's this?" I pull up the photo of Jordan's weird text and hand it to him.

Malik studies it for a while, his breaths getting more and more shallow. He swallows. "Where did you get this?" He shoves the phone back at me, and I nearly drop it.

"It's from Jordan's phone. He got this weird text. I'm not a techie by any stretch, but I thought maybe you'd know what all those numbers are."

He's visibly relaxing as I'm talking. "I have no idea who that was." Then he rolls over and goes back to sleep, hugging his cellphone like a teddy bear.

He is *so weird* when he has a concussion.

19

EVE

"Do I get my car back, too?" Malik asks on the way home the next morning.

I laugh. "Don't get your hopes up. Your dad doesn't know I gave you the phone. That was kind of a spur-of-the-moment, executive decision. Besides, the doctors don't want you driving with this concussion."

He nods and turns back toward the window. He's been unusually quiet. Then again, he did plummet down some stairs and land on his head yesterday. I'm not sure how I should expect him to act, and I'm sure the inability to play football for possibly the rest of the season is enough to shut him down for a while. I decide to just give him space.

We arrive home around ten, and he goes right to his room. I know he's exhausted. *Space, Eve. Give him space.* So I send a quick text to Ruben DeSoto, the trusty IT guy.

Hey, Ruben. When is your break today?

I wait a grueling fifteen minutes for a response. *Sorry, I was installing patches. Good times. My break is during fourth period. How's Malik? I heard he took quite the spill yesterday.*

Me: *Much better, thank you. He's home now. Do you mind if I monopolize your break today? I have more technological questions.*

Ruben: *Sure. I'll be in my office. BYOB*

I chuckle and look at the time. I have an hour and a half to shower this recliner off me, brush my teeth, and turn back into a human.

Thankfully, there's a backdoor entrance to Ruben's office. Not that I have anything to hide, but everyone thinks I'm home tending to Malik instead of working, and I'm neither home nor tending to Malik, and I'm at work but technically not working…

The whole thing raises questions.

Malik seems like he doesn't want any "tending to." Instead of barging in his room before I left, I sent him a quick text: *Running up to the school for a few minutes, k?*

He didn't reply at first, which made me think he was sleeping, but then I got the obnoxious one letter: *K*

Whatever. I rap on Ruben's door before opening it and peeking in. He's sitting at his desk nurturing a foot-long from Subway, his fountain drink dripping condensation and bleeding into his papers.

It's not my problem, so I ignore it. "Hey, Ruben."

"Hey, there," he says in a very patronizing manner, and I remember that I acted like a fool yesterday in Kendall's board meeting. He probably feels the need to pussyfoot around the ticking psychotic time bomb I've portrayed myself as. "You doing okay?"

I smile with a hint of sternness. "Ruben, I'm fine. I promise. I'm sorry I lost it yesterday, but … that subject is something I'm very touchy about for personal reasons. It was a long time ago, and trust me—I'm fine."

He nods. Still patronizing. "I'm glad to hear that."

"I found something concerning, and I think you can help." I pull page nine from my purse, handing it to him and pointing at the highlighted line. "Do you have any idea what this is? This list of numbers that's supposedly a LibertyNet profile?"

Ruben's eyebrows sink behind his glasses as he grabs the paper and studies it, his jaw chewing in figure-eights below his mustache. Anyone suffering from Misophonia would crucify him for this loud-ass chewing.

"What is this, Eve? Where'd you get this?" He swallows his food chunks, the mystifying look growing more intense with each second.

"These are Jordan Sawyer's deleted texts. His stepmom found this and brought it to my attention."

He's staring at me like he wants to punch me in the face. Did I say something wrong? Is he mad at me? I take a step back and manage to squeak out, "Who creates the profile accounts on LibertyNet?"

His face is turning various shades of purple, and he grabs the remaining six inches of his sub and chucks it in the trash can. "I do. And I did *not* create this account."

I'm getting really good at ruining people's lunches.

The purple hue is morphing into red as he grows angrier, and I'm wondering if I should leave. I gasp when he takes an old keyboard and whips it across the room, and it crashes into the wall. I knew he'd be upset, but I've never seen a temper tantrum of this proportion, and I'm married to Alex Hunter. It's almost theatrical—like he's putting on an act. I hold my breath as he throws a few more things, then turns to his computer and starts clicking like a madman.

Keeping a safe distance, I move behind him and gaze down at his screen. He's scrolling through thousands of files, and I've no idea what he's doing. He turns to me, gesturing toward page nine he'd tossed on his desk—even crumpling it a bit in his fury. "These are deleted texts, you said? So it's no longer on his phone?"

"Correct."

"I'm checking the server to find that account and look in the history. I can probably get a location, as well. I'm gonna find out who created this account." He clicks and types a few more minutes before throwing his hands up. "This account doesn't exist. Hold on." He clicks and types even harder, rotating through "nope, nope, fuck" over and over until I'm humming *We Will Rock You.*

He stops and points. "Look. Here's the account right here. Time logs."

I follow his finger. "That's the same day the text was delivered to Jordan's phone."

He drops his finger an inch below. "Yup. Look at the time stamp. Is that accurate?"

I glance at page nine and sure enough, the time stamp adds up.

"It sent that one message, and that's it. Then look. Get a load of this. Account was deleted that night."

"Oh, my god. Ruben. What does this mean?"

The way he looks at me is terrifying. It's sending chills through my bones. "It means someone logged on here and created this account, and then deleted it."

My heart is pounding. "Who else has access to create accounts?"

"No one. I have full administrative access to LibertyNet, the highest set of permissions. I'm the only one who can create and delete accounts."

I take a few steps back. "But you're saying you didn't create this?"

"I did *not* create this. But I'll find out who did. Right now." He turns back to the computer and clicks and scrolls and then snaps his fingers at me. "Write this down. Here's the IP address for the machine that created it."

I grab a pen off his desk and a piece of paper that hasn't fallen victim to the condensation. "Do I need the dots?"

"You need the dots."

I include the dots. "Okay, I got it. Now what?"

"Now hold it for a sec." He minimizes a few windows and clicks a folder on his desktop, opening an excel spreadsheet called PERSONNEL. "This is the list of all the computers in this building. Computer lab, classrooms, media center, offices, everything. If that account was created on this campus, we'll find out now." He pulls up a search box and looks up at me with his fingers hovering over the keyboard. "Okay, give it to me."

I do. He types it and hits enter, and bile rises in my throat when there's a match. He leaps from his chair and circles the room. "No way. No way in hell."

I trip over my own feet, tumbling into his chair and raking my eyes across the spreadsheet. This can't be right. There has to be some mistake. Or has there? Because that IP address belongs to Alondra Hendrick's computer, and with all the shit that's gone down with her in the last couple days, this could actually make perfect sense. And if a guidance counselor with a history of working at schools where kids were committing suicide is suddenly caught creating and deleting profiles to hide communication with Jordan Sawyer, then that crazy, fucking Jill just might be onto something.

20

MALIK

None of that went as planned, and I'm officially the biggest loser in the world. There's so much shit in my head, I can't even control my thoughts. My brain is a constant tornado, spinning and ripping and breaking shit before twirling right back through and doing it all again. Over, and over, and over. I purposely didn't watch *Twister* to avoid shit like this.

That's when I'm awake. When I'm sleeping, the tornado turns into a rollercoaster, and I hate rollercoasters. Always have. And I can't get off it. And it's one where the restraints confine your entire body and you're claustrophobic and your back is smashed against the seat and relentless harnesses are everywhere and you're being flung in all directions.

My mind has disconnected from my body, so it's like my tornado-rollercoaster is watching myself walk around and do all the things I'm supposed to do to stay alive—eat, shower, piss, sleep—but I can't figure out why I'm doing all these things because I don't want to be doing any of them.

A few days ago, playing football was the biggest problem in the world. Then it was getting a speeding ticket. Then Miss Dupree. Then Creed and the baby—ugh, that one makes my stomach turn—and now even Creed's pregnancy seems small because I purposely fell down a flight of stairs because there was no way this life was real and I needed to see if it was real.

Oh, it's real. As real as the bruise on my kidney. It all just escalated so quickly that I needed to be able to control something—I needed it all to stop. I needed the focus to be on me for once, not what I was doing or what I had done. Is it so hard for people to just stop and look at *me*? And see a real person? Not a *thing*?

The first feeling outside the numbness was when my mom handed me my phone. My heart jumped, and that was reassuring—my insides weren't completely dead, yet. The first thing I did was delete the texts with Javi about Miss Dupree, and I had a momentary sense of relief because I thought that was one problem out of my life.

Until my mom started talking about having Jordan's deleted texts. Is that what moms are doing now? Getting their kids' deleted texts? Because if my mom does that, I'm fucked. Then I started stressing about that, not to mention that long-ass number she stuck in my face and asked if I knew what it was. I thought she knew about the conversation I had the night before on LibertyNet, maybe knew about the video I saw, and put two and two together as to why I fell down the stairs. And now I have the added guilt, knowing my parents and everyone would be so disappointed if they knew I did that on purpose.

I'm lying in bed when my phone blings. I tear my eyes from the ceiling and look at the screen. Javier just texted—again. *Yo brother. Hope you're feeling better today. You think you'll be all healed up and ready for playoffs?*

THE FALLING OF STARS

You see? They all want me better, but only because of playoffs. I was hoping to have been injured more so people would leave me the hell alone about football. If I broke my leg like in the video, I'd be out the rest of the season—no questions asked. But I'm expected to make a full recovery by playoffs. And now I feel guilty because I'm missing tonight's game, and if we lose to Braddock, that'll bump us down a seed. I've ruined my life, and now I'm ruining everyone else's.

I don't reply to Javi, but I do call Creed. She doesn't answer. I've texted her a million times since my mom gave me my phone, and she's not responding.

My mom, who's off work today to babysit me, left to go to school for whatever reason. She can't stay away, apparently. I'm the only person in the house. This is rare. I take advantage of the alone time and wander to the kitchen. Xander's cat comes purring and slithering around my legs like a snake. Why do cats move like snakes? Even their tails slither up in the air, and it's disturbing. God, it purrs so loud.

I'm pouring a bowl of cereal when my phone rings and I jump, spilling cereal on the counter. It's Creed. *It's Creed!*

"Hey," I answer.

"Malik, I left my phone in my friend's car last night, and I just got it back. That's why I haven't responded. I heard what happened to you. My gosh, are you okay?"

I can't stop the clown grin that spreads across my face—she's not mad! "Yeah, yeah. I'm home from the hospital now. I'll be fine."

"When did this happen? It must've been right after I … right after we talked."

I swallow. "It was. Those stairs right where we were talking. Man, I don't know what happened. I just couldn't wrap my head around everything you told me and I just … fell."

"This is all my fault." She's crying.

197

Motherfucker, now what've I done? "Creed? Listen. I know I'm not that guy who has to be in charge all the time, and I'm generally pretty easy going, but right now, I'm taking control and you need to listen to me, you understand?"

She's quiet for a sec. "Yes."

"*Nothing* is your fault. No matter what anyone says, or whatever happens with us or this baby. You are perfect, and this whole mess falls on me. I take full responsibility for it. And that's what it is. You got it?"

She doesn't answer.

"Creed!" I yell, trying to sound intimidating like Alex, but I'm nowhere near as badass as he is.

"No," she finally states. "You didn't impregnate yourself. It takes two, you know that. We both did this. I'm so sorry about yesterday. I'm sorry I hit you. I was just so scared. I just took the pregnancy test and was still absorbing it all. I don't know what to do." She's crying like crazy.

"Leave school. Uber to my house. No one's here, and we can talk. I would come there, but I'm grounded and I have a concussion. So it's just not written in the stars for me to drive."

"I can't skip classes. I'll get in trouble."

"There're only two left for the day, and trust me. Once your parents hear you're knocked up, they'll forget all about these two classes you skipped," I joke.

She actually laughs, and it makes me feel things. Oh, god—I'm feeling things!

"Fine," she says. "I'm ditching now. Text me your address and I'll be there soon."

It's an ominous euphoria. The happiness surging through my body—it's synthetic, like my protein shakes. I push it aside and bask in the fact that I'm feeling something. This is good.

Creed arrives, and I run out the front door and scoop her in my arms the moment she steps out of the Uber. I can't help it—I kiss her. I pick her up and spin her and try to make it romantic like the movies, but I realize she's crying again, and why the hell can't I do anything right? I pull my lips away from hers and set her on the ground, brushing her hair out of her face. "What's wrong?"

She looks up at me with pain in her eyes that I put there. "Malik, I'm going to have a baby. Our baby. I'm still in shock. Everything's going to change. What are we going to do?"

I place two fingers under her chin and tip her head up. This sudden burst of euphoria is giving me strength I haven't had in a long time, and I'm going to make this okay. "We'll do whatever you decide to do. If you want to raise it, I'll raise it with you. If you don't, we'll find a family to adopt it. Maybe we can even see it from time to time."

She wrings her hands and whispers, "What about an abortion?"

I swallow. "It's an option."

"No, I need to know what you think. Because if I get an abortion, I'll never even tell my parents it happened. I can have someone take me down to a clinic and it'll be one and done. No one will ever know." She's looking at me with hope in her eyes, like she wants me to give her the word and she'll go.

"How about we think about it for a week or two? You don't want to rush into anything you may regret."

Awkward silence.

I turn toward the house. "Do you want to come in for a while? My parents aren't here."

She appraises my house and bites her lip. "So this is where the Hunters live."

I roll my eyes and grab her hand, dragging her into the house and through the kitchen, and she's just staring at everything. I mean, our house is fine but it's nothing impressive.

"I can't believe I'm in Malik Hunter's house."

I laugh loudly and continue toward the patio. "Well, you're carrying Malik Hunter's child, so there's that." There's a weird noise, and I turn to see that she's fallen to her knees, her head in her hands, sobbing. I rush to her. "What happened? Creed?"

She's hyperventilating. "Oh, god. Oh, god. Oh, god. I'm carrying Malik Hunter's child. Oh, god. Oh, god…"

I literally pick her up off the floor and cradle her face in my hands. "Shhh, Creed. You have to stop. It's going to be okay. *Listen to me!*"

Her eyes snap up to mine, and I'm seeing she responds to authoritative demeanors. That may be a problem, because I'm not that person. I mean, I can be, but I don't like to be. I usually leave that shit to Alex.

"Everything's going to be fine. We'll work through this." I lead her through the French doors, and we sit in the hammock together and look out over the pool.

"Do you know how many girls would love to be in my position?" she says through her tears. Her voice sounds miserable, and it makes me chuckle. "I'm carrying Malik Hunter's baby." She says it slowly this time, resting her hand on her abdomen and whispering, "Oh, god."

"Please stop saying it like that. It's weird. I'm right here, you don't have to keep saying my name—both first and last."

We're quiet for a minute before she says, "I don't want to make this decision, Malik. I want you to decide. Please. I'm not strong enough."

For some reason, her faith in me makes my heart plummet. I threw myself down a flight of stairs yesterday. I can't even make my own decisions, let alone anyone else's. "You don't know what you're saying. You're the one who has to carry the baby, so the decision needs to be yours."

I wait for her to look at me, but she doesn't. She's clutching the hem of her shirt, and her hands are shaking. She finally says, "I was serious yesterday. With what I said. The part about how I love you." And she's purposely not looking at me. "The easiest thing is to terminate the pregnancy and forget it ever happened. No one would ever know. But I do—I love you." She pauses because she's crying. Again. "And if you want to keep it, I'll go through all the hell to keep it. Telling my parents, the pregnancy, the delivery ... all of it. Because I love you."

Now she looks at me.

I hold her gaze. That took some fuckin' strength. She's one strong woman, and I admire her courage. But what am I supposed to say back? *Yes, Creed, crucify yourself to keep the kid for my benefit. Oh, and by the way, I don't love you back, but you're a swell gal.* I like Creed more than any girl I've ever met in my life, and I could totally fall in love with her someday. She's gorgeous and unassuming and talented and sweet.

But I can't say that I love her. And I can't help it that I can't.

I waited too long to answer. She's dropped her eyes back in her lap, and I feel like a big, fat, flaccid dick. I crushed her, and she sits there like her heart hasn't just been broken into a million pieces. I hate myself right now.

I pull her in and kiss her forehead. "Listen, you are the most amazing girl I've ever met. You're hands-down my favorite person in the world. I love everything about you, and every time I find out something new about you, I fall even harder for you. You impress me with everything you do. But we're sixteen. We don't know shit about love. We still have two years of high school left after this, and by the time we go to college, we'll be completely different people. You may hate the sight of me by then. You may be so disgusted by me that you won't believe you ever had sex with me." I grin at her, jostling her shoulder a little.

Her head is down so I can't see her face, but a tear drips onto her black fingernails, and she whispers, "It's because I'm not like the popular girls."

At that, I rocket off the hammock, then I have to stand still for a sec because concussions don't care about teen pregnancies. "Creed, what the fuck! I like you *because* you're not like they are! How many times do I have to say that? I would so much rather be some normal guy that no one's ever heard of and has never touched a football in his life, so that our worlds wouldn't be lightyears apart, and the stars might actually line up for us. But that's just not the way it's been."

"So are you gonna date me now, Malik? Now that we're pregnant? I mean, the stars lined up for that much, didn't they?" She's jumped off the hammock, too, and has planted herself in front of me, waiting for my answer or proposal or whatever she's expecting.

I tip my head up and spread my hands across my face. The splint on my wrist scrapes across my cheek, and now my cheek stings. "We just found out about this baby less than twenty-four hours ago. We both have to sit back and think about stuff, Creed! There's a lot more to think about than whether we should start dating."

She nods, and there's an air of finality in it. "Well, then. I would never want to make you do something you don't want to do." She hugs herself around her middle and turns toward the house, but I grab her arm.

"You're not going anywhere."

She halts.

I hate that she makes me be this person. I steer her by the arm until she's facing me again. "I'm not saying I don't want to date you. We've basically been dating the last two months, anyway. I know it hasn't been ideal conditions, but I certainly haven't taken any other girls out. I haven't been kissing or sleeping with other girls, either. I've been all yours. Yes, there's a baby involved now. And we need to focus on that more than we need to focus on labeling things. Our lives don't change now that there's a baby. We're still sophomores, I still play football, we still go to school. None of that will stop. Do you understand what I'm saying?" I realize I'm gripping her arm stupid tight, and I relax my grip before I end up leaving bruises on her, and then being that guy who knocks a girl up and leaves bruises on her.

She nods, and for once, she's not crying. "I'm sorry."

I pull her into my arms and hug the shit out of her. "Why the hell would you be sorry about anything? Don't say stupid things." I kiss the top of her head.

"I just freaked out, Malik. You could have died yesterday. You've been in the hospital all night, and you have a long recovery ahead. And I'm making it even more difficult—"

I press my lips into hers because Creed Holloway needs to shut the fuck up. She's fucking pregnant. I caused all my own problems—she doesn't know that, obviously, but she's gotta deal with nine months of pregnancy and then whatever the hell girls go through afterward. My mom was a hot mess for like six months after she had Xander.

But I'm not thinking about any of that right now because Creed has lips that taste like sugared sex, and a tongue that turns me the hell on. I rip my splint off because I need to touch her face with both hands. I run them down over her little Creed breasts, down her little Creed body, and pull her hips into me. I drop my hands a few inches lower until I'm double-fisting ass cheeks.

I back her into the wall, pushing my dick into her pelvis because she needs to feel what she does to me. She makes these moaning noises that drive me crazy, and slips her hand between us and runs it along my pulsating dick, and I can't take it anymore. "Let's go to my room."

She pulls her mouth off mine, and her eyes do that cute little girl thing they do when I say something that shocks her. "What if your parents come home?"

I put my lips against hers and grin. "Then it'll be the perfect icebreaker to tell them you're pregnant."

I knew the euphoria was ominous. I thought about it the whole time I was fucking Creed in my bed. I made her come twice before I came, and even that was euphoric. Right in the middle of coming inside her, I had a brief thought—and I mean brief, like, one-one-thousandth of a second—that I can come in her and it won't matter because she's already pregnant, and it made my orgasm even more fantastic. And then I realized that was a fucked-up thing to think, and so that made me feel a little kinky, which also prolonged my orgasm. If Creed wasn't pregnant before, she's having six of my babies now.

But now she's gone, my splint's back on, my parents are home, Xander's carrying his cat around, and I've plummeted from cloud nine right into the depths of hell. I'm feeling things, though—I'm conscious of every bruise on my body, I can pinpoint the exact spot where my wrist is sprained, and my head throbs a host of church choirs singing that I have a concussion, and it's fresh, and it just happened yesterday, hallelujah, praise the Lord.

My parents move about the house, doing their due diligence: cooking, cleaning, interacting, parenting, and they have no idea they're about to be grandparents. The guilt is so heavy I almost wish I was numb again.

My mom makes Beef Wellington again. That's twice in one week. She said she feels sorry for me that I'm hurt and can't play football, and Alex keeps looking at me and asking, "How you feelin', buddy?" And no matter how many times I tell him I'm fine, he keeps coming over and looking into my eyes, monitoring my pupils, and voicing his updates. "Your pupils are the same size today. That's great." And, "They look to be the normal size. Xander, come here. Let me compare your pupils to Malik's."

THE FALLING OF STARS

At nine o'clock, the guilt is overwhelming, and I tell my parents—right in the middle of the movie they begged me to watch with them—that I'm going to bed. They turn their heads from the couch where they're snuggling. "Aw, are you feeling okay?" my mom asks.

"Yeah, just tired."

Alex nods, his eyebrows scrunched into a pair of caterpillars in a faceoff. "Get some rest, son. Have you been taking your painkillers?"

"Yes." No.

"Good."

I look at Xander, who's asleep in the chair, his cat coiled in his lap like a goddamn snake again. I smirk and point at him, and my parents look at him as I continue out of the room, arguing over who has to carry him to bed.

I shut my door and notice my sheets look like sex happened. My heart plummets further. I sit at my computer and log onto LibertyNet. I know nobody's on because it's Friday night, but I want to see if anyone posted videos of the game I missed. But before I can even get to the video page, this idiot freaking messages me again.

I know you fell down the stairs on purpose.

Tingling begins in my fingertips and toes and works its way toward my core. I stare at the message for a solid thirty seconds.

Malik, answer me.

I thought I blocked this freak?

You did it because of the video I showed you, didn't you?

Maybe this is a different screenname—and by screenname, I mean metric shit-ton of numbers—but I obviously don't know, because I didn't memorize them. I do grab a pencil and jot it down, though, then type: *What makes you think I did it on purpose?*

Because I saw you.

Holy Mother of God. I know that I know *that I know* there was no one in that mezzanine when it happened.

And there was no one at the bottom, because I lay there for a solid two minutes before Mr. Lorrey ran up and called 911. And he even asked me what happened.

If you saw me, then why didn't you help me? I write.

Because you did what you wanted to do. Why would I interfere?

I want to block him again, but if he's just changing his username each time, it'd be pointless. Plus, if he knows I fell on purpose, he's got blackmail against me. *Are you ever going to tell me who this is?*

Him: *Let's play a game.*

Me: *I have a concussion, a sprained wrist, and a bruised kidney. I can't play any games until the doctor clears me.*

Him: *This isn't a joke. We're playing. For the rest of the weekend, you'll set your alarm for four AM. At that time, I'll send something to your phone. At the end of the weekend, if you've completed the exercises I've sent to your phone, I'll tell you who I am.*

If this bastard thinks I'm waking up at four in the morning, he's batshit crazy. *No, thanks. Sounds like a fun game, but I forfeit.*

This will determine what type of star you are. You need to know in order to start the healing process. Tonight and tomorrow night. Then Sunday night, I'll tell you who I am. I can help you, Malik. Admit it, you need help.

Oh, yeah? Kinda like he helped me right down the stairs? But I have to retract that—I threw myself down the stairs. Sure, it may have been inspired by his video, but it's not like his video was of people throwing themselves down stairs. That was all me. But what's his deal with the stars? And how can he help me?

Set your alarm for four AM. You'll have something in your inbox. There are specific instructions attached, and I'll know whether or not you do them. So beware.

And what if I don't? I ask.

Him: *There are secrets you're hiding from your parents I have no problem exposing.*

Aw, hell, naw. What else does this asshole know? Creed? Miss Dupree? Is he just bluffing? He knows I fell on purpose, even though I'm not admitting that. In fact, I'm not admitting anything. Nope, not playing his game. *Bullshit. You don't know jack shit.*

Him: *I'm on your side, Malik. I'm trying to help you. Don't make me your enemy. You need help.*

I stare at the blinking cursor until my concussion taps me on the shoulder and reminds me it's still alive and kicking. I blink away the trance and go to log off. But I realize something, and it needs to be said: *You didn't help Jordan Sawyer.*

He responds immediately: *Jordan was a different type of star. His decision to take his life had nothing to do with me. I tried helping him, but he was already beyond help. You are stronger than he was. Four AM. I'll talk to you then.*

He logs off.

21

EVE

I may or may not have had a panic attack in front of
Ruben DeSoto after finding out Alondra was
responsible for the alternate profile. Except I totally did.
That's two in the last two days. I haven't had these in
years. I blame it on everything that's happened lately—
Jordan's passing, Jill's conspiring, Petra's cheating,
Kendall's raping, Malik's falling—and I grabbed Ruben by
his Subway-stained tie and made him swear he wouldn't
tell anyone about my panic attack.

He swore, because I had him by the tie.

Jeremiah left campus for the day, so we decided to go
to him Monday and take the weekend to mull it over, and
now I'm driving home doing the opposite of mulling. I
feel like I'm on the brink of a third panic attack. I pull in
the driveway just behind Alex, and Xander spills out of his
car just as I stumble out of mine. "Hi, Mom!" he calls,
flinging his backpack onto his shoulder and shuffling into
the house.

"Hi, Xan!" I wave and continue toward Alex, who's looking at me sideways.

"What are you doing?" He runs his hands through his hair, and he either had a really rough day at school, or a really rough car ride with Xander.

"I went to see Ruben DeSoto in his office. And listen to this." I'm about to pull out my page nine when Alex holds up his hand for me to stop.

"Eve, why were you at the school today? You were given the day off to take care of Malik. You know how Jeremiah is about this, and you went up to the school anyway?"

Now it's my turn to hold up a hand for the shutting-up ceremony. "If you'd listen, you'd know why I had to go. Malik's fine. He shut himself in his room and doesn't want company. Besides, I had to show Ruben this." I point to the highlighted text on page nine, explaining how Ruben discovered it was Alondra all along, but the look on Alex's face doesn't change. He's frustrated. I feel like he didn't hear a word I said.

He snatches page nine from me and crumples it up, tosses it, and grabs me by both shoulders. "Eve, honey. Listen to me. You're doing it again."

I blink at him. "Doing what? Doing *what?*"

He shakes my shoulders gently. "You've been doing great the last few years. You haven't had an episode since shortly after Xander was born. But they're happening again, and that's okay. The psychiatrist said they would." He moves his hands from my shoulders to my face.

I try shaking my head, but he's got a firm hold on my face, like he knew I'd deny it. "Alex, it's only because of what Kendall said in that meeting yesterday. She made me snap. I'm sorry—trust me, I hate it more than you do that I told everyone what happened. Now people are treating me like a delicate little flower, and I hate it. I'm fine with what happened to me. If anyone knows that, you do."

Alex nods enthusiastically. "Yes, yes! You're right, I do know. And I'm so proud of you for how far you've come. A lot of women never go on to get married and have kids, or even have sex again, and you've managed to have an entire family because you're the strongest woman I know." He kisses my forehead. "But it's okay, sometimes, to not be fine."

"What's going on?" I ask.

He drops his hands from my face, taking a small step back. "Ruben called me just now. He said you had a panic attack in his office."

My jaw plummets. "He promised he wouldn't."

"That's two, Eve. One yesterday, one today."

I feel like I should be crying, but instead, anger surges through my tear ducts and every other tube in my body. "Dammit, Ruben! He promised! Alex, my attacks are induced by crimes committed against Jordan Sawyer. He was surrounded by a bunch of snakes! That's what's pushing me over the edge. Not the fact that I was—" Now the tears rush to my eyes.

He's right. He saw it, even before I did.

I've been in denial.

He pulls me into a hug, and I cry because I know I need to. I don't want to be, not at all. It's been almost seventeen years and I want nothing more than to get past this, but I know in order to do that, I need catharsis. To grieve from time to time. Apparently, now is the time.

Trauma isn't one of those things you just get over one day. It's not like a test, where you take it and fail, and you study harder and retake it and fail again, then study even harder and eventually pass. It's something you have to wake up every day and handle. It's like adjusting to life after losing your sight or hearing. You have no choice but to do it. It doesn't make me a strong person—I'm NOT strong. I do this because I have to. Because I have two children that I never want feeling the fear and pain I did. I do this because the other option is dying, and I'm not cool with that. I wasn't cool with it seventeen years ago when it almost happened, and I'm not cool with it now.

Alex hugs my head into his chest as I cry. He's humming; I'm not sure what song. It doesn't matter. My crying out-sings his humming. We stand in the driveway like two dancing idiots, only we're not dancing and the cars fly by like they do in Miami, the sun scorches our scalps, the humidity clogs our respiratory systems, and nothing stops for you when you've been raped. It brings a whole new meaning to the word *relentless*, and being relentless is a very disrespectful thing, no matter what the situation. It's not the situation or the aftermath that kills people—it's the sheer relentlessness of it all. The constant harping. Forever and ever.

I feel myself being scooped off the ground and carried inside. I feel the ice-cold sheets under my body, all my pillows and goose down and comfort welcoming me as Alex removes my clothes and tucks me in, telling me what a good job I'm doing and to just keep crying. And he scoots in next to me and quits talking. He just holds me. And Alex screws up a lot of things, but this one—this, he's got like a champ.

I roll over in bed, glancing at my phone and seeing I've been sleeping for three hours. I stumble into the kitchen, and he's pulling a baking sheet of puff pastry-wrapped steak from the oven. I smile. "Thank you, Alex. I completely forgot I had Beef Wellington in the fridge to cook."

He grins and arranges the steaks on a serving tray. "Malik is happy he gets Beef Wellington twice in one week."

THE FALLING OF STARS

I move to the stove and see that Alex has made a vegetable-rice medley and a salad with all sorts of nuts and fruits. Damn him for being a better cook than I. "I'm sure he is. I felt sorry for him." I shrug, and Alex gives me a look.

"I heard how sorry you felt for him. He's got his phone."

I shrug lazily and bite into a snap pea. "I gave it to him when he was in the hospital."

Alex moves the food dishes to the table, shaking his head. "That kid will never understand consequences if you keep undoing all his restrictions."

I grab plates and utensils, following him to the dining room. "Please. He's been without his phone for almost a week, and he still doesn't have his car. I doubt he'll be speeding again anytime soon."

Alex smirks as Xander comes in the room holding his kitten like it's a baby. That little thing is already growing. "Me and Biscuit are hungry. Is dinner ready?"

Yeah, he named his cat Biscuit. I totally won that bet.

"Biscuit doesn't get people food, Xander. Will you please go tell Malik it's time to eat?"

Xander jets from the room as Alex serves the food and reenters, kittenless, followed by a groggy, tentative Malik.

Alex takes one look at him and stops. "Have you been sleeping?"

Malik rubs his face. "Uh, I'm not sure."

"Well, have you or not?" I prompt.

He pulls his chair out and sits, surveying the table. "Yeah, I fell asleep for a while."

Alex and I exchange concerned looks before he moves over to Malik and squats down, demanding to look at his pupils for the eight thousandth time since he fell. "Follow my finger," he commands, and Malik's going to get a concussion just from all the finger following Alex makes him do.

Alex stands and meanders to his chair. "Your eyes seem fine. But *you* don't seem fine. Is everything else okay?"

Malik reaches for the salad bowl, nodding and keeping his eyes down.

"Malik?" I call.

He stops and looks at me.

"Your dad asked you a question."

"Oh," Malik stutters like he just forgot who he was, and turns his eyes to Alex for that eye contact we find so polite for our children to maintain. Is that too much to ask? Really?

"Yes, sir. I'm fine." And even though his eyes dropped before the word *fine*, we leave it at that.

"Mom, will you help me? Again?" Xander asks, frustrated because he can't cut steak and whenever we have it—which is now twice this week—he needs assistance.

I begin sawing at his meat, but Alex isn't having it. "Xander, you're eight years old. Your fine motor skills should be well-enough developed to cut it. I think you're being lazy."

"Pshh. You'd think that, but I'm not allowed to play with knives, so ... not so much, with those fine motor skills."

It takes everything inside me not to burst out laughing at his smart mouth. Malik has no such luck. He's gripping his knife with the back of his hand pressed against his mouth, his head turned in attempt to hide his amusement, which isn't working.

I gain control—quickly—and drop Xander's utensils on his plate. "Well, here you go. You can practice now. Smart Alec." I glance at Alex, whose posture is rigid and his hands flat on either side of his plate. He's darting his eyes from Xander to Malik, and I don't know who he's going to reprimand first.

THE FALLING OF STARS

Xander's getting a kick out of his big brother laughing at him, and he's making this situation worse by grinning from ear to ear as he attempts to cut his meat and watches Malik losing it. This isn't going to end well.

"Xander," Alex growls, and the moment the word is out of his mouth, I feel another panic attack. Alex is ripping into Xander, but I don't hear him. I'm gripping the table with all my strength until my knuckles are white, staring at where my water glass touches the tabletop. I'm trying to focus on breathing—I have breathing exercises, but I can't think of them—they're short and shallow and I'm losing where I am.

Someone's tapping my knee. It's relentless, the tapping. Relentlessness is so rude. The silent killer. I blink and turn toward the source of tapping, and it's Alex. "It's rude to be relentless," I tell him, then I remember he's just been *relentlessly* hounding Xander, and the boys probably think that's what I'm talking about. They didn't see the onset of my panic attack, nor did they see Alex stop it from under the table. I turn to Xander and say breathlessly, "Xander, did you hear me? It's rude to be relentless."

Both his and Malik's eyes pop up to me, because that didn't make any sense whatsoever.

"Your smart mouth. It's relentless." I push my food around my plate because I'm putting all my effort into calming my heart and relaxing my breathing.

"Also, it's rude to have a smart mouth *at all*," Alex concludes.

Malik shakes his head and pushes his cleared plate away. "This is the weirdest lecture I've ever heard. Someone just pop the kid in the mouth already so it can stop."

"No one's popping anyone in the mouth," Alex says in a much softer tone, and I feel his eyes on me, watching me engaging in the breathing exercises I finally remembered.

He squeezes my leg, and we continue eating until this incredibly awkward meal is over.

22

EVE

I try taking the weekend to relax, but it's Sunday and I'm stressing about approaching Jeremiah with the crap we uncovered on Alondra.

Alex and I are having brunch in Coral Gables, and we somehow end up with both mimosas and sangria, and we haven't even gotten our food yet. This is going to get interesting.

I love the Gables, and if I were rich, I'd live here. It was built in the 1920s (which is old for South Florida) and is an elegant mixture of Mediterranean Revival and Spanish Renaissance. Twisty, ancient trees line both sides of the streets, their canopies draped over them, making a stunning, green nature-umbrella and the most beautiful scenery in Miami. The downtown area boasts a modern flair amongst the old, Spanish architecture—bridal shops, boutiques, and restaurants nestled along Miracle Mile. It's haunting and rich and splendid, and I breathe in the view as we sit outdoors on the patio of a French-fusion café.

A soft breeze deters the mid-morning humidity as I ask, "So what do you think about Alondra creating that profile?"

He shrugs. "It's definitely worth looking into." Our appetizer of avocado toast and smoked salmon arrives, and as much as I need it to offset the double-fisting of alcoholic beverages, I refrain and observe him clamping a square between his fingers and chomping down on it.

"Alex, you're acting like this isn't a big deal. Let's recap. We found out last week that Alondra is under investigation for assisting in Jordan's suicide. We then discovered she was fired from a school where four suicides happened in a two-year timespan. She was arrested. Now, Ruben DeSoto, the IT guru and creator of LibertyNet, has determined that she created and deleted a profile that definitely reached out to Jordan shortly before he died. And you're dining on avocado toast?"

Alex widens his eyes innocently and snatches up another square. "I just think this all sounds shady. It's one, very unassuming text. There was no more activity on that profile, and it was deleted a few hours later, so obviously nothing happened. Alondra Hendrick, no offense, is not the brightest crayon in the box when it comes to computers. I mean, her profile can't create accounts, so regardless of the IP address Ruben claims was the location, it wasn't her account."

I grab a piece of toast before he eats it all. "It wasn't her account, it was his. She logged onto his account and created the profile. Alex!"

He thrusts his hands out defensively. "What? I heard you. And that's definitely a possibility. It just seems like a stretch. She doesn't seem like an undercover computer genius who would hop from school to school disguised as a guidance counselor for the sole purpose of getting kids to commit suicide."

Why does he have to do that?

"I think Jeremiah's a smart guy. He would've caught onto that during her interview."

"He didn't catch jack shit when interviewing Kendall Dupree."

"Touché," Alex remarks as our food comes, and I lose him to some egg skillet as I'm presented with a Belgian waffle.

I eat about a third before I'm full, and I push it away and look back at Alex. "Will you come with us tomorrow? When we tell Jeremiah?"

Alex nods. "Sure. Don't know how much of a help I'll be, though. It'll be pretty cramped with three of us in there, tattling on Alondra."

But it turns out it's not so cramped, because Ruben's running late Monday morning. So Alex and I are standing in front of Jeremiah in his elaborate office while he gazes up at us from his desk. I clear my throat. "Mr. Lorrey, we—Ruben DeSoto and I—discovered something very disturbing last week. I don't know exactly what Ruben did on his computer, but it seems Alondra Hendrick created a fake account on LibertyNet and reached out to Jordan Sawyer before he passed away."

Jeremiah nods slowly. "Yes, I am aware of the situation."

I start, and Alex shifts next to me. "I'm sorry, what?"

Jeremiah exhales a long, deep sigh. "This was brought to my attention Friday night by Ruben, then again Saturday, and again Sunday, and again this morning when he called to inform me he would be tardy." He lifts his eyebrows and turns one corner of his mouth into a half-smile.

Damn, Ruben! Worst secret-keeper ever. He spilled every single thing we swore to secrecy Friday, and I'm going to ring his fat little neck.

Jeremiah rubs his hands together, looking between Alex and me. "I hesitate on which route we should take with this. While the account creating constitutes investigating, the content of the message sent to Jordan doesn't elicit bullying. And since that's the only message we found, we can't pursue that route."

Alex and I drop into two chairs in front of his desk.

Jeremiah places a hand over his mouth and drags it down until he's pinching his chin. "We need to really dig into this before jumping to conclusions."

I'm confused. Are we talking about the same thing? "It seems as though Ruben has done enough digging to at least confront her about it."

Jeremiah considers this, and Alex sits up in his chair and asks, "Have you found anything of interest in the investigation we already have open on her?"

"Actually, that investigation closed last week, like we assumed. We—"

The door bursts open, and Ruben flies in the room. "Sorry I'm late." He's huffing and puffing and acts a little surprised to see Alex. I feel like he pushed himself harder than normal because he was looking forward to plopping himself in that chair, but it's now occupied by Alex's butt so he recovers by leaning each arm on the backs of our chairs, respectively. "So did we fire her yet? Alondra? Is she gone?"

Jeremiah's offended by the way Ruben burst in so unprofessionally, but he doesn't address it. Instead, he says a bit irritated, "I was just discussing with Mr. and Mrs. Hunter the information discovered in Alondra's investigation. As we know, from Alex's research, she used to go by the name Evelyn Gomez. She worked at a school that had four suicides in two years, and she ended up getting arrested. But her charge had been expunged." He gestures to Alex for confirmation, and Alex nods and props his ankle on the opposite knee.

"Since that time, I have done further investigating, and our initial allegations are true. Her arrest was unrelated to the suicides," Jeremiah concludes, and all three of us perk up, because we didn't know this—not even Alex.

"Why was she arrested?" Alex asks.

"Minor drug charge, a misdemeanor. Cannabis." He flicks his hand like it's no big deal, even though I could never picture Jeremiah Lorrey smoking out or even condoning it.

"Still. It's weird that it's just now surfacing. What about the name change?" I ask.

Jeremiah stands and paces the room, adjusting his tie. "Evelyn Alondra Maria Guevara-Gomez was her full name when she came here from Venezuela." He chuckles. "She had a variety to choose from, so technically she didn't *change* her name—just went by a different one of her many to help clear her reputation after the arrest. When she became a citizen, she officially dropped Evelyn. Hendrick was the man she married shortly after that. He passed away a year later, and she came here to Miami."

Ruben scoffs. "She probably killed him."

Jeremiah huffs. "He was in a fatal car accident. It killed multiple people, unfortunately."

Ruben folds his arms, his annoyance manifesting through the way he's bouncing on his toes. "How many? Four? Were they teenagers?"

Jeremiah is getting more irritated, and Ruben just doesn't get it. Alex holds up a hand to stop Ruben from getting himself fired. "Okay, so what you're saying is, with this newfound information, Alondra's cleared from having any fault in Jordan's suicide?"

Jeremiah sits back down. "I was able to get my hands on her notes she took during her consultations with Jordan. She followed protocol and did everything she could for him."

"Whoa," Ruben and I both say at the same time. I hold up a finger to Ruben and turn back to Jeremiah. "Why would she write in her notes her plan to get Jordan to kill himself? Of course, her notes will line up with school policy. Surely you—"

"How did you get ahold of her notes, anyway?" Ruben interrupts, because apparently he can't hold it back anymore. "Isn't that illegal?"

Jeremiah is leaning back in his chair, rubbing his bottom lip with his forefinger. "Protocol alters during an investigation, Ruben. You must understand that. And as far as your concern, Eve, you're absolutely right. But unfortunately, we can't go back in time and be a fly on the wall during her sessions with Jordan Sawyer. We have absolutely no reason to believe that her counseling sessions with him had anything to do with his suicide."

"Yeah, well … now she's tampering with my intranet. Creating that profile under my name for reasons only God and Jordan Sawyer know." Ruben stands up straight, and I have to turn my head to see him moving around behind us.

"I'll open another investigation, and we—"

Ruben interrupts Jeremiah and points harshly at the ground. "We're going to confront her! I have solid evidence that Alondra's computer was used to log onto my LibertyNet admin account and create a fake profile. These faculty laptops have two-factor authentications. She has a username and password, as well as a security pin. So it's not like anyone could've just gotten on her computer and logged in as me."

Alex is bouncing his foot now, staring at the floor in concentration. "But if someone had somehow gotten your login credentials for LibertyNet, couldn't they also have gotten hers to set her up?"

Why haven't we just asked her? I don't understand…

Ruben looks at him like he's crazy. "That's too risky. Sure, anyone could get anyone's credentials with a key logger or any of the various ways to steal passwords. But to risk going into her office during school hours to create an account, message people from it, and go to all the trouble deleting it hours later? Surely Alondra's never out of her office for hours at a time."

Jeremiah's been twisting semicircles in his chair as Alex and Ruben go back and forth. "How do you know it was hours later?"

Ruben plucks a folded piece of paper from his pocket that I imagine is damp with sweat. He opens it and slaps it on Jeremiah's desk. "The timestamp. Look at the date—the Tuesday before Jordan died. We were all here. Time—created at eight in the morning and deleted at eight that evening."

I scrunch my eyebrows. "She's not here until eight in the evening."

Ruben turns his judgmental gaze to me. "It's a laptop, Eve. She could have easily taken it home."

"Or someone waited for her to leave and logged on then. Did anyone ever go into Jordan's profile to see if he actually did chat with anyone that day, right after the timestamp?" Alex asks.

Ruben is flailing like a balloon animal. "And by 'anyone,' you mean me, right? Do you know how long that would take me? I'd be spending hours reactivating his account, recovering—JUST ASK HER!"

Jeremiah waves his hands. "This is getting out of hand. Ruben, I understand your frustrations, but your behavior is nothing short of insane. The first step is to get your anger under control. I understand your annoyance at having something you've worked so hard at building being tampered with. But we will do this the democratic way, and we will reopen the investigation and get to the bottom of this. There is a method to handling these situations, and as an honest establishment, we need to follow it."

Ruben is breathing again. God, it's so loud. "What about Miss Dupree? There was no protocol with her. We threw her to the wolves the second she was under fire."

"No, we didn't. We held a meeting, and she confessed. Fair and square. Remember, Kendall was caught red-handed. We had many texts between her and Jordan that were way more explicit than this one vague, unthreatening message that we're assuming is Alondra. That's all we have. That and some computer activity. Alondra will be confronted with these concerns, but she is a middle-aged professional who is innocent until proven guilty. Kendall was a hormone-driven child. She was treated as such, as will Alondra be. If it comes about that she is guilty of these things, we will adjust accordingly."

This is why Jeremiah Lorrey is the founder of this establishment. I feel myself nodding throughout his entire speech. Alex knew this, too. I've been too emotional, too biased toward Jordan to see that this is a democracy and people should be treated as such.

Ruben's still not having it, and I get it. He's also emotional and biased toward LibertyNet—his baby. He spent two years creating it for someone to come in and abuse it. But he's a decent guy—I'm sure he'll come around after he calms down.

Jeremiah looks at his watch. "It's about time for school to start, and we all have places to be. Per usual, we must keep this among ourselves, folks. I need you to trust me to take the proper steps to getting to the bottom of this."

Alex and I are nodding, but Ruben is just breathing and pacing.

"Mr. DeSoto, I sympathize with your frustrations, really I do. But I need your patience. We must do the right thing."

Ruben takes one last loud-ass breath before nodding. He shoots his gaze over to me, and I give him a sympathetic look. He returns a subtle nod, and the three of us file out of Jeremiah's office.

Homeroom starts in five minutes, so Ruben bustles off in the opposite direction toward the media room, and Alex and I head upstairs toward our classrooms. "This is getting weird, isn't it?" Alex finally says.

THE FALLING OF STARS

I nod. "It's been weird. My head is constantly pounding."

Alex chuckles as we reach his classroom. "Speaking of pounding heads, how's Malik?"

I shrug and turn toward Mr. Forbes' room where Malik has homeroom. "I'm going to check on him. With this being his first day back after his accident, we need to keep an eye on him." I trot toward Malik's homeroom and peek in. He's surrounded by four or five people, and I wave to get his attention.

One of his teammates sees me first and taps the back of his hand on Malik's shoulder. "Yo, Hunter. Mommy's looking for you."

Malik looks up and tosses his head up at me, like I'm one of his idiot friends. I motion for him to come, and his buffoons start cackling. "Ohhhhh, Malik's in trouble!"

I roll my eyes as Malik ignores them and saunters up to me, shoving his non-splinted hand in his pocket. "'Sup?"

I smile. "I'm just making sure you're feeling okay. Does your head hurt?" I avoid touching his face, for embarrassment reasons.

He shakes his head. "Nah, I'm good."

"Okay. Dad and I will be checking on you throughout the day. Please, no roughhousing with those morons." I gesture to the buffoon pack, who's already being told to settle down by Mr. Forbes, and homeroom hasn't even started yet.

Malik turns to look at them and giggles when he sees CJ and Javier wrestling in the middle of the floor. He looks back at me, his grin still lingering. "I won't, Mom."

I roll my eyes and wink at him, turning from his homeroom and heading toward mine. I pass the girls' bathroom and stop when I hear a voracious noise. It happens again. It sounds like someone's throwing up. Concerned, I step inside and sure enough, a pair of Converse are planted in front of a toilet and someone's vomiting. I move to the stall and push the door open, and there's Creed Holloway with her hands pressed against her chest, shaking, hovering over the toilet while liquids spew from her mouth.

"Oh, my gosh. Creed, are you okay?" I ask, holding my breath. "Can I get you some water or a wet rag or something?"

Creed turns to me, her red, watery eyes opening in alarm when she sees me. "N—no thank you, Mrs. Hunter. I'm okay." She turns back to the toilet and spits a couple times before erecting herself, flushing, and leaning against the wall.

I place my hand on her back and feel sweat through her uniform blouse. "Are you sure? Would you like to go to the nurse's station? Do you need to go home?"

She grabs a piece of toilet paper and wipes her mouth. A chill runs through her body. "I'm really okay. Thank you."

"Let's at least get you some water," I suggest as the bell rings, and she's late to homeroom. I shake my head as I help her out of the stall. "Don't worry. I'll give you a late slip to give to Mr. Forbes."

"Thank you."

I run in my room as she's drinking at the water fountain and hold a finger up to all the juniors sitting prettily. "Give me one second, guys." Then I grab a late slip and fill it out for Creed. When I go back in the hallway, she's leaning against the water fountain. "Creed, are you sure you're not sick?"

She shakes her head. "I just ate something that didn't agree with me." Then she smiles about as brightly as one can after puking up one's guts.

I shrug and walk her to Mr. Forbes' room, handing him the slip. "She was with me," I whisper, watching Creed mosey to her desk.

Mr. Forbes nods, and I take a quick peek at Malik, who looks at Creed, then at me, and he looks like he's about to throw up, too. I shut the door and go back to my classroom. Whatever Creed has, I hope Malik isn't catching it.

23

MALIK

I had a dream with Jordan Sawyer.

We were kids, riding our bikes through a forest (in a forest-less Miami, go figure), and I was following him. He was around eight, which would've made me nine and a half, but I felt like I was the same age I am now.

He kept turning back, grinning and asking me, "Do you see them? Do you see them?" I didn't know what he was talking about. He finally stopped and got off his bike. "The ghosts," he explained, his face glowing with excitement. "Look. They're everywhere." His head tipped back and turned in all directions, like he was watching fireworks all over the sky. But I looked around and saw nothing. Just trees.

"I don't see any ghosts, Jordan," I said, a spooky feeling descending on me.

But Jordan was spinning, his arms thrust upward and a huge grin on his face. "Wheeeee!" he kept saying, and now he's around five years old. "Come get me!" he yelled gleefully, but he wasn't talking to me. Then Jordan disappeared, and I was left in the forest alone.

That dream ended and another one picked up in Jordan's living room. I was spending the night at his house. We were older now, maybe eleven or twelve. We were by ourselves, sitting on his couch, surrounded by these floating red orbs. But we weren't startled by them. It was like they were supposed to be there, like Christmas decorations or something. They weren't big, maybe the size of a fist, but there were like twenty of them. "Just wait for it," Jordan was saying, and we were fixated on the wall. "There it is!" He pointed to the wall and turned to me. "Do you see it? The writing? Look!"

I didn't see any writing. I tried squinting at it. "You mean the shapes? The shadows from the orbs?"

Jordan shook his head and pointed harder. "No, look. Read it."

I turned back to the wall, and it had transformed into what looked like a projector image of the night sky. There were galaxies, constellations, planets. The orbs had disappeared. "Whoa," twelve-year-old me muttered. "Look at the shooting stars."

"And falling stars!" Jordan said, satisfied. "You can read it?"

"Yeah. It says *shooting stars and falling stars*." Although I wasn't reading anything phonetically; somehow I knew that's what Jordan was reading. That's what he wanted me to see.

Then I woke up. This was Friday night/Saturday morning, and I was staring at the ceiling when my phone made a noise. I picked it up, and the first thing I noticed was that it was four a.m. The second was that I had just received a text from the long-ass number @libertynet.org. *Log on now. Don't reply. Delete immediately.*

This was what happened to Jordan. I felt him now more than ever, more than I did in that dream. It was like Jordan was in the room with me. And reading that text—

the same one Jordan read—filled me with a reverent fear. I didn't set an alarm; Jordan woke me up. He wanted me to do this. So I needed to do this for him. I felt like I was living through him, living for him, when he was no longer living. So I logged on. I did it the following night, too. And again last night.

This person is sending me videos every night. They're not too long, maybe between seven and ten minutes. When I clicked play the first night, a warning popped up: *BY CONTINUING TO THIS VIDEO, YOU ARE AGREEING TO ENTER THE GAME. ONCE YOU ENTER, THERE IS NO BACKING OUT.*

That warning didn't show up on the videos the next two nights. Apparently, I was already in "the game." That was the only difference between them, though. They all open with just a black screen. There's creepy, slow music in the background, sometimes echoes of people screaming. They're so fucked up, but I'm always entranced. I feel like I'm back with Jordan, and that somehow I might learn something, experience something he did, and I could somehow pay tribute to him.

So, I'd continue staring at the black screen. It would eventually flicker, then there'd be a shot of a dead body. The setting was always different—lying on frozen ground, lying on concrete, lying in a pile of rocks—but always mangled as if it had fallen off a building. More noises. More bodies. All various angles, all torture-faced, dead-eyed, and I'd watch and watch because it was like I was staring at the inside of my mind. Of Jordan's mind. I felt an eerie connection with the videos, with Jordan, with my dreams.

Then the video would end and I'd exit out, delete it, delete any trace of it, and fall back into some sort of miserable sleep-trance, trying to fit back into this world where I don't belong.

It's Monday, my first day back to school since falling. In a way, I'm glad to be back. I need to be out of the dark cloud that is my bedroom, my thoughts. But I haven't even been here a full hour and I want to leave.

My jackass friends decide that it's actually pretty fucking hilarious I fell down the stairs. *You're a fucking retard, Malik. You can dance circles around eleven football players, and you can't even walk down stairs?*

I laugh along and tell them to shut the fuck up because that's what I'm expected to do, but they have no idea what the hell they're doing.

Malik, you can't even write with your arm in that splint. How do you wipe your ass? How do you jerk off with that thing on? Or did you break your dick when you fell, too?

And I roll my eyes theatrically and give whoever said it the finger, and comment how his mom jerks me off just fine, and that kinky bitch loves it when I finger her with my splint.

Then they shut up for a while until something triggers a comment about my concussion, and round and round it goes. I'm already exhausted, and it's even more exhausting having to pretend like this is all one big joke and coming up with good comebacks so they'll shut their goddamn holes.

And something happened with Creed and my mom. She came in late to homeroom, and my mom was with her and excused her. Creed looked like she'd been crying. But the killer was that my mom gave me some weird-ass look as she walked out the door. Would Creed tell my mom I knocked her up?

I can't wait for third period algebra so I can talk to Creed. But when it finally gets here, she's not in class. Five minutes in, she comes in with another late slip, her eyes red and her face pale. She slips into her desk next to mine.

"Hey," I whisper.

She twists her head toward me, and she's looking at me, but I feel like she's looking through me. That's freaking creepy. She sighs super loud—for sure people are looking.

"You okay?" I ask.

She shakes her head and turns back to her algebra book.

I watch her through the entire class, and when the bell rings, I grab her elbow before she can escape. "Hey, what's going on with you?" I ask softly. We move slowly down the hall now; it's lunchtime so we don't have to rush to any classes.

"This is awful," she moans.

I move my hand to her lower back, guiding her to her locker, and I think this is the closest we've been to each other in school. "I know it is. I feel you. Hey, what did you tell my mom this morning?"

She's right in the middle of shoving her books in her locker when she just drops them, and papers scatter all over the floor. She turns to me, and those tiny red slits she's had for eyes all day are bulging and angry. I start, glancing around the hall to see who's witnessing, but almost everyone's gone to lunch. "Is that what this is about? You're worried I told your mom?"

I marvel at how I can never do anything right—I mean, *NEVER*—and go into my routine of denying. "No, no. I just thought it was strange she brought you into homeroom. I've never really seen you guys interact outside of English, and you looked like you'd been crying."

"I wasn't *crying*, Malik. I'd just puked up my entire soul. Your mother was gracious enough to come into the bathroom and help me. But way to go and make this about you." She slams her locker door and turns to leave, but I grab her arm and turn her back around.

"I'm not making anything about me! All I'm doing is asking what's going on?" I let go of her arm, because bruises, and wait for her to run, but she doesn't.

"Do you know anything about pregnancy?" she asks.

I shrug. "No."

She's looking at me cynically. "Well there's this thing called *morning sickness*, and it's like having the freaking flu for twelve weeks. You feel like crap, you can't eat anything because the thought of food makes you want to puke, but you're so hungry that you want to puke, but when you try to decide what sounds good, nothing does and you puke." She's yelling at me, and I can't keep up with her. "And I just have to pretend like I don't have the flu and keep going to school like normal. Not to mention my hormones are going a buck twenty and I want to cry all the time, and normally, girls have their family and friends to offer support but I don't have any of that because I can't tell my family, and the one person who does know is the one who is responsible for all this, and is too busy worrying about himself and thinking I told his mom."

I take a step back and reach my hands behind my neck. What the fuck have I created? "Creed, I mean, I'm sorry. If I could take the sickness away, I would. What happened? I thought we were cool when you left on Saturday? I had no idea you were so mad at me."

She drops her head back in frustration. "How did you make this about you again?"

I don't understand what I'm doing wrong. Creed's sick, I get it, but she's mad at me like it's my fault, and while it is, it's not like I fucked her with the sole intention of giving her the flu for twelve weeks. Neither of us asked for this.

"I'm not making anything about me. I'm just confused. I have no idea what the hell's going on or why you're screaming at me. Can you just tell me?"

Tears fill her eyes. "I already did." She turns to leave again.

Instead of stopping her, I follow her. "Tell me what to do to make this better. Do you want me to sit with you at lunch today?"

"Not going to lunch. Can't stand the smell of the cafeteria," she says like I should have figured that out. She's beelining down the hall—I'm even having a hard time keeping up with her fireball pace.

"Then what do you want? Do you want me to take you to the abortion clinic? You want me to marry you? Just tell me what to do and I'll do it."

Creed stops in her tracks. I somehow screwed up again, because she's shutting her eyes and squeezing her fists at her side. Then she leans over a trash can and stares at me the entire time she pukes up who knows what the fuck kind of liquid.

I just stand there and watch her retching, her eyes burning holes in my soul. This is straight-up *Exorcist* shit, and I purposely didn't watch that movie to avoid shit like this.

She finally stands and wipes her mouth, but she's still staring at me and I'm just staring back because no matter what I do or say, it's the wrong thing. I wish she'd just tell me what to do to make this better, because I'd do it, like, a thousand times over. She finally goes into the girls' bathroom and leaves me standing here like an idiot.

I'm not gonna wait for her to come out. That'd probably just piss her off, too. I think the only way Creed would be happy right now is if I were dead.

She's not the only one.

I'm still expected to attend football practice, even though I'm not cleared to play. This is not what I intended. I wanted to just get rid of football completely, but this arrangement sucks even worse. I wish I was just playing again so people would stop being such fucktards. Javier and Tyler are alternating quarterback position, and neither of them can throw for shit, so they're just doing handoffs and short passes. I feel like I'm watching a peewee league where they don't know their heads from their asses.

Coach Jay still manages to yell at me, because he wants me to teach these guys the proper turns for each of the handoffs and remind them which ones are reverse and which ones are double reverse and which are fake handoffs and which end up being passes to the slot receiver. But you can't teach jack shit to a couple of apes, and all they're doing is fighting, and I'm about to throw all their asses down a flight of stairs. I'd have better luck coaching Xander and Pillsbury, or whatever the fuck he named that damn cat.

My head hurts.

King, the offensive coach, trots up and stares into my pupils. "You okay?"

"No. My head hurts." I'm glaring at these dumb fucks, but King mistakes it for wincing from the sun. He motions to Coach Jay, who finishes screaming at the D-line and jogs over.

"What's the problem?" he barks.

"Malik needs a break," King states, and I don't want to look like a pussy, so I shake my head and say, "Nah, Coach. I'm good," but make sure to shut my eyes and push on my temples.

Coach Jay smacks my ass. "Get your ass in the locker room and out of this sun. Practice is almost over, anyway. Who's taking you home?"

I point to the smaller of the two assholes (ironic, since he's the biggest asshole ever). "Javier."

Coach nods and tells me to get the frick off his field, and I bow out of the idiot circus and head to the locker room. But the second I open the door, I see Mr. Lorrey tinkering on his phone at the sink, and I duck out before he sees me. I don't feel like being drilled by him, too, about how I'm feeling or the size of my pupils.

I head to the baseball dugout and plop on the bench, teetering on this brink of infuriating reality and the place I've been going while watching those videos.

THE FALLING OF STARS

Jordan went to this place often, too, before he died—I know it; I feel him there. I'm more connected to him now than ever. I'm drawn to this sad, sad place because it understands. It's a mental torture chamber full of demons that hold you when you cry, when no one else would bat an eyelash. Especially those idiots on the football field— my alleged friends. They'd turn it into some joke and mess with me, but they didn't see the looks on the faces of those bodies that fell from wherever they fell from in those videos. I understand those faces, and they understand me. I recognize that look in their eyes, the one that says this world is full of horrible things that no one else sees. But you have to endure it every second of every day, and there's no escaping it because it's living and breathing just behind your face, looming in your skull as a constant reminder that no one understands and that you. Are. Alone.

It's relentless.

Homework blows tonight, because I didn't pay attention in algebra or chemistry today. I don't have the energy to figure it out, so I do the best I can and say fuck it.

I log onto LibertyNet to upload a paper and see what's due in history, and I text Creed for the sixth time. *Hey, answer me, please. I want to make sure you're ok. I'm not the bad guy here, I promise. I'm sorry for the asshole things I said earlier.*

Even though I have no idea what asshole things I said. I'm trying my damnedest to be patient with her, but it's getting hard. It's not my fault that girls get pregnant and guys don't! She doesn't let me react for a second—if I do, I'm making it about me. And she won't tell me what she wants from me. I apparently have to be the strong one and make all the decisions and know the perfect things to say and the exact time to say them. I couldn't do any of that before she was pregnant, so I don't know why she expects a miracle now.

I've just uploaded my homework when a chat pops up with the weird number. Before reading it, I grab the paper I wrote the last set of numbers on and compare the two.

They're definitely different numbers.

The first eight or so are the same, the next two are inverted, then they end pretty much the same. This is a different profile each time, and I think it always has been. This idiot knows how to avoid getting blocked. I write this one down, too.

Welcome back to school, the message says.

I don't want to engage, so I continue navigating to the history portal to see what my dad assigned.

You have a history paper due in your dad's class.

The fuck? I look around the room, searching for hidden cameras or perverts peeking in my window, then turn back to my computer. *How did you know I was looking up history homework?*

I guessed.

This is voodoo shit, right here. I consider logging off, but I remember something. *Yo, I watched your videos. You promised you'd tell me who you were if I watched them.*

Him: *One more series of questions, and I'll tell you. I want to talk about your dad.*

Me: *My stepdad? Alex?*

Him: *Yes. Do you think he really loves you?*

My fingers dart to the keyboard. *Of course I do.*

Him: *How do you know? You have no biological dad to compare him to.*

Again, how does this guy know anything about my life? But it's probably common knowledge, considering I look nothing like these gingers I live with. *Because Alex wanted to be my dad. He raised me like his own child.*

Him: *He seems strict. Is he?*

No need to hesitate here, either. *He's strict AF.*

THE FALLING OF STARS

Him: *Why? You're not a problem child. You're a good student and a good athlete. You respect authority. Most parents would kill to have a teenager like you. So why is he so strict with you?*

I stare at the screen and consider that question. *I don't know.*

Him: *Mr. Hunter's all about appearances. He wants the world to think he has a perfect family, and he'll go to any extreme to get people to think that. He chose your mom because she was pretty and popular among kids and staff. Then he met you, and you were an athletic, fatherless child—the perfect specimen for him to groom into an all-star athlete. Look how he brags about you in school. You have no privacy, Malik. You're always on display because he created you. He's your puppet master. If you embarrass him, like with the buckets, he cracks down on you. If you make him look good, he doesn't praise you—he takes all the praise for himself. He doesn't care about you. He doesn't love you. He uses you and your mother.*

These are all popping up as separate messages, one after the other after the other. I just finish reading one when another pops up, and by the time I'm done, my jaw's in my lap. There's no way that's true. Alex has done too much for us—he's sacrificed his entire life for us. *I disagree* is all I type back.

Him: *Then now we're at the next phase of The Game. Prove to me I'm wrong.*

Me: *How?*

Him: *Find one area in your life he doesn't exploit.*

I nearly laugh out loud. *That he's my history teacher. We don't even discuss it. I don't ask for favors, he doesn't offer extra help.*

I wait almost a minute before he responds. *There's a history paper due tomorrow. Your assignment is to get an F on it. You fail it, you win. I'll tell you who I am. But if you get an A, you lose. And there will be consequences.*

I can't even wrap my head around that proposal. If I fail, I win? If I ace it, I lose? What kind of ass-backwards pony did this fruitcake ride in on?

I can easily get an F in history, and Alex will flip out and kick my ass and scream and ground me for the next five lives, and it may just soften the blow for when he finds out he's gonna be a grandpa.

24

MALIK

This fool logs off LibertyNet, and I navigate to my grades. Straight A's. I click on *World History—Mr. Alex Hunter* and see my scores on each assignment, quiz, and test. I have a ninety-five percent or higher on everything. My test average is a ninety-nine. We've taken five tests so far this year, but that seems like a lot. I only remember studying for two or three. Oh, wait—the papers are test grades, and I have a one-hundred percent on every paper…

Back up. That's weird, because I'm not a great writer. I'm a better test-taker, yet my test grades are lower. I click on the first essay we turned in on Nomadic and Agricultural Societies. Alex gave me a hundred. I scan through it and find grammatical errors that my mom would've yelled at me for if she were proofreading it. At one point, I even spelled *societies, societys*. Wow, that's pretty bad. And my dad didn't even circle it.

I pull up the second paper on The Fertile Crescent. One hundred percent.

The third was about Nile River Civilizations. One hundred percent.

And tomorrow I have a two-page essay due on Greeks and Romans. But is Alex not reading them? Is he just giving me A's? I feel like that should make me happy, but it doesn't. Why do I go through all this work if he doesn't even read it?

Ohhhhhh—so I can play football. I'll never be ineligible for grades, and great report cards go a long way on college applications. He's trying to do me a favor, I know. But that's so ... teacher. I'd understand if Coach Jay were my history teacher and he just gave me A's in everything. But this is my dad, the man who lets the entire world know that just because I'm his son, I get no special privileges.

Alex is constantly harping about how *school is so important, and that's something I've instilled in Malik since he was a child, and cheating is never the answer, and if Malik ever got caught cheating, there'd be hell to pay.* And everyone would nod and say, *Oh, that's why Malik is such a good kid. He's got such a stand-up man raising him. Go, Alex!* But isn't giving me A's without reading it a form of cheating? Or if you give a kid an A in a forest, and no one is around to hear you not grade it, is it really cheating?

Yo... Is that what this idiot online has been trying to tell me? Does he know my dad doesn't read history papers? And is it just my papers he doesn't read, or everyone's? And why do I feel like a hole just got punched through my heart? Over something as stupid and pointless as a history paper? *The place* is reaching out from the depths of my brain, telling me I'm all alone.

Well, we'll see. I Google the history of the Romans and Greeks and go batshit crazy, writing about the Battle of Corinth, the Byzantine Empire, Constantine the Great, and then in the second to last paragraph I change it up a bit...

THE FALLING OF STARS

Alex, you're my dad. You're the only dad I've ever known. Please, with everything that is within me, read this paper. Tell me you read it. Give me an F, because I used the word fuck in a history paper. Whatever you do, don't give me an A. If you do, I'll know you didn't read it. And if you don't read it, I'm going to kill myself, because I've been suicidal for a while now. And I need you to help me. Please, Dad.

Then my last paragraph begins with the typical, *In conclusion...*

I click back to the homework section to see if he wants this one uploaded or if we're to turn in a hard copy, wondering how the hell I'm going to explain this when he reads it. But part of me wants to know. And I'm willing to get an F if it'll guarantee that my dad cares enough to read my history papers.

He wants a hard copy, so I print it out and stick it in my binder, wondering what the hell has happened to me?

The next few days of school all blend together, and I don't remember anything. I've left Creed alone. I don't know what to do with her. She's just throwin' shade, so I'm giving her space.

I feel horrible ghosting her. Or, I would feel horrible if I still felt things. But I've been numb for a while now. I don't care that I knocked her up, I don't care that I fell down the stairs, and I don't care that my biggest confidant right now is a psycho on the school intranet. I have no idea who it is, and I don't care. Girl, guy, teacher, student ... no clue. I mean, I picture him as a student, and obviously a guy, since I'm always referring to him as *him*. He hasn't said anything about Creed being pregnant, so I can rule out one person—God.

It's Friday, and I'm sitting in my mom's English class waiting for the bell to ring when Creed walks in and takes her seat next to me. She's lost weight. I wonder if anyone else notices, but I check myself—Creed isn't in the spotlight like I am. People know when I'm in the bathroom taking a shit. Even now, the biggest gossip is, *What's wrong with Malik lately? He hasn't been the same since he fell down the stairs. You think something happened that permanently altered his brain when he fell?*

Jesus Christ.

Creed hangs her hair across the right side of her face to avoid me. That's cool. I took my splint off yesterday because I was sick of it, so I'm able to write now, and I rest my head on my left hand so I don't have to look at her, either.

At lunch, she's not with her friends where she usually sits, probably because she's still sick. I'm sure those two girls know she's pregnant, because they were there when I found her the day she told me. They probably know I'm going to be a father, and my own parents don't even know. And you know what's even more messed up? I don't even know those girls' names.

I'm looking down at my tray of lasagna, ignoring Javier and Camila engaged in a dirty-talk contest (it's actually really disgusting and I'm losing respect for both of them), when I feel a tap on my shoulder. My eyes immediately go across the table to Javier. He and the guys are looking behind my head with confused stares, and I turn around to see the tapper.

Creed. "Can we talk?" she asks.

I turn back to the guys, who all look like they're stoned—their jaws slack, their eyes glazed, because they have no idea why Creed Holloway is standing at their table, asking Malik Hunter if they can talk.

"Yeah, sure." I abandon my cold lasagna and follow her out of the cafeteria. She shoves through the side doors and takes me outside to the benches at the bottom of the stairs of Lafayette Hall—you know, *those* stairs.

She sits, and I sit next to her, staring at the ground.

"Did I embarrass you in front of your friends?" she asks coldly.

"Nope."

I don't know what she's expecting from me, but whatever it is, she's not getting it. She leans away and pukes in the mulch, and I sit here with my elbows on my knees and my fingertips tapping together until she's finished. She chugs a bottle of water, then apologizes.

"What are you sorry for?" I ask, my eyes fixated on my hands. I'm so glad I took that stupid splint off. My wrist still hurts, but my god, with that splint.

"For puking."

"Don't be ridiculous. You're pregnant." My voice is completely monotone. I take this opportunity to administer a little physical therapy, and I open and close my fist, bending my wrist around and monitoring the mobilization. It feels good, considering I stretched some tendons so bad they nearly snapped. It's creepy, though, watching my body heal from falling down the stairs while my mind gets more injured every day.

She's watching me. "How's your wrist?"

"Fine."

We're silent for a sec. Then I hear her sniffling and squeaking—good god, she's crying. I sigh. Women. They're Molotov cocktails. "What's wrong?" I ask without looking at her, continuing my self-inflicted therapy. If I'm not careful, I'll be back in football soon.

"I just can't believe you're doing this to me," she sobs.

Now I look at her. "Doing what?"

"You got me pregnant and now you're ignoring me."

I roll my eyes. "Creed, I'm not ignoring you. I'm giving you space. When I tried to help Monday, you acted like you hated me. You won't return my texts. So what am I supposed to do? I have my own shit I'm dealing with, and you want me to pretend I don't have feelings so you can feel validated, and I just don't have the energy for that. I'm sorry if that makes me a dick, but this is the first time I'm in this situation, and I need some direction. And when I ask for guidance, you get mad. When I take initiative, you get mad. You know I want to be in your life and the baby's life, so stop acting like I'm being abusive with you."

Her stomach makes a rumbling noise and I think she's going to puke again. She chugs more water, twisting the cap back on slowly. "I'm sorry."

"Now what are you sorry for?"

"For being mean to you. For rejecting your attempts to help. I told you, my hormones are all over the place. I hate this, Malik. I'm in my own personal hell. I feel like a complete outsider, because nobody knows what I'm dealing with, not even my parents."

I crane my head to look at her. "Creed, hello? What do you think I'm going through?" I drop my head in my hands.

"I've been going to counseling."

My head snaps back in her direction, and this is the first time moving my head that fast doesn't make me dizzy. More irony—my head's getting better when Creed just said something that made my head worse. "Where? For what? With who?"

"I've gone twice this week. To Mrs. Hendrick."

I slap my hands over my face as my stomach drops into my ass. "You told Mrs. Hendrick you're pregnant with my child?" I can barely get the words out—it's like I have to squeeze them out with energy I don't even have to begin with.

"I had to tell someone, Malik. I—"

"Me, Creed! You can talk to me about this! I'm the only one in the world who knows what you're going through. And whenever I try talking to you, you bite my head off. You know Mrs. Hendrick works with my parents, you know that, right? She's going to tell them, because that's what adults do." I've jumped off the bench and am pacing around her. I cannot believe she did this. I want to shake her.

She looks like an oscillating fan, watching me pace back and forth. This is the first time I've ever yelled at her; I've never even raised my voice, outside of those couple times I acted firm with her just to calm her down. But now I'm actually pissed. And I don't even care.

"Are you making this about you again?" she asks quietly.

"Yeah, I am. Because it's *my* parents she's going to tell. Not yours. This is a conflict of interest for her. Yeah, she's supposed to keep student stuff confidential, but you've put her in a position because now she knows that the son of her friends and coworkers has impregnated another student."

Creed shakes her head, dropping her gaze to the mulch. "It's not like that. She's not going to tell them."

Why does she immediately act rational whenever I take control with her, but when I try to act nice and loving to her, she gets mad? I don't understand girls, and I don't think I want to.

The bell rings and lunch is over, and I haven't eaten anything since yesterday. Whatever. My appetite went to shit anyway. We just stare at each other because we know this conversation is over because life goes on and we have to go to classes now.

We wait for each other to say something, but neither of us do.

I finally grit my teeth and punch the side of a locker, yelling, "Fuck!" and storm off to history, where I get to stare at my dad for fifty minutes and wonder if he knows I knocked up a girl and he's doing that thing where he makes me wait, or if I'm freaking myself out and he doesn't know jack shit.

I'm already in my seat when Javi slides in the desk next to me. "What the hell was that thing at lunch? What did that freak want?"

I tap my pen on my desk and look over at him. "She wanted help with algebra. She's having trouble ... multiplying."

He makes a face. "She's so weird, dude. Why wouldn't she just ask you for help? Why'd she want you to leave the table?"

I drop my pen on my desk. "Maybe because she knew you'd say some smartass comment to her, because you're mean to her."

I can tell he's butt-hurt, but the bell rings and that's the end of it. My dad is walking around the room handing our papers back, commenting on how impressed he was with the majority of them, and I don't hear one more thing for the rest of the day because he walks by my desk and drops my paper on it with the biggest freaking A+ 100% scrawled across the top.

This is the second time I've gone to the locker room just to throw things and cry like a little bitch. I'm going crazy, and yet there's a small part in this clusterfuck that is my brain that knows I'm doing this because I got an A on a paper, and Malik is being a dramatic little shit. But that small part gets lost in the mob of the rest of my mind that lost it a long time ago because the moral of the story is that fucking Internet weirdo is right and I'm wrong.

Alex doesn't give a shit about me. It's all about him. All these years I thought he was my proof there was a God. But now I feel like Xander when he found out there's no Santa Claus.

THE FALLING OF STARS

I skip my last two classes and Uber home. I guarantee no one'll notice—not my parents, anyway. They're too busy being wrapped up in themselves to know I left school. And they'll come home later—my mom with Xander, my dad with his trusty briefcase—and no one will say a word because they'll think Javier dropped me off.

And that's exactly what happens.

My mom makes burgers for dinner, but I can't eat much because I haven't eaten since yesterday morning. She and Alex keep asking if I feel sick, and I keep saying no. And the only reason I don't just say screw it and storm off is because they'd come back and ask me why I'm acting so erratic, and what's really wrong.

So I excuse myself like a good little puppet and go to my room. I have no intention of doing homework, but I log onto LibertyNet anyway. It takes twenty minutes before he sends me a chat, and I immediately compare this eighteen-digit number to the last two I'd written down. This one's different, too.

You lost, Malik.

For some reason, that makes my heart rate flutter. My fingers move across the keyboard: *Yup. I lost.*

Him: *I told you there would be consequences if you lost.*

Because apparently finding out your dad doesn't love you isn't punishment enough. I swallow and type: *What are they?*

He's not responding right away, and that's making me nervous. Will it be bad? Like, is he gonna hurt me? Ruin my life?

My phone blings with a text. It's from him and his new long-ass number. *Set your alarm for four AM. Send me a screenshot so I know you did it.*

He does realize I could send him a screenshot of my alarm set, and then just turn it off, right? But I have a feeling I shouldn't piss this guy off. So I do what he says.

He texts back: *Good. Four a.m., you'll receive your punishment.*

And now I'm not gonna sleep at all tonight.

It's three in the morning, and I haven't slept. Creed, Alex, this impending punishment that I have no idea what the heck it's going to be... How sick is this guy? C'mon—he sent me videos of dead people.

I'm considering just telling my mom about him, but she'll be pissed that I didn't tell her when she showed me Jordan's texts, then she'll end up finding out about the videos and waking up early, and that won't end well.

Besides, no punishment can hurt as bad as finding out your dad cares more about himself than he does you. If this guy took a baseball bat to my head, I wouldn't feel it.

I must have dozed off for a few minutes, because I'm startled by my alarm. I jump up and silence it before my parents or brother hear. Within two minutes, a text pops up: *Log on now.*

I slip from my bed to the computer and enter my credentials for LibertyNet, and I have a new message. He's sent me a video. A short one—it's only thirty seconds. I take a deep breath and click PLAY.

For the first five seconds, I can't tell what I'm looking at. It looks like a bowl of bloody hamburger meat or something, and when I realize what these images are that are flashing in front of my face, my limbs start shaking. I can't breathe. They're aborted fetuses. The screen blanks, and words pop up in red font: *Tell her to do this.* *#consequences*

He knows about Creed. He's making me abort the baby. He isn't a he at all. He's a she, and this is Mrs. Hendrick because Creed told her.

25

EVE

It's been over a week, and we haven't heard a word on Alondra's investigation. We hesitate to bring it up, simply because Jeremiah requested to keep it among ourselves, and well—Alex, Ruben, and I are hardly ever just the three of us. But Alex and I talk about it all the time.

Argue about it, more like. I want to pursue things and he wants to just back off, because the whole thing seems weird and we should let Jeremiah handle it. But I reciprocate that Jeremiah isn't going quickly enough, and this murderess could be doing this to other people, and Alex says, "Really? You honestly think she's in her office, conning teenagers into killing themselves?" and I just stay quiet.

I watch Alondra parade about the school without a care, as middle-aged and professional as ever, and yet I swear on the Holy Scriptures she's avoiding me.

It's Wednesday, and I'm sitting in the teachers' lounge during my seventh-period break. I generally spend it alone, now that my previous break-partner is being charged with statutory rape. I'm sipping coffee and going through Snapchat filters when the door opens and Ruben storms in.

He stops when he sees me, and I nearly spit coffee back into my mug, completely ruining the cat ears and glasses I was virtually adorning myself with. "Eve!" He throws his hands up and races to the table. "Finally! What's happening? Have you heard anything?"

I shake my head. "Nothing. And Alex won't let me ask."

"Well, whatever it is—"

The door opens again, and in walks Alondra holding a mauve mug. She smiles and scuttles toward the coffee, taking the pot of hot water and pouring it in her mug. She tosses in a teabag and Ruben is kicking me under the table, and why he thinks I have shins of steel I'll never know, but I quickly divert my legs to the other side of the chair.

His foot swings aimlessly beneath the table now, and he looks at me when he realizes his thunder-toes aren't connecting with my shinbones. I give him a dirty look and mouth "*Ow!*" and he gestures toward her, like I don't know she's standing there.

"Good afternoon," she says politely, and I swear on the Holy Sword she's avoiding eye contact with me.

"Hello," I say, and Ruben's silence is louder than any insult he could throw at her. "How are you, Mrs. Hendrick?" I say over his rudeness.

She rolls her eyes dramatically, bobbing her teabag in her ugly mauve mug. "Never a dull moment in a school full of teenagers!" She turns back to the fridge and pulls out a container of heavy cream, and Ruben takes the opportunity to send me a million telepathic messages, none of which I properly decipher.

"Sooo … anything exciting happen lately?" I ask lamely, and Ruben shoots me a look like I just killed any chance of a confession with my stupid question. I give him a small shrug—*it's not like you're trying anything*—and give her the warmest smile I can muster when she turns to me.

She shrugs uncomfortably, like she's about to lie. "Not really. You?"

I shake my head. I'm not even looking at Ruben anymore. It's stupid.

She's stirring her tea like crazy. There has to be a category five hurricane in that mug. "I—I do think we should chat, Eve. About—well, what we talked about before. There's some stuff you should know."

Oh, shit. This is it—she wants to talk about Jordan. She knows I'm onto her! *She knows!* "What's your availability?" I croak.

She takes a sip of tea and looks thoughtfully at the ceiling. "Let me check my calendar and I'll text you. Oh, that reminds me! Mr. DeSoto, my Outlook isn't working properly. Is that something you can help me with?"

Ruben finally turns to her and can barely hold eye contact for three seconds before turning forward again. "You need to update to the latest format," he mumbles. "It should prompt you automatically. When it does, just follow the steps to update it. You'll probably have to restart your computer when it's finished."

He's being such a dick.

Alondra sighs. "Hopefully it'll work. I have the worst luck with computers." Then she chuckles and gives me her best *am-I-right?* look before walking out the door.

There's no way in hell I'm cooking tonight. This is the never-ending week, and it's only Wednesday. I suggest ordering Uber Eats, and Alex bitches about spending the extra money on delivery and tips, but I tell him I'd pay a million dollars to not cook, and he's not making any attempts in the kitchen, so pick an entrée and figure out what the kids want and order that shit.

Malik has his car back, and the doctor cleared him to play football—just in time for playoffs. He seems a little apprehensive, which concerns me and frustrates Alex. He keeps asking Malik what he's afraid of, and Malik says he's not afraid, just cautious. Then I have to come to Malik's defense because I agree with him, and that's not a conversation I want to have over Uber Eats tonight.

But when the food arrives, I send Xander to get his brother from his room, and Xander comes back announcing that Malik is asleep.

"What? It's not even eight o'clock," I say as I pull boxes from plastic bags.

"Well, Malik does have a pretty tough life," Xander remarks, accepting the bowl of mac-n-cheese I hand him. "May I eat this in my room?" he asks, and I'm impressed with his proper use of *may I*.

"Yes, you may," I reply, and Xander escapes before Alex can rebut with some new rule about not being allowed to eat in your room or something.

"It looks like it's just you and me tonight, sexy." I pull my grilled chicken salad from the bag, and the condensation has already made it soggy. Alex does an evil laugh as he opens his box of fajitas, and I pour us each a glass of wine.

We eat in silence until my phone chimes a text. I nearly choke on my wine when I see that it's Alondra, letting me know she has tomorrow at lunch available. Alex looks when he hears me sputtering, and the asshole reads my text.

"Eve? No! What are you doing? I told you not to get involved!"

I cannot stop coughing. Wine is the worst to choke on. Now my nose and throat are drunk. "I'm not!" I finally cough out.

Alex laughs. "You're the worst liar ever! It's right here!" And he holds up my phone.

I shake my head and wipe my eyes. "No, *she* approached *me* today, and asked when we can talk again. She said there's some stuff I should know."

Alex sets my phone next to my salad. "Well, let her know you're no longer having marital problems, and stay the hell away from her, Eve. Please. Until this investigation's over."

"I can't avoid her for the next five years! This investigation is turning into an investication."

Alex looks to the ceiling with a puzzled expression. "Is that a combination of investigation and vacation?"

I shrug and make a face. "Kind of. It was supposed to be a play on staycation, but I don't think I pulled that off very well."

Alex pooches his lip out and nods. "That wasn't too bad. You've come up with worse. Like when you were priorganizing. Organizing your priorities."

"Shut up. That was gold."

He presses his lips into mine—his fajitas merging with my salad—and I don't even care because it's still hot. But then he whispers against my lips, "You're not going to see her."

I sit back. "Then I'm going to Jeremiah. I think he's forgotten."

"He hasn't forgotten! I told you, this is a process. He's working on it. A hacker is very sneaky, Eve. Someone of that caliber would hide their tracks a little harder. If you're hacking into the administrator's account and creating and deleting profiles, you've got quite an intricate agenda. Again, Alondra is the first suspect, but there are some T's to dot and some I's to cross." He crosses his eyes and winks at me, because he said that stupidly on purpose.

I suppress a grin and turn back to my salad. "It bothers me that neither you nor I are involved in this. Who's helping him, anyway? Why wouldn't he involve

Ruben? He's the one who discovered her IP address, you'd think Ruben would be a key factor in this *invest-stay-cation*."

Alex pops me on the nose. "You're a dork." Then his phone rings. He pulls it from his pocket and turns to me with wide eyes. "It's Jeremiah."

I watch him as he answers and speaks with our boss, and it's literally thirty seconds before he hangs up and looks at me. "Tomorrow, after school. Faculty meeting regarding Alondra Hendrick."

We high-five and finish our food.

Now that I know Alondra's "trial" is today, I actually go out of my way to *avoid* her. And of course, the day goes by ridiculously slowly.

Something's wrong with Malik. He slept at least ten hours last night, and he's dragging through his classes today. I notice when he's sitting in my English class with his head propped on his hand the entire hour, staring at his notebook. Maybe he should go back to the doctor. I hope he doesn't do that in Alex's class, but if he does, Alex had better not embarrass him and call him out.

I decide to send Alex an email saying just that, because I know he'll check his school email before he'll check a text message. He's one of *those* employees. But when I try to open my Outlook, it doesn't load. Damn.

Then I remember Ruben telling Alondra that we need to update Outlook, but I'm getting no popups like he talked about. I try clicking things, but I only have a few minutes before students begin piling in, so I pick up my phone and call Ruben.

"Yellow," he answers.

"Hey, Ruben. Can you help me update my Outlook? I can't do it."

He's eating again; I'm not surprised. "Sure thing, Eve-bola."

"That's disgusting. Don't ever call me that again."

He swallows whatever he's eating. "Are you running the click-to-run version?"

I pinch the bridge of my nose. "Please don't ask me things like that. I don't even know what that means. Maybe we should just wait. I have another class in a few minutes."

"Actually, I can just do it for you real quick, if you want."

"No, it's okay. You're eating, and by the time you get up here, my next class will have started."

"Shut up and prepare for magic. Just watch your computer screen. Hang on."

I swear out loud when my cursor starts moving and clicking things all on its own. "Ruben? What's going on? My computer's possessed."

He laughs. "No, it's not. It's me. I'm remotely accessing your computer through this software. It's installed on every computer in the school. It's so much easier for me to fix your stuff when you destroy it by just mirroring your screen instead of having to come to your room."

I'm almost in a trance watching my computer pulling up screens and clicking prompts I've never seen in my life. Text is appearing in text boxes, access is being granted, programs are restarting ... this guy's a genius.

"There you go. Should all be up to date."

I'm staring at my Outlook inbox with all my emails. "You're amazing, thank you," I say, wondering how to boot him off so I can have control of my computer back. But the cursor clicks on *Compose* and a new email pops up. He starts voicing everything he's typing.

"To ... alex-dot-hunter-at-libertynet-dot-org. Subject ... I love you, Honeybunches. Message ... You are the best. Love, Eve." Then he clicks send. The box disappears.

I start laughing. "Did you seriously just send my husband an email from me?"

"Sure did," he says as a new message from Alex pops up in my inbox. It just has two question marks.

Ruben and I crack up laughing. "Okay, Ruben. You've done your job. Now get out of my computer, please."

"Ha, ha, I just did. You have complete control now. Plus, your email."

"Perfect timing. The kids are pouring in now. Thank you."

We hang up, and I hurriedly send Alex an email to be nice to Malik. I'm still shocked at how Ruben can just take control of people's computers like that. He can pretend to be anyone.

He can just…

…oh, my god.

Is it … is it Ruben? Could Ruben have mirrored into Alondra's computer and contacted Jordan?

Alex is always saying Alondra isn't computer savvy enough, and that's a point of his I can never argue. Ruben's the one who created LibertyNet, and he's the only one with an admin account. Why was he never a suspect?

Then I remember that melodramatic temper tantrum he threw the day I showed him, when he threw stuff across the room. He was so angry, it scared me. I thought it was a righteous indignation that someone tampered with his creation to harass a depressed teen. But was it because I caught him? Was that his way of threatening me?

He could've easily hacked into Alondra's computer and read her notes on Jordan. And by accessing Alondra's computer remotely, it would direct to her IP address if anyone ever caught him. That explains why (despite his rage) he was so complying to humor me in checking out Jordan's text initially, because he knew it would point back to her computer, even though it was his account. It was his cover-up.

THE FALLING OF STARS

He's been so adamant about throwing Alondra to the wolves. Way worse than I've been. No wonder Alex and Jeremiah have been so cautious about convicting her. There is absolutely a method in pinpointing this on someone, and holy shit—Jeremiah wasn't even involving Ruben in the investigation. I bet it's because he figured it out, and he hasn't been able to say anything because Ruben is constantly harping him about it.

Oh, lord. I have to tell Alex.

26

MALIK

Mrs. Hendrick got fired today. When I first heard my parents talking about it tonight before dinner, I was so relieved I almost started crying. No more harassing me on LibertyNet. No morbid videos at four in the morning. No chance of her telling my parents about Creed.

But that quickly turned to more anxiety. What if they go through her computer and find her messages to me? Or the notes she took from Creed's counseling sessions? My parents would kill me and then revive me, just to kill me again even harder. What if I somehow go to jail for all this? I mean, it could happen. I'm sure I've done *something* illegal, and if Alex thought speeding was worth two weeks of grounding, I'm probably better off in jail.

I don't have the mental stamina to continue thinking about this. Or the energy. I skipped practice again today. I'm supposed to be playing again, and I haven't been going. Coach Jay called when I missed practice yesterday, and I just sent him to voicemail. He didn't even call today. I'm somehow going to end up in jail for that, too.

Creed and I have been texting. Small things, pretty much. *Hi, how are you feeling, how was your day,* typical bullshit. But this one she sent me just now—not so much.

I think it's time to tell my parents about the pregnancy.

Motherfucker. I sigh, like it's the last breath I'll ever take. I text: *You'll probably feel a lot better after it's all out.* But I'm shaking like a leaf.

Creed: *I doubt it. Will you do something for me?*

And like an idiot, I respond with: *Always.*

Creed: *Will you be here when I tell them?*

Fuck me. I purposely didn't watch *The People Under the Stairs* to avoid shit like this. But I knew this day was coming. I mean, Creed's been barfing and freakin' miserable for a while now, and I'm sure her parents have noticed. Her belly's gonna start growing. And she's going to need to go to the doctor. I write back: *Sure. When?*

Creed: *Tonight.*

Fuck me now.

My parents didn't even give me a hard time when I left fifteen minutes before dinner. I thought my mom would be all like, *"But Malik? Dinner is almost ready!"* And my dad would be all, *"Sit your ass down, son, and eat your dinner without being a disrespectful little shit,"* but they both just got this concerned look and nodded when I told them I'd be studying with a friend. I didn't even have any books with me. Like, how bad of a liar am I? But I guess it just proves even more that Alex doesn't care about me. He has his wife and his biological son. That's all he needs.

I text Creed when I pull in her driveway, but she doesn't respond. So I go knock at the door, scanning my eyes across her house. It's nice, one of those typical cookie-cutters that builders keep building in like four months all through Miami, even though there's no room left. I can even see the shoddy craftsmanship along the exterior—the cracks near the windows by laborers forcing glass into squares they don't fit in for pennies an hour. But these McMansions go for over a half a million bucks, and I'll never understand it.

She opens the door, looking scared as all hell.

"Hi." I give her a hug.

She reaches up to wrap her arms around my neck. I have to force myself not to smell her hair. She pulls me in the house, and both her parents are sitting on a sofa and now I'm about to shit myself. I don't even try to predetermine if they're cool or not, because at this point it doesn't matter. Not with what we're about to confess.

She leads me to the sofa across from them and forces me to sit. "This is Malik Hunter. Both his parents are teachers at my school. He's the quarterback on the JV football team."

Her parents eye me and nod slightly at her resume-like introduction. "Hello, Malik," her mother says. Her dad says nothing.

"Hello." I give a little wave.

Creed stands up. "Malik and I ... well, I'm pregnant."

What the fuck.

I drop my head in my hands because I can't even look at their faces. All I know is her dad is yelling and her mom is crying and Creed is pleading and why the *fuck* did I agree to do this? Dads shoot boys who impregnate their daughters, it's common knowledge.

I'm literally experiencing my life ending. Parents know. Shit just got real. Her dad is shoving tables and chairs and storming toward her as Creed holds her hands up, begging, "Daddy, please! Calm down!" And the mom is sobbing on the sofa like a useless blob.

Her father makes an abrupt turn toward me, and I put my head back in my hands as I feel him hovering over me. "Get up, Malik Hunter! Stand up and be a man!"

And here's where I'm gonna get my ass kicked. I drop my hands and stand, staring him in the eye. We're about the same height. I'm trying to determine if I can take this guy while Creed's grabbing his arm, begging him to stop.

"I am so sorry I did this to your daughter—"

"Oh, yeah? Were you sorry when you stuck your cock in her? Or did you just fuck my daughter because you're an asshole who has no respect for women? That is my *daughter!*" He shoves his finger in Creed's direction, and I have nothing to say.

The mom is sobbing even harder on the couch, listening to the dad say all these vulgar things I did to their child. Creed is behind him, pleading for him to leave me alone. I'm gonna die.

"Are you even dating her?" he yells.

"I told Creed I'll do whatever she wants me to do. I'll be whatever she wants me to be." I'm holding up my hands, actually backing away from him because I swear to God he's gonna start throwing punches soon, and I'm just going to have to take them because I can't hit a dude whose daughter I knocked up.

He finally turns to Creed, shaking her off his arm. "What the hell are you gonna do with a baby? Is this why you've been so miserable lately? Because my *baby girl* is *pregnant?*" He picks up a candle jar from a table and throws it across the room. The rest of us jump as it smashes into the wall, and this just keeps escalating.

I turn to the mom, waiting for her to get control and put a stop to this insanity. But she's curled up like a fuckin' shrimp cocktail, letting her husband turn into a monster. So many more things make sense about Creed, now. I watch as her dad stands over her, screaming. I'm just waiting for him to put his hands on her so I can fuck him up.

"This is not good for the baby!" I holler.

THE FALLING OF STARS

Everyone stops what they're doing—crying, screaming, pleading—and looks at me. Of all the things to say, and I just said that.

Her dad comes at me again, and when his hand comes up, I flinch. But he points toward the door. "Get out! Stay the hell away from my daughter, or I'll get a restraining order!" He pushes me toward the door, opens it, and shoves me so hard I nearly tumble down the porch stairs. The door slams.

Fuck, fuck, fuck.

I can't leave. I need to make sure he doesn't hurt Creed. Or the baby. I wish he'd punch the mom, if he's gonna punch anyone. But as I stand on the porch, I just hear him yelling. *How could this happen? I raised you better than this! How can you raise a child when you're barely sixteen? How many times did this happen? Did he rape you?*

I roll my eyes at that one.

"He didn't rape me, Dad!" Creed says.

His following remarks send ice daggers right through my heart: "So you voluntarily got knocked up by some stupid kid with dreadlocks? What sort of low-class trash are you?"

I can't listen anymore.

I'm being raised by the whitest family in America, but when shit goes down, everyone points their finger at the kid with the dreads.

My legs move toward my car, and I eventually stuck the key in and started it, and somehow I backed out of the driveway and drove, because I'm currently sitting in a Target parking lot, bawling my head off.

I've already decided I'm not going to school tomorrow. I walk in the house after sobbing for who knows how long, and my parents and brother are all in the kitchen. I can't look at them.

"Malik?" Alex says.

I stop without turning to them. "Yeah?"

"Is everything okay?"

Tears return to my eyes. They can't see this. I reach both hands to the top of my head. I'm shaving these dreads off. "Uh, yeah. I'm just really sick. I'm gonna go to bed. I don't think I can go to school tomorrow." My back is to them, and I'm waiting for them to yell about their coveted eye contact. They're not, though.

I hear my mom's feet moving across the floor toward me. There's nothing I can do when she steps in front of me and looks up into my face. "Baby? What's going on? Come, eat. I saved you a plate." She links her arm through mine and leads me into the kitchen. "Talk to us, Malik."

I let her guide me halfway to the kitchen until I look up to see Alex seated at a barstool, twisted toward the one next to him like he's anticipating putting his arm around me once I sit there, and Xander perched on the one next to that, his little eyes creased with concern—even with a kitten slithering in his lap.

I could confess everything—right now. Tell them the millions of ways my life has gone to hell, and how I brought it all on myself. I can tell them about the pregnancy, because I know as pissed as they'd be, they'd never in a million years act like Creed's dad. But where would I stop? Would I tell them about falling down the stairs? About Miss Dupree? And Mrs. Hendrick reaching out to me online?

I've kept too many things from them for too long. I'll get no release from this torture by telling them anything, because I'll always have secrets to be hidden. I'll never be able to have an open, honest relationship with them, because I'm not the person they think I am. I'm not Malik Hunter—the great scholar and athlete. I'm Malik Hunter—the fucked-up multiracial kid who doesn't fit in anywhere in this world, not even in this family. I would single-handedly crush their entire lives in one sitting if I tell them all this.

I'm too weak. That's the bottom line—Creed has bigger balls than I do. I can't do it. This family is better off without me. I'm a huge failure who has done nothing but rain disaster and disappointment on the perfect family.

"No, Mom. I'm not hungry. I just want to take a shower and go to bed." I shimmy my arm out of hers and turn, but then turn back. "I really don't want to go to school tomorrow."

She assesses my face and rests her hands on both sides of my neck. "You're warm. Your eyes are red; it looks like you've been crying." She pauses and cocks her head. "Have you?" she asks softly, like she's scared of what my answer might be.

I shake my head, because what's one more lie? "No, I just have a migraine. I think I'm just getting sick."

She pulls my face down and kisses my cheek. "You can stay home tomorrow."

Xander jumps off the stool. "You want Biscuit? She's a good snuggler. She'll purr in your ear."

I chuckle. "Naw, thanks Little Dude. You keep your cat." And I accidentally make eye contact with Alex before turning away. He's looking at me, and I hear everything he doesn't say. Biological dad or not, Alex and I have always had this nonverbal man-language. It's pretty primitive, and usually involves him showing his dominance over me. Kinda like, *I'm your dad, and I'll fuck you up if you challenge me.*

But right now, his message is loud and clear: *I'm your dad, and I'll fuck up whoever has done this to you.*

Joke's on him, because I've done this to myself.

27

EVE

Today's been an absolute shitshow.

We had the faculty meeting for Alondra, all right. But it was nothing like Kendall's. It was short and to the point—to inform us that Jeremiah had *already* fired Alondra this morning for "gaining unauthorized access into the school's intranet."

I may or may not have made another scene, much akin to the Kendall Dupree one. Except I totally did. To the point where Jeremiah sent everyone out of the room except me, Alex, and Ruben. But in my defense, Ruben was making a scene, too.

"This is unbelievable!" Ruben shouted. "There was so much more to what she did than simply 'gaining unauthorized access.' She was—"

"Shut up, Ruben!" I screamed, then turned to Jeremiah, pointing at Ruben with my biggest tattling finger. "It was him, Mr. Lorrey. Ruben DeSoto, our beloved and intelligent IT technician, pinned this on Alondra Hendrick!"

Both their faces twisted into a hybrid of shock and confusion, and Alex slapped his hands over his face. Jeremiah, who was struggling to stay in control, folded his hands. "Mrs. Hunter, why would you assume that Mr. DeSoto has set up Mrs. Hendrick?"

"Because. Because of *remote accessing*. He installed this software on everyone's computers, and he sent my husband an email from my email address while controlling my computer. Ruben is the only one with an admin account. Alondra doesn't even remember her own password."

Ruben gripped the top of the mahogany table. "Are you accusing me of cyberbullying Jordan Sawyer into committing suicide? You evil bitch."

Alex was out of his seat in a second. "Don't talk to my wife like that!" And Jeremiah stood and placed his hand on Alex's chest, ultimately dismissing all three of us and excusing Ruben and me from coming in tomorrow on a leave of absence until further notice.

And now Malik comes home, looking like he just witnessed a murder. I've never seen him like this, and as I place my hands on either side of his neck, I feel his pulse beating through the arteries in his throat. His skin is damp from sweat. His eyes are red and look like they've experienced a lifetime of torture camps. He's really ill, and I'm concerned.

Malik's asleep within the hour. I put Xander to bed, reading him a chapter of *Harry Potter* before hitting the hay myself. Alex and I collapse into bed, neither of us with enough energy to turn off the lamps on our nightstands.

Alex squirms next to me. "It might not be a bad thing to get back on anxiety medication," he says, then immediately throws the covers over his head, as if protecting himself from my reaction.

But I'd be lying if I said I hadn't considered it already. So I throw the covers over my head, too, and now we're in a fort. "I think I might," I whisper. "Malik needs to go back to the doctor. I think there're still some lingering effects from when he fell. This isn't him." I feel my face getting even more solemn.

I didn't think he could see it, since we're in a fort, but he places a finger on my nose. "We'll take Malik wherever he needs to go to get him well again. I already told Coach Jay to back off, because we think the doctor may have been wrong to clear him to play. He understood. Kind of."

I sigh deeply.

"One thing at a time, Eve. You know the drill. Let Malik stay home from school tomorrow. You'll be here, anyway. We have this other mess to handle now."

Suddenly I can't breathe. I jerk the blankets off my face and suck the cool air into my lungs. "He fired Alondra. He did it *before* the board meeting, Alex. We didn't even get a chance to confront her. Or Ruben. I don't understand."

Alex turns on his side toward me, scrunching the pillow under his head. He looks like a pinup model. "Eve? No offense, but you keep making scenes during faculty meetings. I'm not surprised he did it privately."

I roll my eyes and turn away, and he takes the opportunity to spoon me. "I'm not done with this, Alex. Not until I get to the bottom of who was getting to Jordan. I know it was Ruben. It makes so much more sense than Alondra ever did."

Alex's whole body tenses. "If Jeremiah let her go, it was because he had enough evidence on her. How long did her investigation last? This wasn't on a whim."

"I'm sick of this turning into a game of Clue. Jordan Sawyer? He's still dead. Jill Sawyer? Has asked me to find out if her son was bullied. And guess what? I'm finding out that he was. This shouldn't be a game, Alex. Why has this turned into a game?"

"Because you won't leave shit alone." Then he yawns.

I brush his hands off me and roll away, flipping off the lamp on my nightstand.

"Oh, c'mon, Eve. I'm sorry. I was joking—"

He's cut off by my phone ringing, and I unplug it from my charger and look at the screen. It's Jill. I jump out of bed and leave the room, because God forbid Alex be entertained by my continuous not leaving shit alone. "Hello?" I say once I'm in the hallway.

She sighs. "Hi, Eve. I'm not bothering you, am I?"

"Not at all. What's up?"

"I just need to talk. Petra's working tonight. This is unbearable. When does it get better?"

I flip on a lamp in the living room and collapse on the sofa because my stomach has sunk to the bottom of the ocean floor. "I'm sorry, Jill. I'm sorry I haven't been good at staying in touch."

She sighs again from far away. "I understand, you're busy. Have you found anything? Anything at all? I can't sleep, Eve. Knowing there's someone out there who's done this to him. Knowing they could be doing it to someone else as we speak. Please tell me you've found something."

Oh, no. This is the conversation I've been avoiding. "I—I've been working on it. I've gotten the school involved, and they're investigating things. As soon as the investigations are over, I'll let you know what they discovered."

"But you think it's something, right?"

I'm not telling Jill I have a list. A list with Petra, Kendall, Alondra, and Ruben on it. How would I tell her there are quite a few people involved, including her wife? "I think you're his mother, and you knew him better than anyone. And if you think there was foul play involved, then I'll do everything I can to get to the bottom of it."

She's quiet, so I continue. "Jill? Can I ask you a question?"

"Sure."

"What if ... what if you don't like the answer?"

"What do you mean?"

I stand and pace around the coffee table. "What if … what if it's not what you thought? What if it's someone we don't expect? Like, it ends up being someone we trusted, and maybe it's worse than we thought? What if I don't think you can handle it?"

She's silent, and I look at my phone to make sure we're still connected.

"Eve? My son is dead. He's never coming back. There's nothing in this world that someone could tell me that's as horrible as that truth. Everything else … it's just background noise."

We talk until nearly four in the morning, and when we hang up, I feel like I have a mobile of depression in the shape of little circus animals twirling over my head and rocking me into a sound despair. I sneak into Xander's room. He's sprawled out in bed, his pajamas twisted and bunched in the most uncomfortable places, and I brush his hair aside and kiss his sweaty forehead. Biscuit purrs at his head, curled into a ball, and pops her head up when I don't kiss her. So I do, and I thank her for giving my youngest son such happiness.

Then I sneak into Malik's room. I don't care what a giant he is, I'll come in his room when he's sleeping and kiss him whenever I want. He's stretched out on top of his covers, his fan aimed right at his face and he's probably freezing. But when my lips hit his forehead, he's burning up. I back away and look at his face; he looks like he's dreaming. His face is scrunched in concentration, like he's disturbed.

His phone buzzes from his nightstand, and he has it face down, so I see the light brink the edges from whoever just texted him.

Who would text him at four in the morning?

I reach for his phone, but am startled when his entire body jumps, a whimper escaping his lips. I freeze—he's still sound asleep. His face crumples like he's going to cry, or like he is crying, and I don't know what to do. Should I wake him up?

I'm alarmed when his hands make tight fists, the tension in his body manifesting as he writhes on his sheets, his teeth grinding. He's moaning, his head jerking back and forth.

"Malik," I whisper, sitting on his bed and jostling his shoulder. "Baby, wake up. You're dreaming. Malik!"

His breathing regulates and he opens his eyes, darting them around the room before landing on me. "What?" he says in his fog.

"You're dreaming. It's okay. You're here, I'm here, everything's fine." I scoot closer and gather his sweaty, bare chest in my arms. I haven't done this since he was a child.

I hug him, making shhh noises and rocking him. What would've happened if I hadn't come in here? Does he do this often? What's going on with my son? "What were you dreaming about?" I whisper in a voice usually reserved for Xander or Biscuit.

His hand wraps around my back and clings onto my hair. It almost hurts, but I don't say anything. "Jordan," he responds. His body quivers every few seconds.

"You were dreaming about Jordan?"

"Yeah." And now he's officially pulling my hair.

I gently pry his fingers from the roots at my scalp and hold his hand. We haven't discussed Jordan since the funeral. I don't even think he's mourned him yet. I should've had this conversation with him long ago. "It's a very sad thing, Malik. I'm sorry. I wish there was something I could say to make it better. But it's over, and now we just focus on our own lives, and not making the same mistakes Jordan did."

I stop when I realize he's sleeping again; this time he looks calm, his breathing soft and normal. "I love you more than you'll ever know, sweet boy." I plant another kiss on my son's cheek and lie across from him in his queen-sized bed, because if he has another bad dream, I'll be right here to make it better.

28

MALIK

I wake up in the morning to the weirdest thing—my mom is sleeping on the other side of my bed. Then I remember—I was dreaming. I was with Jordan, and we were kids again. We were camping and had pitched a tent. There were no adults, just us.

We were in our sleeping bags, and I guess we were like "screw the tent," 'cause we were lying outside next to a sad, twisty tree, looking at the stars. Jordan kept pointing up at them, talking about each one like they were people, like he knew them personally. Like they were his long-lost family or something.

Every time I looked at the sky, the stars looked different. Sometimes there were tons of them—galaxies, constellations—the whole sky was lit up. Other times, I saw no stars at all. Just pitch black. But he just kept talking about them like they were his best friends.

But then shit got weird. Jordan would call out to them. Talk to them, like he'd talk to me. I'd dart my eyes around our campground, and I realized we were in a forest again—like from my first dream. But check this out—the forest was alive. The trees would move, the ground would shake, and Jordan was in tune with everything. He would interpret shit to me, telling me what the trees were saying. Telling me they were angry. That I had pissed them off, we both had. "Malik, they want to know why we left them? Why did we become these people? The people are evil." Jordan got out of his sleeping bag and came to sit on top of mine. He crossed his legs and stared at me, and suddenly I couldn't move. My sleeping bag was too tight, and Jordan was watching, and the trees and stars were closing in on me, all saying how the people are evil. It was a legion of voices, all coming out of Jordan's mouth. But his mouth wasn't moving.

The people are evil.

Then it changed.

Shooting stars, falling stars. Shooting stars, falling stars.

Then my mom had woken me up. It was the first time I hadn't felt alone in I don't know how long. She talked to me like she did when I was a kid, and it was so comforting I must've fallen right back into a dreamless sleep.

Apparently, she knocked out, too, because she's curled up in the corner of my bed.

Light pours through my blinds, and I know I told them I wasn't going to school today, but shouldn't she be there by now? I reach past her and grab my phone to check the time.

I got another text.

20495278111043310821@libertynet.org: *If she doesn't have the abortion, you will suffer the consequences.*

What the hell? I thought Mrs. Hendrick was fired? Why am I still getting these? It was sent at four in the morning. She sent another video, and I can tell by the still-shot it's another one of aborted babies.

I'm not watching it. My mom's in my freaking bed. Delete ... and ... delete.

THE FALLING OF STARS

I get out of bed and remember I wanted to check the time. It's after nine. She's definitely late. I cross the hall to my parents' room, and Alex is gone. Biscuit meows at me when I peek in Xander's room. I toss my head up at her. "'Sup?"

Ah, geez. I talk to cats now.

Alex wouldn't let Mom oversleep, so she's home for a reason. I'm not waking her up. I move to the kitchen, and there's like this calmness creeping into my gut. It's insane, like I don't even care about Creed's dad or this stupid threat on my phone. I haven't felt this hopeful in forever. Is it because my mom was there in the middle of the night when I needed someone? I feel like it is, but isn't that weird? I should be disturbed that I was rocked to sleep by my mom at age sixteen, but what the hell—I'm a cat whisperer now, too. Whatever it is, I feel human today. I'm hungry, and I haven't felt hungry in weeks. So I pour a massive bowl of cereal.

I think about the text from the weird number. Was I wrong about Mrs. Hendrick? Would Creed have told anyone else about the baby? I decide to text her, make sure she's okay after confessing to her parents. But when I try sending it, a message pops up: *This number is not receiving messages at this time.* Holy hell, she blocked me.

I try to think of this coherently, because I feel like I can. I haven't felt coherent in a while, so now that my brain is making simple connections, I feel like Einstein. I talk myself down, telling myself her dad made her block me, and she'd never do this on her own. I need to make sure she's okay, but I don't know how. Then my mom comes staggering out, looking like a zombie.

"Hi," she slurs as she moves to the Keurig.

I chuckle. "Hey. Not going to work today?"

She shakes her head as the machine comes to life and makes the kitchen smell like coffee.

"Why not?" I say through a mouthful of Corn Pops.

She turns to me. "You're sick. I'm staying home with you today." She smiles and winks through her sleepy stupor, and I can't help laughing. Her hair looks like someone jumped in a bale of hay, froze it, and stuck it on her head. And she's got this huge line down her face, running from her forehead, through her eye and down her cheek.

"My bed is pretty comfortable, huh?" I joke.

She pours creamer in her coffee and joins me at the island. "Sorry, I must have fallen asleep in your bed when you were dreaming. You scared me. How often do you have these dreams?"

I shrug and push the cereal away. "It's happened a couple times now."

She's staring at me. Her gaze is piercing through my temple and penetrating my brain, and I'm scared she can see the haunted insane asylum my mind is. I turn my eyes to hers, and it's like the world's...

Biggest...

Epiphany.

She was pregnant at our age. She's experienced this. She was in Creed's shoes! And she's fine! Oh, my god— I'm telling her. I've experienced rock bottom, there's nowhere to go from here but up. She's going to fix this, she's gonna save my life. *I'm telling her!*

I can feel the weight lifting off my shoulders as I determine how to drop this coincidental-but-not-hilariously-so bomb.

"Mom, can I ask you something?"

She leans toward me. "Always."

"Can we talk about when you got pregnant with me?" I look at her, and her face has contorted into a haunted insane asylum of its own. She leans back—away from me—and her eyes are on her coffee, but not on her coffee.

"Mom?"

She tosses glances at me, but she can't maintain eye contact. I'd tease her and tell her she's being a hypocrite, but she's kinda scaring me.

"Have you—have you heard anything about it recently? At school?"

"What? School?"

"Oh, man. I've brought this on myself." She totally just whispered that to herself. Then she blinks, her eyes refocusing and landing on me—like, urgently. "Malik? I've never lied to you, okay? What have I told you about your biological dad?"

I shrug, kinda regretting going this route. "Um, not much. That he's dead. Multiracial with light eyes. Maybe from South America?"

She nods. "All that is true. They don't know where his dad was from, but he was born and raised in Kentucky where his mom was from. And he died when you were two."

Her eyes are filling with tears, and I'm feeling really bad for bringing this up now. "I'm sorry. Do you miss him, or something? Did you love him?" I ask.

Tears drip off her chin, her lip is quivering. God, what have I opened?

She shakes her head violently. "Oh, god, I don't know how to say this. Your dad was executed. The day he died was one of the happiest days of my life."

I'm so confused, I don't even know what to say. "What did he do? Did he kill someone? Did he hurt you?"

Tears stream down her face. One, after another, after another...

And any renewed hope I felt this morning is being shattered eight thousand times by a goddamn sledgehammer. "Were you raped? Mom? Am I a product of rape?"

She reaches a shaky hand to wipe her face. "I was sixteen. He was nineteen. He attacked me one night and would've killed me if I hadn't gotten away. Other girls weren't so lucky."

But I don't wanna hear this. I must've shoved the cereal bowl across the island, because it smashes on the floor. "Are you fucking kidding me? You never told me this? You never told anyone? You just let everyone think you got knocked up by your boyfriend in high school? Do you know the jokes I've had to listen to my entire life about what a whore you are?"

She doesn't even bat an eyelash. "I don't care what people think of me. I was never trying to protect myself, Malik. I was trying to protect *you*."

As my heart is shattering, so many other things are falling into place. That's why my grandparents hated me; that's why she doesn't speak to them. I really have been a charity case to Alex all these years, and that's why he's so fucking strict—he thinks I'm gonna go out and start raping people because I have rape DNA. Oh, my god—I'm the son of a serial rapist and murderer. I'm gonna throw up.

I am the product of the worst thing that could ever happen to a woman.

A man raped a teenager one night, and that's why I exist.

I'm an abomination.

She must think about it every time she looks at me.

I'm rape personified.

This is why I've always felt I don't belong in this world. Because I don't.

I should've never been born.

My existence is disgusting.

She's talking, but I've no clue what she's saying. I can't believe she kept this from me all these years. I storm to my room and throw on a shirt, grabbing my keys and stepping into my slides. She's followed me, still talking. She stops when I turn around and look at her. "I always thought you were a whore, but you're just a damn liar." I push past her and her face is falling, and I hate myself for saying that because none of this is her fault and she didn't ask for this, but neither did I and she could have told me.

She chases me out of the house in tears, begging for forgiveness, insisting she loves me, asking where I'm going, what I'm doing, but I just jump in my car and leave.

My headlights sprawl across my house at one in the morning. It's such a cute little thing, our house—with the palm trees and the landscaping and the plantation shutters ... it's fucking hell. Fuck this place and fuck the people inside it.

I went to the beach. It was a dumb idea; it's not like you can "get away" in Miami. There's no place to just step back from all the bullshit and traffic and concrete and heat and pissed-off people. They're everywhere.

So yeah, I went to the beach. Walked through the shitty sand and nasty seaweed. I walked. And walked. And walked. I waited for something, someone—a sign, an angel—anything to offer some hope. I even looked to the planes flying above pulling the banners. They all advertised a new night club, and not one of them said *Jesus Loves You* or anything.

My skin felt heavy, my bones dense, the blood pumping through my veins pointless busywork. I was a large, piece-of-shit mass taking up space on that beach, crushing perfectly good sand with every step, gulping air I had no business breathing. I walked, apologizing to the earth for occupying it, for being a blasphemy to its existence.

I kept thinking, I could just walk out into the ocean and never come back...

But now here I am, in front of my house and wishing I did let the ocean swallow me up.

I go inside, ready to be attacked by Alex so I can punch him. But everyone's asleep. No one cares that I've been missing almost an entire day.

On the way to my room, I hear whimpering from behind Xander's door. I stop for a sec and listen. He's definitely crying. I tap on his door and open it, and he's sitting on the edge of his bed with his face in his chubby little hands. I sit next to him and hug the little guy. "Hey, Little Dude? What's wrong?"

"Biscuit's gone," he sobs.

"What? What happened to Biscuit?"

Snot's running out his nose, and I look for a tissue before it gets on my shirt. "I don't know. When we got home from school, I looked for her, and I can't find her anywhere."

I'm glancing around his room, searching for glowing cat eyes under a pile of clothes or toys or furniture. "She's gotta be around here someplace, buddy. Don't worry. We'll find her."

Xander shakes his head frantically. "We looked everywhere. We even laid her favorite treats around the house. We looked outside and inside, and Dad posted pictures of her online and nobody's called." He hiccups, and the snot. It's on me now.

"Hey, bud. We'll find her, okay? I promise. But it's super late, and you should be sleeping. You shouldn't be sitting here crying all alone like this. Let's lie down, okay?"

He snorts up his snot and complies. "Will you lay with me, Malik?"

"Sure." Even though I have no idea how I'm going to fit in his twin bed. I scoot in next to him, my ass hanging off, and I have to tighten every muscle in my body to keep from falling.

I look at his little face when his eyes close, and he looks like one of those fat little cherubs on Valentine cards. "Hey, Xander?"

"Hmm?"

"Promise me something, okay? Promise you'll never sit here, crying all alone like this again. You have people who love you. You're never alone."

"'Kay."

I wait until he's asleep before leaving, and you'd think I'd be hurt that he was so upset over a missing cat, and not a missing brother. But I'm not. In fact, it gives me an eerie sense of peace. He won't miss me. He'll be okay.

I go in my room and log onto LibertyNet, I don't really know why. I think I just want to remember what it was like to be a normal kid. A kid whose biggest worries were football, schoolwork, girls, and not getting grounded by my dad.

I want to message Creed, but there's no trace of her name. She's blocked me here, too.

A message pops up from him/her/it, and I'm surprisingly relieved because it's the first time someone's reached out to me today.

You didn't watch the video I sent last night, did you?

Great. I've pissed off the only guy/girl/thing that cares about me. *No, my mom was in the room.*

Him: *Creed hasn't gotten the abortion. I told you there'd be consequences.*

Me: *She blocked me. I have no way to get ahold of her.*

Him: *You entered the game at your own discretion. You knew there'd be consequences to failing. And you failed this.*

Me: *So now what?*

Him: *They already happened. Your consequences.*

My heart's beating kinda faster. *What did you do?*

Him: *Meow.*

My breaths are choppy and I'm pissed. He broke into my house and hurt my brother by taking his cat? *What the hell did you do with my brother's cat? He's sitting in his room bawling.*

Him: *You hurt the ones you love, Malik. That's all you ever do. Every decision you make impacts your family, and you always let them down. You are a failure.*

My throat tightens. He's right. Again. *Did you kill the cat?*

Him: *No, but I can. And I won't stop there, if you keep failing.*

Me: *What can I do for you to give my brother back his cat?*

Him: *We haven't even gotten to the ultimate part of the game. You still have a chance to save everyone and everything that matters. But you have to realize what does and doesn't matter. It's time to choose what type of star you are. Imagine that every person in the world is a star. That's what we are, Malik. In the grand scheme of things, we're celestial stars, lighting the way, bringing joy and awe to others, writing myths and legends in our constellations. Leaving our marks in the sky.*

I think about my dreams with Jordan and shiver—they always involved stars.

But there are some people—like you—who are shooting stars, falling stars.

He stops. I'm not getting any more messages. So I type back: *What do you mean?*

Him: *First, tell me. What's the difference between a shooting star and a falling star?*

I cheat and Google it. *They're the same thing.*

Him: *Wrong.*

I toss my hands up and let them fall to the desk. Now he's gonna kill the cat or something.

Him: *Have you ever seen a shooting star? A falling star?*

Me: *Yes. When I was little, and we lived on a farm in the Redlands. Stars were a lot clearer out there without all the city lights.*

Him: *What did you think of it?*

Me: *Idk, I'm sure I thought it was cool or something.*

Him: *Why?*

Me: *Because it's a star that's moving across the sky. And it was super bright. All the other stars just stay in one spot and aren't as bright.*

Him: *So would you say being a shooting star is more special than being a celestial star?*

THE FALLING OF STARS

Great, now he's trying to cheer me up. I humor him and type: *Yeah, I guess.*

Him: *Wrong.*

Mother—

Him: *They aren't even really stars at all. They're dust. That's all you are, Malik. You're not an eternal flame in the sky, like other stars. Your existence is meant to be an instant—just a few seconds worth of a flash of light. You're a meteoroid falling toward Earth and burning up. Everyone else is an eternal, celestial star. You are just dust. Falling. You like to fall, right?*

Breathing hurts. Existing hurts.

Him: *You are the product of rape.*

The bones of my soul shatter. I burst into tears.

Him: *You and Jordan were very similar. He was a shooting star. He understood it, he accepted it. Now, Malik—you get to choose. Will you be a shooting star? Or will you be a falling star? That's the last question in this game. Go to your Instagram profile.*

With fingers that don't feel like mine, I click the icon on my phone. All my posts are gone. Like they never existed. Like *I* never existed. I message him back: *My profile is empty.*

Him: *Yup. Just like your life. It's a symbol of what you are, and what you will be. Your light is about to go out. Your existence soon will perish. All that's left will be memories. Go into your photos.*

I audibly swear when I click on them and there's nothing. He remotely accessed my phone and deleted all my photos. A message pops up before I can even respond:

Your phone is an empty shell of what you once were. So is your body. Your mission is set. Will you be a shooting star? Or a falling star? You need to decide the difference, and you need to become one of them. Once you decide, you will save everything. Your family. Your baby. Your brother's cat. You will win. Do it. Soon.

He logs off. I look back at my phone, and a strange peace floods over me. He's been right about everything. I've known for a while that my life isn't like everyone else's, my existence just a glitch in the overall quest of the universe and humanity. I navigate to my text messages and delete them all. I don't use Twitter or Snapchat, but I delete them off my phone.

I stopped wishing for death once I realized I was living it. If this is life, I'd rather not. I'll be doing everyone a favor by ending it all. I've done nothing but bring heartache to every single person in my life. I let my football team down a long time ago. Creed—the one girl I actually liked—I was horny and selfish, and I destroyed her. My brother is cute, but all he needs is a cat. He doesn't need a depressing older brother, someone he has no business looking up to. My parents can have another kid, then Xander can be the older brother. He'd be a great big brother. And Alex has given enough of his life reforming me and making sure I don't turn into the rapist my real dad was. He has Xander—his biological son. And my mom, well, it's pretty obvious she never wanted me. I am a living, breathing reminder of the worst day of her life. She can have her parents back, her family, and she can go on living without the sickening abomination that I am.

He's giving me time to decide, but I already know. Jordan was a shooting star, but me? I love gravity.

29

EVE

I can't stop crying. What have I done? What is wrong with me? I had to go crazy and tell everyone I was raped, and I assumed they figured Malik was the product. So when he brought it up this morning, I freaked out and thought someone told him.

I should've never told him. I should've told him a long time ago. What is the right answer, here?

I text Alex the moment Malik leaves, after he said those horrible things, which I completely deserved.

CALL ME ASAP.

The call comes an hour later, during his break.

"Alex, I messed up. I told Malik I was raped."

He doesn't say anything, and I can picture him slamming his palm into his forehead like I've caused him to do so often. "Eve, what is wrong with you? You've been doing the weirdest, most impulsive things lately. Why would you tell him that when he's already been so out of it?"

I grit my teeth and hop in place. "Ugh, I don't know. He asked me about it, which he hasn't done since before you. And I just told him. He left, Alex. I don't know where he went. But he's so mad at me." I start crying again.

"It's okay. He's not going far. He just needs to get away, and I don't blame him. Give me one second. I'm going to track his phone."

"Okay." I wait a few moments.

"He's heading east on the 836 about to get on 395 toward the MacArthur Causeway. It looks like he's going to the beach."

I huff a huge sigh. "You think that's all he's doing? You think he's with anyone?"

"I'm sure he's by himself, hon. All his friends are here—Javier, Tyler, CJ—even all the girls." I hear his smile through the phone, but I'm getting another call.

"Alex, I gotta go. Bye." It's Ruben DeSoto. What the hell does this guy possibly have to say? Curiosity wins; I answer. "What?"

"I'm under investigation now because of you, Eve. How dare you accuse me of this?"

I feel my lip curling into a snarl. "You're the only one with an admin account, Ruben! You mirrored my computer. You made sure every computer in the school had that software so you could pin anything on anyone. You're the king of IT in this place, and it was you."

"You think I'm guilty? I'll prove to you now that I'm not."

I smirk. "How?"

"I'm at the school. I've been here all night, hacking into my own system to see what the heck is going on. I've found some realllllly interesting things."

"We aren't supposed to be at the school. We're on leave. So it just seems you don't care much about rules, regulations, and protocol."

"Can you shut your damn mouth and get down here? Do you want to see what I've found or not? We're talking about someone cyberbullying a teenager into committing suicide. This is serious. And I have a feeling this is still going on."

I swallow and consider all this. I don't trust him. But he's right—this is serious. "If I come down there, I'm coming in the backdoor. I don't want anyone seeing me."

"Do whatever you need to do, but if Jordan's mom is looking for proof that someone cyberbullied her son, I've struck gold."

I was planning to shave my legs today, but screw it. I take the world's quickest shower and throw on a pair of jeans, rock a bun and BB cream, and Uber to the school. I can't risk anyone seeing my car or recognizing me.

I tell the Uber driver I'll give him an extra tip if he sits in the parking lot for a few minutes while I crouch down and wait for the enrollment director, Mrs. Chavez, help Mrs. Steinson carry boxes from her car. Then there's the groundskeeper, Mr. Wilmur, taking trash bags to the receptacle and hauling around a rake. Mother-loving rake.

But after a few minutes, I realize the Uber driver doesn't speak English. He's looking around nervously, making more of a scene than if I were to just get out and walk normally. I slip out of the car, hunching over and scampering toward the door leading to Ruben's office.

But when I step inside, he's standing there holding a knife.

I freeze. "What are you doing?"

He holds it up and cocks his head, trying to look like a mafia hitman, but he just looks like a fat guy with a crooked head holding a knife. "What? You're the only one with trust issues? You want me dead, Eve. I know it. I want to make sure you're not armed." He takes a step toward me, spinning the handle of the knife.

My body starts shaking when I realize he's going to frisk me. "Ruben, so help me God, if you put your hands on me, I will—"

"Relax, I'm not going to touch you. You've made your scene, I get it. Just set your purse down there by the door." He uses his knife as a pointing device now, aiming it at the door like I don't know it's the freaking door.

I look at him suspiciously. "Why would I do that? Guns aren't allowed on school premises."

"Did Jordan Sawyer die as a result of this school?"

"I believe so, yes."

"What did the autopsy report say again as to how he died?"

"Gunshot wound to the head."

"Set your purse down over there." He gestures toward the door again.

I roll my eyes. "That's stupid reasoning. Just look in my purse. Ignore the tampons." I open my purse, and now his knife is being used as a prodding device. "You're an ass," I say when he finds no guns or deadly weapons.

"Give me a piece of that gum, and we'll call it even."

I throw a stick of Trident at him and march toward his computer. "What did you find?"

And now I have to listen to him smacking on gum, and I swear his jaw never stops masticating shit. He sits at his desk and maneuvers his mouse. "I went back to when Jordan first enrolled here. Back when I created his account. I've tried reviving everything he's ever done, especially in the chat." He whistles. "That boy talked to a lot of girls, if you know what I mean."

"Ruben, please."

"Right. Anyway, it was like two weeks into school when these weird numbers started reaching out to him."

"You mean the one from that text I showed you?"

"That's the thing!" Ruben twists his chair until he's facing me, holding up an "ah-ha" finger. "That's just one of many eighteen-digit numbers that reached out to him. She would have one conversation with Jordan, then the account would be deleted immediately. So Jordan never had a conversation with the same profile twice."

"She?"

He gives me a bored expression. "Alondra Hendrick."

"Oh, right. Ugh. Do you have any cigarettes?"

His face scrunches, making his mustache look like a pencil sketch of an inchworm. "Gross! You smoke? I never pegged you as a smoker."

"I'm sorry, I can't hear you over all that ketchup on your shirt. You said something about gross?"

His face flattens, killing his worm 'stache. "Anyway! Back to Alondra—she knew exactly what she was doing, because it's a lot harder for me to trace a gazillion different profiles with eighteen different digits as the username. So far, I can only go by what comes up when I check the history of Jordan's profile."

"So what did *she* say to him that makes you think she's the reason he killed himself?"

"Get a load of this—"

Ruben's door swings open, and Alex spills in the room. "Eve! What are you doing here?" He jerks his head toward Ruben. "You're both on leave! You're not supposed to be on this campus."

"How did you know I was here?" I ask.

"Apparently, half the staff saw you sitting in an Uber for like ten minutes." Alex shoves Ruben's shoulder. "And your car is sitting in the parking lot. What the hell is the matter with both of you? Ruben, you're under investigation, so the fact that you're here in your office, tampering with all this is not going to bode well for you. Get out. Now!"

Ruben shuts down his computer and silently trots to the door like a dog with his tail between his legs, the latch clicking behind him. He even left his phone on the desk.

Alex turns his frantic eyes to me. "You cannot be here conspiring with this guy and end up being guilty by association. Just get your ass home, Eve! Now! They're coming!"

"Who?" I ask as he's pushing me toward the door.

"Security! I heard Mrs. Steinson and Mrs. Chavez and Mr. Wilmur telling the security staff. God! You're the worst sneaky person I've ever met in my life!" He grabs my hand and hauls me toward the door.

"Alex, I don't have a car to get home!"

He halts. "Sweet Baby Jesus. Here." He shoves his keys in my hand. "I'll Uber home, too, I guess. And pick up Xander at dismissal, for the love of Christ!" He slams the door behind us.

I'm practically running, trying to keep up with his fast pace toward his car. I hit his key fob and he opens the door, lowers me into the seat, and slams the door, sprinting back to the building. I hightail out of the parking lot before any security guards or tattletales catch me. I'm never going to find out what happened to Jordan.

Alex keeps sending me updates on Malik's whereabouts throughout the day, riddled with quips about tracking my phone, as well. I pick Xander up from school, and when we get home, he's screaming about his cat within five minutes.

"Mommy! Biscuit's gone! I can't find her anywhere!"

We look and we look and we look. The damn cat has disappeared.

Then Alex gets home and we fight. We fight and we fight and we fight, and at midnight I can't take any more. I take an Ambien and knock the hell out.

I wake up early the next morning, and the stress picks up right where it left off. I need to make sure Malik made it home. I run to his room, and tears rush to my eyes when I see him sleeping in his bed. *This can get fixed, Eve. It can. Just breathe...*

THE FALLING OF STARS

Then I peek in on Xander, who's also knocked out. My heart breaks because there's no kitten snuggling with him. Biscuit was like his security blanket. I quietly shut the door and go to the kitchen, plopping on a barstool with my head in my hands.

So much has happened the last few weeks, and I've let it spiral out of control. I need to step back and organize my priorities. Priorganize. Why doesn't Alex see what a wonderful word that is?

I hear a door open, and my heart flutters. It's Malik. I jump off the barstool and rush to him. "Malik, baby, you scared me. I'm so sorry about yesterday, I—"

He waves his hands to cut me off. "Don't worry about it, Mom. I was just surprised, that's all. I'm sorry for the mean things I said. Let's not talk about it, okay?"

The only move I make outside of the erratic blinking is my mouth slowly morphing from hanging open to twisting into a stupid grin. This seems too good to be true. Malik is forgiving me? He's accepting the horror I gave him yesterday as to why he's even on this earth? I thought we'd need to go to counseling—talk to a therapist, at minimum. But he's okay and he's not mad, and my eyes are filling with tears as I hug his waist.

He hugs me back, and I feel my first glimmer of hope. I've screwed up a lot the last few weeks, but I've priorganized, and this weekend will be all family. I can't think about Jordan, Jill, Petra, or Ruben. Every breath I take will be devoted toward my children and husband.

30

EVE

It's Sunday, and I get a call that I'm to report back to school Monday. My initial thought is to start plotting—going to Ruben's office, talking to Jeremiah, getting to the bottom of this insanity. But this weekend has been so relaxing and healing, I decide to milk the last few hours.

It was Malik's idea to take Xander to the animal shelter and let him rescue a kitten yesterday. He picked out a white one and named it Snow. Malik's been so calm and content; it's like he's back to his old self. I'm so happy. My heart is full. For the first time in a long time.

Alex redeems himself three-fold by sneaking into the shower with me well after the boys are sleeping. Any lingering animosity rinses down the drain while my eyes close, my head tilting as his mouth brushes my neck. His whispers send chills across my skin, despite the scalding water.

He slowly peels my wet hair from my shoulders. "Eve, you are my everything."

My undoing.

I don't remember getting out of the shower, but we obviously did because we've continued our sexcapade in bed, rolling in the sheets until they're a mangled heap on the floor.

Needless to say, I'm well-rested when my alarm goes off Monday morning.

I'm nervous to see Jeremiah. I'm embarrassed that I keep having outbursts, enough to get me a leave of absence. But he's not at school this morning; at least, I don't see him. So I go about my day, and no one mentions my absence Friday. At lunch, I get a text from Alex: *Come to Ruben's office after school. Immediately.*

And now my day's ruined.

Of course, the remainder of the day crawls by, and the moment the bell rings, I start journeying toward the other side of Lafayette Hall toward Ruben's office. My heart's pounding right along with the clicking of my heels.

It's quiet at this end of the building—so quiet, I can hear both their voices coming from his office. I strain to hear the words, but I can't decipher them. Just as I'm about to enter the room, another set of footsteps echoes through the hallway, and I turn to see Roy Leeman, the Head of Security, approaching. I stop and stare at him, completely caught off guard.

"Mrs. Hunter, you're wanted in a board meeting immediately."

"Excuse me?"

"Mr. Lorrey has called an emergency board meeting, and you're to be in attendance."

I place my hand over my heart and begin walking away from Ruben's office toward the boardroom. "Oh, my gosh. Is it about the LibertyNet hack? Did he find more information?"

"I believe so, Mrs. Hunter."

I fall silent as my head spins. This is it. I'm finally going to find out what happened and give Jill some closure. Justice will be served, demons can be put to rest.

THE FALLING OF STARS

We exit Lafayette Hall and head toward The Easton Building. A huge crack of thunder erupts overhead, and the winds are blowing like crazy. Thank goodness there's overhang along the walkways, or I'd be drenched in this sudden downpour. "Wow, where did this come from?" I shout over the noise of the storm.

"Tropical depression," Roy answers.

"This is more like a hurricane." I jog the rest of the way, as quickly as I can in heels and a pencil skirt. We finally enter the foyer of The Easton Building, and Roy continues to escort me to the boardroom entrance. "Thank you, Roy. I've got it from here."

But he grabs the handle and opens it for me.

"Th—thank you."

I step inside and glance at the circular mahogany desk. Jeremiah's seated in his center spot, and the rest of the seats are filled with the usual faculty and staff, minus Alex's and Ruben's seats, but I know where they are. They're all looking at me with a hint of irritation.

I clear my throat and scurry toward my seat next to Jeremiah. "Sorry I'm late. I was just informed of this meeting. Did you want Alex and—"

"Mrs. Hunter," Jeremiah interrupts.

I halt halfway to my seat.

He gestures in front of him. "Please. Take your place at the podium."

I jerk my eyes toward the podium of condemnation and turn back to him. "Excuse me?"

He nods toward it this time, his hands back in their usual folded position. "I kindly ask you to take your place behind the podium."

I gaze back and forth between the podium and the circular table of coworkers, their eyes critical and judgmental. Much how mine probably looked when Kendall Dupree and others walked this same path. But what's happening? What did I do?

I look to Alex and Ruben's chairs—glaringly empty. "Shouldn't we wait for—"

"Mrs. Hunter! Everyone is present. Now please. Take your place behind the podium."

I swallow and scan the room again before acquiescing, my movements labored as I do the walk of shame. I approach the podium and stare down at the surface, wondering how many others have pictured themselves throwing up on it, like I'm doing now.

Jeremiah clears his throat. "Mrs. Hunter, it seems you have been participating in activities that are against policy here at Liberty School of Excellence, and you are hereby subjected to employee discipline, the severity to be determined by the present board members, and if decided, can result in dismissal from our staff."

"*What?*" This has to be a joke. Where are Ruben and Alex? They must be in on it—this is Alex punishing me for coming to the school Friday, Ruben's revenge for blowing his cover. I'm gonna kill them both.

He retrieves a folder from his briefcase. "The first incident dates back nearly a month, when a staff member witnessed you sneaking into the personnel file and tampering with Mrs. Hendrick's file."

My jaw drops as I remember Mrs. Steinson walking in on me with Alondra's file. I pan across the semicircle until I find her. "You saw that?"

She diverts her eyes as a hushed murmur spreads amongst the staff, and Jeremiah speaks over them. "Is that an admission to this accusation?"

"That's ridiculous. Alondra was under investigation, I was just trying to help."

"Mrs. Hunter, an employee's files are confidential, and may only be viewed upon permission from upper management. Now, did you receive permission to look in her file?"

"Why are you just now bringing this up? That was weeks ago."

"Please answer the question. Did you receive permission?"

I toss my hands out and slap them on the podium. "No, I didn't." Then everyone in the room starts scribbling on their stupid papers.

"The next incident happened shortly after, when you attacked an employee right here in this room."

"*What?*"

"There are many witnesses present who can confirm that you accosted Miss Dupree, putting your hands around her neck in a violent manner, intent to do bodily harm. Right in the precise spot you're standing, as a matter of fact."

This is a joke, for sure. I start laughing, but stop when nobody joins in. "Mr. Lorrey, with all due respect, you and I have had many one-on-one conversations since both of these incidents, and not once have you mentioned this." I scan the room again, pointing at each person sitting in their judgment seats. "You were all here, you saw the situation. Kendall Dupree was a sex predator who cost Jordan Sawyer his life. And if that's not enough reason to accost someone, she then tried twisting the situation by making herself a victim."

I turn back to Jeremiah, who's tapping his pen on his lips. "Are you quite through?"

I nod. "Yes. Again, you were all—"

"So is this an admittance to the second accusation?"

I look at him sideways. "You know I had my hands around her neck, you were the one to pry me off. And I'd do it again. So in short—*hell,* yes."

Down go the pens, scratching across the papers.

I grit my teeth and clench the sides of the podium, wishing I could shoot laser beams from my eyes as I pan across the god-forsaken circular desk.

Jeremiah makes a meal of sorting through the thousands of papers in my file, and pulls out another one.

"Mrs. Hunter, is it true you were on this campus Friday while on leave?"

"Yes."

Scratch, scratch.

"Is it true you accused Mr. DeSoto of cyberbullying Jordan Sawyer—shortly after you accused Mrs. Hendrick of the same act—by participating in another outburst during a staff meeting, the only evidence you had being that he had remotely accessed your computer, and you found that to be suspicious?"

"Yes."

Scratch, scratch.

He strums his fingers on the table. "You seem to have a pattern of annihilating the careers and reputations of your coworkers. You meddled in many affairs for which you were unauthorized, and yet your meddling was ultimately the demise of three employees at this establishment."

Three? That must mean he fired Ruben. Good. I give him a dirty look. "You're welcome. None of them should've been employed here. And if somebody was doing his due diligence during the hiring process, maybe he could have avoided hiring these deplorable people altogether, and I could have stayed in my room and focused on teaching English and literature instead of doing his job for him."

A few snickers leak throughout the room, and even Jeremiah looks a bit taken back. "Touché, Mrs. Hunter," he says with a grin. "I would ... agree with these sentiments you so vehemently expressed, if not for one. Small. Detail."

"What?"

"This behavior straddles the line between keen observance and utter insanity. Both extremes are admirable, in their own ways, but motive is the ultimate factor here. And the question begs, what was your motive?"

"To find out if someone was cyberbullying Jordan Sawyer."

He cocks his head in the other direction. "So Liberty School of Excellence has never been your ... target?"

"Target?"

"Mrs. Hunter, the day your son fell down the stairs and was taken to the hospital, I overheard a conversation you had with Jordan Sawyer's stepmom in the cafeteria regarding her filing a lawsuit against the school. You said, and I quote: *I don't care, either way. She has every right to file a lawsuit against them, and I'll still support her.*"

"Finish the quote, goddammit!" I scream over the gasps throughout the room, slamming my fists on the podium. "I said I hoped she didn't!"

He's nodding, like he's got me right where he wants me. "So, you've just admitted to saying that. You're not going to deny this accusation? It's your word against mine. There is no paper trail, security footage... Just one man's word against yours."

That little fucker. He tricked me. He purposely omitted part of what I said so I couldn't deny it altogether. I've already stuck my foot in my mouth. Already dug my grave. Pens are scribbling, heads are shaking, and where the hell are Alex and Ruben?

"You see, Mrs. Hunter, that one small confession paints a whole other picture as to why you continue to sabotage employees here at Liberty. It seems your intention is to uncover anything you can about this fine establishment and ruin our reputation through scandal."

"That's ridiculous. I've worked here for ten years, and I've been nothing but loyal to this school. I met my husband here, I have my son here, I—"

He holds up a hand. "This is a democracy, Mrs. Hunter. You are innocent until proven guilty. So, as per regulations, those present will vote on the extent of your discipline, and the ruling will be as such."

This is bullshit. Kendall Dupree fucked students, Alondra Hendrick was a druggie who lied on her resume and "counseled" Jordan to death, and I'm being treated like a murderer. And there's absolutely nothing I can do. I'm rendered useless as I stand here and watch them scribble away and fold their papers and pass them to Jeremiah, who opens each one and records the verdict.

It's all finished within five minutes. "Mrs. Hunter, the board votes that you shall receive the maximum penalty for these acts, and has convicted you guilty for defamation of the school's character. As of today, you are no longer an employee here at Liberty School of Excellence."

31

MALIK

It's better this way. Everyone may think they're sad at first—I mean, no one likes teenage funerals—but they'll come to see I did the right thing. Creed can keep the baby; Xander will get his cat back. I'll make everyone's lives perfect again.

It's exhausting, the constant war in my head. And no one knows. Nobody sees that my body hates me. You always hear that suicidal people are self-loathing, but I don't hate myself—my*self* hates *me*. My body won't let me die. My heart keeps beating, the blood keeps pumping, all feeding into the never-ending torture my mind reels day in and day out. Nothing is connected, nothing makes sense.

I've tried the self-help crap. Doesn't work. I've read the articles on Twenty-Five Ways to Beat Depression, and they're cool and all, but they're not for me. Those are for people with normal minds, people who are salvageable. My mind is dead. It's like reading an article on all these ways to deal with diabetes, but if you don't have diabetes, you can only be happy for everyone who does and reads the article.

It's storming on top of Lafayette Hall like crazy, but that's okay. I feel the rain and the wind. I'll never feel storms like this again, not even inside my head. That'll be nice.

But that's the difference between the storm and me. The storm has a purpose. The storm belongs here. I don't. I'm the bit of dirt flying through the universe among all the celestial beings—I'm disguised as a star. I don't belong, I never have.

I step up onto the ledge, and my stomach flips. I step back down, but only for a second. I chide myself—who am I kidding? Every atom that makes up my being is a waste. I apologize to my hands every day. The fingernails that continue to grow, the fingers that are so intricately designed with bones and muscles and tendons and ligaments—what a waste they are. These hands can throw a football fifty yards, and yet can grope a girl's body and destroy her life.

If my stomach flips, it has no right to. It's just a bag inside a rotting corpse. I step back onto the ledge. My stomach doesn't flip as much. I push my toe to the edge, and realize I'm wearing old-school Jordans. How symbolic. I wonder if anyone's ever died in old-school Jordans? I wonder what condition they'll be in when I hit the bottom…

Enough of this. It's time. I've memorized his instructions he sent at four this morning, and I'm on the second-to-last one—the Instagram post. I've found the perfect photo. With shaking hands, I post it with the hashtag, then power off my phone.

Now for the last step. Ha! Pun intended. I push my toe out farther until my whole foot is dangling over the edge. I feel good about this.

Jordan was a shooting star. But I'm a falling star. And no one chases a falling star. No one even remembers a falling star.

32

EVE

I can't even wrap my head around this.

What just happened? I just got fired for no reason. Where's my husband? I'm frozen in shock.

Jeremiah dismisses the meeting, and just as people are standing, the backdoor bursts open and uniformed officers pile into the room.

Oh, my god. They're going to arrest me.

My hands immediately go in the air as the officers march toward me, but my confusion skyrockets when they continue past me and head toward the circular table. My panicked gaze pans across the room—there are six officers total. One standing at each of the three entrances, one approaching the front of the table, and two moving behind it.

The one in front is dressed as a civilian, but the badge around his neck doesn't play. He's the one who speaks. "Jeremiah Lorrey, you are under arrest for murder in the first degree and conspiracy to commit murder for directing the death of Jordan Sawyer. You have the right to remain silent. You have the right to an attorney…"

I don't hear anything else; I'm on my knees. Heaving. Falling forward. Forehead on the floor. I'm going to be sick.

Even when Alex puts his blazer around my shoulders, I can't stop shaking. He's rubbing my arms as we sit in Ruben's office.

The frenzy has died down; Jeremiah's been taken to the station. Two detectives are questioning Alex and Ruben—who both managed to uncover the whole conspiracy.

Detective Solis is the smaller of the two, and he's sitting at Ruben's computer while Detective Campos stands behind him. Solis pauses, listening to the Bluetooth in his ear, then turns to Ruben. "He used a key logger to obtain your password, Mr. DeSoto. They just found it in his office now."

Ruben sighs. He hasn't stopped rubbing his mustache. "I knew it. It's the easiest, most foolproof way. I've got the system protected against brute force, but the guy's a genius. He could've created LibertyNet himself. He worked it like a three-p.m. hooker! I think he only kept me around as a scapegoat. Same with Alondra. People to blame when shit hit the fan."

"So what happened?" I ask.

Alex massages my shoulders. "He hacked into Alondra's files and read the notes on the students she was counseling. He found the weakest one—Jordan Sawyer— and used the issues Jordan divulged to her to manipulate him and gain control over him."

"How was he doing that?" Campos asks.

THE FALLING OF STARS

Ruben points at me. "This girl figured that out. He was remotely accessing Alondra's computer and doing all his dirty work through her machine. Creating fake accounts and deleting them shortly after making contact with the victim, making them harder to trace. So if someone was adamant about tracing them far enough—" he turns to me again, shaking his finger and grinning— "it would point back to Alondra's computer, making it look like she was capitalizing on Jordan's secrets and bullying him into suicide."

"How did you trace it back to Jeremiah?" I ask.

"Now that took some thinking," Ruben says proudly, interlacing his fingers behind his neck and giving us a front-row view of his pit stains. "A lot was involved, but the main thing had to do with timing. Jordan was getting these messages at four a.m. So I had to go through each device and see which was active at those hours of the morning."

I lean forward. "Hang on, did you say he was sending Jordan messages at four in the morning?"

"Yup!" Ruben claps.

"Why did he do all this?" Campos asks.

Ruben gestures to Alex for this one. Alex stands and begins pacing the room. "If there was any doubt that Jeremiah Lorrey was the person behind all this, it's squashed with this." He leans across Solis and navigates to something on the computer. "A manifesto."

"Shut up," I say.

"It's five pages long," Ruben hoots. "Eerily, it looks a lot like the school's mission statement."

Alex continues. "The gist was that this school was founded upon *perfection*. The humans that represent the Liberty Lords shall be of the highest tier of humanity. Anyone who would sully the good name of Liberty by being worthless to society—like Jordan, according to him, since he was depressed, underprivileged, and had an alternative home life—wasn't worthy of the status it upholds, and he felt he was—are you ready for this?—'cleansing the earth of waste.'"

Those of us sitting lean back. Those standing step back. Someone does a low whistle.

"That's some messed-up psycho stuff," Campos says.

"That's why he was in such a hurry to fire you, Eve. You were on to him. He knew you would eventually blow his cover. He fired Alondra, thinking you'd leave things alone, but then you started saying it was me, and he just needed to take you out at that point. You were relentless." Ruben cackles like a hyena.

It's the relentlessness that kills us.

But my mind is still whirling. "If he had this … this manifesto, does that mean he's doing this to more kids? I mean, he didn't do all this just for little freshman Jordan Sawyer, right?"

Detective Solis stands and rubs his chin. "I guarantee he's been doing this to other students. We still have a lot more investigating to do, patterns to pick up on."

I'm becoming entirely too uneasy. I've chewed my lip so hard I'm tasting blood. If Jeremiah was sending messages at four in the morning, and if he's doing this to other kids…

The detectives are going back and forth with Alex and Ruben, and I still have so many questions, but I reach for my phone in my pocket. I hide behind Alex's blazer as I unlock the home screen and tap my Instagram icon, navigating to Malik's profile.

There've been many times in my life I thought I'd die of fright. But none compare to this.

Malik's profile is wiped clean, save one photo he posted two minutes ago. It's a stock photo of a galaxy, much like the one Jordan posted. And his caption: *#fallingstar*

I drop Alex's jacket and tear out of the room. I'm sprinting across campus in the pouring rain toward my car, calling Malik's phone, but it's going right to voicemail. I navigate to the app we use to track him. Nothing's showing up. "His phone's off. Oh, no. He posted a photo two minutes ago, and now his phone's off." I swallow the excess saliva gathering in my mouth and gaze around the student parking lot.

Malik's car is there.

He's on campus. *Think, Eve.* He and Jordan posted the same picture. Jordan shot himself. Malik's on this campus, and the only way he has a gun is if he got mine out of my glove compartment. I race to my car; it's still in there. So what's he doing?

Think, Eve! I get back on Instagram and go to Jordan's last picture, and I notice his hashtag is different. #shootingstar

Jordan shot himself.

Malik's is #fallingstar.

Oh, lord. He's going to jump.

33

MALIK

No one is coming to help.
  No one is coming to help.
No one is coming to help.

The rain is relentless. The ledge is slippery. I stand, then I sit. Now I'm standing again. Because no one is coming to help. I've dangled this Jordan over this ledge twice now, the third time's the charm. I'm going.

Because no one is coming to help.

No one is here to stop me.

I shut my eyes, leaning into the storm. This is it.

"Malik!"

Someone came to help.

I open my eyes.

"Malik!"

I turn around. My mom is running toward me, and she stops when I see her. She's soaking wet, but there's a gun in her hands. She holds it up for me to see. Then she deliberately cocks it, and puts it to her own head.

34

EVE

"I wasn't kidding, Malik. It wasn't a joke what I said at Jordan's funeral. I made you promise you'd put the gun to my head first! You lied! I guess we're both a couple of damn liars."

He's staring at me, his face as blank as if he were already dead. He's silent, standing on the edge of the tallest building on campus—two floors above the mezzanine I'm now convinced he threw himself down.

I push the barrel of the gun harder into my skull. "I'll do it! So help me God, I'll pull this trigger if you don't get down from there right now!" I'm nearly ten feet from him now, but I'm scared if I step closer, he'll fall. This wind, it's relentless. It's going to push him, and I need him to step down now, God, please!

He finally speaks. "Where did you get that gun?"

"I bought it when I was released from the hospital seventeen years ago."

"You never wanted me."

"You are so wrong. Malik, I always thought the night I got raped was the scariest, worst night of my life. But no. This is! Right here! I would go through that night every day for as long as I live, again, and again, and again, if I knew I'd end up with you as my son. You are the love of my life! There were so many nights after it happened that I would scream and cry, and I'd wish he had killed me. Then I had you. And you changed me. Baby, please! Don't do to me what he almost did! If you die, then I should have died seventeen years ago. But I didn't. You saved me. Please come down."

My breathing hitches when he turns toward me. "I got Creed Holloway pregnant."

I gulp and force a smile. "Baby, that's okay. We'll help you. We'll help Creed. And you will see the love a parent has for their child. One day at a time, Malik. I did it with you, and I'm so glad I did."

"I fell down the stairs on purpose."

My smile falters. "I kind of figured you did. That's how I found you here."

"I don't want to play football."

I shake my head. "You don't ever have to touch a football again."

"Someone's been harassing me on LibertyNet. They stole Xander's cat."

"It was Mr. Lorrey. He's been arrested. We'll get Biscuit back. I know everything, Malik. Everything will be okay."

He stands still, and instead of stepping down, he begins sobbing. "I can't do this anymore, Mom! No matter what you say, nothing makes this pain go away. Nothing makes it better."

I take another step toward him; I could reach out and touch him now. "Malik? *I understand.* You think you're alone, but I know *exactly* what you're going through. I went through it myself. Sometimes I couldn't breathe because the pain was so heavy. I didn't have parents who supported me. I only had my nightmares—the only things that stayed with me. I'd lie there at night with nothing but my tortured mind and cry, thinking no one was coming to help. And then someone did. You."

I finally see a light click in his eyes, and he swallows and says, "And then you came when I thought no one was coming to help."

"And I will every day for as long as I live. Son, you were my falling star. I wished upon you, and you made my dreams come true." And slowly, I reach my hand out to him.

He looks at it...

...and places his hand in it. His other hand wraps around the gun at my head and pushes it down toward my side, and he steps down from the ledge and I can't wrap my arms around my son's body fast enough and I'm never, ever letting go of this child.

35

EVE

The sun glares on my shoulders as I stare at Jordan's new headstone. "It's beautiful, Jill." I reach over and squeeze her hand.

She sighs. "I hope he's at peace."

I swing our linked hands back and forth. "You know, he visits Malik in his dreams a lot. And Jill? He's happy." I glance at her staring at the grave. A bit of color has come back into her cheeks, but I know that will come and go. I'm not getting my hopes up. There's no complete healing, but the moment you accept that it's a war that comes and goes for the rest of your life, you've already won the majority of the battle. It's just about taking control of it. Staying in charge. People appreciate it—you don't think they do, but they do.

"You really came through for me, Eve. I can't thank you enough for all the trouble you went through. I always thought it was me. I didn't provide enough for him. Didn't love him enough. But this—I mean, I can't say I feel better about it, but I'm more at peace. I just wish I could have stopped it before it happened."

Petra wanders over and grabs Jill's other hand.

Jill looks back and forth between us. "Do you guys mind giving me a moment alone with him?"

"Of course not," I say, and we hug her and walk toward the car. "She looks good."

Petra nods. "I think she's making progress. When you and Alex told her everything, that gave her closure. Thank you, Eve. You went over and above your duty as a friend."

I hate it when they thank me. I never know what to say. *You're welcome* doesn't seem appropriate. So we walk in silence to the car. The weather is so beautiful, you'd never know a tropical depression just went through here a few days ago.

"I'm going to tell her," Petra says. "Even though we found things in the texts."

I smile. "I think you're doing the right thing."

She snorts. "I have a lot of wrongs I have to right."

We look back at Jill, who's kneeling next to her son's grave. My heart breaks for the millionth time. But again, hearts will always break. It's knowing that life goes on once they do, and then they'll break again, and life will still go on. Things will always get better; nothing stays the same.

Jill joins us after a few minutes, and I silently drive them back to their house. I walk them to the door, and as I hug Jill goodbye, she says, "Do you want to come in for a while?"

I shoot Petra a glance, and she has tears in her eyes. She shakes her head. "Actually, Jill, I have something I need to talk to you about."

"I can come over tomorrow, Jill. Just call me whenever you need me, okay? I'm always here for you." I give them both one last hug and run to my car. I need to get home to my family.

TWO AND A HALF YEARS LATER

MALIK

I'm not going to tell you my life got easier when I stepped down off the ledge. It actually got fucking harder. The next few months were the worst of my life. There were times I wished I did jump, and those were the times I swear to God, my parents read my mind. Alex would talk to me. No yelling, no lecturing, no punishing—he let me be myself and tell him whatever I wanted to say. He'd physically restrain me when I wanted to end it all, and he'd stand by and watch me struggle as I grew stronger and was able to restrain myself, offering silent support. He broke down sobbing when he read the things Mr. Lorrey accused him of. "I was trying to cut you a break, by giving you A's! I thought I was being a good dad.

I had no idea, none, and if I could do it all over again…"
But I told him there was no need. He's my father and my
best friend.

And my mom—what's there to say about her? She's a
hot mess, but she's my guardian angel. My savior. I'd be
dead without her. Literally. She's the strongest, wisest
person I know, and she's my mother-effing hero (she
won't let me say the F-word).

The court cases were the worst. I purposely don't
watch *Law & Order* to avoid shit like that. I had to testify
about all the shit Mr. Lorrey fed me online, and apparently,
this guy was the jack of all psychos. Liberty was a fuckin'
cult. This guy had been plotting to brainwash students for
two years, when he first asked Mr. DeSoto to create a
website where the student body could chat with each
other. And while he was busy micromanaging Mr.
DeSoto's creation, he hired Mrs. Hendrick, knowing her
unfortunate history, for the sole purpose of exploiting her
if someone ever discovered what he was doing. Then he
found Jordan: the misfit, the boy with two moms, the boy
who slept with teachers (although Miss Dupree was a
monkey wrench—he really would've never hired a
pedophile because of the scandals), and he hounded him
to actual death. Me? I was the next misfit. The bastard
child, a different race, an introvert living an extrovert's life.
We were the "stains on society," according to that
narcissist.

Yeah, the narcissist—his "investigations" included
himself and no one else. No staff, no authorities, he was a
one-man band. He purposely held off on firing Mrs.
Hendrick for so long because he was waiting for me to kill
myself to pin that on her, too. If he fired her when my
mom wanted him to and I killed myself after, questions
would arise again. But my mom had to go screw all that
up, so he fired her, too. He basically stalked me—
monitored all my activity on LibertyNet, followed me
around campus (which was how he knew I purposely fell

down the stairs and conveniently was the one to find me), and snuck into the locker room while I was at football practice and deleted my Instagram posts and photos off my phone. I want to punch myself in the face every time I think of that day during practice when Coach sent me in the locker room, and I saw him in there and darted off to the baseball dugout. He was on my phone then, and I fuckin' ran away. But whatever. The guy was a nut job. So … he'll be doing life. I'm not even kidding. He should write a book, though. He's one smart and manipulative SOB.

My mom and I went to therapy—no shame in that. Sometimes together but mostly separate, we learned to handle our demons. And hey, the demons won't go away. Mom's been dealing with hers forever, and they keep coming back and she's okay with it (she's got her pills now). Mine will, too. But nothing lasts forever. Just understand this crisis will be over, then another one will come along. That's what life is, isn't it? A series of challenges that you always pass, one way or another. Even if you fail them. Either way, it's over. But it's all about taking control of your emotions, not letting your emotions control you.

That shit's exhausting.

I'm driving Xander home from football practice when my phone dings for like the nine hundredth time today. The news of my scholarship to the University of Alabama has traveled quickly, but any news of mine usually does, so I don't mind. Besides, Crimson Tide!

"You shouldn't text and drive," Xander says as he grabs my phone. "I'll read it for you. It's from *Creed*. Who's Creed?"

"No shit! She's an old friend."

"*She*? Who names a girl Creed?"

I laugh and smack him on his shoulder pads. "Hush. What's her text say?"

Xander swipes right. "It says, 'Do you want to see Ethan?'" He looks at me. "Who's Ethan?"

I grip the steering wheel with both hands as I pull into the driveway, feeling my grin stretch from ear to ear. "Write back to her, 'Yes, I do.'"

"I'm not writing anything until I find out who Ethan is."

I snatch my phone from him once I kill the engine and text her back as I sprint into the house. "Mom! Hey, Ma!"

"What?" she calls from the bedroom. She comes out folding one of my football jerseys, followed by Snow and a very pregnant Biscuit. I show her the text, and her eyes light up. "Can I come? Please? When are you going?"

My fingers dart across the phone, and I can't lose this shit-eating grin. "Of course you can. She said today! His birthday party. Matheson Hammocks Park, in one hour."

Creed's the first person I see as my mom and I head toward the pavilion decorated with Ninja Turtles and giant balloons shaped in the number 2. She's walking from the other parking lot carrying a gift, and I stare at her legs as she moves across the grass. She's gotten taller, her legs are slimmer.

"Is that Creed? She looks fantastic," my mom whispers.

She catches me watching her, and at first, I'm nervous. It's been two years since I've seen her, and the last meeting didn't go so well. But her lips turn up into that gorgeous smile that I loved, and she skips over to us, wrapping her arms around my neck.

I hug her and kiss her cheek. "Your hair is long. I like it." I run my fingers through it, and she blushes behind her glasses. God, she's beautiful.

"Thank you. You look great. You're taller. More built. Hot damn, Hunter." Then she turns to my mom. "You better watch out with this one, Mrs. Hunter. He's trouble."

My mom laughs as she accepts Creed's hug. "You don't have to tell me that," she says and smacks me in the chest.

"Stop it, you two," I say, grinning, and they both crack up like a couple of women.

The three of us continue toward the pavilion. "How's South Miami High?" I ask her. "You ready to graduate soon?"

She rolls her eyes. "I've always been ready to graduate. I saw your last game against Gulliver. You did amazing! Although I still think you made a fantastic quarterback…"

Now it's my turn to roll my eyes. "Ha! No, thanks. QB is all right, but it's not for me. I was done playing football until my parents took me to Columbus and Coach Hill talked me into it. He's a good guy."

Creed giggles. "I heard about your scholarship. Congrats! Running Back?"

"Yeah. And Receiver."

She looks at my mom. "How's Liberty, Mrs. Hunter?"

"It's called Greater Falls Charter now," my mom says proudly. "And it's fantastic, now that Mr. Hunter and I are administrators. We kept some of the Liberty staff. Those who didn't want me fired, anyway. So basically, just Ruben."

"I'm glad. So Malik, you didn't want to attend your parents' school?" she says playfully.

"Hell, no."

They laugh, and she squeezes my hand as we approach the pavilion. The first thing I see is a woman carrying a small boy who is a perfect mixture of Creed and me. My heart soars. She sees us at the same time, and her face lights up. "Ethan, look!" she says, pointing to us. "Those are your birth parents! And your grandma!"

I can already tell my mom is crying behind me. Creed, too, for that matter. But I just stand in awe, looking at this little boy who's the most gorgeous thing I've ever seen. Creed reaches for him first, and I just stare at Creed because being a mom comes naturally to her. She would've been the best mom to Ethan.

The woman's name is Danielle, and I've only seen pictures of her and her husband, from when Creed and I were choosing the adoption family. She looks at me with tears in her eyes, and there are too many crying women here, and I'm gonna lose it pretty soon, too. I purposely didn't watch *Steel Magnolias* to avoid this shit. "Malik, I never got to thank you for choosing us. You changed our lives. We're unable to have children of our own. And your selflessness changed all that for us. We're in the process of adopting another baby—a girl. So Ethan will have a little sister."

I can't even respond. Giving up the baby was the hardest thing in the world, and Creed and I fought about it a lot, but ultimately Creed's family was torn apart by this pregnancy. Her parents divorced, and both my mom and I had been preoccupied with therapy—me focusing on my suicidal tendencies and my mom dealing with her past. So we decided to look into adoption, for the baby's sake. And when we saw this family, we just knew. It was written in the stars.

Creed hands him to me, and he actually reaches for me as I take him. "Hi, Ethan," I say, and my mom cries out that she wants a picture. I pull Creed in next to me, and we put our arms around each other with our baby, taking our first-ever family portrait.

Danielle takes the phone from my mom. "You get in there, too, Eve!" I hand Ethan off to Creed and pull my mom into my other side.

"Send me those pictures, Mom," I say.

"Me, too! Please," Creed adds.

We spend the next couple hours together with our son and his family. My mom holds him the most, because she's pretty much the brattiest grandma in the world. Probably the youngest, too.

When the party's over, we hug and say our goodbyes to Danielle, promising to keep in touch. I can't stop hugging Ethan. I can't believe Creed and I made that. He's so perfect and beautiful, and I know what my mom meant now. I'd put a gun to my head over him, too.

That whole thought process that your family would be better off without you? It's the biggest lie. That's Satan shit, right there.

"You ready?" my mom asks me, and I nod.

Creed joins us as we walk toward our car. "So, you think we could hang out sometime? Maybe get something to eat? I know you don't like coffee, so I won't even suggest it."

I laugh loudly. "If you want to drink coffee, you know I'll drink coffee with you. I told you back when we were sophomores. I'd do anything for you."

She smiles satisfactorily, the smile widening the more my words sink in. "Really?"

I grab her hand and squeeze it. "Really."

She starts heading toward her own car, causing our hands to stretch and eventually pull apart. "Call me later?"

I nod and grab my mom's hand, heading toward my car. I'll call Creed tonight. And we'll chat. It's been a long time, and we've got a lot of catching up to do on each other's lives.

PLEASE CONTACT THE CARING PERSONNEL AT THE NATIONAL SUICIDE PREVENTION HOTLINE IF YOU OR A LOVED ONE ARE EXPERIENCING SUICIDAL THOUGHTS OR DEPRESSION. THEY ARE THERE FOR YOU. THERE IS HELP. THERE IS HOPE.

CALL 1-800-273-8255

OR TEXT HOME TO 741741

ACKNOWLEDGEMENTS

Jesus Christ, who saved my soul over two thousand years ago and continues to save it daily. I can do all things through Him.

Robert, whose unconditional love outshined my self-loathing. Thank you for showing me my worth. You've created a monster.

Robbie and Andrew, who make me feel loved and needed in the most unorthodox ways. You boys are the bones of my bones and the flesh of my flesh.

Twenty-One Pilots, who will never read this, but saved my life with the album, *Vessel*. Someone tell someone to tell someone to tell ol' Tyler and Josh I said thanks.

Stephanie Drewry, who loves my books as if they were her own. You may have joint custody, Brian. I love you!

Tarryn, who will forever be my always. Crème brûlée, all day.

Michael Platt, for allowing me to share his beautiful adoption story. And for schooling me on all things IT ... when we were IT coworkers. See how that job went for me?

My beta readers: Cassie Sharp, Willow Aster, and Jenna Walker, who validated me and pointed out my ignorance more than I'd like to remember. I love you ladies something fierce!

Erica Russikoff, my puzzle piece and other half. I'll stop there, to keep the acknowledgements G-rated. But you know the rest...

Jenn, Sarah, Brooke, Daisy, and the Social Butterfly PR crew, who move mountains for me—at an eerily fast pace.

Jammie Morris, who guided me through this journey with Tarot cards and sweet tea. Thank you for teaching me to breathe.

And you. Whether you know it or not, you've moved my soul. Thank you.

Made in the USA
Middletown, DE
27 March 2020